Regency Brides
Collection

2 Sparkling
Regency Romances

The Youngest Dowager
by Francesca Shaw

Master of Tamasee
by Helen Dickson

Regency Brides

A collection from some of Mills & Boon
Historical Romance's most popular authors

Regency Brides

Collection

Francesca Shaw & Helen Dickson

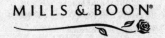

MILLS & BOON®

First published in Great Britain 2004 by
Harlequin Mills & Boon Limited,
Eton House, 18-24 Paradise Road,
Richmond, Surrey TW9 1SR

REGENCY BRIDES COLLECTION © Harlequin Books S.A. 2004

The publisher acknowledges the copyright holders of the individual works as follows:

The Youngest Dowager © Francesca Shaw 2000
Master of Tamasee © Helen Dickson 1992

ISBN 0 263 84080 8

138-0804

Printed and bound in Spain
by Litografia Rosés S.A., Barcelona

THE YOUNGEST DOWAGER
by
Francesca Shaw

Francesca Shaw is not one, but two authors, working together under the same name. Both are librarians by profession and they first began writing over ten years ago under a tree in a Burgundian vineyard. Their shared interests include travel, good food, reading and, of course, writing.

Also by Francesca Shaw
in Mills & Boon Historical Romance™:

A SCANDALOUS LADY
THE REBELLIOUS BRIDE

Chapter One

Whiting swung closed the great oak double doors, cutting off the view of the funeral cortège as it began its stately progress down the long drive to the Southwood family chapel.

The late March sun had not yet reached the front of the Hall and the last sound Marissa heard as the door closed was the sharp crack of carriage wheels breaking the icy puddles on the gravel.

'Shall I bring tea to the small parlour, my lady?' the butler enquired, sympathy colouring his usually grave tones. He wondered if he should send for her maid, for the Countess looked so pale, a fragile figure of black and white lost amongst the chequerboard of the great entrance hall, dwarfed by the towering classical statuary.

The Dowager Lady Southwood raised wide hazel eyes to meet his anxious gaze and almost yielded to the temptation to retreat to the cosy sanctuary of her morning room, the little fire, her pile of books, the undemanding affection of Gyp, her King Charles spaniel.

'No, Whiting.' Her sense of duty, as always, reasserted itself. 'Please bring my tea to the Long Gallery: I must be there when they return from the…chapel.'

Holding her prayer book in her clasped hands, Marissa moved slowly across the hall, up the curving stairs into the Red Salon, then through into the Long Gallery, which ran the entire length of the west front of the great house.

After two years of marriage she was too used to the chilly splendours of Southwood Hall to even notice the towering columns, the perfect geometry of every room and the exquisite correctness of each detail of decoration and drapery. Restoring his grandfather's Classical masterpiece to its original impeccable state had been an obsession of her late husband's, but try as she might she could admire the Hall, but she could never love the soulless integrity he had created.

To reach her chair in the Long Gallery Marissa had walked almost a hundred yards. She was nineteen years old, yet today she felt nearer ninety. Every step dragged as if she had a lead weight attached to her black kid slippers, and she sank gratefully down on a red satin chair.

Upright and graceful, she opened the prayer book at the Psalms and composed herself to read, but when the footman brought in her tea she realised with a start that she had taken in not one single word.

'Thank you, James.'

'Thank you, my lady. Will there be anything else?'

'Not for the moment. Go and see if Mrs Whiting needs any assistance with the refreshments.'

As he left James inadvertently let the heavy pan-elled door slam, startling Marissa out of her chair. How her lord would have hated that discord! She al-most expected to hear his voice issuing a quiet, chilly rebuke. But she would never hear the third Earl of Radwinter speak again. She shivered: by now the vault door would have slammed shut with force and finality, leaving him to the silent keeping of his ancestors.

She moved restlessly to the window, which gave a sweeping view across the trees of the park to the salt marsh and the faint line of the grey sea beyond. The movement behind the bare trunks of the limes forming the Great Avenue marked the return of the cortège of carriages bearing the gentlemen mourners. They would be back soon: Marissa chided herself for her morbid, almost Gothic thoughts when she should have been bent on the consolation of prayer. As she watched, her hand resting on the fringed brocade of the draperies, another carriage approached from the east. No doubt this would be her husband's aunt Au-gusta, coming to pay her respects to a nephew to whom she had hardly spoken a word during the latter part of his forty-five years.

Although she hardly knew the formidable spinster, Marissa was grateful to have female support during the ordeal of the funeral meats and the inevitable read-ing of the will. The late Earl had disliked the idea of a female companion for his wife and the intrusion upon his privacy, and the spinster cousin she had invited to join her in her widowhood had not yet arrived from Cumbria.

Marissa stepped back from her vantage point: it was most incorrect to be gaping from the window, not behaviour becoming to the widow of the Earl of Radwinter. She paced slowly back to the head of the flight of semi-circular steps which led down to the hall and waited for her guests.

As she stood, smoothing her skirts of dull black silk, she was aware of the subdued bustle of the staff all around her. Footmen were carrying trays into the Long Gallery, Whiting was supervising the arrivals and the maidservants were whisking away heavy coats, hats and gloves from the chilled guests.

'My dear child!' It was Aunt Augusta, red-faced from the cold and long days in the hunting field, her clothes curiously old-fashioned. But she was so alive, thought Marissa with envy. Alive, vital, noisy and interfering, a woman who cared not a fig for anyone else's opinion or for convention, despite her fifty-seven years.

Marissa hardly knew the half-sister of her lord's father, but that did not stop her liking her, and she took her hand with a look of speaking gratitude as the redoubtable spinster stood beside her.

'Chin up, girl! You are doing splendidly.' And indeed, on the face of it, her niece by marriage was. A courageous child, this widow of her cold fish of a nephew. Far too young for him, of course; far too young, they had all said, to be mistress of this great mausoleum of a house. Yet she had coped with dignity and grace. Augusta glanced sideways at the composed profile as Marissa spoke to each of the guests in turn. Could she really have been happy?

Every line of the widow's gown as it skimmed her tall figure was perfect, every lock of what Augusta suspected was a veritable mane of black hair was disciplined into a smooth coiffure, and the pale oval of her face showed nothing but the solemn calm suitable to the occasion. Did she ever smile? the older woman wondered. Let alone break that composure with a spontaneous outburst of either laughter or tears?

Once all were assembled in the Long Gallery the footmen began to circulate with trays of sherry, Canary and Madeira. Marissa, looking at the pinched features of some of the older men, wished she had defied convention and ordered mulled wine to be served to warm their blood. But that would have presented far too festive an appearance, and that would never do.

The older Mr Hope, the senior partner of the solicitors who had served the family for generations, was at her elbow, clearing his throat in a meaningful way.

'I think we should progress to the reading of the will, my lady. If those concerned and the staff assemble in the library, ma'am, I will deal with the bequests to the servants first. They can then leave us to the greater matters in privacy.'

The solicitor turned to catch the eye of various people, and Whiting was already marshalling the staff to move into the book-lined room when James appeared and, hastening to the butler's side, bent to whisper in his ear.

This indecorous behaviour caught the attention of the assembly, and, following the butler's astonished gaze, thirty faces turned as one towards the closed double doors.

They swung open and a man stepped into the gallery, pausing on the threshold to survey those within it with calm interest. He was tall, long-legged, immaculate in black superfine and silk cravat. Dark blue eyes scanned the room from under brows slightly raised at the startled expressions which greeted his arrival, until his gaze met that of the Dowager Countess.

Marissa felt the blood leach from her face and a high-pitched singing start in her head. With an almost physical effort she dragged her eyes up from the man framed in the doorway to the portrait which hung above. Charles Wystan Henry Southwood, third Earl of Radwinter, stared haughtily down, blue eyes chilly in a white face below raven black hair. Beneath, come back from the vault, he watched her with those same eyes, hair bleached by death.

With a little gasp of horror Marissa let the darkness engulf her, falling heedless towards the hard parquet floor.

Her aunt seized Marissa in her strong, horse-woman's grip, but even as she did so the man was there, catching Marissa up in his arms. Augusta was not a woman to be scared of ghosts, but even she was severely shaken by the stranger's appearance as he stood there, showing no sign of effort as he held the tall girl against his chest.

'Where shall I take her, ma'am?' he enquired, his voice cultured, deep, yet with a slight exotic lilt.

Lady Augusta pulled herself together. 'Through here, in the library. There is a chaise longue. Whiting, send for her ladyship's maid!'

From the black depths of her swoon Marissa was faintly aware of being caught up in a strong embrace, of a feeling of warmth and safety and the hot scent of sandalwood. She murmured something indistinguishable and snuggled closer. The grasp tightened, then she was laid down and the blackness swirled over her again.

Lucian Southwood backed out of the room, his gaze lingering on the porcelain features of the woman who lay so still. His blood was stirred by the recollection of her body against his, of the trusting way she had clung to him, of those parted red lips, almost the only colour in her deathly white face.

'I assume I am speaking to a member of the Southwood family?' a dry voice enquired at his elbow.

'Yes, I beg your pardon, sir. I am Lucian Southwood, cousin of the late Earl, newly arrived from the West Indies.' There was no mistaking the other man's profession. 'Am I addressing the family's legal representative?'

'You are, sir. Gabriel Hope at your service. A letter from me is even now on its way to you in Jamaica; we had no idea you were in England.'

The two men were alone together, the rest of the party having tactfully withdrawn to the far end of the Long Gallery. Lucian was aware of the curious glances being cast his way and the low-voiced conversations, no doubt speculating on the identity of this stranger.

'I arrived in London three days ago with my sister. I had business to transact, but had no intention of bringing myself to the attention of the Earl. You may be aware, sir, that my father fell out with his family and the two lines have had no contact since he made his own fortune in Jamaica. Imagine my surprise when I opened *The Times* yesterday to see the announcement of my cousin's death and the notice of today's funeral. It was too late to send a message, but I felt it my duty to attend.'

He glanced over his shoulder to where a feminine bustle now surrounded the form of Lady Southwood on the chaise longue. 'However, Mr Hope, please believe I would have stayed away had I any idea of the effect my arrival has obviously had. Mr Hope, please can you enlighten me as to why the Countess reacted as she did?'

In reply the solicitor took his elbow and turned him to face the door through which he had newly entered, and the portrait that hung above it.

'My God!' Lucian stared up at the features that might have been his own. Only the colouring was different, one so dark, the other so fair, as though an artist had drawn an exercise in opposites. Lucian's hair was naturally a dark blond, but over the years the unrelenting Caribbean sun had bleached it to the white of coral sand. The long spring voyage had diminished his tan, but even so he made the man in the portrait appear ghostly pale.

'You have, if I may so observe, sir, the Southwood features, if not the colouring.' Mr Hope nodded towards the many oils which hung in the Gallery, depicting generations of Southwoods.

'I had no idea,' Lucian said slowly. 'My father always said I favoured my grandfather, while he himself took after his mother's family. It is astonishing, especially as my father and the late Earl's father were only half-brothers. But what an appalling shock for her ladyship, so newly widowed! If I had had the slightest notion I would never have come.'

Mr Hope was looking at him assessingly. 'It is perhaps as well you have, sir. You cannot be unaware that you are the heir presumptive.'

'But surely my late cousin had children?'

'No, he was not so blessed in his lifetime. However—' Mr Hope became even drier '—we must make no assumptions until several months have passed.' He coughed in a meaningful and somewhat embarrassed manner.

Again Lucian looked at the woman on the chaise. He could not see clearly into the other room, but it appeared she was now sitting up. Despite that slender figure, could she be carrying her late husband's child?

Something was tickling the back of his hand. Lucian brushed his fingertips across the dark superfine cloth and pulled away a long, springing dark hair. As he pulled it it curled like something alive into the palm of his hand. Absently, still talking to the solicitor, he wound it around his little finger, trapping it under the band of his signet ring.

In the library Marissa pushed gently at the hands that were trying to keep her on the chaise longue. 'No, I must get up! My guests…I must go back…how foolish to faint! I cannot think what came over me!'

'Well, I can,' Augusta declared with her typical bluntness. 'I nearly fainted myself when I saw his face. He must be Richard's boy—he's the spitting image of your late father-in-law. No, sit still a minute, you foolish girl, and sip the water Simpson has brought for you.'

Meekly Marissa took the water and tried to make sense of the last few dizzying minutes. 'Who is Richard?'

'My late brother. I last saw him in '78; he was only eighteen when he left for the West Indies. He and my father never got on, but they had one final, irrevocable row about money and Richard swore never to set foot in Southwood Hall again. And he did not,' she added reflectively. 'He was buried in Jamaica, and by all accounts made himself a fine fortune before he did so.'

Marissa rubbed her fingers across her aching forehead, as if it would clear her thoughts. 'So,' she began slowly, 'the man out there is my lord's cousin…'

'Indeed. I think he has a sister as well. I suppose they are half-cousins, if there is such a term, because Richard and I were the children of our father's second marriage.'

So that explained the almost supernatural likeness.

Marissa made a supreme effort and stood up. Her hands went up to her hair, tucking the few wayward strands which had escaped firmly back into the tight chignon. The late Earl had hated to see her with her hair out of place.

Her eyes met the stranger's direct gaze, and for a long, long moment everyone else in the room ceased to exist. He made a movement towards her, then checked it, and Marissa realised he was afraid of alarming her again. She found she was holding her breath and released it with a soft sigh.

Mr Hope touched Lucian's arm with a murmured, 'Might as well get it over with now,' and led him forward to be introduced.

'My lady, may I present the Honourable Lucian Southwood, newly arrived from Jamaica. The late Earl's cousin,' he added meaningfully. He only hoped it would not be an unpleasant surprise to the Countess to meet the man who, if she were not carrying a male child, would inherit her late husband's title and estates.

Marissa found her small, cold hand engulfed in a strong, warm, tanned grip. The warmth seemed to spread through her chilled body, and the remembrance of being caught up and held in an enfolding embrace caused her heart to lurch for a moment. It must have been Mr Southwood who had carried her to the chaise.

The colour rose in her cheeks and Lucian thought it was like seeing a marble statue suddenly come to life. Even as he thought it the colour ebbed and she freed her hand. 'Sir, you are welcome to Southwood

Hall. I am only sorry that it should be in such mournful circumstances.'

Lucian bowed, and found himself, along with several others, being ushered back into the library by Mr Hope. Lady Augusta sat firmly beside Marissa and the gentlemen ranged themselves around the desk at which the attorney seated himself.

Mr Hope produced a pair of eyeglasses which he set on his nose after fussily polishing them. He extracted a key from his waistcoat pocket, unlocked a brass-bound box which had been placed before him, and gazed impressively over the spectacles at the assembled company.

Lucian suppressed a smile, covering his mouth with long fingers. The old boy was milking the situation for all it was worth, no doubt to justify the large fee he would eventually charge the estate.

'As you know,' Mr Hope began gravely, 'we are gathered here to hear the testamentary dispositions of the late Charles Wystan Henry Southwood, third Earl of Radwinter, newly deceased.' His clerk emerged from the shadows, produced an impressive document tied up in red tape from the box, broke the seal, handed it to his principal and effaced himself again.

'Harrumph. I shall begin with the bequests to the staff.'

There followed several pages of gifts, small pensions and life interests in estate cottages. Lucian reflected that his cousin had made very correct, if not generous, provision for his faithful servants, but wondered at the total absence of any personal mentions or expressions of gratitude. He glanced across at the widow and saw she was sitting with absolute rectitude, her gaze fixed on the carved over-mantel of the fireplace. She looked composed, almost frozen, but as he watched he became aware that the jet drop earrings were trembling against her white neck. He wondered if she were normally so composed or whether her deep grief had frozen her heart.

He did some rapid mental calculations. As far as he could recall his cousin had been forty-five years old: this girl could scarcely be more than twenty.

Mr Hope had droned his way through the minor bequests and the servants had filed out of the room, leaving only the immediate relatives, Dr Robertson and the family chaplain, the Reverend Mr Field.

After another four more pages of interminable legal phrases Mr Hope regarded his stupefied audience over the top of the vellum and announced, 'In essence the position is straightforward. The title and the estate, both entailed and unentailed, with the exception of that in the Countess's marriage portion and the Dower House, descends to the male heir of the late Earl.'

Marissa transferred her gaze sharply to his face. 'But…'

Mr Hope swept on, a touch of colour staining his sallow cheeks. 'The matter is delicate, but none the less it is my duty to tell you that under these circumstances it is normal…' he paused '…and prudent, to wait a certain number of months before the succession can be…clarified.'

It suddenly dawned on Marissa that Mr Hope, that

dry lawyer, meant that they all had to wait to see if
she was pregnant. Without thinking, she blurted out,
'But there is no need to wait!'

Lady Augusta gasped, 'Hush, my dear! Not in front
of the gentlemen!'

But Marissa was adamant. The thought of the whole
household watching, waiting, studying her looks, her
health, her mood, week after week, for signs she was
with child, was insupportable. Better to get it over
with now. 'I can assure you, Mr Hope, that there is
no vestige of doubt that my lord is without a direct
heir.'

Mr Hope snatched off his eyeglasses in agitation
and looked wildly at the doctor and Lady Augusta.
They stared blankly back at him. At length he managed to regain some composure and asked, 'Dr Robertson, Lady Augusta, perhaps if I may prevail upon
you to retire to another place with the Countess and
discuss this matter further…'

Scarlet to her eartips, Marissa swept out of the room
towards her bedchamber, followed by a bemused and
embarrassed Lady Augusta and a scandalised doctor.
Her head high, she dared not look at anyone else, but
she was acutely aware of Lucian Southwood as he
rose when she passed him.

Then all thoughts of anyone else left her as she sat
in her room, whispering answers to Dr Robertson's
tactful questions. But her mind was only partly with
him. It was in this very chamber only a week ago she
had had to tell her lord that once again she had failed
in her duty and that she was not carrying his heir.

He had never reproached her in words, but his disappointment had sent him out to ride furiously across the frozen parkland where small drifts of snow still lingered. It was one of these which had concealed the rabbit hole which had tripped his horse, pitching the Earl head-first onto the iron-hard ground to break his neck in an instant.

Marissa knew it was her failure as a wife, her lack of duty to her lord, which had killed him. Her eyes filled with tears at the thought and Lady Augusta, seeing this, held up her hand to stop the flow of questions from the doctor. 'Enough. Surely you are satisfied with what the Countess has told you?'

'Indeed, indeed.' The doctor leaned across and patted her clasped hands in an avuncular fashion. 'You have been very brave and very frank, my dear, and in doing so have been a great help to those administering the late Earl's estate. But it is a melancholy thought that the direct line must cease—' He broke off as Lady Augusta gave him a sharp kick on the ankle and one solitary tear rolled down the young widow's cheek.

Dry-eyed, and with her head held high, Marissa resumed her seat in the library and the gentlemen hastened back to their positions. The doctor had a rapid, whispered conversation with the lawyer, who nodded and took up his papers once more.

'I am in a position to tell you, ladies and gentlemen, that the title, honours and estates of the third Earl of Radwinter pass immediately to his heir, the fourth Earl, Lucian St Laurence Southwood of Jamaica, who by great good fortune is with us today. My lord.' He stood up and bowed to Lucian, who acknowledged the salute with equal gravity.

Marissa was conscious of a huge sense of relief, as if a great weight had been lifted from her shoulders. Now she could relinquish this great house, this mausoleum which so chilled her soul and deadened her spirits, and move to the Dower House. It would be someone else's responsibility to manage the impeccable running of the Palladian splendour which her husband had created. She wondered how swiftly such a move could be effected.

Lucian, watching the brief play of emotions over the pale countenance, was unable to interpret the expression. Surely it had not been—could not have been—relief? No, it must have simply been thankfulness that this ordeal of the will-reading was finally at an end. He was acutely aware that his own presence, his very appearance, must be a painful reminder to her of her loss. But he could not now take his leave, return to the West Indies, for he was responsible now for this huge estate and all its people, including her.

Whiting was announcing luncheon and Lucian held back to allow the Dowager Countess and her supporters to precede him to the dining room, where the great table was laid out with the funeral meats. But Marissa turned and waited for him. 'Mr… My lord…' and he realised she was expecting him to take her arm and lead her in. Once again he marvelled at the strength of will and composure in one so young. Her hand, resting on his sleeve, was taut with tension; he felt she was like a violin string, stretched almost to the point of breaking.

The place at the head of the table was laid, but the chair was draped in black, and Lucian led Marissa to her place at the foot of the long board, taking the place to her right.

The chaplain said grace and the party settled with a thankful collective sigh. Gradually the volume of conversation rose as everyone relaxed and tongues were loosed by the consumption of fine wine.

What the devil did one talk about under these circumstances? Lucian wondered, helping the widow to roast beef. Back home in Jamaica even a funeral meal was more relaxed, more informal and emotional. There was something about the heat and the sunshine, the vibrancy of colour, the closeness of nature—a dangerous nature—that would make this sort of rigid formality impossible.

And what a brutal way to treat a grieving young woman, to expect her to maintain a rigid composure surrounded by this sombre flock of dark-coated old men. He shivered slightly and instantly she was all attention, the perfect hostess.

'My lord, you are cold.' And yet he had seemed so warm when he touched her... 'Whiting, more logs on the fire. This country must seem very chill after the heat of the West Indies.'

'Indeed, yes, madam. My sister declares she will never feel warm again, but now I have been back in England for almost a week I find I am becoming accustomed.'

Marissa cut a minuscule portion of beef and raised it to her lips. She wondered if she would ever feel warm—or hungry—again. 'You have a sister, my lord? I am afraid I know nothing of your family—are there others still in Jamaica?'

'No, madam, there is only Nicole and myself. I intended bringing her to London next year to do the Season, when she is seventeen, but she plagued me so much to bring her on this trip so she could see the sights and buy some London fashions that I could not resist her.'

Marissa saw the fond smile on his lips and envied the ready affection in his voice. How wonderful to have a loving brother like that, to have such a bond with another person. 'You are very fond of your sister, my lord, I can tell.'

Lucian, surprised by the longing in her tone, glanced at her quickly, but her face was closed and he answered lightly. 'She is the bane of my existence, madam. I have spoilt her to death and now I must pay the price. When you meet my sister you will be in no doubt that we had a French mother!'

'I hope to meet her very soon. You will be sending to London for her?'

'I must think what to do. All this has come as a great shock to me and I am entirely unprepared. I visit London every few years on business, and that was my purpose on this occasion. Now I will have to return to Jamaica to place my affairs there fully in the hands of my agent. I will have to meet with your—' he caught himself '—the estate manager here, and with

Mr Hope, so that I can be confident that all will be well in my absence.'

There was a long pause. Lucian twisted the wine glass between long brown fingers. Marissa found she could not take her eyes off his hand, nor forget the warmth of his touch through the silk of her gown. What would it be like to be held in his arms again…? She caught her errant thoughts with an inward gasp of horror. How could she entertain such longings? It was wrong, wrong…and in any case it was a delusion that comfort lay in the arms of a man…

'Lady Southwood, when you feel able, I must speak with you about your wishes. Needless to say I would not want you to feel you must make any change in your arrangements. This is your home and you must stay in it as long as you wish.'

Marissa looked him straight in the eye and said with utter conviction, 'My lord, I have lived here for only two years. It is the Southwood family seat, but it has never been my home. My cousin Miss Venables will be joining me soon from Cumbria. When she arrives I will move to the Dower House.'

She realised she must have startled him with her frankness, but all he said was, 'It shall be as you wish, naturally. You must instruct the estate manager to move whatever you want from the Hall into the Dower House, and to have whatever resources you need for your comfort there.'

'Thank you, my lord. Would you wish me to continue to oversee the housekeeper in your absence?'

'That would be most kind, if it would not be an

imposition. We will speak of this tomorrow, and of course you must decide which servants you wish to take with you.'

Marissa thanked him, and turned to her other neighbour. Throughout the rest of the meal they spoke of nothing but inconsequential matters, and with her mind relieved of the need to guard her every word she found her attention wandering to the man at her side.

His manners were correct and impeccable, as befitted a gentleman, but there was a foreignness too. Perhaps it was the slight French accent on certain words, the lilt that came into his voice when he spoke about the West Indies. He was a handsome man—all the Southwoods were, to judge by their portraits—but this man had a dangerous, vital energy that radiated even in this sombre company.

Under the pretext of dabbing her lips with her napkin, Marissa stole a sideways glance from under her lashes. His hair curled over-long on his collar, the blond hair shot through with the warmth of the tropical sun. His face was lean and tanned and there were white lines at the corners of his deep blue eyes, as though he often screwed them up against the sun-dazzle on the Caribbean sea. His nose was straight, his mouth was as firm as her husband's had been, but the new Earl's lips looked as though they more readily curved into a smile than tightened in displeasure.

He was attractive, dangerously so. But he was also a man, and that meant that whatever face he showed in company there was another, darker side to his character, as there was with all men. Marissa reminded herself that was something she should never forget.

Chapter Two

Marissa gave up on the unequal struggle to sleep and threw back the heavy silk coverlet, wincing as her feet touched the polished boards by the bed. She padded across to the banked glow of the fire and held out her hands in an attempt to draw its warmth into her restless body.

In time she supposed the numbness would pass, but for the moment she was gripped by a strange sense of unreality. Only the routines and duties of the chatelaine of a great house made everyday existence possible: she had never been so grateful for the sense of duty which had been inculcated in her from childhood.

But in her chief duty she had failed, and failed repeatedly. Marissa gazed into the flickering red depths of the fire and remembered again her lord's cold disappointment that she had once again failed to conceive the heir to Southwood. Not that he had shown anger: the Earl had never allowed himself to show his emotions, least of all to his wife. And he had expected the same restraint from her.

At least that discipline had enabled her to bear the embarrassing ordeal of the doctor's questioning yesterday, the knowing eyes of the men in the library as the will was read. Her cheeks burned hot and Marissa turned from the fire to cool them. As she did so her eyes fell on the door which led, via a suite of dressing rooms, to her lord's bedchamber, the Master Bedchamber. On an impulse she hurried into her dressing room and opened the connecting door. The key, as always, was on his side. With a swift twist of her wrist Marissa pulled it out, closed the door and locked it from her side.

It was a foolish, pointless gesture, barring the way into that empty suite beyond with its black-draped bed and mirrors veiled in mourning for the dead Earl. But it was her room now, hers at least until the man who occupied the Red Bedchamber, the best guest room, decided to take control of his inheritance. And by then she would have long gone to the Dower House.

The view from her windows showed an expanse of parkland glittering with frost under a chill moon. The windows were already rimed on the outside; by morning the frost-fingers would have crept up the panes inside too. Was the new Earl able to sleep in the big bedchamber, his warm Caribbean blood cooled by this unseasonable spring? Doubtless he would have been snugger in the Radwinter Arms at the park gates, where he had originally left his valise. But it was unthinkable that the fourth Earl should not sleep in the house of his ancestors.

A familiar restlessness filled her. Marissa felt the

urge to run, to feel the blood sing in her veins, her heart beat wildly in her chest—to let go of all the rigidity and formality which had kept her confined these past few days. She slipped her long white silk peignoir on over her nightgown, pushed her feet into kid slippers and opened the door onto the corridor.

All was silent, then the sound of the hall clock striking one reverberated through the corridors. The night watchman would have done his rounds of the house by now, checking for open windows and guttering candles, and would be dozing quietly in his hooded porter's chair by the front door. Occasional lanterns illuminated the galleries and the moonlight flooded in through the long windows.

The patterned marble floor stretched enticingly long and clear before her. Marissa picked up her skirts and ran, ran as she had so often done in the freedom of the night. Her feet made only a slight pattering on the hard floor as she flew, hair loose, skirts billowing. She took the newel at the top of the stairs in both hands as she passed and swung round it, a bubble of laughter beginning at the back of her throat. Her eyes shone with exhilaration, with the freedom of the movement.

Marissa paused, panting slightly, between the doors of the Library and Long Gallery, trying to decide which way to go. She could dance in the Gallery under the disapproving eyes of the marble goddesses. But then she remembered the equally disapproving eyes of the ranked Southwood ancestors and her child-like enthusiasm waned, leaving her feeling guilty that she should be behaving so in a house of mourning. She was alive, vital, while they were all consigned to dust.

Her shoulders drooping, Marissa turned to retrace her steps in a more decorous manner. She never knew what stopped her: perhaps some sound, or the mysterious sense of another presence close to her. There was someone in the Gallery.

Tiptoeing in, she paused in the doorway. In the strong moonlight the figure by the south window was plain to see. He had his back to her, but there was no mistaking that burnished head, the width of the shoulders, the height of the man emphasised by the sweep of his heavy brocade dressing gown.

Lucian Southwood was standing braced with his hands on the mullions on either side of the long window. His head was bowed, as though the weight of the world was on his shoulders. Marissa had an impulse to run to him and throw her arms around his waist, to tell him that, whatever it was, she would make it all right. She took half a step, then checked herself. What was she thinking of? She did not know him, but she did know that one thing you never dared do was to show you had seen a sign of weakness in a man. She had only made that mistake once…

The stone mullions were chilling his hands to the bone, but Lucian scarcely noticed the additional discomfort. It was so damnably cold—yet he sensed that Southwood Hall would chill him even in the height of summer.

His life had been turned upside down in a matter of hours: his rambling home by the deep blue sea, his estates, the fleet of ships, his friends, the relaxed, unconventional society of Jamaica. All those were lost to him. He was responsible now for this great estate and all its people. He was the keystone that an entire economy rested on.

And his cousin's widow, so young, so beautiful, so vulnerable—and now his responsibility too. She appeared to have no family to support her, no friends to comfort her in a grief that must be devastating. And he, Lucian, was in the position her own child should have occupied. What a bitter reminder he must be to her, not only of her childlessness but, in his astonishing likeness, of the husband who had been taken from her so abruptly.

The die was cast; there was nothing to be gained by dwelling on it and he had never been a man to rail against the inevitable. His duty was clear. Lucian pushed himself away from the window, absently rubbing his chilled hands, and straightened his shoulders. Tomorrow he would send for the steward...

The skin on the back of his neck prickled: someone was in the room with him, watching him. He spun round, his sword hand reaching instinctively to where his rapier would have been, then froze in amazement.

For one mad moment he thought a ghost had appeared. The figure poised for flight in the doorway was almost elemental in its whiteness, save for the cloud of black hair framing the face and the dark-shadowed eyes. Then he recognised her.

'Lady Southwood! Please...do not go, I am sorry to have startled you.' He held out a hand to arrest her movement and saw the tension in her body relax slightly. 'I should not be wandering about the house at this hour, but I confess I could not sleep,' he added lightly, searching for a way to make this extraordinary encounter ordinary.

'Why should you not wander as you will? It is your house,' she replied matter-of-factly. Marissa found herself stepping into the room, drawn by some strange compulsion, when she knew propriety ruled that she should bid him goodnight and return to her chamber immediately.

Lucian came to meet her halfway, noting the tinge of colour in her cheeks, the rise and fall of her breast. Why, he must have scared her half to death, for she was breathing as though she had been running for her life.

'I hope your room is warm enough, my lord. I do appreciate how chilly you must find it after the warmth of the Caribbean. Let me ring for a servant to make up your fire.' She made as though to tug the bellpull.

'At this time of night? Surely no one is awake?'

'But of course. There is always a footman on duty throughout the night in case anything is required.'

Lucian laughed down into her face, imagining the staff at White Horse Cay if he demanded that they sat up all night just in case he wanted some small service performed. His father had freed his slaves, much to the scandal of the surrounding planters, but none of the staff had left him, regarding themselves, quite correctly, as just as much part of the family as they had ever been. Most of them had known Lucian since he was a child, and still tended to treat him, at the age of twenty-eight, as a faintly irresponsible boy.

Charmed by the infectious amusement in his face, although completely ignorant as to its cause, Marissa found herself smiling back.

Lucian caught his breath at the transformation. The hazel eyes sparked green, the serious little face was suddenly warm and full of life, the dark cloud of hair seemed to crackle with vitality. Without thinking he took her face between his palms, bent his head and kissed her full on her smiling mouth.

It was so unexpected, so startling, so pleasurable, that for a brief, shameless moment she kissed him back with soft, generous lips. It was as if his warmth was flooding her veins, touching the icy core of her with the heat of the sun and of him.

The realisation of what they were doing seemed to hit them both simultaneously. Even as she began to pull back she felt his hands release her. Lucian, his face sombre with shock, took two rapid steps back.

'Madam, I cannot begin to apologise for my outrageous behaviour,' he began. Her eyes were enormous with shock, her lips—the lips that had quivered against his—were parted in dismay. Without a word Marissa turned and ran.

Lucian strode to the wall and hit his fist hard into the unyielding wooden panel beside him. 'Damn, damn, damn…! You bloody insensitive fool!' How could he have succumbed to a moment of weakness like that?

She was his cousin's widow; only hours before she had buried her husband. He had already scared her into a faint by his unexpected appearance, had witnessed her humiliation at the reading of the will. He must be a constant reminder of the loss of her husband and the absence of an heir. And then, instead of offering her his brotherly support, he had taken her in his arms and kissed her!

And she, shocked, grieving, without affectionate friends at her side, had for a brief moment gone into his arms seeking consolation. Lucian stalked back along the corridor to his bedroom, ignoring the pain in his bruised fist, furious with himself. 'You bloody fool, what are you going to say to her in the morning?'

On the other side of the Inner Court, Marissa slammed her door behind her and leaned, panting, against the panels. She pressed her fist against her mouth as if to stem the tide of tears gathering at the back of her eyes. What had she done? She had *wanted* to kiss Lucian, to be held against that warm strong body, never to have those gentle lips leave hers. She ran to the mirror, turning her face anxiously, expecting to see the marks of his fingers branded on her skin. There was nothing to show, yet she could feel them as if they still cradled her face.

How *could* she feel like this? It was improper, humiliating, shameful. Not only had she let him kiss her, but she had kissed him back! Even if she had, however briefly, accepted his embrace, she should never have answered it. No lady should ever allow herself to show passion in any form. Two years of marriage had reinforced that lesson well. How could she have felt so safe in his arms? How could kisses as gentle as those lead, as she knew they did, to the reality of the marriage bed?

Marissa let herself fall into bed, dragging the covers tight around her ears as if to block out her own tumultuous thoughts. How could she face him tomorrow?

But face him she had to. With the house full of guests, Marissa made a special effort to be early at the breakfast table, but even so the new Earl was before her. Whiting removed a plate bearing the remnants of a large beefsteak and placed a basket of fresh rolls in front of his lordship.

'My lady! Good morning.' Whiting bowed and moved to pull out Marissa's chair. Lucian rose to his feet and waited courteously for her to take her place at the oval breakfast table.

He watched her as she sat, her hair haloed by the weak sunshine that streamed in through the breakfast parlour windows. She might have been carved in marble for all the animation in her figure, gowned in deepest unrelieved black.

'Good morning, my lord,' she remarked calmly. 'I am sure Whiting has been looking after you. No, Whiting, I will just take tea.'

'Chocolate will be more sustaining, my lady,' Whiting coaxed, conscious that Mrs Whiting had given him strict instructions to make sure his young mistress ate properly. 'And a sweet roll, my lady—it is a bitterly cold morning, ma'am.'

'Very well. I will take a roll. But no chocolate, Whiting.' The thought of the rich liquid made her stomach roil. She could crumble a roll without the butler noticing she was scarcely eating a morsel…

Lucian buttered a roll while keeping a covert eye on the widow. Neither of the things that were uppermost in his thoughts could be carried out. The first was to apologise unreservedly for his behaviour last night in the moonlight; the other was to do it all over again. Then he saw how she was crumbling the roll and hiding the pieces under her knife. If she had been his sister he would have taken her on his knee, put an arm round her shoulders and coaxed her to eat. But she was not his sister; she was his cousin's widow.

Marissa's words broke into his thoughts. 'My lord…'

'Will you not call me by my given name?' he asked abruptly, scandalising Whiting, who was standing immobile by the sideboard. 'After all we are related, if only by marriage, and I am not used to this formality.' He saw her dubious face and added, with a charming smile, 'Will you not take pity on a stranger in a foreign land?'

Marissa doubted if his lordship was ever out of countenance, but once again found herself yielding to the charm of that smile. 'Very well…Cousin Lucian.' The door opened at that moment and Whiting, storing away this almost revolutionary informality to recount to Mrs Whiting at the earliest opportunity, busied himself with seating Mr Hope and some of the less elderly second cousins, who had decided against taking breakfast in their bedchambers.

Lucian stood up and bowed. 'If you will excuse me, Cousin, gentlemen, I have an appointment with the steward.'

Marissa managed to maintain a flow of polite smalltalk for a few minutes, before excusing herself to go and talk to the housekeeper. As she made her way towards the green baize door which separated the servants' quarters from the main house she reflected that she had never been so glad to see Mr Hope as when he had come into the breakfast parlour just then.

How assured Lucian had been! He seemed not to have the slightest self-recrimination for his behaviour last night. And as for asking her to call him by his given name! She should never have agreed so readily, yet how could she have snubbed him in front of Whiting?

Marissa's heels clicked on the stone floor as her pace increased to match her growing irritation with both herself and Lucian. That smile, the glint of white teeth in his tanned face, the slight exotic accent... Oh, yes, he was charming all right, and he used that charm very easily, too easily. Doubtless young women fell into his arms with such facility that what had happened last night was nothing remarkable to him...

She had worked herself up into such a state of righteous indignation that when she rounded a corner and found herself face to face with the object of it she made no attempt to hide her frown.

'Cousin Marissa! As you can see, I have become

lost looking for the estate office.' His smile was charmingly apologetic, inviting her to laugh at his inability to navigate the big house.

'If you retrace your steps to the first door into the courtyard, cross the courtyard itself, then it is the green door in front of you,' she directed in clipped tones. Finding herself alone with him again was embarrassing; she was aware of a tightening knot of anger in her chest, though whether at herself or him she could not analyse.

'Cousin, is something amiss?' Lucian moved closer, not hiding his surprise at the coolness of her mien.

'You can ask me that after last night?' she demanded, her colour rising.

'I had thought perhaps I had been forgiven after you agreed to call me cousin this morning,' he began, only to be interrupted by Marissa's sarcasm.

'Oh, forgive me, my lord, if I have misled you. I foolishly believed it would be better not to discuss our…encounter…in front of Whiting. I should, of course, have regaled him with the entire episode! As it is, you put me in a position where I have scandalised him by agreeing to a form of address which can only be regarded as quite inappropriately informal. But doubtless in the West Indies you do things differently, so we must all learn to make allowances for the new Earl.'

'Why, you little madam!' Lucian stood and stared at her, amazed irritation replacing his look of rueful apology. 'I thought you were in need of friendship and some brotherly support…'

'Brotherly!' Marissa stamped her foot. 'Sir, what you did last night was not brotherly!'

'*I did?* It was only your good manners, I suppose, that led you to kiss me back?'

Marissa drew herself up to her full, unfashionable, five feet six inches, eyes ablaze. 'Why, you… you…you may be the fourth Earl of Radwinter, but you are no gentleman!'

Lucian stared down at her through narrowed eyes. 'If you were my sister I would put you over my knee for that! I have no time for spoilt young women whose every whim has been indulged by doting middle-aged husbands. I am truly sorry for your loss, madam, but do not think you can twist me round your little finger as you did my cousin.'

For a long moment she stared at him, speechless, and in her eyes he caught a look of such desolation that he caught his breath. But before he could say anything there was the sound of footsteps in the corridor behind him. He turned to find Poole, the steward, hurrying towards him, and when he looked back Marissa had vanished.

Lucian cursed his fiery temper: he was easy to rouse, but all his family, friends and servants knew his rages blew over as fast as they arose. He would have to try and explain to Marissa, but now was not the time.

'My lord, I do apologise. I was not in the hall to show you to the office.' The steward was obviously alarmed, and Lucian realised his face must still be thunderous.

'Not at all, Poole.' He clapped the man on the shoulder. 'I was irritated with myself for losing my bearings. I swear a man needs a compass to navigate this place! Come, let us get down to business, for we have much to talk about.'

Marissa meanwhile swept downstairs to the housekeeper's room on a tide of hurt anger. So, he thought her an indulged child, did he? A bitter laugh escaped her tight lips at the unfair irony of the accusation. One thing she had never been was indulged. Left motherless at an early age, she had been raised by a father whose irritation at being saddled with a daughter had been eclipsed only by his determination that she be brought up in a manner that would ensure she would marry well and as quickly as possible. Her own preferences, not that she had ever been asked to express them, had been entirely irrelevant to her father's plans for her.

But as she entered the cosy parlour where the housekeeper was scanning the linen lists she felt her bitterness ease in the face of the familiar warmth and comfort that she always found there.

'There you are, ma'am!' The housekeeper pulled up a chair by the fire. 'Now, you sit down there, my lamb, and warm your hands. I know you didn't eat your breakfast: even if you fool Whiting, you can't fool me. Just bide there and I'll cut you a slice of my fruit cake and pour you some of this tea.'

Absolutely scrupulous in maintaining her young mistress's dignity in front of the other servants, in private the housekeeper treated her like a granddaughter.

His late lordship had been a great nobleman but not an easy gentleman to live with, with his exacting standards: not a speck of dust, not a vase out of place, not a servant out of line. And woe betide the mistress if it was. Mrs Whiting had made sure that everything within her purview was as near perfection as she could make it, because any shortcoming had been visited not on her head, but on Marissa's. And she loved this young girl as if she was her own.

Something had upset her now; that was for sure. The porcelain-pale skin was flushed above the cheekbones, and her breathing was slightly ragged.

'Now you eat that up, my lady, while I finish these lists.'

'Thank you, Mrs Whiting. But there is so much we must discuss— Mmm!' She broke off to take another appreciative bite of the cake. 'This is delicious!' And it was the first thing that had not turned to sawdust in her mouth over the past week.

The older woman eyed her, then began to work round to the subject that had been uppermost in her mind for days. 'It must have been such a shock, his lordship's accident...I don't suppose you'll have had a chance yet to think about what you want to do now. And his new lordship arriving like that out of the blue, and everyone thinking he's off in those foreign parts...'

'Oh, I know exactly what I am going to do,' Marissa said with surprising conviction. 'I have sent for my cousin, Miss Venables, and as soon as she arrives we will move into the Dower House. His lordship can then do as he pleases without needing to refer to me.'

Mrs Whiting pursed her lips at the hint of irritation in Marissa's voice. So, she didn't take to the fourth Earl! That surprised her, for she thought him a well-set-up, very pleasant gentleman, even if his ways were a bit foreign.

'Had you thought about staff for the Dower House?' The housekeeper tried to keep her voice neutral.

Marissa pulled herself together and gave the question her full attention: she had wanted to speak to the Whitings about this. She knew, however much she disliked formality, that as the Dowager Countess of Radwinter she had a duty to maintain a proper household.

'I will need a butler and a housekeeper, three footmen, kitchen staff, chambermaids…Mary, of course, will come with me. But it is the butler and housekeeper who are the most important to decide upon. What a pity that Matthews from the London house is not married: his lordship will not want to keep it fully staffed while he is out of the country…'

The two women discussed the possibilities half-heartedly; no one seemed appropriate, but Marissa knew that because of her youth she would need to select her senior servants carefully. Even with a respectable companion like Miss Venables she needed the dignity of experienced and mature upper servants.

Eventually the housekeeper cleared her throat and ventured, 'I know Whiting was going to raise this with his lordship, but as we're talking about it, my lady… He and I feel we're getting on in years. This house is a big responsibility, and his lordship's bound to want to bring his own people in. Would you like it if Whiting and I were to come with you to the Dower House?'

It was the perfect solution. Marissa looked at the housekeeper with shining eyes, but then doubt crept in. 'But you have a position here. This is one of the great houses of East Anglia—surely you would not want to descend to looking after a mere manor house?'

'I'd like nothing better, my love,' said Mrs Whiting with transparent honesty, then added cunningly, 'And my poor old joints aren't what they used to be…'

'Then I will be delighted if you will come with me.' Marissa hugged the housekeeper, who was therefore unable to see her face as she added, 'I will speak to his lordship about it.'

And as soon as possible, she thought as she walked back to the small parlour which did duty as a morning room. As she opened the door Gyp, her Cavalier King Charles spaniel, jumped down from the window seat with a sharp bark of joy and danced around her feet, plumed tail waving. Marissa scooped up the little dog, laughing as he tried to lick her face, rubbing her fingers through his silky hair.

'There's a good boy! Has James taken you for your morning walk, then? We will have a run after luncheon, I promise. Now, sit down while I look at the accounts.'

Gyp, recognising that he was not going to be taken

out just yet, settled down in front of the fire with a sigh and promptly fell asleep. Marissa sat at her little French bureau in the bay of the window and opened her account book. But she made no attempt to total the columns of figures, or to puzzle out why the cost of wax candles had become so high.

As she had thought, she could see clearly across the frosty courtyard into the estate office window. If she kept an eye on it, she would be able to intercept Lucian when he left and speak to him before luncheon. After all, she reasoned, biting the end of her pencil, she could hardly speak about the Whitings moving to the Dower House in the presence of the butler himself. And one or two of the relatives who had come for the reading of the will had decided in view of the inclement weather to wait a few days for the harsh frost to thaw; they too would be at the table.

But the truth was that Marissa felt bad about her bitter words to Lucian in the corridor: this was no way to deal with the man who was now master of Radwinter and, apart from her father, her closest male relative. He would be returning to London and thence to Jamaica within a matter of weeks. And by the time they met again that awkward encounter in the Long Gallery would be long forgotten…

Lucian appeared to be pacing the small office; she could see him passing and repassing the window, occasionally gesticulating with both hands to drive home a point. It appeared to be a perfectly amicable conversation. When she caught a glimpse of Poole, the steward was nodding in agreement.

At eleven o'clock a footman crossed the courtyard, balancing a tray with some caution. The cobbles were rimed with frost in the shadows which still lay around the edges of the courtyard and Marissa suppressed a smile at the sight of the man mincing along in his leather-soled buckled shoes, while struggling to keep level the tray laden with two tankards and a platter of bread and cheese.

The arrival of the food did not appear to halt the discussion: Lucian continued to pace, despite the tankard in his hand. Almost an hour later the door swung open. With a clap on the steward's shoulder Lucian strode off, leaving Poole looking somewhat dazed in the doorway.

There was no doubt that Mr Poole was finding that dealing with the fourth Earl was a very different proposition from dealing with his predecessor. Charles had made his expectations crystal-clear and had then interfered only on the rare occasions when they had not been met.

Marissa dropped her pencil and whisked out of the door, running downstairs to waylay Lucian before he reached the Hall. 'My lord! Could you spare me a few moments?'

'Of course, Cousin.' He bowed politely and waited for her to precede him. Her earlier irritation appeared to have vanished, yet she seemed agitated, slightly out of breath. Her normally impeccable gown had a light sprinkling of golden hairs on the shoulder and one lock of her disciplined coiffure had come loose. Lucian curbed the urge to unpin the rest of it and set the whole cloud free around her shoulders.

'I realise it is unusual to receive you in my parlour,' Marissa began as she pushed open the door to her sanctum, 'but I have a particular reason for wishing to speak to you alone.'

At the sight of the answering glint in his eyes she sat down hastily by the fire and gathered Gyp onto her lap. The spaniel curled a lip at the intruder, but Lucian, sinking into the chair opposite, snapped his fingers and the little dog jumped down and trotted over to sniff at his feet. After a moment he curled up again, his chin comfortably on one of Lucian's boots, and went back to sleep.

'Well, I must say!' Marissa was indignant at her pet's perfidy. Gyp disliked men generally, although he tolerated the footmen who took him for walks, and he had particularly hated the late Earl.

'I do not know why you should object,' Lucian observed mildly. 'He is much more of a handicap to my improper behaviour lying on my feet than he ever was in your arms.'

Marissa could feel a flush rising to her cheeks. 'I think we should forget that incident, Cousin; put it behind us and pretend it never happened.'

'Feel free to pretend what you like,' he returned ambiguously.

'Er…yes, well, what I wanted to speak to you about was the Dower House.'

'I too wished to discuss that with you. Poole tells me it is in good condition and well furnished, if not in the latest style. That will be rectified. Of course you must stay here for as long as you wish. I will be gone for many months, perhaps a year, in Jamaica, and when my sister and I return there will still be no need to drive you from your home. You have only to say which suite of apartments you wish to retain and they are yours…'

'No!' The word burst from her before she could contain it, and Lucian looked at her in surprise. 'I mean, no, thank you, Cousin Lucian. The Dower House will do me very well, and I intend to move there as soon as my companion, Miss Venables, arrives from Cumbria and the funeral party disperses.'

Lucian steepled his fingers and regarded her gravely over the top of them. 'I do beg your pardon, Cousin. I should have realised that this house must hold unbearably painful memories for you now.'

Marissa dropped her gaze to her hands clasped tightly in her lap. 'Indeed, yes,' she said quietly. 'I will be glad to be gone from it.' After a moment she rallied slightly and added, 'But of course I will regard it as my duty to oversee the housekeeping here in your absence.'

Lucian noted her use of the word 'duty' yet again. She was so young to be so serious about her duty. He could imagine her over the coming year, clad in her unrelieved mourning black, forcing herself day after day to revisit Southwood Hall in pursuit of her duty.

'This is a charming room,' he remarked, in an attempt to ease the tension. The colours were soft: rose-pinks, delphinium-blue, touches of coral. There was

an Aubusson rug on the polished boards, the furniture
was in the country style, and the upholstery bore the
marks of Gyp's scrabbling claws. It was warm, cosy,
slightly untidy, with books overflowing the table,
Gyp's drinking bowl in the hearth, a sewing basket
with the lid askew and skeins of thread spilling out.

'It is a very untidy room.' She laughed suddenly.
'But then, my lord never came in here…' She stopped,
aware she was in danger of saying too much, revealing
too much about her marriage and herself.

Rather hastily she went on, 'But the reason I wished
to speak to you alone is the question of the servants.
Mrs Whiting has told me that she and her husband are
finding this big house too much for them now. They
would like to come with me to the Dower House, but
we are all conscious that you must have reliable staff
in place. Perhaps you would be bringing your own
staff from Jamaica?'

'I have my own butler, Edward Jackson: I could not
leave *him* behind if I tried! If the Whitings wish to go
with you, then they do so with my blessing. Is there
a reliable couple you could recommend to take their
place here? It will, after all, be very quiet here for at
least a year whilst I am away and you are in mourning.'

'The butler at Grosvenor Square—Matthews—is a
good man and Whiting considers him ready for greater
responsibility. And I imagine you will close the London house while you are away. However, Matthews
is unmarried, so you will need to engage a housekeeper. Mind you,' Marissa added thoughtfully, 'Mrs

Wood, our cook here, is quite capable of managing the housekeeping while there is no one in residence. And with the Whitings close at hand, if she and Matthews have any difficulties they will have ready advice.'

Satisfied with such a neat solution, Marissa sat back against the cushions with a sudden happy smile which illuminated her face and made her look absurdly young. Gyp started out of his doze, as though the foot he was resting against had moved, and Lucian said abruptly, 'An admirable solution. Shall we visit the Dower House after luncheon?'

Chapter Three

Marissa asked Mrs Whiting to accompany them on their expedition to the Dower House. It was, of course, entirely proper to take a chaperon, but, that aside, Marissa recognised in herself a growing susceptibility to Lucian's charm that made her wary of spending too much time alone with him. It would never do to become accustomed to his company, she chided herself.

The housekeeper was delighted at the opportunity to survey her future domain. 'The Dower House was the home of Miss Anne Southwood for many years, my lord,' she explained as the carriage made its cautious way along the frozen drive. The coachman was concerned about the horses' legs on the iron-hard ground, and the slow progress made the three occupants of the carriage glad of the footwarmers and thick fur rugs they were wrapped up in.

'She died just before you came here, my dear...my lady, if you recall. But the house has been well looked after, so we should not find much to concern us.' She chatted comfortably on about how she had instructed the elderly married couple who had stayed on after their mistress had died to light fires and to clean and air all the rooms. 'For once you let damp in—with us so close to the sea, my lord—you never get rid of it.'

'It seems strange that we are so close to the sea yet cannot see it,' Lucian remarked. 'I can smell it when the wind is onshore, but I can neither hear nor see it, and I am used to doing both at home in Jamaica.'

'Yes, the land rises so gently to the house, and there is over a mile of saltings and marsh before the beach, so that you must ride almost to the dunes before you see it,' Marissa explained. 'If it were not so cold I would suggest going down there, but the wind will cut like a knife without the protection of the trees.'

'I find it hard to believe it could be possible to be any colder,' Lucian said with a grimace as the avenue of holm oaks widened out to reveal the neat little Queen Anne Dower House, sitting like a doll's house in a hollow surrounded by its walled gardens.

The Bishops, the elderly couple who were caretaking, were on the look-out for them, and the chilly party found themselves whisked into a snug hall with a fire burning in the grate and cheerful brocade hangings shutting out the draughts.

Mrs Bishop soon took Mrs Whiting off to discuss the vexed question of the kitchen range and its persistently smoking chimney, leaving her husband to conduct his lordship and the young Dowager around the house.

'I had forgotten how charming this house is!' Marissa exclaimed in delight as they entered the drawing room. She walked across to look out of long windows which opened onto what would be a flourishing rose garden in the summer. 'And how nicely you and Mrs Bishop have kept everything!'

Bishop, much flattered by the attention, proudly conducted them round every one of the three reception rooms, the little library and the six bedrooms.

'This will do me very well,' Marissa declared as they climbed the back stairs to check that the servants' accommodation was in good order.

'I agree. It is a charming house, and very home-like and comfortable,' Lucian agreed. 'But, Lady Southwood, do you not feel it is perhaps a little old-fashioned, especially in contrast to the Hall? Shall I order a complete redecoration and refurnishing to be set in train?'

Privately he found the house delightful, and did not find the worn fabrics or faded paint objectionable. It was welcoming, a house that had been home to happy people. Southwood Hall, in all its Palladian magnificence, was a rich man's showpiece, an ice palace. How he was ever going to make it a home for himself and Nicole he could not imagine.

'No! Leave it as it is!' Marissa spoke vehemently, and then saw the quickly suppressed look of surprise on Lucian's face at her warmth. 'I mean...I would prefer to live here a while and get to know the house before I decide on any changes.' Seeing that his lordship was still regarding her quizzically, Marissa fell back upon a tactic she had always found mollified Charles. She dropped her eyes and murmured, 'I will be guided by you, my lord, but at the moment I feel too shaken to make any decisions…'

There was a pregnant pause. Marissa kept her eyes down, sensing that this man was not convinced by a show of feminine weakness from a woman who had only hours before been most decided in her plans to leave the Hall, engage a companion and arrange her own domestic staff. However, he merely replied blandly, 'It will be as you wish, Lady Southwood. You have only to command the steward when you have decided what you want to do.'

Mrs Bishop bustled in, dropping a curtsey before addressing her husband vigorously. 'Now then, Bishop! What are you about? Keeping my lady and his lordship up here in these attics! Come you down, ma'am—I've laid tea out in the little parlour.' She led them down, chattering as she negotiated the winding stairs, and pushed open the baize door into the main house. 'Not that the little parlour is the right room for afternoon tea, I knows that, but it is the cosiest on a day like today, there's no denying that…'

As the door closed behind her Lucian enquired with a laugh, 'Does that woman ever stop talking?'

'Probably not, but Mrs Whiting knows how to manage her. Tea, my lord?'

'Thank you.' He leaned across to take it, his fingertips just brushing hers on the rim of the saucer. 'I thought we had agreed that you would call me Lucian when we are alone?'

Marissa regarded him over the tea table with steady hazel eyes. 'And I thought I had consented to call you cousin.' She really could not afford to be sent into a fluster every time she found herself in his company. It was the informal manners of the West Indies, of course; that was why he seemed so warm, why his conversation seemed so intimate. But underneath it all he was a man, and they all had the same expectations, the same demands. On the surface Lucian Southwood simply had a different style.

They fell silent, sipping tea in the warmth of the parlour, and gradually Marissa relaxed, letting her mind fall to wool-gathering. Lucian could not tell what Marissa was thinking, but he thought he had never seen her look so…so… He groped for the word in his mind… So *real*. When he'd first seen her she had seemed another marble statue in the gallery, or one of the portraits come to life. Everything about her had been constrained and stiff; now, in this cosy little parlour, he felt he was with a real flesh and blood woman.

The fire had brought a glow to her cheeks, her shoulders were no longer set as she leaned back against the faded chintz, and one tendril of hair had worked loose and hung behind her left ear.

'Will you not be lonely?' he asked suddenly.

'Lonely? Living here?' Marissa was taken aback. Loneliness was a state to which she was accustomed; it was her normal condition. 'Why, no more than usual… I mean, I will have Miss Venables, and Mrs Whiting, of course. And Lady Augusta will visit, even though we are in mourning.'

'No, I mean... Forgive me, but do you not have any friends of your own age?'

'No, my lord,' she said simply. 'I came straight from my father's house in Hampshire: I met my lord at the start of my first Season, so I had no opportunity to make close friends amongst the other debutantes. And my lord, being older than myself, had his own circle of friends, which of course became mine.'

Lucian cursed himself for his tactlessness, for this conversation had brought a tautness to her face and the old wariness back to her eyes. Her devotion to her late husband was unquestionable, and he was a fool to keep reminding her of a pain so newly inflicted.

To cover the awkward moment, he said bluntly, 'Would you advise me, Cousin? I have an idea in my mind concerning my sister Nicole which I would like to venture with you. She is very young—only sixteen—and she found the sea voyage very distressing. Despite being used to inshore boats all her life, she was sick from the moment we reached deep ocean, and I know she dreads the return journey.' He leaned over to put his cup down, a deep furrow between his eyes. 'Now I have to tell her that we must return almost at once, that she must say goodbye to her home and friends and face yet another onerous ocean journey.'

'Oh, poor child!' exclaimed Marissa with ready sympathy. 'What an awful prospect for her—and for you to see her suffer so!' It was obvious to Lucian that Marissa's idea of his sufferings—those of a caring and sensitive brother—were far removed from the reality of living with a wilful and tempestuous girl. Nicci had been allowed to run wild, and so far had never been asked to face anything unpleasant in her life. There would be endless rows, sulks and tears from the moment he broke the news until they arrived back in London—perhaps a year hence.

'I want—I would like—to leave her here in your care, and not to expose her to the rigours of both the journey and the pain of parting from her home again.' He leaned back in the chair and watched Marissa's face, gauging her reaction. 'I know it is asking a lot, to take on the care of a young, high-spirited girl under any circumstances, let alone these…' He watched the calm, thoughtful face before him and realised with a start that Marissa could only be three years older than Nicci, and had married scarcely older than his sister was now.

Had she always had this grave air of reflection, of inner constraint? Had she ever been a headstrong young girl, and, if so, what had it taken to effect the change in her?

'But of course she must come here to me!' Marissa exclaimed. 'I could not bear the thought of her suffering so!' In her unknown cousin's plight she felt again the terror of being plunged into an unknown world, of having to learn the rules and expectations of a new way of life, cut off from everything that was familiar. 'Poor little thing! She must be so homesick, and missing you. With whom is she staying?'

'A West India merchant by the name of Montfort and his wife. It is my habit to stay with them on my visits to London, and fortunately they have several children, including a girl of Nicci's age.'

'It must be a comfort to you to know she is in the care of friends. Mrs Montfort will be helping her to buy her mourning, I expect.'

Lucian reflected ruefully that if Mrs Montfort was succeeding in getting Nicci to concentrate on anything as dull as buying mourning, let alone wearing it and behaving in a manner befitting her new station in life as sister of an earl, then he would eat his hat.

'I cannot tell you what a comfort it will be to have her living quietly in the country. I just hope it is not an imposition on you in your present state of mourning.'

'Oh, no, it will be a pleasure to have her here.' It would be a novelty too, to have someone to look after. And sixteen was such a vulnerable age for a young girl trembling on the threshold of womanhood…

Marissa woke the next morning with an unfamiliar feeling of pleasurable anticipation. Not only would Miss Venables be arriving soon, and they would be able to make the move to the Dower House, but planning for Nicole Southwood's stay was a delightful novelty. It would be like having a little sister.

Gyp, delighted to be admitted to his mistress's bedchamber, snored at the end of the bed. He had always been banished to her little parlour at night, but now there was no one to object he was becoming a familiar shadow at her heels wherever she went in the house.

Mary was already pulling back the drapes to reveal

a foggy morning. 'It's set in a thaw overnight, my lady. Much warmer, but there's this danged fog, and the mud is something dreadful.'

'Language, Mary!' Marissa reproved half-heartedly. 'You will never make a London lady's maid saying words like "danged".'

'Yes, my lady. Sorry, my lady. Here's your chocolate, ma'am. Mrs Whiting asked me to say, ma'am, that she would like a word this morning about what you wish done with his late lordship's suite.'

'Yes, please tell Mrs Whiting I will speak with her after breakfast.'

Half an hour later, fully dressed for breakfast, Marissa hesitated on the threshold and glanced back at her dressing room door. If she were to discuss her lord's chambers she had better take a look around them now. She could not face walking into that suite for the first time since his death with anyone else there.

Her hand shook slightly as she turned the key and opened the door into the formal sitting room which lay between the two dressing rooms. It was a characterless space, used by neither husband nor wife. She hurried through it without a glance; it held no memories, no threat to her equanimity.

His dressing room was immaculately tidy, just as his valet had left it. The door into the bedchamber beyond stood ajar, opening into the darkness of the shrouded room. Before she could change her mind Marissa strode across and wrenched back the heavy curtains from the windows. Foggy light poured across the floor behind her.

Marissa turned slowly on her heels to survey her lord's chamber, her heart thudding in her chest. To her heightened imagination it felt as though he was still there. She could sense the sharp tang of his cologne. Every item on the bedside table was perfectly aligned. Nothing had been removed or changed since his death; all was as he would have demanded it should be.

Then, as she turned, Marissa's heart gave a painful lurch. There on the side table lay his gloves, his riding crop, his hat, just as though he had walked in and put them down a moment before.

'My lord!' she whispered, but there was no answer in the high-ceilinged chamber. Her hand crept to her throat as she was gripped by a powerful sense that he was not dead. Dr Robertson had prevented her from seeing the body; she realised now he had feared she might miscarry if she was with child. And no lady ever attended the actual interment.

Marissa ran from the room and was halfway along the corridor to the main stairs before she could calm herself, control her breathing. By the time she reached the breakfast room she had outwardly regained her composure, but inwardly her fantasies battled with her common sense.

Like an automaton Marissa passed bread and butter, made conversation with the elderly relatives who were taking their departure that morning. By the end of the meal she had decided that she would walk down to the chapel and visit the family vault. Of course he was dead, she knew that, but perhaps if she saw the tomb with her own eyes she could lay to rest this spectre.

The dining room door opened and Lucian entered. He had been out already: there was colour in his cheeks from the raw cold and his hair curled damply from the fog. He took a cup of coffee from Whiting and wrapped his cold fingers round the porcelain, addressing the guests who were finishing their breakfast. 'I hope, gentlemen, that this fog will not impede your journeys. Will you not stay a few more days until the weather clears?'

'It will be better once we are away from the coast, sir,' Sir Thomas Cribb, a distant cousin, declared. 'The sea fret lies heavy here, always does. Too damp, this spot; I've always said so,' he added under his breath.

'Should I not ring for your valet, my lord?' Marissa enquired. 'This cold fog seeps through damp to one's very bones.' And, she reflected, was enough to produce pneumonia in someone used to tropical climes. Not that the Earl was looking unwell; far from it. Used to her husband's pale skin and immaculate hair, to her, Lucian's tan and unruly crop seemed vibrantly alive and healthy. Try as she might, she could not become used to the physical similarity between the two men which underlay these differences.

'Thank you, no. I intend going down to see the Home Farm once our guests have departed—if we cannot persuade them to stay. I must confess I had not appreciated the scale of the estate here: there is much to put in hand before I leave.'

Marissa, enfolded in a thick wool cloak with a bonnet and muff, waved goodbye to the last of the guests from the front steps of the Hall and waited while Lucian mounted and cantered off in their wake towards the Home Farm.

Whiting was hovering, waiting for her to re-enter the house. 'Thank you, Whiting. I shall take a turn round the pleasure grounds for some air.'

As the front door closed Marissa walked briskly down the gravel path that wound into the shrubbery. The evergreens dripped with fog moisture and the snow lay in depressingly grubby patches against their trunks. She increased her pace and emerged onto the open greensward that fronted the little stone family chapel.

As she laid one black-gloved hand on the latch of the gate the cold struck through the fine kid, yet she hardly noticed it. She stopped, in the very act of opening the gate. What was she about? she chided herself. Why was she suddenly prey to this ridiculous compulsion? Of course Charles was dead, his neck broken in his fall. And it was her fault: once again she had disappointed him; once again he had ridden out in cold fury at her failure as a wife... Why had he ridden over the Common when only the other day she had heard the gamekeeper remarking on the extent of the rabbit holes and the damage they were causing? It could only have been because he had been distracted by yet another disappointment; yet again there was no sign of an heir to displace the estranged cousins in Jamaica.

Marissa turned to leave, then hesitated. If she went in now, saw the vault, it would make an ending to her life at the Hall. She could start again, afresh…

The door creaked open on reluctant hinges and the cold, damp air rolled out to meet her. Shuddering, Marissa huddled deeper into her cloak and stepped inside. The chill pressed up through the soles of her sturdy walking shoes as she walked slowly towards the great vault, hung with wreaths of laurel.

The family always worshipped in the parish church which lay on the boundary of the estate: the chapel was used only for family interments. All around were the slabs and monuments denoting the resting places of many generations of Southwoods, back to Sir Ralph, lying in his armour, his dog at his feet.

Her lord's grandfather had constructed this new vault with its great iron-bound door. The space for a new plaque was empty, awaiting the carved tribute to her lord, but a hatchment with his coat of arms hung above, and a painted board stated simply: *Charles Wystan Henry Southwood, Third Earl of Radwinter, 1770-1815.*

How well the marble mausoleum suited him in its cold, classical perfection. Yes. He was dead. For the first time Marissa truly believed it. She was free of him. A tiny glow of warmth burned inside her as she tried the word under her breath. 'Free…'

For two years she had longed to be free, longed to wake up and find, not that he was dead—never *that*— but that he had gone, vanished from her life by some miracle. For two years he had dominated her by his will, controlled her every act, wrung out every drop of spontaneity and warmth from her, given her only wealth and status, demanded only perfection—and an heir.

She had married him determined to be a loving and dutiful wife, but she had found that only duty was expected of her. And, however hard she'd tried, she had never been able to please his exacting standards— by day or by night.

The vault seemed to be full of his personality as Marissa stood there, relief and a dreadful guilt that she should feel like this flooding through her. Then there was a step behind her and the door, which she had left ajar, swung open with a thud.

Marissa whirled round, and for one hideous moment believed she saw him standing in the doorway.

'My lord!'

Then she saw it was Lucian, his breath curling warm on the cold air, a look of concern on his face as he took in the expression on hers.

Marissa drew in one difficult breath and then burst into tears of shock, guilt, relief. After one horrified moment Lucian strode across and gathered her in his arms, holding her tight while she sobbed, cursing himself under his breath. He had done it again, scared the poor child by coming on her unawares, reminding her at the worst possible moment of what she had lost.

Riding back from the Home Farm, he had seen the chapel door standing ajar and had come to secure it. He should have realised it might be Marissa, visiting her husband's grave to mourn in peace. He had broken in on her grief and by doing so had broken her composure and the control that had been helping her to cope with her loss.

Trying to explain and apologise would only make things worse. Gently Lucian urged her towards the door and out into the open, where the sun was at last penetrating the fog in fitful rays. He closed the door firmly behind them and found a handkerchief.

She spoke, her voice muffled against his greatcoat. 'He has really gone, has he not? He will not be coming back?'

Later it was to strike Lucian as an odd choice of words, but then he hardly noticed it as he patted Marissa gently on the back until the sobs subsided and she took his handkerchief with a watery smile.

He offered her his arm. 'Come, Cousin, let us walk back slowly past the lake. The sun is finally beginning to warm that west-facing bank.' And it would give her time to regain her composure before facing the servants.

They walked on in silence, Marissa's hand tucked warmly into the crook of his right arm, his horse ambling quietly behind them. The fog was curling up off the surface of the lake like smoke, and the fringing reeds stood brittle and dead in the still water. Flocks of duck were dotted across the lake and rose in panic at the sight of the people.

Marissa blew her nose and struggled to find a suitable topic of conversation. She ought to feel awkward, yet she did not, and the Earl seemed quite unperturbed by her sudden tears. Perhaps having a sister had made him adept at soothing agitated females and more tolerant of emotional outbursts than fathers or husbands would be. Charles would never have tolerated tears, whatever the cause, and her father would simply turn and walk away if any emotion was shown.

A pheasant suddenly flew out of the tussocks around the lake with a strident alarm call, and across the meadow came the plaintive bleat of sheep carried clearly on the still air.

Agriculture seemed an unexceptionable topic. 'Did you see all you wished at the Home Farm, Cousin?'

'Thank you, yes. Everything appears to be in excellent order. My late cousin was obviously a good landlord.' If not a well-liked one, he added to himself. Everyone he'd spoken to had been as one in agreeing that this was a well-managed estate, run to the highest standards. No one had spoken to him of a sense of loss, or with any warmth of the late Earl. Yet every one of the estate workers he had encountered had enquired anxiously and with obvious respect after the welfare of the Countess.

Lucian glanced down, but the rim of the bonnet hid her face from him. Her hand rested trustingly on his arm, the kid-gloved fingers surprisingly firm. It seemed as though she was the only person who had found something in his cousin to mourn: there was no mistaking the genuineness of that flood of tears or the cold hurt in her eyes. This was no rich young widow weeping for form's sake.

They discussed the estate and its workers as the great house loomed into view. Lucian was impressed again by Marissa's depth of knowledge of the families at Radwinter: who was related to whom, who had a daughter in service in London, which of the pensioners suffered from arthritis and needed help in his garden...

'If you want to know more about sheep husbandry, then Reuben Childs is your man; he knows all about it. I imagine that sheep are not common in the West Indies? He is Mary's grandfather; she is my maid... Oh, look, another carriage. Perhaps it is Miss Venables arrived at last! Poor thing, what a cold and long journey she must have endured.'

It was indeed her spinster cousin Jane, daughter of her father's elder sister, who had made a most regrettable marriage to an impoverished curate. She had compounded the offence this had given her brother by living happily in their rambling Cumbrian vicarage and producing a bevy of equally happy and unambitious children.

Despite Sir George Kempe refusing to acknowledge the existence of his sister or her family, Miss Jane, the eldest of five girls, had written to congratulate her young cousin on her marriage and they had fallen into the habit of exchanging greetings on birthdays and at Christmas. Miss Venables, in her early forties, had been earning her own modest living as a governess, but had confessed to Marissa that she did not find it a congenial existence and was hoping to find a position as a companion.

Marissa's first action, once the immediate shock of the Earl's accident had died away, had been to write to Miss Venables urging her to join her and enclosing a bank draft to hire a post chaise and postilions.

Miss Venables was standing in the front hall as Marissa and Lucian arrived. Her modest pelisse and bonnet were matched by the few items of luggage which stood beside her, yet she did not appear overawed by the splendour of her surroundings, which she was regarding quizzically, nor by the host of superior servants who were bustling around her.

Marissa hurried forward, her hand outstretched in welcome. 'Cousin Jane! How very glad I am to meet you. I do hope you have not had too fatiguing a journey! Please, let me make you known to my husband's cousin. My lord, Miss Venables, who has so kindly hurried to support me. Cousin Jane, the Earl of Radwinter.'

Miss Jane's thin eyebrows rose a further fraction as she returned his lordship's bow with a demure curtsey. She might be a spinster of forty-two summers, but that did not dull her discernment of good looks or breeding, and the Earl had both in abundance.

'Shall we go up to your rooms, Cousin?' Marissa enquired as the footmen carried the luggage out of the hall. 'Luncheon will be in about an hour, but I am sure you would like a cup of tea to warm you.'

As soon as they were alone in Miss Venables's rooms, Marissa turned a look of glowing gratitude upon the other woman. 'I cannot express how much I am obliged to you for coming to support me in such haste! I do hope it did not cause any inconvenience to your employers.'

'I had already given them notice,' Jane replied, removing her pelisse. 'For, although I loved their children, I could scarcely tolerate the parents. Your letter could not have come at a more apposite moment, my dear Lady Southwood...'

Marissa crossed and impulsively took her hands. 'You must call me Marissa, for I hope and believe we shall be good friends.' She found her fingers gripped warmly in response.

'I do believe it too, Marissa.' Miss Venables, a shrewd judge of character, had liked her young cousin on sight. But there was something very wrong. Something that transcended the shock of recent bereavement. She could sense it, but now was not the time to probe.

Mary came in and dropped a curtsey. 'Shall I unpack now, ma'am? James has put the tea tray in your parlour, my lady.'

'Thank you, Mary.' Marissa turned to her cousin. 'Mary will see to your needs until we can find a suitable girl of your own. Now, let us go down to my sitting room—the fire should be well alight by now.'

Seated either side of the hearth, with Gyp curled up on Miss Venables's feet, they found themselves slipping into an easy conversation as though they had known each other for years.

'You are honoured indeed by Gyp's attentions as footwarmer! He is normally most wary of strangers. Although perhaps he is mellowing, for he likes his lordship too.'

'One can quite see why,' responded Miss Venables.

'From the little I saw of him just now he seems to be a gentleman whose manners and appearance are such as to be universally appealing.'

She sipped her tea, then, looking up, caught Marissa's eye and was intrigued to see the young woman blush. That was interesting: Marissa did not strike her as a person who could shrug off the loss of a husband, even one so much older, in order to flirt with an attractive man.

'Why, I declare this fire is almost too warm,' Marissa murmured, pushing her chair back and fanning her warm cheeks.

'It must be disconcerting to have a stranger, however amiable, in the place of your husband,' Miss Venables observed. 'And presumably his lordship will be bringing his wife here as soon as possible. Has she remained in Jamaica?'

'Lord Southwood is not married, but he does have a young sister who has travelled to London with him. He has asked if I will be willing to have her live with us while he returns to the West Indies to settle his affairs, for he expects to be away for quite some time.' Marissa realised that her original letter to Miss Venables had been of the briefest, and added, 'I did not explain when I wrote, but I am moving to the Dower House in the grounds as soon as possible.'

Miss Venables placed her cup on the table before replying calmly, 'It will be most pleasant to have a young person with us, I am sure. But will you not regret leaving your home? It is truly…er… magnificent.'

'How tactfully you put it, dear Jane!' Marissa laughed. 'Since you ask me, I will answer you candidly: I hate this mausoleum. It is cold, impersonal, and has never felt like my home. I do hope you will like the Dower House as I do. His lordship has said I may redecorate it as I wish, but it is like this room: comfortable and a touch faded, warm and just big enough.'

'I like it already, my dear.'

There was a tap at the door and Whiting entered. 'Luncheon is served, my lady.'

Lucian got to his feet as the ladies entered. The conversation was general as soup was served and replaced by a platter of cheese and cold meats. Then he turned to Marissa. 'I trust it will not be inconvenient, Lady Southwood, but with the weather turning milder I thought it would be as well to leave for London after this meal. I should reach Downham Market before it is too dark. I will put up at the King's Head there, rest the horses and push on first thing.'

'Your sister will be so pleased to see you, my lord,' Miss Venables remarked. 'I collect that she is rather a young lady? To be in a strange city, even with friends, can be unsettling.'

'Indeed, ma'am,' Lucian rejoined blandly, although the person to be unsettled was most likely to be Mrs Montfort, charged with keeping control of an impetuous young lady who was all agog to explore Town when she should have been choosing mourning gowns.

Marissa listened to the conversation with something

approaching dismay. Why had Lucian not mentioned his intention to leave today? Had her outburst of emotion repelled him? He had behaved with great tact and kindness at the time, but, like all men, would find such displays distasteful. Of course she had known he was going up to Town to fetch Nicole, but somehow she had not expected it to be so sudden. And she had not expected to feel so bereft.

Doubtless it was because she was so used to having a man in charge of affairs: she would soon become accustomed to his absence when he left for Jamaica. Her little household of ladies would by then be well ensconced in the Dower House and she would be so busy she would not notice.

After luncheon Miss Jane declared her intention to rest a little in her room, and bade farewell to his lordship. They exchanged a few words about the route and Marissa drifted across to the windows, gazing out over the grey, dripping parkland which echoed her mood so well. She did not want Lucian to go! It was so strange to feel like this: always before she had been happy to be left alone, left to her own thoughts and devices.

As the door closed behind Miss Venables Marissa turned, a bright smile on her lips, her hand outstretched. 'Well, I trust you have a safe journey, my lord. Please do everything in your power to assure your sister of the warm welcome that awaits her here.'

'You are very formal, Marissa,' he said with a twinkle in his eyes. 'But I will give Nicci your message.'

He took her hand in his firm, warm grasp and bent to give her a cousinly salute on the cheek.

The soft, satiny skin seemed to quiver at the touch of his lips; the scent of her filled his nostrils and he heard her sharp intake of breath. Neither knew which of them moved, but suddenly she was in his arms and his lips had fastened on her mouth in a deep kiss that held a wordless question. Marissa responded, her hands grasping his lapels to draw him deeper in, her senses drowning in the realisation of his strength, his warmth, his power.

And then he broke away, his face darkened with anger, his fist slamming hard down onto the dining table sending the china jumping and a fork bouncing onto the floor.

'Damn it! I must have lost my senses!' And he was gone, the heavy door slamming behind him, cutting off the sound of his booted feet on the boards.

Chapter Four

'I do think we could begin to move into half-mourning now, my dear,' Miss Venables remarked as she buttered her breakfast roll. 'It has been thirteen months, after all, since the third Earl's sad demise. This lovely weather makes one think of summer and light gowns—'

'And here we sit like three moulting crows in our sad blacks!' Nicci interrupted her, springing to her feet and pulling back the drapes at the breakfast room window even farther, to let the sunshine stream in.

'Nicci, dear,' Miss Venables protested, although more out of habit than any real expectation of being heeded. Thirteen months in the company of Miss Southwood had left both Marissa and Jane inordinately fond of the young woman, but still struggling to tame the natural high spirits which her unconventional upbringing had fostered.

Nicci was charming, polite and warmly affectionate, but also headstrong, outspoken and still struggling with the social *mores* of English country society.

Fresh, pretty, blonde and spirited, she was a favourite with the daughters of the surrounding gentry and had a coterie of friends, all, like her, seventeen and on the verge of their come-out.

Constrained as they were by the rules of mourning, the ladies had spent a quiet year, only attending the most private gatherings. But time had still flown. The Dower House had been refurbished to their liking, and if pretty dress silks had been missing from their lives there had still been the excitement of choosing furnishing fabrics and arguing amiably over colour schemes.

'Is it this morning that you are joining the Vicar's daughters for your dancing class?' Marissa enquired, sipping her breakfast chocolate. Nicci was learning dance and deportment with the two Misses Woodruffe, the Vicar's daughters, and Miss Catherine Ollard, the Squire's youngest. Miss Venables had taken the rest of her education in hand, declaring Nicci to be woefully ignorant of most of the knowledge required of a fashionable young lady.

'Yes, but when I get back please may we write to the silk warehouse in Norwich for some samples of dress fabrics?'

Miss Venables watched Marissa as she laughingly agreed to write that very morning. What a difference a year had made to her dear cousin! In company Marissa was still grave, poised and reserved, but when they were alone the young widow allowed her warm, funny, caring nature to blossom and the house was often full of laughter. She never referred to her late husband unless she had to, and then only in the most formal terms. Miss Venables felt she understood that marriage no more now than she had at the beginning.

Occasionally she found Marissa deep in thought, a little smile playing wistfully round her lips, but as to the object of her musings, she could only guess.

'I think we could go as far as fawn, pearl-grey, violet…all with black edging, of course,' Marissa was saying as the door opened and Whiting entered with a salver.

'This morning's postal delivery, my lady.' He proffered the letters to Marissa, who began to sort through them.

'Aunt Augusta…yet another account…the oddest handwriting on this one…two for you, Jane dear. Nicci, here is one for you, a little battered from its travels.'

Nicci reached for the package eagerly. 'It is from Luc!' she cried joyfully, slitting the seals with her butter knife and tearing open the wrapper. 'He is coming home! Oh, Marissa, Jane—Luc is coming home at last!'

'Where was it posted my dear?' Jane enquired calmly. 'Do take care, you are getting butter on your cuffs.'

'When?' demanded Marissa abruptly. 'I mean… when was it posted?' For some reason her heart was beating erratically and she felt breathless. She pressed one hand to her bodice, briefly, as if the gesture would still the sudden turbulence in her breast.

'It was posted in Kingston, and he says he expects

to be in London...' Nicci was scanning rapidly '...why, by this week!'

'My goodness!' Miss Venables sprang up, her napkin dropping unheeded at her feet. 'There will be so much to do at the Hall! All the rooms under Holland covers and nothing aired! Matthews must be apprised of this immediately... Marissa, my dear, are you quite well?'

'Er...what?' Marissa pulled her scattered wits together and focused her attention on her cousin. 'Yes, everything you say is eminently sensible, Jane. Perhaps we should ask the Whitings to lend a hand. Matthews has managed admirably, but there is all the difference in the world between Southwood Hall without the family at home and what his lordship will require.'

She got up gracefully, leaving her unopened letters unheeded on the table. 'Nicci, we will travel in the gig with you and drop you at the Vicarage before we call at the Hall. Pull the bell for Whiting, would you, please, and then we must fetch our bonnets and wraps and be off.'

Nicole, as usual, took up the reins of the gig, but was soon relieved of them by Miss Venables. 'Really, my dear Nicci, you will have us in a ditch, and that poor pony does not know whether it is coming or going!'

'Oh, but I am so excited!' Nicci surrendered the reins without demur, but sat jigging on the seat. 'Must I go to my class? How can I concentrate on dancing and deportment when Luc may even now be within sight of shore!'

'Even if he is landing in Bristol as we speak,' replied Miss Venables repressively, 'it will still take him at least three days to accomplish his journey. And surely he will want to spend at least one day in London on his way.'

'He would not!' Nicci wailed. 'He could not be so cruel as not to come to me at once!'

Marissa sat silently listening to the interchange, her feelings alternating between dread and excitement. She had spent the last year imagining the moment when Lucian would return, yet thirteen months from their parting she was still no clearer as to what she felt for him.

At night her lips burned with the guilty remembrance of his kisses.

But by day she remembered all too clearly the anger in his voice and the sound of his fist crashing onto the breakfast table when they parted. She had behaved shamelessly, no better than a hussy, and she had disgusted him.

It was in their nature that men had carnal desires, but it was unthinkable that a woman of breeding should exhibit the slightest passion, incite caresses, offer warmth and passion in return. Her lord had made it perfectly plain early in their marital relations exactly what was required of her, and she had learned quickly that any attempt on her part to change that would be met with swift retribution.

Perhaps the passage of time had erased the memory of her behaviour from Lucian's mind. None the less, she must guard against ever letting him see the warm, passionate woman inside her well-modulated exterior.

Still distracted by her thoughts, she was scarcely aware that they were bowling briskly up the Vicarage drive. Miss Venables, who had an unexpectedly dashing driving style, was thoroughly enjoying herself, her sallow cheeks tinged with pink and her eyes shining.

A tall figure was walking slowly towards them, and Jane drew up as they came abreast of him. 'Mr Ashforde, good day to you! A lovely morning, is it not?'

The Honourable Reverend Crispin Ashforde was probably one of the most beautiful young men any of the ladies had ever seen. The second son of Viscount Bassingbourn had scandalised his noble papa by choosing the church over the army or government office, and was currently setting every susceptible heart in the surrounding parishes aflutter.

Black-haired, white-skinned, with a perfect classical profile, he looked as though he had stepped from a plinth in Southwood Hall. Yet Mr Ashforde's disposition was such that the patent adoration of young ladies was lost on him. Serious, studious—and, in Miss Venables's opinion, thoroughly boring—he was regarded by all the matchmaking mothers as a perfect catch. Nicole, however, possibly the least eligible female for an earnest cleric that could be imagined, had caught his attention. And she, dazzled by his looks and piqued by his serious nature, had fallen head over heels in love.

Miss Venables knew puppy love when she saw it and was tolerantly inclined to ignore it.

'My lady, Miss Venables, Miss Southwood.' Mr Ashforde raised his hat and bowed. 'A very clement morning, is it not? One is put in mind of the words of Horace in the *Odes,* is one not?'

'Frequently,' Miss Venables responded drily. 'But you must excuse us. Miss Southwood is already late for her class.'

'But wait!' Nicci was blushing prettily. 'We must tell Mr Ashforde our news!' She turned her radiant face to him and blurted out, 'My brother is expected home from the West Indies at any day.'

'What marvellous news! I shall look forward to calling upon him at the earliest opportunity,' Mr Ashforde assured her earnestly. 'Good morning, ladies.'

As Marissa and Jane regained the coast road the older woman sighed heavily. 'Oh, dear, I do believe the young idiot will be asking his lordship for Nicci's hand as soon as he sets foot over the threshold of the Hall. I fear the Earl cannot but be displeased with us for allowing such an attachment to develop.'

Marissa was startled at the thought that his lordship might think them at fault. 'But Mr Ashforde is not ineligible, Jane. After all, his father is Lord Bassingbourn, and although he is the second son I believe he has a not inconsiderable fortune from his late great-aunt. And he is such a nice young man, so gentle and serious.'

'My dear Marissa, you sound as if you approve! I had not felt any anxiety, assuming that it was a mere youthful flirtation. But I am made uneasy by the speed with which Mr Ashforde announced his intention to call. Nicci is far too young to think of marriage, and her upbringing has left her immature and sheltered from Society. You cannot wish her away on an earnest young curate, however well connected. She has her whole life before her. And,' she added tartly, 'you cannot wish her on him! What a dance she would lead him, poor boy.'

Marissa did not argue, but whatever Miss Venables said, she could not but feel that Mr Ashforde was a safe choice for Nicci. Her young cousin must never know what marriage to a sophisticated, demanding older man could bring. She would never allow Nicci to experience the heartache and the loneliness that such a disparity in ages and temperament would mean. She knew the girl must marry, but Marissa's heart was full of fear for her and she was determined to favour the curate's suit.

Miss Venables, noticing with concern her silence, and the ebb and flow of colour in her cousin's cheeks, reined in at the gates of the Hall. 'There is no necessity for you to be cooped up talking to Matthews about setting the house to rights. Why not walk down to the beach? It is a lovely morning and the sea air will do you good.' She expected Marissa to protest that it was her duty to see to the arrangements, but to her surprise her cousin nodded.

'Thank you, Jane. I will make my own way back to the Dower House in time for luncheon.'

Thinking about marriage had recalled all the early memories of her lord's courtship, if it could be described thus. The Earl had asked her to dance twice at Almack's, and at first she had been flattered that the eligible, wealthy and handsome Earl of Radwinter should show her such attention. But formal observance had been all he ever showed, and after two months of impersonal conversations when they met she had been stunned when her father informed her that he had accepted on her behalf an offer of marriage from the Earl. Marissa, as a dutiful daughter, had had no say in the matter, and in a matter of weeks had found herself the Countess of Radwinter.

An unseasonably warm breeze blew over the salt grazings on either side of the track. Marissa flicked back the fronts of her wool pelisse and strode out, the fresh air filling her lungs. Fortunately she had put on stout walking shoes, and after a few minutes the megrims had left her and she was filled with the promise of spring and the excitement of Lucian's return.

He would have forgotten that disgraceful encounter the day that he had left, she assured herself. He would settle at the Hall with Nicci and the estate would come to life once more. From his letters to Nicci she had a vivid picture of his life in Jamaica, of the warmth and the vibrancy, of his energy… And she and Jane would continue their comfortable life in the Dower House, gradually mixing more in Society as the mourning period came to an end.

The saltings were cut off from the sea by a ridge of old sand dunes, now covered in tufty grass and gorse bushes and crowned by a ridge of Corsican pines, bent and gnarled by the wind.

Marissa scrambled up the steep landward side, the

sand slipping and shifting under her boots. She was panting by the time she gained the summit and stood there, one hand on the rough red bark of a tree, the other shading her eyes as she gazed out across the wide beach to the glitter of the sea beyond.

The dunes swept down in a low shallow slope to the beach, an almost irresistible invitation to run, to swoop down like a bird, free in the spring sunshine. Marissa cast a swift glance around, but there was no one in sight, not even a fishing boat. She untied her bonnet strings, unbuttoned her pelisse and set both under a gorse bush, and then, gathering up her skirts, she began to run down the long slope.

Almost immediately her foot caught in a twisting root, half covered by the shifting sands. She fell, rolling on the slippery turf. After one startled moment Marissa let her body go with the movement, eyes shut, rolling down the dune as she had seen small boys do many a time in this very spot.

Her eyes were tight shut, her hair shedding its pins, and sand was getting everywhere, but she did not care, laughing aloud with the sheer exhilaration of the sensation.

At last, with a gentle bump, she landed at the bottom, resting against a tree trunk. She lay panting on her back, her eyes still tightly shut, the vanilla scent of the gorse blossom filling her nostrils.

Her breathing steadied and she relaxed, the sunlight red through her closed lids. The picture of the broad, empty stretch of beach and sea filled her mind. Gradually a small incongruity dawned on her: there were no trees below the point where she had started to run...

Cautiously she opened her eyes and found herself looking at a pair of travel-stained leather boots. Her gaze moved upwards to take in buckskin breeches covering long, strong legs. Horrified, Marissa snapped her eyes shut, then, hardly daring to do so, she opened them again and looked up into the man's face.

It was Lucian. His eyes were vivid against a deep tan, his teeth showed in a wide, white grin of amusement. With perfect formality, as though he were meeting her in the drawing room, he bowed and said, 'Good morning, Lady Southwood. I trust I find you in good health.'

The lilting accent of the West Indies was back in his voice. Marissa's bones felt as though they were melting; she could not move, speak, could hardly breathe, so overwhelmed was she by his unexpected appearance. Somehow, in thirteen months, she had forgotten the sheer physical impact of his presence, the force of his personality.

Lucian's amused gaze was travelling down the length of her dark brown walking dress. Marissa could feel it was twisted tightly around her body, and from the feel of the breeze she realised with horror that her legs were exposed to the knee. She dared not look, but she had a horrible fear that her garters were showing.

She struggled to sit upright, knowing that the very action was causing her bosom to heave and the dress to cling more tightly.

'Allow me.' Warm hands grasped both of hers and Marissa was pulled to her feet in one easy motion.

'My lord…' She found her voice with an effort. 'Thank you. I lost my footing at the top of the dune. I could not stop…'

He smiled without speaking and Marissa's voice trailed away as she stood looking up at him. His hair was overlong again, shot through by the sun with gilt. Around his eyes the tiny laughter lines were paler against the tanned skin, and she noticed for the first time how his dark lashes were tipped with gold.

He must have set out that morning early, and in a hurry, for he had not shaved. She had to fight down the urge to trace the stubble above his upper lip with her forefinger to discover whether it was rough or soft to the touch.

Marissa felt as though she was enmeshed in a feverish dream. Even her feet felt trapped by the soft sand. With an effort she took a step away from him and stumbled.

'Are you hurt? Have you twisted your ankle?' He was at her side again, one hand burning even through the twilled cotton of her sleeve.

'No…no… It is just this soft sand. My goodness,' she laughed shakily, 'I must look a regular fright. Whatever must you think of me?'

'I think you look utterly—' He broke off, the laughter gone from his eyes, his expression strangely intent.

Unable to cope with the silence, Marissa blurted out, 'What are you looking at?'

'You…' Then he laughed. 'And the twigs in your hair.'

'Oh, no!' All her awkwardness was forgotten as Marissa hastily ran her fingers through her dishevelled curls, realising that all the pins had fallen out in her headlong tumble. Twigs showered out and fine sand ran down her neck. With an impatient 'tut' Marissa brushed at her skirts, shaking what seemed to be a pound of sand out of her petticoats.

Tactfully Lucian turned his back, striding up the slope to rescue her bonnet and pelisse from the bush where she had left them. Flushed, but feeling more in command of herself, Marissa buttoned the pelisse and pulled on her bonnet, doing the best she could to bundle up her loose hair inside it.

Her fingers were on the bonnet strings when Lucian said, 'Stop.' She froze in obedience, not even asking why. He was close again, his eyes fixed on her face. 'You have sand on your cheekbone,' he murmured. 'Here, let me…'

Before she could raise her hand his fingertips were stroking the fine grains from her skin, gently brushing them away from her eyes. The warm, gentle touch hypnotised her into closing her eyes, and for a long moment she stood there, his fingers tracing the curves of her face.

Marissa turned her face into his hand, and in response his palm cupped her cheek. His breath whispered warmly on her mouth and she waited…

There was the thud of hooves on the turf and a rattle of carriage wheels. Marissa opened her eyes to find

Lucian standing a good three strides away from her and a groom hastening around the edge of the dune where the track petered out onto the beach.

'My lady! Miss Venables sent me to tell you that— Oh, your lordship, I did not know you were here. Begging your pardon, my lord, Miss Venables was wishful of letting her ladyship know you had arrived, sir.'

'Yes, I saw her ladyship on the dunes and rode down to greet her.' Lucian turned to hand Marissa up into the gig and swung up onto his patiently waiting horse. 'I will ride with you,' he informed the groom as the gig moved off along the sandy track.

Marissa pulled herself together with a supreme effort and remarked, 'I am sorry we were so ill-prepared for you, my lord. Nicole received your letter this morning and we had not looked to see you for at least the next three days. Miss Venables is even now at the Hall putting in hand preparations for your arrival. Your sister, I am afraid, is at the Vicarage—at her dancing class.'

She felt she was prattling mindlessly, and was acutely conscious of the presence of the groom beside her. The man cleared his throat, 'Pardon me, my lady, but James has gone in the carriage to collect Miss Southwood: Miss Venables sent him off as soon as his lordship's baggage coach and carriage arrived.'

Miss Venables was once again rising to the occasion, Marissa thought with relief. She could be relied on to know exactly what to do under any set of circumstances, which, considering that she herself could hardly string two words together sensibly just at the moment, was a very good thing.

'Your journey was smooth I trust, my lord,' she enquired, finding her eyes fixed on his hands, strong and brown on the reins. Unaccountably she could not meet his eyes, the embarrassment of being caught out in her hoydenish behaviour almost paralysing her. She had intended meeting him graciously, assured in her new role as the Dowager, and instead had been discovered romping in a way which would have been inexcusable even for Nicci.

'I was fortunate with the winds and landed in Bristol a week ago. I can only assume that the ship bearing my letter was delayed.'

Marissa was all too well aware that men rarely considered the problems of domestic arrangements and all that was involved in making a great house ready for its master and could well believe it had not occurred to Lucian to write from Bristol. 'What a delightful surprise for Miss Southwood,' she said weakly.

Luc turned in the saddle, blue eyes creased in amusement. 'That is a very polite way of telling me I should have sent word from Bristol, and that I have caused the household a great deal of work,' he remarked. 'I have no doubt that I will be due a severe scold from Miss Venables! Tell me, how should I best make my apologies?' His smile was broad and white and quite shameless.

Marissa, very conscious of the groom beside her, was constrained in her reply. 'Southwood Hall stands ready for your lordship whenever you choose to ar-

rive. But I can only apologise that the London house
was so unprepared. As you will recall, Matthews is
here at the Hall, and there is only a skeleton staff left
in Town.'

'No matter. I had no intention of setting everyone
in a bustle for one night: I stayed at Fenton's Hotel
and was perfectly comfortable.'

Marissa was taken aback by such consideration for
the servants. Her late husband would have expected
to be able to walk into any of his establishments at
any hour of the day and night and find all in perfect
readiness and order.

'And how is my sister? Has she led you a merry
dance this past year? From her letters I have lived in
daily expectation of a communication from you desir-
ing me to remove her from your household immediately.'

The groom repressed a snort with great difficulty,
bending over the reins to hide his broad grin. Miss
Southwood was a rare handful, not but that she wasn't
a nice young lady it was a pleasure to serve. Always
a smile and 'please' and 'thank you'. But she was full
of mischief and he was just glad she wasn't *his* sister!

'It has been a pleasure to have her with us,' Marissa
said repressively. What had Nicci been writing? 'We
have been living very quietly, of course: I can only
hope dear Nicole has not been intolerably bored.'

Luc did not reply, merely smiled, reflecting that
Nicci's letters had indeed shown all the frustration to
be expected from a lively young woman suddenly
placed with strangers in a cold, new world of formal-

ity. But his sister had soon stopped bemoaning her
life, and gradually a picture of a happy trio of ladies
had emerged. It had intrigued him to see Marissa
through his sister's innocent eyes. Nicci had written a
few months ago:

> *I love her very much. She is kind and funny,*
> *but there is a great sadness at the heart of her*
> *which I do not understand. She never speaks of*
> *his late lordship, but it cannot be that, surely, for*
> *he was very old…*

Luc had smiled wryly at the thought that a man of
forty-five could be considered 'very old' and could
only assume his sister saw him, seventeen years
younger than the earl, as middle-aged.

'There's Miss Southwood now, ma'am,' the groom
observed, pointing to the coast road where a small
carriage had just turned out of the Vicarage drive.

'My lord, please ride to meet your sister; I will join
you at the Hall.'

Lucian needed no further prompting. He urged the
horse into a brisk canter and had soon intercepted the
carriage. Even at that distance Marissa could hear
Nicci's shrieks of delight as the girl came tumbling
out of the carriage in a flurry of petticoats and flung
herself at her brother's horse.

Luc had dismounted by the time Marissa's gig came
up with them, and was laughingly attempting to dis-
entangle Nicci's arms from around his neck before she
throttled him. The narrow road was completely

blocked by horse, carriage and gig, but the arrival of a carter with a timber wagon soon dispersed the reunion.

They formed quite a procession on the way back to the Hall, Nicci hanging out of the carriage window animatedly bombarding her brother, who rode alongside, with questions. Marissa shuddered with despair at the girl's unrestrained behaviour but knew that there was no hope of curbing it in her present high state of excitement.

The baggage coach and the travelling carriage were pulling away from the front of the Hall as they drew up, but the great doors stood open and the scene glimpsed through them resembled nothing so much as a disturbed anthill.

Miss Venables, flanked by Matthews, stood in the centre of activity, directing footmen and maidservants as they scurried to disperse the piles of baggage which stood heaped around. Marissa, following Lucian and Nicci up the steps, became aware also of Whiting, who was regarding two male strangers with as near to horror on his well-schooled countenance as she had ever seen.

A dapper individual guarding a dressing case was doubtless his lordship's valet, but it was his companion who was causing Whiting's discomfiture.

Marissa was not surprised. The man was evidently, from his immaculate clothing, an upper servant, but the correctness of his dress was totally belied by his features. Built like a prizefighter, he was standing with folded arms, the upper muscles straining the cloth. His

face, tanned like leather, was crossed by a wicked scar
which bisected his eyebrow from temple to cheekbone
leaving a slash as white as his cropped hair. Standing
in the hallway surrounded by classical perfection and
the scurrying English servants he appeared foreign,
dangerous and utterly out of place. In fact the only
place where Marissa could envisage him looking at
home was on the deck of a pirate ship.

Nicci, spotting him, dropped her brother's arm and
with a shriek of 'Jackson!' threw herself into his arms
to be enveloped in a bear-like hug. Miss Venables's
eyebrows rose almost to her hairline at this unseemly
and inexplicable behaviour, but before she could protest Nicci was set firmly back on her feet and the man
was admonishing her in a surprisingly cultured voice.
'Lady Nicci, please conduct yourself with decorum.
What will Miss Venables be thinking of you?'

To almost universal amazement Nicci lowered her
eyes and said meekly, 'Yes, Jackson, but I am so very
pleased to see you, you know.'

'Well, you can best show that by helping Miss Venables,' the man replied repressively, but with a twinkle
in his grey eyes.

Jane Venables crossed the chequerboard tiles to
greet the Earl. 'My lord, welcome home to Southwood. It is a great pleasure to have you back amongst
us.'

'Thank you, Miss Venables.' He smiled down at her
over their clasped hands. 'I must apologise for my lack
of forethought in advising you of my arrival, but I see
that the usual high standards here have not slipped.'

He nodded pleasantly at Matthews and Mr and Mrs Whiting. 'Matthews, I would like a word with you this evening after dinner about the future domestic arrangements, meanwhile Jackson and Laurent will accompany me to my suite.'

'Very good, my lord.' Matthews bowed. 'A cold collation is set out in the small dining room if you and the ladies would care to partake.'

'Lady Southwood, if you would excuse me for half an hour to remove the dust of the road from my clothing, I will join you shortly.' Lucian bowed and was gone, his two servants at his heels.

Alone in the dining room, with the hubbub of the hall shut out, Nicci burst out, 'Oh, I am so pleased that Luc brought Jackson with him. I was so afraid he would leave him to look after the Jamaica estates.'

Miss Venables fixed her with a gimlet stare from her position in one of the window seats. 'And just who is this Jackson, if I may enquire?'

'Why, our butler, of course!' Nicci exclaimed in surprise. 'But he is much more than that! He has been with us for years, originally as captain of one of my father's schooners. But no one is quite sure where he came from—he will never speak of it. And then when Luc was seventeen he saved his life when the schooner was attacked by privateers. Jackson was terribly injured, almost given up for dead, but Luc brought him back home and he has been our butler ever since old Peters had his heart attack. Why,' she added disingenuously, 'Jackson has almost brought me up. He is terribly strict, you know.'

Miss Venables shuddered. 'I am not reassured. No doubt this Jackson is a good man, in his rough way, but he is hardly suitable as butler in a great house.'

'Wait and see! You will get used to him,' Nicci promised airily. 'Oh, where is Luc? I am starving!'

'Nicole, dear, ladies do not speak of their appetite; it is most improper.' Jane appeared to become aware of Marissa's appearance for the first time. 'Why do you not remove your bonnet and pelisse, Marissa?'

Reluctantly Marissa did so, sending her hair tumbling onto her shoulders and releasing a small shower of fine sand onto the polished boards.

'Marissa! What have you been doing?'

'Rolling in the sand by the look of it,' Nicci said gleefully. 'Luc did not see you, did he, Marissa?'

'I tripped,' she replied with uncharacteristic shortness. 'I must go and tidy myself before luncheon.'

She was very conscious of two pairs of eyes—one censorious, one gleeful, and both speculative—as she left the room, and was still feeling flustered when she returned, her hair brushed and pinned and her face washed.

Luc arrived at the door as she did. He was freshly shaven and dressed in clean riding clothes. Marissa kept her eyes down as he opened the door for her and ushered her to her place at table.

They all ate hungrily, helping themselves from the cold meats spread out before them. The meal was punctuated by the tale of Luc's journey and the many people he had brought messages from for his sister. Marissa watched him from under her lashes, her heart unaccountably beating faster in his presence. He seemed to bring warmth and energy with him and to infect everyone around him with his vitality. It was as though the warm Caribbean sea and the hot sands were just outside this chilly mausoleum of a house.

'You must have a dance, to celebrate your return,' Nicci was suggesting as Marissa came back to herself with a start.

Miss Venables coughed warningly, and with a swift look at Marissa Lucian turned to his sister. 'I do not think that would be appropriate Nicci: we are still in mourning.'

Nicci bit her lip in mortification, instantly catching his suggestion that she might be upsetting the widow. 'Oh, I am sorry, Marissa. That was very thoughtless of me. I did not mean…'

Marissa leaned across the table and touched her hand. 'Do not worry, Nicci, I know what you meant. But it would be a pity indeed if our neighbours did not have the opportunity to meet the Earl as soon as possible. I do not think a small dinner party would be out of place, if his lordship consents.'

'A capital idea,' Luc agreed, sitting back and smiling at all three ladies. 'How long would it take to arrange such a dinner, and—' he grinned at Nicci '—order your new gowns?'

Chapter Five

Laurent smoothed an imaginary wrinkle from the dark blue superfine cloth across his master's shoulders, then stood back and viewed the finished effect critically.

'For heaven's sake, man,' Luc protested as the valet made another dart forward with the clothes brush. 'We have been at this long enough; the guests will be here shortly.' He grimaced down at his legs. 'Knee breeches! Anyone would think we were in London instead of the depths of Norfolk.'

'It is *à la mode,* my lord,' Laurent demurred. 'It is expected, and, after all, it will be a social event spoken of for months afterwards in the neighbourhood.' He gave a final, unnecessary polish to his lordship's shoe buckles and added gloomily, 'After all, what else is there to talk of in this place which *le bon Dieu* has undoubtedly forsaken?'

Lucian fixed him with a stern eye. 'If I have to learn to be a respectable earl, then you must learn to be a respectable valet, Laurent.'

'Pah!' The man picked up his lordship's discarded linen and stalked towards the door. 'I will be respectable, my lord, but do not demand that I like this place. I will die of the pneumonia, *sans doute,* if I do not first expire from the food.'

Luc grinned at his own reflection in the glass. The man had been with him for years: he had tried to encourage him to stay in Jamaica, knowing he would hate England, but the valet had insisted that his place was at his master's side, although it would be the death of him.

Not that Luc couldn't see his point: he too yearned for the warmth, not just of the weather, but of the people. The social *mores* of English society came hard when one had lived a life characterised by informality, driven by the climate and the dictates of nature. And he missed the Caribbean sea: the cold, grey waves washing against the coast here bore no resemblance to the inviting blue depths of Jamaican waters, filled with fish as bright as jewels.

There was little point in dwelling on all that: it was past, and his new life as the fourth Earl of Radwinter was waiting for him. Tonight's soirée was his first foray into county Society, and for the sake of Nicci's future—and his own—he had to make it a success.

Lucian strolled over to the window, resisting the urge to run one finger under his collar, resenting the control that the formal evening suit imposed. But Marissa would be expecting to entertain in this style and he could not let her down. He had not failed to notice the air of rigidly suppressed excitement under her perfect poise. Like a cat's fur in a thunderstorm, her mass of hair seemed to crackle with energy under the restraint of its pins. It reminded him of the night she had found him in the Long Gallery: the one long hair that had curled itself around his finger like a living thing was still where he had placed it, between the pages of his pocketbook.

A mile away across the park Marissa too was completing her toilette. Seated in front of her dressing table mirror, she watched Mary's deft fingers capture, twist and pin up her hair. On an impulse Marissa reached up and teased out the short curls around her hairline.

'Oh, that *is* pretty, my lady!' Mary exclaimed in astonishment. Never had she known the Dowager permit the slightest curl to escape from its tight chignon, but it well became her, emphasising her cheekbones and softening the curve of her brow.

'Yes…that will do,' Marissa decided, rather surprised at her own reflection. 'Now, the diamond set, I think, Mary.' The maid fastened the diamond necklace around her mistress's neck, then began to secure the coiled hair on her crown with matching combs. Marissa adjusted the cold stones on her throat, then lifted the drop earrings and fastened them to her lobes. She had never particularly cared for the set, although her husband had insisted she wear it often. Now, against the severity of black silk, the stones sparked with a hot fire she had never seen before.

Mary helped her button her shoulder-length white kid gloves, then clasped a diamond bracelet around her wrist. As she stood Mary bent to tweak out the heavy flounce around the hem, then puffed up the little sleeves before draping a white silk stole with a long fringe over Marissa's elbows.

There was a knock on the door and Miss Venables entered, resplendent in deep plum satin, two spots of colour staining her cheeks. 'My dear, you look lovely! The carriage is here, and we must be off, for it is six o'clock and we promised his lordship that we would be there to help him receive.'

The shadows were lengthening in the park as the barouche pulled up at the front door. Marissa was suddenly seized by the odd sensation of arriving as a guest at what, until so recently, had been her own house. She was looking forward to this dinner party, for it would be the first where she would not have to sit in constant fear that some detail would be found wanting, a shortcoming that would be visited upon her later by her lord. It was not the only reason for her anticipation, but it was the only one that she was prepared to acknowledge to herself.

The door was opened by Jackson, dignified in evening black, but still managing to look dangerously out of place. He bowed the ladies in, handed their cloaks to a footman, and conducted them past a small string ensemble who were tuning up on the landing and into the Salon.

'Lady Southwood, Miss Venables, my lord.'

Lucian felt his jaw drop and pulled himself together rapidly. For a moment he had not recognised the dazzling young woman in the doorway. He had seen Marissa virtually every day for the last fortnight, but she had always been the Marissa he had come to know: poised, rigidly groomed, controlled, friendly yet distant.

But this was a different woman. Her hair sparkled in the candlelight, her skin, always so white, seemed creamy against the diamonds, and with a shock he realised that she was not much older than his sister.

Marissa saw Lucian's admiration in his face and her eyes sparked green with pure pleasure. For the first time she felt the sensation of being admired without any obligation to anyone else. She was not in the marriage mart, obedient to her father; she was not presenting herself as an adornment of her husband. She was herself, and she was revelling in it.

Nicole, who was wearing a pretty gown of midnight-blue appropriate to a young lady who was not yet out, gasped audibly. 'Oh, Marissa, how pretty you look!' She dashed over, caught Marissa's hands in hers and turned to implore of her brother, 'Do you not think Marissa looks pretty, Luc?'

'No, I do not,' he drawled, his eyes on Marissa. His sister gasped indignantly, but before she could protest he took the wind out of her sails. 'I think she looks beautiful.' Marissa blushed rosily, her heart suddenly beating more quickly, and she could only be relieved when he turned to her friend. 'Miss Venables, may I be so bold as to compliment you on the elegance of your gown?'

Miss Venables was responding with a gracious inclination of the head as Jackson entered and announced, 'There is a carriage approaching, my lord.'

Hastily the party assembled themselves to receive their guests and before long the Salon was alive with the sound of chattering voices and the swish of silk.

When they had constructed the guest list Marissa had been apologetic about the lack of distinguished company. 'With the start of the Season so close our more fashionable neighbours are up in Town,' she had explained. 'The Blackwoods, the Exeters... I wonder if the Scotts have left yet...'

In the end the guest list had included the local squirearchy and professional people, with a touch of aristocratic eccentricity in the form of Lady Augusta, who now had Sir Henry Ollard trapped against the mantelpiece and was berating him over the state of his coverts.

'How you expect to enjoy a decent run if you cannot provide the cover for the foxes I do not know!' Sir Henry, a mild man, was protesting faintly that his keepers were doing their best, but was making no headway.

Lady Ollard, making polite conversation with Mr and Mrs French, raised her eyebrows but passed no comment, being well used to Lady Augusta. The Frenches, more recent arrivals on the local scene, tended to start nervously when Lady Augusta approached them. Mrs French, having moved from the bustling heart of the City, where her husband had made a substantial fortune, was finding it difficult to adjust to an entirely new social scene.

Her sons Stephen and James, however, found the country perfectly palatable: still at the age where country sports held more appeal than the company of young ladies, they spent their days with their new friends and were dragged reluctantly to parties.

Miss Catherine Ollard was attempting, not very successfully, to engage Stephen in conversation, but as both he and his brother were more interested in Mr Ashforde's description of a recent shooting trip her efforts were wasted. The Misses Woodruffe, probably the only young ladies in the neighbourhood who remained uncaptivated by Mr Ashforde's startling good looks, were chattering to Nicci about clothes, but she was only half listening, her shining eyes fixed on the perfect classical profile of the young curate.

Lucian, politely extracting himself from a discussion of a local political scandal which was engrossing Dr Robertson, Mr Hope and Miss Venables, strolled across to where Marissa was standing by herself, watching the group of young people.

'And what is my little sister up to now?' he enquired softly.

'Oh, nothing.' Marissa smiled tolerantly, her focus still on Mr Ashforde. 'She is enjoying the party, which is only natural. I am afraid it has been so very dull for her at the Dower House this past year, and she really has been very good.'

The child deserves a diversion, she thought, and Mr Ashforde, so kind, so gentle, might prove to be more than that in time. Her lips curved in a soft smile and Luc, following the direction of her gaze, frowned suddenly. He said abruptly, 'Is that the curate? What's his name…Ashton?'

'Ashforde,' Marissa corrected. 'He is very much a favourite hereabouts, quite an embellishment to local Society. He is the second son of Viscount Bassingbourn, but so unlike his elder brother. Mr Ashforde is dedicated to his calling, and so erudite.'

'Popinjay!'

'Oh, no, never that! I admit his quite extraordinary good looks draw more attention to him than he would wish.'

'You think him good-looking, then?' Luc eyed the white skin, classical features and elegant figure of the curate with distaste and an uneasy feeling that with his black hair and cultured manners Mr Ashforde must offer a reflection of the late Earl to a woman who was still mourning her husband.

Marissa turned to Luc in surprise. 'Good-looking? Why, certainly, he is perhaps the most handsome man I have ever seen: he could take his place on a pedestal here in the sculpture gallery and rival Adonis.' Luc's expression mystified her. What had Mr Ashforde done to displease him so? It was so much accepted that Mr Ashforde combined excellent manners with physical perfection that it seemed quite natural to discuss him as one would any other beautiful phenomenon. Not finding herself attracted to the curate, it did not occur to Marissa to be self-conscious in the way in which she discussed him with Luc.

Luc still seemed strangely out of humour to Marissa's acute eye when Jackson announced that dinner

was served. Luc offered Lady Augusta his arm and
Marissa found Sir Henry, who would sit at her right
hand. Gradually the party sorted themselves out and
processed past the string quartet into the Small Dining
Chamber, a cavernous room only slightly less imposing than the Grand Dining Chamber. Luc, having
viewed the larger room, had announced flatly that he
would not use it, and had instructed Jackson to move
the best silver to the Small Chamber.

Huge fires blazed at either end of the room, despite
the mild weather outside, and a myriad of candles reflected off the polished mahogany and massed silver.
Marissa took her place at the foot of the table, facing
the new Earl. She had protested when he had asked
her to act as hostess, but Nicci was not yet out and
Luc had flatly vetoed her suggestion that he ask Lady
Augusta to preside.

Luc's eyes were on Marissa as he listened to a lec-
ture from Lady Augusta on the probable shortcomings
of his cook. Judging by the array of dishes that the
servants were even now bearing in, Mrs Wood could
stand up to the worst criticisms from her ladyship.

Marissa could not help herself worrying about the
arrangements, but relaxed as the dishes were laid out.
Stuffed soles, a fricassee of veal, chickens, curry of
rabbits, a vegetable pudding, sweetbreads, buttered
lobster and a fat goose created a cornucopia of local
fare which Marissa hoped would show Luc the best
that his estate could offer.

She met Jackson's eye and saw a glimmer of satisfaction in their dark depths. The footmen were re-

moving covers and pouring wine. The volume of conversation began to rise and with a sigh of relief she smiled down the length of the table at Luc. At that distance the likeness to her late husband disappeared; all she was aware of was Luc's mane of blond hair, caught by the late evening sun, the relaxed grace of his body, the broad set of his shoulders. Despite the formal evening clothes he still managed to radiate a dangerous sense of exoticism.

And yet she felt safe with him. If it had been Charles in that seat she would have been picking at her food, her stomach churning with nervous anticipation of an error, a slip by the servants which would mar his expectations of perfection.

Luc caught the smile, read the pure, uncomplicated pleasure in it and his irrational jealousy and bad humour vanished. Of course she was not hankering after that young puppy of a curate! Nor, for the first time since he had known her, did she seem trapped in some sad memory.

His attention was distracted momentarily by the giggles of the Vicar's daughters and Miss Ollard. They, and Nicci, seemed so much younger than Marissa. He had resigned himself to the thought that sooner or later he was going to have to go up to London, brave the Marriage Mart and find some suitable young lady to be mistress of Southwood, mother to his heir.

He looked again at Marissa, almost luminous at the other end of the table, her skin glowing in the candlelight, the diamonds glinting at her throat and in her dark hair. Why had he not thought of her before? There was no bar to marriage with a cousin's widow. She was beautiful, intelligent, mature beyond her years, well used to running a large establishment. Nicci loved her, that much was plain. And she was not averse to him—when he had kissed her it had been as though a fire had kindled into life.

Yes…why not indeed? Why not broach it this evening after the guests had departed?

Marissa was too far away to read his expression, but she noticed his sudden stillness, the intensity with which he was gazing at her, then he seemed to recollect himself and began to talk to Lady Ollard on his left-hand side.

It was time she stopped daydreaming and paid attention to her guests, Marissa chided herself. She listened intently to Mr Woodruffe's knowledgeable suggestions for plants for her refurbished gardens at the Dower House, charming him with the graceful deference she showed to his experience.

'Now roses are always safe on these heavy soils, and of course you are sheltered from the worst of the winds in that dip. Lavender, now, might suffer, although if you get your gardener to dig in plenty of gravel that will stop any root-rot…'

He was well away, needing only occasional nods and murmurs of encouragement. Marissa glanced down the table and frowned slightly to see Nicci's heightened colour. Her laugh was becoming rather shrill and she had been talking to Crispin Ashforde almost exclusively. It would never do for her to be setting her cap at him too obviously, especially when Lucian seemed disinclined to like the young man. She would have to do something to change that opinion, for she was still convinced that the curate would be the ideal husband for Nicci.

The servants were removing dishes, re-laying the table with an array of sweetmeats and desserts. Syllabubs, jellies, a confection reproducing the frankly hideous fountain in the West Court in sugar, baskets of pastries and custards were set before them. One of the footmen lifted the heavy epergne loaded with fruit from the sideboard to place in the centre of the table. It was off balance, and another man hurried to help him, but before he could do so the top layer of fruit spilt over, thudding onto the table and scattering between the chair-legs.

Footmen scrambled for the fruit, Jackson seized the epergne and set it firmly on the table and Luc laughed out loud. The guests, cheerfully fielding fruit as it rolled in their direction, joined in.

Still laughing, Luc looked down the table and saw Marissa, white as a ghost, hands gripped onto the arms of her chair, her expression one of stricken horror. He had seen that look before, on the face of a servant expecting to be whipped by a neighbour of his who was notorious for his brutality. Even as that impossible comparison came into his head she had collected herself and was apologising graciously to the guests on either side of her.

The old Marissa was back, the shield of social propriety was in place, and the spontaneity and joy he had seen on her face had utterly vanished. The meal seemed to drag on, and throughout the dessert course he noticed she toyed with three grapes on her plate and never lifted a mouthful to her lips.

Luc rubbed his temples as he cudgelled his brain for an explanation of the dramatic change in Marissa's mood. He was still puzzled as she rose, catching the eye of Lady Augusta, and led the ladies out, leaving the gentlemen to their port.

Marissa struggled to regain her composure as they entered the Salon. Mechanically she encouraged Lady Augusta in her efforts to set up a four for whist, and found music for the young ladies to play later.

Was she never to be free of Charles? Would her husband always haunt her, dominating her in death as he had in life? She shivered as she remembered what had always followed any domestic transgression for which he held her responsible. The late Earl had believed that physical punishment was necessary to discipline servants, hounds and his wife. He would never show the slightest sign of displeasure in public: chastisement belonged in the bedchamber...

Half an hour later, when Luc led the gentlemen back in to join the ladies, the whist table was already established and Miss Catherine Ollard was turning over the pile of music sheets on the piano, rather too obviously hoping that she would be asked to perform.

'Will you not play for us, Miss Ollard?' Marissa asked, seeing the young girl's eagerness.

'Oh, well, that is, I do not know if my playing is... Oh, well, if you insist, Lady Southwood.' She sat at the piano, settling her skirts and opening a volume of ballads on the music rest before her.

The younger Mr French came forward with alacrity. 'May I turn for you, Miss Ollard?'

The Woodruffe sisters raised their eyebrows at each other, but sat politely to listen, and the other gentlemen disposed themselves about the room.

Luc came and sat next to Marissa on one of the pair of sofas flanking the fireplace. He stretched out his long legs, folded his arms and whispered out of the corner of his mouth, 'Did you *have* to do that?'

He was rather too close for convention, the sleeve of his coat almost touching her gloved arm. Marissa felt the warmth of him, smelled the sandalwood cologne he wore and felt her heart begin to thump. Somehow she managed to give him a reproving stare and whisper, 'Shh!'

Under cover of the opening bars he leaned closer and whispered in return, 'You look even more magnificent when you frown at me!'

'Do not be ridiculous!' She could feel the colour rising up her throat and turned her head away. Why he should be flirting with her she could not imagine, but that was undoubtedly what he was doing. She might never have been involved in flirtation before, but she could recognise it when it was happening!

'There is nothing ridiculous about it; you must know how beautiful you look this evening.' His eyes rested appreciatively on her averted profile.

'I know no such thing!'

'Fishing for compliments, my lady?'

The sheer audacity of it brought her head round, her eyes sparking with indignation. 'My lord!'

'But no young lady appears at a social occasion with a new hairstyle unless she is well aware of how well it becomes her.'

She could hear the laughter in his whispered teasing and it only served to add to her indignation. 'Sir, I am not a *young lady*. I am a Dowager.'

'Surely the youngest and most beautiful in the land.' He broke off to applaud the end of the ballad. 'Well done, Miss Ollard, a very pretty air indeed! Will you not favour us with another?'

Miss Ollard flushed and began to rise from the pianoforte. 'You are very kind, my lord, but I believe it is time to make way for someone else. Or…Miss Woodruffe, if I were to play, will you not sing?'

Having restored peace with her friend, whose meaningful looks she had been only too well aware of, Miss Catherine struck up an Elizabethan love song. Miss Woodruffe warbled prettily, causing Luc to moan softly in anguish.

'Luc, you are impossible,' Marissa hissed, while maintaining an appreciative social smile. 'You will have to get used to this sort of thing.'

'Remind me to have the pianoforte chopped up for firewood,' he retorted, low-voiced.

Marissa could not help but smile. 'Miss Sophie Woodruffe plays the harp, and she often brings it with her.'

'Oh, my God!' He dropped his head into his hands in mock despair. 'Then I shall invest in a pair of earplugs at the earliest opportunity.' The air came to an end and before they could embark on another Luc was on his feet, leading the applause. 'Ladies, thank you, that was delightful; it almost moved me to tears.'

Neither young lady could work out why, but somehow it did not seem appropriate to continue playing, and at that moment Jackson forestalled any further entertainment by ushering in the footmen with the tea tray.

Marissa was dutifully circulating around the room, exchanging pleasantries with the guests, admiring Lady Augusta's winnings at the whist table, where they were playing for penny points, and congratulating the young ladies on their musical performance.

Seeing that the Earl was within earshot, she added wickedly, 'And I do hope you will bring your harp to the next soirée here, Miss Sophie. His lordship has just confided in me that it is quite his favourite instrument.' She looked him square in the eye, her face alight with laughter.

As he passed her he bent his head and whispered, '*Touché,* Marissa.' His eyes followed her slender, elegant form as she moved around the room, gracefully putting everyone at their ease, taking the opportunity to thank Jackson for the success of the arrangements as she passed him.

No, it would be no hardship being married to Marissa, and the contrast with the immature young girls only pointed up her obvious advantages. He would ask her to marry him tonight, find an opportunity to speak to her alone.

He found Sir Henry at his side, the older man also watching the Dowager Countess. 'Good to see her enjoying herself again,' the baronet observed. 'I've missed seeing her out riding, you know: damned fine seat on a horse. Of course your cousin would never permit her to ride with the hounds. Great stickler for decorum, the late Earl.'

Luc looked thoughtful. 'Tell me, Sir Henry, I am not familiar with the fine details of English social niceties yet, but would it be considered inappropriate for Lady Southwood to be seen riding at this stage in her mourning?'

'Good grief, no! It's been well over a year, has it not? Perfectly acceptable, and it seems a shame to deprive her of something she enjoys after all she has been through.'

Luc clapped his guest on the shoulder. 'Sound advice, Sir Henry. I am obliged to you.'

Marissa accepted a cup of tea from Jackson and went back to her place on the sofa. Luc, waving aside the offer of refreshment, joined her. 'Tell me, Marissa, do you miss riding?'

Taken aback, she exclaimed, 'Oh, yes, very much! I used to ride every day when the weather permitted.'

'Surely it would be acceptable for you to ride again now?'

'I suppose so…yes. I must think about buying a horse.'

'You must have had a horse. Is it not still in the stables here?'

'My lord preferred me to ride a variety of mounts,

depending on the occasion and the season.' With some constraint she added, 'My lord viewed a rider in the landscape as being part of the composition of the parkland.' Seeing his puzzlement, she expanded, 'In autumn, for example, against the backdrop of the newly ploughed fields and reddening foliage, I rode the red roan in a chestnut-brown habit. In winter, he wished me to ride in garnet-red on the grey.'

Her face was serious as she explained his lordship's detailed rules for creating a landscape almost Palladian in its perfection, in order to set off the house like a jewel in its box. Luc would have laughed out loud if he had not been so fearful of offending her. He had heard wherever he went murmurings of his late cousin's eccentricities, but had put them down to the whims of a dilettante rich enough to indulge his every desire. Now he was beginning to wonder if the third Earl had not been…unbalanced.

'That being so, I will send instructions to the stables that any mount you choose should be at your disposal.'

'Why, thank you, my lord! That would be wonderful. I shall so much look forward to that. I have missed my rides out about the estate. Oh, I see Lady Augusta waving; I believe she wishes to converse with me. Will you excuse me, please?'

Luc watched as Marissa crossed to where the older woman was now rising from the card table, ready, it seemed, to take her leave.

'I'll be leaving now, my dear. I can't get used to the French fashion of late dining; it plays havoc with my digestion. But I've had a splendid time, particularly when the footman dropped the fruit, eh? Didn't get that sort of entertainment with stuffy old Charles!'

It was as though a bank of freezing fog had swept into the room. Marissa had forgotten that incident, and the memories it had evoked, the fear of her lord's cold, studied, anger. Yet here she was, surrounded by friends, admiration, laughter. It was madness to be afraid of Charles now; she was beyond his reach, and his retribution. She was free now, free to rebuild her own life, and she never need be in the power of another man again as long as she lived.

The guests had begun to leave. Marissa detached Nicci from a rather too intimate conversation with Mr Ashforde and the two of them joined Luc at the head of the staircase to see the guests off to their waiting carriages.

Marissa was still mulling over the words she had heard pass between the young couple as she had approached them. It had sounded suspiciously like the arrangement for a tryst, but when the curate had shaken hands with Nicci Marissa had been able to detect no trace of anything other than normal courtesy.

Miss Venables put a hand on Marissa's arm. 'Will you wait for me for a few minutes, my dear? I have just remembered that Mrs Wood promised to give me a chicken pie for Widow Smith down at the wood-cutter's cottage, and if I take it now it will save me the extra journey tomorrow.'

Marissa smiled back at her. 'Of course, my dear Jane. Now, Nicci, you should be off to your bed.'

'Indeed, my lady,' Jackson concurred, coming up behind them. 'You will get black circles under your eyes, Miss Nicci.'

Nicci sighed theatrically, but did as she was told, kissing Marissa affectionately before skipping off to recount the highlights of the evening to her patiently waiting maid.

Luc had descended the stairs for a last word with Sir Henry and was still below, talking to one of the footmen. Marissa took a deep breath and made a resolution: she would lay the ghost of her lord once and for all. She would stare that portrait in the face, exorcise her fear. She only had to convince herself: he was not coming back and had no power over her life any more.

In the Long Gallery all was still, quiet, dark. She set down the branch of candles she had snatched up from the corridor and for a long moment stared at the painted likeness over the door. There: it was nothing but pigment on canvas; that was all that remained of his cruelty and control.

'I am free of you, Charles,' she said out loud. 'There is nothing you can do to me…'

As she spoke the candle flames flickered in some draught, and the painted eyes glinted as if alive. Shadows chased across the thin mouth as though the lips were forming words: cold, unemotional words calculated to wound and crush her spirit.

All her defiance dissolved. Marissa felt the tears of despair welling up in her eyes before they broke in a storm, coursing down her cheeks to drop onto his cold diamonds which encircled her throat. She was not free, she would never be free, the fear and the guilt would live on in her heart for ever.

In the doorway behind her Luc stood stock-still, his hand still on the doorknob, the slight draught he had caused in opening it still eddying around him.

He checked his instinctive desire to gather her in his arms, kiss away her pain. But he had no right, and she would not welcome his intrusion into her grief. How could he have been such a fool as to think that the mere passage of time had healed the loss of her husband? And how could he ask a woman who was so obviously in love with her dead husband to marry him?

He backed quietly away, cursing himself for a fool. He could not offer her anything to make up for the love she had lost, and it seemed cold-blooded in the extreme to suggest to Marissa that a marriage between them might be mutually convenient.

A few moments later, unaware that she had been observed, Marissa resolutely dried her tears and pushed back the damp tendrils of hair from her temples. She turned her back on the portrait and walked steadily from the Gallery. Behind her the painted eyes seemed to follow her exit.

Chapter Six

Sunshine flooding through the muslin drapes at her bedchamber window roused Marissa from a deep, but surprisingly dreamless sleep. Sitting up against the pillows, she gazed out at the burgeoning fresh green of the Home Wood and chided herself for the state she had got herself into the night before in the Long Gallery.

Why, it was perfectly Gothic, worthy of a sensational novel! She could not spend the rest of her life dwelling on what had gone before. Marriage to Charles had had…dark moments, but it was spring, and time for a new beginning. And on a beautiful day like today the best remedy for the megrims was fresh air and exercise.

'Mary!' Marissa called, swinging her legs out of bed and stretching like a cat. 'Put out my green riding habit. I shall walk up to the stables after breakfast.'

Marissa arrived in the stableyard, flushed from her walk and quite unconscious of the attractive picture she made as she picked her way across the stone-flagged yard.

Peters, the head groom, alerted by a stableboy to her ladyship's presence, emerged from the tack room wiping his hands on a rag as he strode across to meet her. His weather-beaten face was alight with pleasure.

'My lady! This is a welcome visit after so many months!'

'Not a visit, Peters—I have come to ride. His lordship has kindly put a horse at my disposal.'

'Well, my lady, you know them all, none better. Do you have a fancy for a particular one, or shall I have some led out for you?'

'Oh, lead them out, please, Peters! I have missed them so.'

Minutes later she was taking chunks of carrot from the groom and feeding the roan, feeling its soft muzzle nibbling gently at her gloved hand. She ran her hand over the arched neck, enjoying the strength and vitality beneath the warm hide. The grey mare, jealous of the attention its stablemate was being paid, nudged Marissa none too gently and she laughed.

'Yes, you may have some too, Tempest! I remember you well! Is she still such a handful, Peters?'

'Indeed she is, my lady! Had young Ned off three times yesterday, just because she took agin that herd of cattle in the Long Meadow. Very wilful she is, ma'am, but as I recollect you never had any trouble handling her.'

Marissa ran her thumb down the centre of the grey's nose, managing to tickle the most sensitive spots and reducing the animal to a state of docility that belied the flash in its eye.

'She tried to unseat me once or twice in the beginning, before we came to an understanding—didn't you, my pet? I'll take her, Peters. After all, I do not think it would be wise for Miss Southwood to ride her, and she is not up to his lordship's weight. There is no reason why the Dower House stables cannot house her, is there? Allen can take care of her along with my carriage horses. I will take her out now and perhaps you would be so good as to have the rest of her tack and so on moved down this morning.'

'Certainly, my lady. Ned! Sim! Come and saddle up Tempest, and Ned, get the rest of her tack shifted down to the Dower House stables as soon as may be and tell Allen to make up a loose box.'

Marissa touched his arm and said quietly, '*Both* saddles, please, John.'

The head groom's grizzled eyebrows drew together in a worried frown. 'Is that sensible, my lady? His new lordship's not going to like that.'

'His new lordship is not going to know, any more than my lord did.'

'Yes, but, ma'am, his late lordship was away as often as not, and this one isn't! What's he going to say if he finds out you are riding at night, by yourself and…' he hesitated and dropped his voice still further '…astride.'

'Do not worry, John. I will take care.'

'I'll see to the saddle myself, ma'am. And I'll have

a word with Allen; he's a good lad—he'll keep his mouth shut and not go gossiping.'

Marissa let Peters toss her up into the saddle and held Tempest with a firm hand while she arranged the long skirts of her habit to her satisfaction and the groom adjusted the girth and stirrup leather.

The mare was skittish, and determined to see what she could get away with. She took exception to the muck barrow which Sim was wheeling across the yard, behaved as though the stable cat was a dangerous tiger and tossed her head impatiently at being made to stand.

Deliberately Marissa forced her to walk out of the yard and across the spread of gravel before the house. She was concentrating so hard on the horse, on ensuring that her seat on the side saddle was perfectly balanced after long months when she had not ridden, that she failed to see Nicci waving from the drawing room window.

'Oh, look, Luc, does not Marissa look fine? I wish I had a habit like that!'

'I wish you had a seat on a horse like that!' her brother retorted drily, but his eyes followed the slender figure in the fir-green habit. 'I hope Peters knows what he is about, letting her out on that mare, and without even a groom.'

'Is that the one you said I must not ride because it was so wild? It seems very docile this morning.'

Even as she spoke a pheasant erupted with a panic-stricken cry right in front of Tempest. The mare threw up her head and backed rapidly in a crab-like movement. Marissa sat tight and calmly brought the mare under control, urging her into a trot and disappearing from sight round the curve of the drive.

'That is why, my dear Nicci, I said you were not to ride Tempest!' Even though Marissa was out of sight Luc remained standing at the long window, his eyes fixed on the spot where he had last seen her. The sight of the slender figure in green, controlling the animal with such ease and grace, had stirred something deep within him. Instead of going down to the estate office to spend an hour reviewing leases, what he really wanted to do was send to the stables for his stallion and follow Marissa into the park.

'What are you doing this morning, Nicci? I have to see Poole for a while, but I can take you driving later.'

His sister gave him a brilliant smile, 'Oh, thank you, Luc, but there is no need. It is such a lovely morning, I thought I should take a walk.'

She was up to something, Luc thought as he crossed the courtyard to the steward's office, although what the devil it could be, he knew not. The sooner they were in London and that little madam had some of her hoydenish ways curbed the better. Although for the life of him he could not think who he could get to chaperon her.

One of the footmen was setting out a tray with sherry in the steward's room. 'Please send to the stables and tell Peters to send round my horse for eleven, James.' He would have his ride after all, and combine it with a visit to look at that drainage ditch Poole had been worrying about...

An hour later, after a long gallop through the park, Marissa reined in on a rise which gave her a view across the back of the house and the formal gardens. The golden stone shone in the spring sunlight, the gardens lapped green at the foot of the terraces and the garden boys were out raking the gravel walks into a perfection that would be entirely lost on their new master.

How her lord would have disliked her riding without an escort. How he would have disapproved of her habit, just the wrong shade of green against the new foliage. And how wonderful it was not to have to care what anyone thought! Tempest snorted and shook her head, but Marissa kept her standing, enjoying the warmth of the sun through her jacket, uncaring that her hair was coming down at the back and that her cheeks were flushed with the exhilaration of the ride.

As she surveyed the distant gardens she became aware of a black-clad figure, small in the landscape, making its way through the rose garden. As the man came within sight of the house the doors from the small salon opened and Nicci ran down the steps and joined him.

It was Mr Ashforde, Marissa realised, screwing up her eyes against the light. The two began to walk up and down the rose terrace between the still-brown beds of pruned bushes.

How very odd that he should have come to the back of the house, Marissa mused. And it was almost as though Nicci had been waiting for him. Oh, dear, she did hope this was not a clandestine meeting—it would be fatal to the young couple's hopes if Luc discovered such a tryst had taken place. She was more than ever convinced that the kind and noble Crispin Ashforde would be the ideal husband for Nicci, but this was not the way to go about it.

She collected up the reins and urged the mare into a trot, following the track worn by the sheep and the deer until she reached the fence around the pleasure grounds. The young couple were now easily discernible, and she was close enough to see the distress on Nicci's face as she broke away and ran into the house.

Marissa threw her leg over the pommel, slipped to the ground and tied Tempest's reins to the fence. Mr Ashforde was standing gazing into an ornamental pond, a dispirited sag to his shoulders.

'Mr Ashforde! Good morning!'

The curate was so startled that he nearly dropped his hat into the water. 'Lady Southwood! Good morning to you. A fine day, is it not?'

'Yes, it is. But never mind that.' Marissa was in no mood for social chit-chat. 'What is the matter with Miss Southwood? She seemed distressed.'

Mr Ashforde smoothed back his hair from his brow, his handsome face creased with worry. 'May I be frank with you, Lady Southwood?'

'Of course! You must know I regard Nicole in the light of a sister, having none of my own.' She smiled encouragingly at him.

He fingered his hat-band, much of his normal air of quiet confidence dissipated. 'I must confess to having formed an…attachment to Miss Southwood, and I have the honour to believe that my feelings are reciprocated.'

Marissa felt a momentary impatience with his formality. 'You are in love with each other?' she demanded.

'So I believe.' He blushed rosily. 'I must confess that I have never before felt an attachment of this nature...so I can only assume it to be the tender passion which animates me.' He added earnestly, 'You must believe that I only wish the best for Miss Southwood.'

'I do believe that, Mr Ashforde, although I must warn you that his lordship is likely to take a less charitable view than I of your meeting Nicole unchaperoned like this.'

The young man's blush deepened. 'I too am deeply conscious that such a meeting could be construed as improper, but Miss Southwood was in such distress last night that I felt I should meet and talk with her where we could be private.'

Marissa was puzzled: she had no recollection of Nicci being in anything but great high spirits at the dinner party, but perhaps the eye of love had seen a deeper emotion... 'But why is she upset now?'

'Because I told her that I did not feel we should declare our feelings for each other until she had come out into Society. She is very young,' he added, somewhat ponderously.

'Oh, no,' Marissa cried. 'I am sure you are mistaken! I am certain that the Earl would look kindly upon your suit, for you are so well connected and suitable in every way. And, young though Miss Southwood is, surely a settled attachment with a long engagement would not be unacceptable to his lordship?'

The young man looked startled. 'If you are certain, then I will be guided by you—I had resigned myself to a longer wait, but in view of your counsel....' They had been walking as they talked, and were strolling around the corner of the house. 'Oh—there is the Earl now.'

Luc was cantering across the greensward from the direction of the Home Farm. Marissa gave the curate a little push. 'Strike while the iron is hot! Speak to him now! I will go in to Nicci.'

Nicci was pacing up and down in the Salon, traces of tears on her cheeks. 'Marissa, darling, I am in such despair!' She ran over and grasped Marissa's hands. 'Crispin is so noble, so good, but he is ready to sacrifice our love for convention...for prudence!'

'For heaven's sake, Nicci!' Marissa was aware of an unsympathetic feeling of irritation with the young lovers. 'Do try for a little moderation! You are not going to win your brother round by histrionics; it will serve only to vex him. Men hate such displays of sensibility.'

'But you do not understand! It is hopeless. I cannot convince Crispin that he must speak to Luc, declare for me. He says we must wait until I am older.'

'Do not worry, Nicci, even now Mr Ashforde is speaking to your brother, asking to pay his addresses. I am sure all will be well if you will only—'

She was cut short by the sound of the front door crashing like a thunderclap. 'Nicole!' Luc roared.

The two young women instinctively clutched each other, and were gazing at the door, a picture of guilt, when Luc strode in.

Nicci gave her brother a weak smile. 'Why, Luc, whatever is the matter?'

He had tossed off his hat, his riding coat was open and he stood tapping the riding crop against his booted leg. The steady noise, as regular as a heartbeat, unnerved Marissa.

'You little minx! You know perfectly well what the matter is! You have cajoled that poor boy of a curate into believing himself in love with you, and what must the poor wretch do but ask me for permission to pay court to you. Hah! If it were not so absurd it would be laughable.' Luc strode irritably across the room.

'But we love each other!' Nicci cried dramatically, one hand pressed to her bosom.

'Oh, do not come the Sarah Siddons with me—I have no liking for high theatricals. Are you as much in love with him as you were with your drawing master? Or that young ninny Westlake you mooned over for months?'

'You are so unkind! This is the real thing!' Nicci promptly burst into tears and buried her hot face in Marissa's shoulder. Marissa responded by placing a comforting arm around the young woman.

'Sir, do not be angry with her. Mr Ashforde was only doing what he felt to be right. Why, he told me—'

'So you knew about this?' Luc ceased his pacing

and swung round to face her, his eyes narrowed. 'And you encouraged it?'

'But he is such an eligible young man, so intelligent, so kind...'

'Such a milksop! One of these days that young man is going to be a bishop—can you imagine a more unsuitable wife for a bishop than this silly goose?' He pointed the riding crop at his sister.

Nicci wailed in protest and recoiled dramatically. Tightening her arms around the sobbing girl, Marissa raised her chin and protested, 'Sir, you are cruel and unfeeling!'

'Unfeeling, am I, madam? Allow me to know my sister better than you. Am I to assume you have been instrumental in promoting this touching romance?'

Marissa noted with alarm that he had gone pale with anger under his tan. His relaxed manner had deserted him: now he was a big man in a towering rage. Physically the resemblance to Charles Southwood had never been greater, but with Charles she had never seen hot anger, only cold, calculated displeasure.

The tattoo of crop against leather increased, menacing in the sudden silence. Marissa's heart beat, choking her. She tried to speak, found her voice trembling and steadied herself. Only the instinct to protect Nicci kept her from running pell mell from the room.

'I...yes, I did advise Mr Ashforde to seek your permission to see Nicci. No more than that. They are deeply attached. I had not expected you to be so brutal to the poor child.'

Luc grinned, but without humour. 'Which poor

child? My silly little minx of a sister or poor young Crispin Ashforde? And I will thank you, madam, to mind your own affairs and not meddle in mine. Nicole, go to your room.'

Nicci broke free from Marissa's arms and dashed for the door. 'You are a beast, Luc, and I hate you!' she threw at him from the safety of the threshold.

'And you are a spoilt little hoyden who needs discipline, and I am determined you shall have it.'

He took one step towards her and Nicci fled. Marissa, calling up all her courage, stepped between him and the door, her slender figure rigid. 'No! I shall not permit it!' In her mind the sight of the riding crop in his hand could mean only one thing—she knew only too well what 'discipline' meant.

Luc's face flushed with anger. For a moment she believed he was going to lay hands on her, thrust her bodily from the doorway. Then he turned on his heel and brought the riding crop down in a furious arc to crack across the top of the occasional table which held Nicci's sewing box. The sound in the room echoed like a pistol-shot: the rosewood box fell with a splintering crash to the boards and Marissa fled down the corridor, up the stairs and into Nicci's room.

Marissa swept in without knocking and turned the key in the lock. At the sound Nicci, who had cast herself across the bed, looked up. 'Marissa! Why on earth have you locked the door?'

Ignoring the question, Marissa hurried across and gathered the girl in her arms. 'There, there, do not worry. I will not let him hurt you.'

'It is too late. He has already hurt me! My heart is in pieces!'

Despite the dramatic words, Nicci was already looking more composed. Marissa sat back and regarded her with some puzzlement. 'No, Nicci, I did not mean that... Luc is very angry, but you must not be frightened.'

'Frightened?' Nicci scrubbed her eyes and sat up, staring at Marissa in astonishment. 'Why should I be frightened of my own brother?'

'But he is so angry! His language so immoderate. And he hit the table with his riding crop...' Her voice faltered.

'Oh, so that was what the crash was.' Nicci got off the bed, all tears forgotten. 'He hasn't broken my sewing box, has he? He really is the limit!'

Marissa's puzzlement grew. Nicci was certainly not frightened, and now, looking back, her tears seemed little more than a temper tantrum.

'He does not often lose his temper,' Nicci explained. 'But when he does, we all hide! He once threw the soup tureen at Jackson when they were arguing about one of the ships. It was empty,' she added naively. 'Jackson caught it and threw it back and they both ended up laughing.'

Marissa got up and walked to the window, her back turned to Nicole. 'But he seems so violent...'

'Well, he *is* hard on the china, but he's as soft as butter, really. I've never known him strike anyone! You did not really fear that he would beat me, did you, Marissa?' Nicci came and put an arm around

Marissa's tense shoulders. 'Marissa, I am sorry if we upset you—I'm sure you are not used to this sort of thing!'

Marissa kept her face averted, fearful that Nicci would see how shaken she was.

'Did your husband never lose his temper? I thought we Southwoods would all be the same.'

'He never…shouted.' Three little words that concealed so much pain. Marissa put a determined smile on her face and turned back to Nicci. 'I am so sorry if my advice has served you badly, but do not despair. I am sure Mr Ashforde will wait for you for as long as it takes.'

Nicci looked doubtful, but before she could speak there was a tap at the door, and when it was unlocked Jackson entered with a tea tray, an expression of dour disapproval on his weather-beaten face. 'He's gone out again,' he said without ceremony or preamble. 'You shouldn't have done it, Miss Nicci—he wants to know what I was about, letting you run around on the terrace with the curate and no chaperon! Huh!' He put the tea tray down with a thump and departed.

Marissa gazed after him in bemusement. 'He is very…unusual, is he not?'

'He is just Jackson,' Nicci said, as if that explained everything. 'Tea, Marissa? You know,' she added after a couple of meditative sips, 'I do not feel any longer as though my heart is breaking. Perhaps I am not in love with Mr Ashforde after all. It is a very lowering thought that Luc might be right and that I am indeed a flirt.'

Marissa's brow creased in consternation. 'But, Nicci! I thought you wanted to marry him!'

'I think I shall wait until I am out. It would be a pity to be engaged and not to enjoy Society—I should not be able to flirt at all!'

Marissa sighed, acknowledging to herself that she had learned a lesson that morning. Obviously not all young women were as dutiful as she had been, first to her father, then to her husband.

'I should not think there is much likelihood that your brother will take you up to London for the Season after this upset,' she said sympathetically.

'*Au contraire,* I think it might make him do it sooner. I heard him talking to Jackson yesterday about opening the Town house. And,' she added disarmingly, 'he needs a wife! That is what he means about discipline for me. He thinks his wife would look after me and bring me out.'

Marissa's heart thudded unaccountably. 'Wife? Is he thinking of getting married, then?'

'Well, Diane says he should get married. And he listens to her advice.'

'Who is Diane?'

'Oh, his mistress. Madame de Rostan, you know. She lives on the next estate to us in Jamaica. Her husband died ten years ago—he was much older than she was.'

Marissa set down her cup with a rattle, her colour high. 'Mistr… Nicci, you should not know about such things, let alone talk about them! I am sure Madame de Rostan is simply a close friend.'

She felt very flustered indeed, far more than Nicci's improper behaviour warranted. Luc had a mistress! Well, of course he had; he was a man and men seemed to need such…diversions. At least this woman was in Jamaica. The thought was comforting, but she did not like to dwell too much on why she should care.

Nicci looked at Marissa from under her lashes. 'I am sorry if I offended you, Marissa, but things are more openly known in the West Indies. And Diane is perfectly respectable and received everywhere. I do miss her; it will be delightful when she arrives.'

'Arrives? Here?'

'Oh, no, in London. She has a house over here and comes every two or three years for the Season and to buy clothes.'

Marissa's mind was in a whirl, her emotions in turmoil. Without thinking, she blurted out, 'Why does he not marry her if she is so respectable?'

'Why, Diane says they would fight like cat and dog if they were under the same roof. And besides…' Nicci wandered over to the clothes press and began to finger a pile of lace '…she is *years* older than he is.'

It was some comfort, but not much. No doubt in Miss Southwood's eyes anyone over twenty-five was quite in their dotage. Marissa stood up, suddenly exasperated with the whole Southwood family.

'I must go home, and I have left Tempest tethered to the fence. Will you be all right now, Nicci dear?'

Nicci crossed and kissed her on the cheek. 'Quite all right, and thank you for trying to help. I am sorry Luc was so cross.'

Luc was standing in the hall when she descended the staircase. Marissa faltered slightly at the sight of him, then she walked steadily down, giving him a cool nod as she passed him. He put out a hand, touching her arm, and was shocked to feel her flinch away from his touch.

'I must apologise for losing my temper, Marissa.'

'Please do not concern yourself, my lord. Nicci tells me it is a not infrequent occurrence.' Her tone was glacial.

Luc regarded her ruefully. 'I had hoped you would have forgiven me, for I was going to ask you a favour.' He led her into the study, closing the door behind them. Under his fingers he felt her stiffen; the tension was vibrating from her like a note from a bowstring. Damn it, he thought, she is still overwrought from last night, and now I have taken her into her husband's study. It must be full of memories for Luc had changed nothing, preferring not to use the unwelcoming room.

Marissa stepped away from him, holding herself erect. 'Forgive you, my lord? It is not my place to do so. I made a severe error of judgement in interfering between you and your sister, and it is I who should beg your forgiveness.'

To Luc her tone belied the sentiment: she could not have been colder had she been carved from ice. He knew her bereavement ran deep, but there was something else; he was sure of it. If only she would open up and tell him—but he could hardly ask her to confide in him.

Luc retreated into formality. 'Then we have agreed; we shall speak of it no more.'

A short, uncomfortable silence ensued, until Marissa observed, 'You said you had a favour to ask me, my lord.'

'I have decided that I must take Nicci up to London; she is too restless for the quiet of the country and will get into one scrape after another. The Season has hardly begun; it will do her no harm to come out quietly this year.'

'Indeed? And I understand from Nicole that you yourself will be seeking an eligible alliance.'

It was a palpable hit: Luc coloured and looked away. Damn that little chit, prattling on to Marissa so improperly. And Marissa was making it obvious that she felt not the slightest regard for him if she could speak so dispassionately of his quest for a wife.

'Possibly,' he responded shortly. 'I had intended to ask you if you would consider accompanying us, helping me to launch Nicole into Society.'

'Me?' Marissa's eyebrows rose haughtily.

'And Miss Venables, naturally. But if you feel disinclined, madam, we need say no more. Nicole must wait another year for her come-out.' It seemed to Luc that Marissa must be considerably irked by him still to sound so unwilling.

'Surely you have other female acquaintances who could oblige you?' Marissa enquired, watching his face.

For a moment Luc thought that his wretch of a sister had said something about Diane, then he recovered himself. Even Nicci would not be so indiscreet. 'Unfortunately, no. No one suitable.'

'I will think about it, and also speak to Miss Venables: it may not suit her convenience,' Marissa responded coolly. 'For myself, it makes little difference where I spend my time.'

Luc regarded her, lips tight. She was deliberately provoking him, paying him back with her control for his intemperance earlier. He wanted to take her in his arms, kiss her until the ice melted, make love to her there and then on that wide mahogany writing desk…

Something in the warmth of his gaze made Marissa swallow hard. She gathered up the long skirts of her habit and turned to the door, her slender figure moulded in the tightly tailored costume. 'If there is nothing else, I will take my leave, my lord. Please do not trouble to show me out.'

Luc stood looking at the door which she had closed gently behind her. He raked his hand through his hair, then with a muttered oath poured himself a glass of claret from the decanter on a side table.

Tempest was thoroughly bored with being tied up to the fence, and made her displeasure known in no uncertain terms. Marissa had no intention of leading her round to the front of the house in search of a mounting block so she used a tree stump. The mare sidled and backed every time Marissa attempted to mount, and it took ten minutes before she was in the saddle.

Fighting a bad-tempered horse all the way back across the park to the Dower House, combined with the morning's upsets, did nothing for Marissa's own mood. She stalked into the house and up to her room, calling for her maid as she went.

In her chamber she pulled off her jacket without waiting for Mary. When the girl arrived, breathless from running upstairs, she asked, 'Has Miss Venables waited luncheon for me?'

'Yes, my lady. Let me help you with that, ma'am. What would you like to change into, ma'am?'

'Oh, anything you like, Mary. Just a simple gown. Look at my hair!'

Miss Venables was placidly reading in the dining room when Marissa joined her. 'Your colour is very good, dear,' she observed. 'Did you have a good ride?'

'My *ride* was very enjoyable. I have moved my favourite mare, Tempest, to the stables here. Would you care for some cold meat, Jane?'

'Thank you, yes. If your ride was enjoyable, it sounds as though something else was not,' Miss Venables observed shrewdly.

'I became embroiled in a dispute between the Earl and Nicci over Mr Ashforde, who has asked if he may court her.'

Miss Venables snorted. 'Has he indeed? Silly young puppy! He is no more in love with that girl than she is with him. No doubt his lordship put her right about that!' She buttered some bread and asked innocently, 'Embroiled, you say, my dear? How so?'

Marissa gave her an edited version of the morning's events.

'And his lordship was angry?'

'He was certainly extremely annoyed, and said so,' Marissa supplied. She had made no mention of his flaring anger, of the riding crop and the effect it had had on her.

'Oh, dear, so we are out of favour with the Earl.'

'Far from it, Jane dear. He has asked that we accompany Nicole and himself to London to do the Season and bring her out. I was so taken aback by his effrontery after all that had passed between us that I did not trust myself to give him an immediate answer.'

'Oh!' Miss Venables said, trying to conceal her dismay. 'But it seems an excellent plan to me—just think how much we would enjoy it after this past year. There can be no objection now to you coming out of mourning. We would have a splendid time: balls and parties and riding in the park. And entertainment of a higher kind, naturally. There will be the galleries and exhibitions… And the shopping, dear, think of the shopping.'

Marissa laughed out loud and leaned across the table to take her companion's hand. 'You are so good for me, Jane! We will like it exceedingly, in spite of his lordship. I shall tell him that we will oblige him.'

'At whatever cost to ourselves,' Miss Venables added, tongue firmly in cheek.

Chapter Seven

Marissa, Lady Southwood, thanks the Earl for his kind invitation to join his London establishment for the Season. Miss Venables joïns her ladyship in accepting the Earl's amiable offer. Doubtless his lordship will favour them with full details of his plans at his convenience.

Luc screwed the letter up and tossed it onto the desk in front of him, anger welling within him. He had thought he was making progress in breaking down Marissa's reserve. And he had thought he was offering her and Miss Venables an opportunity for pleasure and diversion after long months of mourning. The cold formality of the note demonstrated just how wrong he had been.

He reached for the crumpled note and smoothed it out, letting his palm rest on it. Marissa was an enigma to him, and her parting words earlier that day echoed uneasily in his mind. She had said she did not care where she spent her time; he recalled her distress in the Gallery before the portrait of her husband. Despite her calm exterior Marissa must still be deep in grief... Was he being cruel in asking her to spend more time with him when his appearance must be a constant reminder of her loss?

Nicci bounced into the Salon without troubling to knock, shattering his reverie. 'Luc, you have quite destroyed my rosewood box! I shall have to send to Norwich for a new one—and if you expect me to pay for it out of my allowance, then I call that mean of you!'

'I am sorry for your box, you provoking brat! You may choose yourself a new box in Bond Street—and pay for it out of the ridiculously extravagant allowance I intend making you in London.'

Nicci whirled across to sit on his lap, wrapping her arms round his neck and planting a big kiss on his cheek. 'You are the most wonderful brother in the world! We can truly go to London? And I will have a truly magnificent allowance?'

'Far more magnificent than you deserve. You have soon recovered from your broken heart, have you not, you minx?' Luc asked, giving her a wry smile.

'You were quite right, brother dear. Mr Ashforde and I would not suit; I see it now. What is that?' She pointed at the letter underneath his hand.

'A note from Marissa accepting my invitation for her and Miss Venables to accompany us to London.'

Nicci jumped up, clapping her hands with excitement. 'I am so glad Marissa is coming, and dear Jane of course.' She regarded her brother from under her lashes and added innocently, 'What a good thing Diane is setting up her own establishment and not staying with us.'

Her brother waved a warning finger at her. 'Have you said anything to Marissa about Madame de Rostan?'

Nicci coloured betrayingly. 'Well...I might have mentioned her in passing. As being one of our dear friends, you know.'

'Nicci!' Luc growled. 'How much have you told her? Have you said that Diane has been...very close to me?'

'Marissa says I should not talk about such things,' Nicci retorted betrayingly.

Luc dropped his head in his hands. 'Oh, Nicci. I really would prefer it if you would strive not to create the impression that my life is littered with mistresses! Or betray that you even know the meaning of the word!' No wonder Marissa was so frosty. After a happy marriage she was doubtless shocked to the core to hear that he had had an irregular liaison.

The next day was unseasonably hot for May: the clouds seemed trapped in the sticky heat, and nothing moved in the still air other than an army of small insects which buzzed irritatingly whenever one opened a window.

Up at the Hall Luc and Nicci, accustomed to the heat of the Tropics, thought nothing of it, but at the Dower House both ladies retreated to the shaded cool of the garden room and drew the blinds, Gyp panting in the corner, too hot to even chase birds in the garden.

They spent a desultory day making lists of things to be done, things to be packed and, much more enjoyably, things to be purchased as soon as they arrived in London.

'Oh, for some lightweight cottons and muslins,' said Miss Venables, fanning herself. 'I shall be so thankful to see the last of these dark colours and heavy fabrics!'

'And pretty straw bonnets, and parasols and little kid slippers,' Marissa said dreamily. She felt so restless, so full of energy despite the heat. She wanted to run, to gallop, but it was too hot to walk and it would not be fair to take Tempest out in the heat and flies. And beyond the parkland and the dunes the cool sea beckoned...

Marissa ordered a late dinner, and it was after ten when they sat sipping their tea. Miss Venables looked at the curtain, just stirring at the open windows, and remarked, 'Thank heavens! The breeze is getting up at last; perhaps we shall not have too unpleasant a night.'

Marissa got up and pulled back the curtains. The cloud had lifted at last, leaving a clear sky, and the full moon bathed the garden with light. The cool stirrings of the air lifted the fine hair at her temples, serving to rekindle her restlessness.

'I am going to retire now, Marissa, the heat of the day has quite sapped my energy. Don't be too long yourself, my dear. We have much to arrange tomorrow.'

'Goodnight, Jane. I shall follow you up soon.'

Marissa stood looking at the moon-bathed land-scape for some time, breathing in the scents of the night stocks and roses, enjoying the peace and the cool. Despite her words to her cousin she felt disinclined to retire to bed.

Many times before, when her lord had been away from home, she had taken a horse out at night and ridden until she had exorcised the restless demons which possessed her and she could trot home, calm and collected and ready to resume the mantle of Countess once again.

Peters, the head groom, had been her loyal if unwilling accomplice in these escapades. At her orders he had sent the man's saddle down to the Dower House stables. Allen worked for her and her alone: if she told him to make Tempest ready he would do so unquestioningly.

Before she knew it she was pulling her breeches and jacket from the bottom of the chest of drawers. Mary had obtained them for her and had loyally guarded her mistress's secret. She buttoned up the linen shirt, tugged on her boots and shook her hair free of its confining pins.

In the light cast by the moon through the long windows she was quite transformed into an exotic creature no one would associate with the elegant Lady Southwood. As an afterthought she tossed a lightweight cloak over her shoulders and scooped up some linen towels from the washstand.

The candle was flickering in the window of the groom's room above the carriage house. Marissa banged on the door and when Allen came stumbling down the steps ordered him briskly to saddle up her mare. 'The man's saddle, please, Allen.'

Briefed by Peters, the undergroom complied immediately, only his unusually wooden expression betraying his surprise at seeing his mistress thus attired at this hour of the night. 'Shall I saddle up the hack and accompany you, my lady?'

'That will not be necessary, thank you. And there is no need to wait up for my return—I am quite capable of unsaddling Tempest and I would not keep you from your bed.'

'Yes, ma'am, thank you, ma'am.' The young man climbed back up to his room reflecting that it was nice of her ladyship to care about his rest, but Peters would have his guts for garters if he went to bed without checking that his mistress was safely returned.

Marissa walked the mare quietly across the cobbles and past the front of the Dower House: it would never do to rouse the household! Once they were through the wood she let the mare have her head and Tempest, with a toss of her head, settled gladly into a canter that sent the wind through her long mane. The cloak flew out behind Marissa and she shook her hair free to catch the wind too, so that mistress and horse seemed as one, flying over the moonlit turf of the parkland, cutting diagonally across the front of Southwood Hall. The big house lay silent and still, lit only by the dim lights of the watchman's lanterns.

In the master bedroom Luc lay, hands behind his head, gazing at the plaster moulding of the ceiling overhead as he had been for the last half-hour. Sleep was unaccountably eluding him and he found his mind turning again to the thought of Marissa, cold and angry, yet curiously vibrant in the clinging riding habit.

He grinned ruefully to himself, reflecting that enforced celibacy was doing nothing for his equilibrium. He and Diane had amicably ended their liaison over two years ago, and since then there had been a number of charming entanglements of which, thankfully, his sister knew nothing. But those too had ended when he had left Jamaica, and the provocative presence of Marissa only served to highlight his lack of intimate female companionship.

It was no good, he had to get up and do some work. There were some suitably soporific estate accounts he had promised his agent he would peruse. As he crossed he room he heard, faintly, the sound of hoofbeats on turf.

Luc threw back the curtains and looked out on the park, so bathed in silver light that it seemed almost as bright as day. A grey horse was cantering across his view, its mane flying. On its back was a slim figure, its cloak streaming behind it, a mass of hair swept back by the breeze.

It was Marissa. There was no mistaking the rider, despite, he realised with a shock, the fact that she was riding astride and clad in breeches.

'What the devil!' he exclaimed, staring at the wild creature who had Marissa's form yet who could not, surely, be that controlled, proper young widow who had so coldly conversed with him that day. As he watched she turned the horse's head towards the coast road and dropped her hands: the mare responded immediately, breaking into a gallop which swept them out of his sight in less than a minute.

His astonishment swiftly turned to fear for Marissa. What had prompted this wild ride? Had her despair finally overmastered her control? He remembered again her torrent of tears in the Long Gallery, the almost too casual way she had said she did not care where she spent her time. It obviously made no difference to the depths of her misery whether she was in Norfolk or in London; she was still in hell.

The image of that cold expanse of sea beyond the dunes was suddenly very vivid in his mind. Luc tried to tell himself he was overreacting, but even as he struggled with his imaginings he was tugging on breeches and boots, shrugging into a shirt.

He ran down the stairs, across the hall and out through the front door, startling the dozing watchman as he snored in his hooded chair. Luc pounded into the stableyard and flung open the door of the stable housing his hunter. He threw the saddle over the startled animal, tightened the girths and was reaching for the bridle when Peters emerged, hair tousled, eyes heavy with sleep.

'My lord?'

'Nothing! Go back to bed. I have a fancy to ride.'

Peters wisely refrained from commenting on his lordship's dishevelled appearance and hastily effaced himself.

Luc swung up into the saddle without putting his

foot in the stirrup and was urging the big chestnut hunter into a canter before it had even cleared the stableyard arch. The park was empty when he reached it, but he knew where she was headed and he urged the horse into a flat gallop, headlong down the driveway to the sea.

On the beach Marissa sat for a moment, breathing in the cool sea air and watching the moonlight laying a path of silver across the waves. The light breeze stirred her hair but it was not cold. The sea would be, she knew, but it was irresistible, and so shallow, even on the rising tide, that it would be safe to swim.

She dismounted, tied Tempest to a branch and pulled off her clothes, leaving them in a heap on the cloak. The breeze caressed her naked body and she stretched like a cat, then walked slowly down the beach, kicking the fine sand, letting it run between her bare toes.

The water struck cold but she did not hesitate, wading out, relishing the chill kiss on her heated skin. The beach shelved so gradually that even after wading several hundred yards the water did not quite reach her waist. The moon was so big, so beautiful that she held her face up to its light and just stood relishing the tranquillity, the freedom, the aloneness.

The chestnut hunter breasted the dunes at the gallop, plunging as it scrambled down the far slope. Luc reined in hard, making it rear, unsettling Tempest who had fallen into a half-doze.

Luc swung down, dropped the reins and scanned the expanse of sea. There she was, standing like a naiad in the moonlight. Her hair cascaded down her bare back, white as alabaster in the cold light. As he watched, transfixed, she raised her hands and lifted the mass of dark curls off her neck, exposing the whole of her naked form before letting it drop once more.

She was beautiful, lovely beyond the imaginings he had striven so hard to control. Her slender waist, the curve of her hip rising from the lapping waves, took his breath away. Then she moved swiftly, disappearing into the water with barely a ripple.

Urgently Luc ripped off his shirt, tore off his boots and breeches and plunged into the water. The shallowness forced him to run, not swim, and he felt as though he were being dragged back with every stride. The cold water splashed up his back and chest as he ran, conscious of nothing but the need to reach her before she sank from sight below the grey water.

Marissa, unaware that she was not alone, floated tranquilly on her back, her fingers gently fanning the water to keep her in position. Vaguely she thought that the wind must be getting up, for she could hear splashing, although her ears were under water and she could hear little.

Frustrated by the impeding water, Luc plunged into a running dive, striking out strongly to where he had last glimpsed Marissa, praying through clenched teeth that she had not already sunk below the grey waters. Half blinded by the salt in his eyes, he surged forward, cutting through the water with powerful overarm strokes. His search succeeded better than he could have hoped as with startling suddenness he collided with a body.

Marissa had perhaps two seconds' warning as she floated serenely, her face to the moon. The surface of the sea rocked in a sudden swell, sending little waves across her face. Before she could react, before she could feel fear, a hard body crashed into hers. The breath knocked from her lungs, she was pushed under the surface of the sea. Water flooded her nostrils, stung her eyes, filled her ears: her bare behind grazed the rippled sand of the sea bottom and as she felt it her panic abated as she recalled just how shallow the water was. Curling her legs underneath her, she found her footing and stood up, coughing and spluttering as she took in air. Wildly she looked round for whatever it was that had rammed her, suddenly very afraid. The local people had tales of sharks in these waters which she had always dismissed as fantasy—now she was not so sure.

But it was not a shark who seized her from behind. Strong arms clamped themselves around her waist and she was lifted bodily from the water. Pressed against hard, cold flesh Marissa kicked, screamed and dug in her elbows. With a muffled curse her assailant dropped her. Marissa's feet hit the bottom and she dug in her toes and spun round to face him.

'Luc!' She was so taken aback that she fell back into the water with a splash. The realisation of her nakedness kept her submerged, crouched so that only her head and shoulders emerged. No such considerations of modesty appeared to afflict Luc, who stood there, hands on hips and chest heaving, regarding her.

'You must be mad! Whatever has possessed you! This is no solution…' He caught a ragged breath and looked at her with a strange mixture of anger and concern.

'*I must be mad?*' Marissa was so taken aback that she half rose, then rapidly remembered her nakedness and fell to her knees. 'What do you think you are about, crashing into me like that? You could have drowned me!' Her hair hung in sodden strands across her face, dripping stinging salt water into her eyes, She pushed it back with both hands, then dropped her arms hastily to cover her breasts.

'Why should you worry about me drowning you when you were hell-bent on self-destruction?' he demanded furiously.

'Self-destruction? Luc, have you completely taken leave of your senses?' Her sense of bewilderment was growing by the second. 'I came for a swim because it has been so hot all day. I am a very good swimmer, I would have you know, and I do this frequently and quite safely.' She looked up at the water-drenched figure. His hair was dark and sleek, pushed back to reveal the strong planes of his face. His powerfully muscled shoulders, moving slightly with his breathing, gleamed as the moonlight struck the water droplets. She did not dare let her eyes stray lower…

He spoke slowly and deliberately, his relief firing his anger as he realised just how badly he had misread the situation. '*Swimming!* You are here in the middle of the night, all alone and you tell me you do this *often?* If you do not care for the risk you put yourself to, do you not have some concern for the impropriety of it?' He could hear how pompous he was sounding, but he could not bring himself to tell her his true fears. 'You have a position to uphold. You are the Dowager Countess of Radwinter. What if someone were to see you? What do the servants think of you riding around in men's clothes?'

'My servants are loyal to me and do what I tell them,' Marissa retorted coldly.

'Well, I shall speak to Peters in the morning and have your horse brought back to the stables at the Hall. We will have no more unsupervised riding.'

'How dare you seek to control my life?' Marissa suddenly, and very satisfyingly, lost her temper. 'I am neither your sister nor, thank heavens, your wife! You cannot command me, my lord. Take Tempest back, if you wish to be so petty-minded; I shall buy my own horse. And Allen—who, if you need to be reminded, is *my* groom—will look after it for me. I ride when and how and where I please.'

It was as if two years of subservience, of fearful obedience to her lord, had dissolved in a flash of anger. All her life men had controlled her. Well, now she was free, independent, able to do what she liked. She was so exhilarated by the thought that she stood up, forgetting her nakedness, intending to regain the shore and leave Luc standing there.

The expression on his face recalled her to her situation. His eyes widened as his gaze travelled down the lines of her form and he became, suddenly, very still. Marissa gasped, her hands springing to cover as much of her chilled body as she could, unwittingly striking the classic pose of a startled sea nymph. She found her eyes locked with Luc's, noticing with surprising clarity how the salt water had spiked his eyelashes.

Shakily she managed to say, 'I have had quite enough of this nonsense. Please turn your back; I want to go back to the shore.'

Luc did as he was bid, turning slowly to present her with a view of broad shoulders, a long, supple back tapering to narrow hips and taut buttocks. Marissa swallowed hard and turned abruptly herself. Too abruptly: her foot caught one of the rare stones on that sandy shore and she stumbled, falling with a loud splash and a cry back into the cold water.

Instantly he was beside her, lifting her up in his arms and holding her tight against his chest. 'You are frozen! You little fool, are you trying to catch pneumonia?'

Marissa could only shiver in response. Now she was out of the water, her wet skin fully exposed to the breeze, she was colder than ever. But it was not only the cold that was making her shiver; it was the nearness of this man, the strength of him, his obvious concern for her that she recognised as the source of his anger at her behaviour.

And something else, something that was dangerous insanity: she was falling in love with him. So this was what it was like, she mused as he made his way through the water, slowly, hampered by his burden and the dragging shallows. She had heard about love, but had never felt it, and now she recognised the months of thinking, dreaming about Luc for what they were.

Instinctively Marissa snuggled closer into Luc's arms, and was rewarded by a tightening of his grip. But as they neared the beach she began to think more clearly. This was a fatally stupid thing to do, to fall in love with this man. He was her husband's cousin, so like him to look at that they could be twins, one dark, the other blond. And, however different his behaviour appeared to be on the surface, all men were driven by the same urges; she had no doubt of that.

Luc had made it quite plain that he was going to look for a wife in London. And men did not expect love in marriage; she knew that. They sought duty, a good alliance, obedience and subservience. If he even guessed she was falling in love with him he would be embarrassed at best, appalled at worst.

As soon as his bare feet touched dry sand Marissa wrenched from his arms and was running to where she had left her clothes and towels piled under a bush at the foot of the dunes. She snatched the largest rectangle of linen and swathed it round her shivering body, keeping her back turned to him. Between chattering teeth, she said, 'Will you please go away?'

'I will, but I would appreciate it if you could spare me a towel, otherwise it will take me rather a long time to get dressed, wet as I am.' The anger had left his voice, leaving only a trace of faint amusement.

Without turning Marissa held out the smaller towel, conscious of just how close behind her he must be as he took it.

Seconds later, right behind her, he said, 'Will you not get dressed? You are shivering.'

'Go away, then!' she implored, her back still averted. 'How can I get dressed with you here?'

'For heaven's sake, Marissa, stop acting the prude! You have been a married woman, when all's said and done!'

'But not to you,' she snapped back.

Suddenly, incredibly, she felt the weight of her sodden hair lifted and strong hands were gently wringing the water out of it. Then Luc began to rub the damp mass with the towel he held, working down from the scalp to the finest tendrils lying on her shoulderblades.

'Stop it!' she demanded shakily, realising only too clearly that if Luc were drying her hair with the towel he was not wearing it himself.

'Stand still,' he admonished gently, carrying on the rhythmic stroking. 'If you will not dry yourself, I will do it for you.'

His hands touched her shoulders and Marissa whipped round, her hands coming up to push him away. They flattened onto the planes of his chest, but she did not push, only stood there feeling the cold skin against her palms, the beat of his heart under her fingers. Luc looked down at her for a long moment, then pulled her tight against him. She felt the heat of him under the cold skin, the hard strength of him, the frightening, arousing, maleness against her. His mouth came down slowly on hers and he kissed her softly, as if asking a question. Her response seemed to give him the answer he was looking for, for he deepened the kiss, his mouth moving sensuously against hers, his tongue probing gently the softness of her mouth.

Shocked, for her lord had never kissed her, except formally on the cheek, Marissa tentatively let her own tongue-tip taste his. The sensation made her knees feel weak, but she was rewarded by the soft groan in the back of his throat as Luc moved his hand in a sweeping caress down her spine. The towel, swept away by his impatient fingers, fell unheeded to the sand as his hands, cupping her buttocks, moulded her to him.

The heat of him was a shock, then a thrill as she caught fire too. Speechlessly she clung to him as he dipped his head to graze a long kiss from her earlobe down her neck to the swell of her breast.

Marissa gasped out loud as his sharp teeth found one peaking nipple and fastened gently on the aroused tip. His tongue teased and tasted her salty skin and Marissa whimpered as it circled and licked the tight bud.

Through her shock and sensuous delight Marissa struggled to understand what was happening to her. Her lord had performed his marital duties on her shrinking body with a haste—and distaste—which had shown only too clearly how she had displeased and disappointed him. Never had she expected that a man could give her so much pleasure—this must be what they did with their mistresses...

But underneath this tide of unfamiliar pleasure there

was something else, a building yearning, a feeling of expectation that there was more to come, a goal to be reached, to be striven for.

Luc pulled her down gently onto the fallen towel, his hands never leaving her body, his mouth returning to hers for a long kiss that sapped her will and sent a frisson of delight pulsating through her being. It was there again, this sense of building pleasure, of expectation. Her body arched under his hands and she whispered, 'What are you doing to me?'

'Making love to you, I had rather hoped,' Luc answered huskily, his voice sounding slightly amused. His breath was warm on her chin, then his tongue was trailing insidiously down the curve of her breast to the other nipple where it recommenced its teasing.

Marissa drew in a shuddering breath, hardly able to wait for whatever it was that was coming to sweep her away. Luc's fingers strayed downwards over the swell of her hip to the softness of her inner thighs, gently parting and exploring with stroking caresses her secret core.

The wave of sensation swept over Marissa, shaking her in every part of her body. She cried out, arching into Luc's embrace, then fell back, lights exploding against her closed lids. As the pleasure ebbed, leaving her quivering in his arms, shudders shook her.

After an age she opened her eyes to meet his, smiling down at her. Marissa smiled tremulously back, reaching up her hand to stroke his cheek. Luc closed his eyes at the caress, then groaned. 'I really do not think sweetheart, that I can wait any longer…'

His mouth fastened on hers, hard and demanding, then his weight was on her, pressing her down into the yielding sand, his long legs twining with hers, separating them, easing them apart.

Marissa's eyes flew open. The man above, the familiar weight on her flinching body, the water-darkened hair and the Southwood features lit coldly by the moonlight—all this was horribly familiar. Automatically Marissa did what she had always done to allow her body to be used. She lay still and passive, not preventing, not welcoming the invasion, her eyes open and unfocused.

Luc froze, as he realised the change in her response to him, then rolled off her body and onto his feet in one swift movement. Never in his life had he taken an unwilling woman, and he was not about to start with this one. He ran down the short beach and plunged beneath the cold water, feeling its cold kiss dousing his heated arousal. He swam hard for two minutes, killing the fire in his veins, before turning back to the shore. As he swam he did not allow himself to think, to feel. As he strode ashore he saw Marissa had pulled on her clothes and was standing with her back to him beside her horse.

'The towels are by your clothes,' she said, her voice expressionless, as she heard him splash ashore.

'Thank you,' Marissa heard him say, his voice neutral. She walked away, leading Tempest to where a tree stump protruded from the sand at a convenient height for a mounting block. Her skin was still damp and her breeches clung uncomfortably as she bent her knee to mount, but she managed it and gathered up the reins to turn the horse homeward.

Luc, now dressed, ran to put a restraining hand on the bridle. 'Wait, please. Marissa, you must believe that I intend to marry you…'

'Indeed, my lord? It is doubtless very honourable of you to make the offer after your actions tonight. However, I have no more desire to marry you than you have shown up to now to marry me.' She gazed down at him with an expression he could not read.

'Desire?' He laughed without humour. 'If we are to talk about desire, madam, might I remind you that yours appeared to at least match mine. And certainly, unless you are a very good actress, you have obtained more pleasure from this night's encounter than I.'

The words were out before he could stop them. She jerked at the reins, sending Tempest plunging away into the dunes, but not before the moonlight caught her face and Luc glimpsed the hurt twist of her mouth, the pain in her eyes.

But she was gone, and after one hasty step towards his hunter he checked himself. There was nothing he could do tonight to make things any better. After a night's reflection Marissa would realise that she had to marry him. For himself, he reflected as he swung up into the saddle, the night's escapade had made up his mind: his cousin's widow would make an admirable wife.

Chapter Eight

The rhythm of Tempest's hoofbeats changed abruptly as she plunged down the bank from the saltings and onto the hard-packed surface of the coast road. It was enough to shake Marissa out of her mindless, head-long flight from the beach, from Luc. She reined the mare in and trotted more gently up the carriage drive until a path led off towards the Dower House through the trees fringing the park.

The moon had disappeared behind a bank of high cloud and Marissa slowed Tempest to a walk to allow the horse to pick its way across the tussocky grass of the park. Now that her instinctive flight had ended she found she was acutely aware of every sensation, every sound. Her wet hair clung to her jacket, soaking through the cloth between her shoulderblades, sand gritted between her toes inside the leather boots and her eyelashes felt salt-sticky. Yet despite these dis-comforts she felt alive, tingling with the awareness of her body. For the first time she felt truly aware of herself, of her skin, of her lips, of her breasts, of the caress of the night air on her cheeks.

She held her hot face up to the breeze as it sighed through the beeches and allowed her mind, at last, to be free, to think about what had just happened, what Luc had done to her.

Through the stillness hoofbeats sounded, almost preternaturally loud in the night. Marissa drew Tempest back farther into the shadows as Luc's hunter galloped by, his master low on its neck. Marissa let Tempest move forward slightly to the edge of the copse and watched as the big horse vanished under the arch of the stable block.

He was angry with her. She had rejected him, not once, but twice. He could never guess—and she could never tell him—why in the end she had rejected his lovemaking when he must have realised that she wanted him. *Wanted him*… Marissa rubbed her forehead in perplexity. It had never occurred to her before that a woman could want—could welcome—a man in that way. With Charles she had feared it, forced herself to do her duty, endured what had passed, prayed for it to be over swiftly.

But Luc…Luc had said he wanted to make *love* to her. He had intended that she should feel pleasure, had done everything to ensure it, been patient with her.

Tempest, sensing her mistress's distraction, began to walk slowly across the park, retracing her earlier route past the front of the big house.

Marissa was unconscious of the movement; her mind was replaying Luc's lovemaking. She shivered as she remembered the sensations that had awakened her body—and her mind. It had never occurred to her that a man would care for a woman's pleasure, would actively incite it, revel in it, enjoy it as much as she.

The realisation, when it came, hit her with the force of a blow. *This* was how it should be. It had been Charles whose warped view of the world had dominated her mind and body in the two years of their marriage. What she had accepted as normal was anything but. Suddenly the pattern of his behaviour was revealed to her as a whole: his demand for perfection in everything, his coldness, his cruelty. There, she had thought the word, for Charles *had* been cruel to her; she could see it now.

He had been unfeeling, self-centred, critical, frozen at the core, incapable of love, or even of caring for another person. He had made much of her childlessness, yet if she had produced an heir for him Marissa sensed that he would have found something else to blame her for.

Well, now he had gone, but he had left a legacy of fear. Tonight Luc had unlocked the door to the prison of her mind and emotions, shown her the daylight, the freedom beyond. But she was afraid of stepping out into the air. When Luc had sought to consummate their lovemaking she had panicked, frozen, rejected him. And just as the sight of Charles's portrait could reduce her to trembling fear, so his shadow would always fall across her bed.

Candlelight shone from a window in the front of the house; a figure moved across the uncurtained casement. It was Luc, returned to his chamber. Marissa gathered up the reins and turned Tempest towards the house, drawn by the light and the thought of Luc.

A figure loomed at the window, staring out blindly from the lit room across the darkened landscape outside. She drew closer, so close that she had to tip up her head to watch him as he slowly unbuttoned his shirt and shrugged it from his broad shoulders. The candlelight glanced off his unruly blond hair, and the recollection of the feel of it beneath her fingers sent a frisson down her salt-sticky spine. She wanted to be there with him, her palms flattened against the strong, satiny planes of his chest, drawing in his warmth, his vitality.

But when he led her to the big bed it would happen all over again; she knew it, the fear would overwhelm her desire for him. And she realised now, loving him as she did, she could not risk that. A man who loved her would be cruelly hurt by the rejection; a man who wanted her would not tolerate her rejection of him. And, after all, Luc had not spoken of love, only of his *intention* to marry her, to make things right after their scandalous behaviour together on the beach.

Marissa turned her horse's head, dug her heels gently into the soft flanks and rode steadily away. No, loving Luc, being with him, was a fantasy. She was irretrievably marked by the past and there was no future for her with him.

A light burned in the stable loft as she wearily slipped off the mare's back. Despite her orders, Allen had waited up for her. Even as she put her hand on the door latch it opened and the lad emerged, tousled and sleepy, hay sticking to his jacket.

'There you are, my lady. It's getting cold out. Let me take her now.'

Marissa handed him the reins with a smile. 'Thank you, Allen, but I did say not to wait up.'

'I've been asleep, right and tight, my lady, in the hay. Mr Peters would have my guts for garters if I had gone back to bed with you out. 'Night, my lady.'

Back in her chamber Marissa peeled off her damp clothes and dropped them wearily on the floor, too tired and drained to do more than get into her bed and fall into a deep, dreamless sleep.

Jackson placed a dish of eggs on the buffet and eyed his lordship cautiously. Normally breakfast was a good time to discuss the household's domestic affairs as Nicci never stirred from her room before ten and peace could be guaranteed. This morning, however, the Earl was looking heavy-eyed and preoccupied. The butler decided this was not the time to raise the matter of the under-footman, who had been found last night asleep on the pantry floor and clutching an empty bottle of his lordship's best port.

He lowered the lids of the chafing dishes silently and was about to take up position by the buffet when one of the double doors opened and James peered round. Jackson raised his eyebrows in silent reproof but the footman ignored the look and beckoned urgently.

'Excuse me, my lord,' Jackson murmured, and left

the room. 'What are you about, James? You know his lordship doesn't like being disturbed at breakfast and he is not in the best of moods today. Can't it wait?'

'I'm afraid not, Mr Jackson. It's her ladyship, you see…'

'You mean, Miss Nicole?'

'No, her ladyship, the Countess. She's here, pacing up and down the hall—and *she's* in an odd mood too, I can tell you.'

'I'll come—and don't go gossiping about your betters, lad. Doubtless her ladyship is experiencing some problem with the travel arrangements up to Town.'

As he neared the head of the stairs Jackson could hear the swish of long skirts on the marble floor of the hall. Marissa was dressed for riding, her long green skirts trailing behind her as she paced. She was veiled, but even so, as she stopped and looked up at his approach, he could see the glitter of her eyes behind the fine mesh.

'Good morning, your ladyship. I hope you have had a pleasant ride. Miss Southwood is in her room: would you like me to send up a cup of chocolate for you?'

'Good morning, Jackson.' Marissa allowed none of her feelings to colour her tone. Now that she was standing still she was conscious of just how her agitated pacing must have appeared to the footman: she must pull herself together; this was no way to behave in front of the servants. She lifted her veil and handed him her gloves and whip. 'Thank you, no. I have come to see his lordship, not Miss Southwood.'

'His lordship is at breakfast, my lady. Will you wait

in the Blue Salon, and I will let him know you are here?'

'Is he breakfasting in his chamber?'

Jackson was taken aback. 'Why, no, my lady, he is in the morning room...'

'Then I shall go up.' She was in no mood to be kept waiting. 'There is no need to announce me, Jackson.'

'Not at all, my lady...' Jackson hastened up the stairs to precede her. Something was up and his lordship was not going to appreciate being surprised at his breakfast table, whatever it was about.

Luc looked up as the doors opened and the butler, looking uncharacteristically flustered, announced, 'The Countess of Radwinter, my lord.'

'I am not at home, Jackson...'

But it was too late. Marissa swept past the butler and said firmly, 'Thank you, Jackson. I can pour myself some chocolate.'

Without risking a glance at his employer Jackson effaced himself, closing the doors behind him. If it was not for the dignity of his position he would drop to one knee and apply his ear to the keyhole. As it was, he withdrew to a discreet distance and waited for the sound of breaking crockery.

'Good morning, Marissa,' Luc said coolly, resuming his seat as she sat, cup of chocolate before her, at the other end of the table. He raised one eyebrow and waited.

For her part Marissa was beginning to regret the impulse which had brought her here. A night's sleep had not changed either her feelings for Luc or her belief that they had no future together. Whenever she closed her eyes it was Charles's face she saw, Charles's weight she had felt as Luc's body moved over hers. And then the fear had come, as it always had before. And in the shifting shadows of the moonlight Luc had looked so much like his cousin.

The overwhelming, wonderful, unfamiliar sensations she had experienced in Luc's arms, and her own instinctive responses to him had shaken her to the core and made it difficult to face him. Luc was watching her now, his deep blue eyes steady on her face. Under his scrutiny Marissa could feel a hectic blush start rising up the column of her throat, up her cheeks, until it reached the curls on her forehead.

'Why have you come, Marissa?' he asked calmly, leaning back in his chair. 'Not that is not always a pleasure to see you.'

Marissa realised she did not know. She had left the Dower House because she could not bear to stay still any longer. She was confused, almost angry, but she did not rightly know with whom. She wanted to be near him, yet his very closeness frightened her. She needed to be in his arms, yet was terrified of what that might lead to…

'Marissa?' Luc prompted gently.

'I cannot come to London,' she blurted out at last.

'Why ever not?'

'Um…' It had only just occurred to her how impossible it would be. How could she live under Luc's roof for months, seeing him every day, watching him as he set about the task of finding a wife when she had fallen in love with him herself? Still fiery red, she muttered, 'After last night…it is impossible. You must see that.'

'I do not see that it is impossible: far from it. You are naturally agitated that I allowed my passions to run away with me last night. We will be married, of course: it is an eminently suitable solution for both of us. You are the perfect mistress for Southwood Hall and, for my part, I can offer you the style of living to which you have been accustomed. If you wish a longer period to elapse before we announce our betrothal, then I accept that, naturally.'

Luc leaned back and smiled at her kindly. An unexpected flash of anger overcame her embarrassment: here was another man dictating her life, dressing up his offer as the perfect solution for her when in reality it was the perfect solution for *him*.

'No! I will not marry you! Last night…we must forget last night. It was a mistake. And there is certainly no need for you to marry me because of it. I do not wish to remarry, not now, not ever.'

'But you must marry.' Luc leaned forward, fixing her with his blue gaze. 'You are young, and beautiful and eligible. You must want children—' He broke off as she went white. 'I am sorry if what I am saying is painful, Marissa, but life moves on. Charles will never leave you, you will never forget what you shared together, but it will become part of your memories as you live your new life.'

Marissa gave a choked sob and jumped up, knocking over her cup. 'No! No, you are wrong!' How could he tell her that she would never forget when her whole happiness depended on her being able to forget Charles, push those awful years into a locked cupboard in her mind so she could start living afresh?

Luc stood, but did not approach her. 'I am sorry, it is obviously too soon to speak of these things. But why will you not come to London? You are overwrought. You need a change of scene and you would enjoy the balls, the theatre, the shops. You have been confined in the country too long and need diversion.' Luc picked up his cup and saucer and strolled to the window, looking out over the rolling parkland. He added lightly, 'And besides, Nicci needs you as her chaperon.'

'Miss Venables would enjoy the role, and perform it far better than I,' Marissa said stubbornly. She wanted so much to go to London, but she did not want to be with Luc. Close to him, under the same roof, how could she disguise the fact that her feelings for him were growing?

The underlying unhappiness in her voice reached him, and he put down the cup, crossing the room to put one arm around her shoulders, drawing her against his warmth and strength. 'Marissa, do not be so obdurate!' he chided softly. 'Let us not fall out over this. Can't you see—you are cutting off your nose to spite your face? I want you to come to London; Nicci wants you to come to London… Damn it, *you* want to come to London!'

Marissa had let her body relax against his for one

self-indulgent moment, then common sense reasserted itself. She pushed hard at his chest and wriggled free. 'Take your hands off me! How dare you touch me…? And after what passed between us last night! Sir, you are no gentleman!'

Luc could not resist it. Confronted by a beautiful, angry woman, with the recollection of the silk of her skin and the taste of her lips still fresh in his mind, he could not ignore the provocation. 'But you, Marissa, judging by your responses on the beach, are all woman.'

She lifted her hand to slap him hard, but he caught her wrist in one hand and pulled her against his chest. His other hand cupped her chin and he bent to kiss her mouth.

Marissa set her lips tight and twisted her face away, fighting the temptation to yield to him, cover him in kisses.

At the sound of the double doors opening slowly and of raised voices outside, Luc dropped Marissa's hand and took a step backwards. Marissa sank onto the window seat and remarked coolly, 'The park is looking quite lovely in the sunshine, my lord, do you not think so?'

Jackson, with Nicci hard on his heels, entered. There was colour in the butler's cheeks and Nicci had an unmistakable air of triumph about her. 'Jackson said you were busy and were not to be disturbed, but I told him that was nonsense, you were only having breakfast, and even if you were grumpy I need to talk to you… Oh, good morning, Marissa, I had not realised you were here! Honestly, Jackson, you are impossible—I would have come down directly if I had known Marissa was here.'

Jackson cast Luc a look of resignation and departed. Nicci was chattering on. 'Well, I am really glad you have come; I need to talk to you about jewellery. Luc is being incredibly stuffy about it; he will only let me take pearls and not Mama's diamonds or the emerald set...'

'He is quite correct, Nicci,' Marissa replied steadily, controlling her agitated breathing. She was relieved that the girl seemed not to have noticed anything amiss. 'You must not be disappointed, but gemstones are not considered suitable for a young lady in her first Season. Pearls will be lovely, and there is no reason why you cannot wear amber or rose quartz beads.'

'Oh, if you are going to be stuffy too, there is no point in arguing, I suppose. I am so excited—is it really only two days until we set off? Are you packed and ready? I am sure I will never be.'

Marissa paused, then explained awkwardly, 'I was just saying to your brother that I am not coming with you to London. But I am sure Miss Venables will be a splendid companion for you...'

With a wail of disappointment and dismay Nicci ran across the room and threw herself down on the seat next to Marissa. 'Marissa, this cannot be true! Why, why can you not come to London?'

Marissa struggled to find an acceptable answer, unconscious that her gaze had strayed to Luc's sardonic face.

Nicci caught the look and swivelled round immediately. 'So that is it! It is Luc's fault, as usual—I suppose he has upset you in some way, Marissa dear, and now he is going to ruin my come-out!'

'No, no, Nicci—please do not blame your brother. It is entirely my decision. I just felt, er, it was too much. It is too soon. I mean…' Marissa's words fizzled out in a trail of lameness. She had not even convinced herself, let alone Nicci.

'Now, Marissa,' Luc interjected smoothly. 'You are being unfair on yourself. Tell my sister the *real* reason why you do not wish to accompany us to London.'

Marissa stared at him in horror. Surely he would not even hint at what had passed between them last night, or what had been said this morning? Her mouth opened; she sought for the right words but nothing emerged.

'Very well, I see I shall have to be brutally honest. Nicci, I am afraid that Marissa feels that you will be too much of a handful for her. Now, I know she wanted to spare your feelings, but you will have to accept that she is going to sacrifice her own pleasure on the altar of your wilfulness,' Luc said solemnly.

Nicci promptly burst into tears. Marissa, with one harassed glance at the girl, left her and marched over to where Luc was standing, one booted foot on the fender, arms crossed—and obviously thoroughly enjoying himself. 'Luc! How could you say anything so untrue and unkind to your sister? See how you have upset her.'

He smiled down into her furious face. 'Yes, I realise

it is not very…gentlemanly of me, but it had to be said for her own good.' If he had hoped to goad her by flinging her accusation that he had not behaved as a gentleman back in her face, he had succeeded.

With a frustrated stamp of her foot Marissa turned back to Nicci, who was drooping miserably on the window seat, sniffing into a lawn handkerchief. 'It is not true, Nicci dearest. Luc is teasing you—and me. I simply said…that I was feeling very tired. I think the arrangements, and the hot weather, have sapped my energy. But do not mind it. I will be better directly: of course I will go to London with you!'

'Well, if you are sure. A change of scenery and occupation will soon chase away these megrims,' Luc said smoothly. 'Although I am certain you will miss the invigorating sea breezes.' He smiled wolfishly, his teeth very white in the lean, tanned face.

'I know what you are about, Luc,' Nicci accused suddenly. 'You are teasing Marissa about something and it is very unfair of you!' She stood, mustering her dignity, and extended her hand to her cousin. 'Come along, Marissa, we shall go upstairs and leave him to his beastly breakfast! I need you to tell me if any of my hats are fit to be seen in London.'

Despite her conviction that she would need an entirely new wardrobe for London, Miss Southwood still managed to pack enough valises to almost fill a travelling coach, and Luc was forced to add two more to the train of carriages that set forth from Southwood Hall on a brilliantly sunny day.

The journey was smooth and uneventful, but none the less Marissa was pleased to see Matthews's smiling face as he stood at the head of the staff gathered to welcome them to the Grosvenor Square house. She had been afraid that he would resent Jackson's arrival to usurp his position, but it soon became clear that the inexperienced young man welcomed direction in managing the Town house now the family were in residence.

The hall was soon full of servants and luggage and Marissa slipped away to the little morning room which overlooked the garden at the rear of the house. She stood by the windows, reflecting how different their arrival had used to be when she was married to Charles. He had hated commotion and disorder, and for that reason the luggage had always been sent well ahead, so that everything would be in its place by the time the Earl and Countess drew up at the front door.

The Grosvenor Square house was still decorated to Charles's exacting taste, yet although it was as cold and impersonal as Southwood Hall the memories it held were not as painful. Marissa had known that whenever they went up to London she would hardly see her husband from one day to the other. Charles had left her to her own devices, in fact had hardly spoken to her. He'd had his own circle, his own interests, and had spent much of his time at his clubs. After his initial courtship he had rarely accompanied her to Almack's or the numerous soirées to which they received invitations, leaving his wife to seek the escort of friends.

Marissa had spent many lonely days in London, but at least she had been free of Charles's dominating presence. And, curiously, here she had never been summoned to his bedchamber as she had in Norfolk.

Matthews's discreet cough behind her recalled her to the present. 'My lady, I was not certain which chamber you would wish to occupy.'

'Her ladyship will, naturally, have her usual suite of rooms,' Luc's voice responded before she could reply.

'No, surely Miss Southwood should occupy those rooms,' she protested, turning to find them both in the doorway.

'I insist. Matthews, see her ladyship's luggage is taken up before any of the rest.'

'Yes, my lord.'

'Oh, and Matthews, order some tea to be sent up: her ladyship is fatigued.'

When the door closed behind the under-butler Marissa snapped, 'Thank you so much for your concern, my lord, but I am quite capable of ordering my own tea.'

'You are as pale as linen, Marissa. I am sorry. I appreciate this must be painful for you.' Luc came and took her hand, leading her to a chair and gently pressing her into it. 'I should have realised you would have an attachment to this house and will find it difficult to see it occupied by others.'

'No, not really.' Marissa was startled into honesty. 'I never cared much for this house. It is not that I dislike it, simply that it has no character, no warmth.

My lord ordered it decorated in the Classical taste, but I cannot but feel that it is not so successful in a house of this scale as it is at Southwood Hall.'

'How true,' Luc agreed drily, casting a critical eye around the morning room. The walls were ice-blue with white mouldings. The curtains, again in chilly blue, were draped with almost rigid perfection around the long casements and two marble nymphs flanked the empty grate. 'I have it in mind to redecorate throughout, but I would not want to do anything you would dislike.'

Marissa looked up with an animated face. 'Oh, yes! That is a splendid idea. I have always felt that this could be made into a real family home. The house has beautiful proportions, but it is not served well by my lord's taste.'

Luc's eyebrows rose. 'So, my impeccable late cousin had at least one failing, then?'

The animation drained from her and Marissa cast down her eyes to where her hands had tightened in her lap. 'As have we all, my lord.'

Luc dropped to one knee beside her chair and covered her taut hands with one of his. 'Marissa…'

She glanced up and found he was looking at her with such compassion that her heart knotted within her. If he would only take her in his arms now, hold her, tell her that her marriage had been a bad dream, that it would not be like that with him…

'Your chamber is prepared, my lady, and I have had the tea tray sent up.' Having delivered this message,

Matthews withdrew as silently as he had appeared, but the spell was broken.

Marissa withdrew her hands from under Luc's fingers. 'Excuse me, my lord, I will go up now.' Luc rose silently from his knees, offering her his hand. Marissa stood gracefully, releasing his light grasp the moment she was on her feet. The moment of intimacy had passed, yet the pressure of his fingers still remained as though imprinted on her skin.

Her chamber, although tidy, seemed very full. Mary was shaking out and hanging up her gowns, a pile of trunks was stacked in the corner and Nicci, obviously too excited to sit, was pacing the room, chattering non-stop to the stoical maid.

'Marissa! There you are! Oh, do not bother with tea—can't we go out to the shops now, or for a drive in the park? Surely it is the fashionable hour to be seen.'

'Nicci, please sit down. You are badly in poor Mary's way, and I declare you are positively giving me a headache with your pacing. Sit down and have a cup of tea, then we must finish our unpacking, have a rest and a quiet family dinner. Tomorrow we shall go shopping, I promise you.'

'But I need so much—I cannot be seen in these clothes. And there is a pile of invitations and cards downstairs already! If I do not have the right gowns I will miss all the parties…'

Marissa regarded her over the rim of her cup. 'This is the start of the Season: there will be time—and parties enough for you to go to. You know your brother will deny you nothing in the way of gowns.' Nicci was looking mutinous, so she added cunningly, 'You would not wish to appear to be a provincial by scrambling to attend every event you are invited to. We will be selective: you must not appear over-eager.'

'Very well. I expect you are right as usual, Marissa dear. Tell me about your come-out. Was it very wonderful? Did you have lots of lovely gowns and admirers?' She took her cup and sank down in a flurry of muslin skirts, ready for a good gossip.

Marissa looked at the girl's eager face and chose her words carefully. 'My lord proposed to me within a month of my come-out. And of course thereafter I always attended functions with him. But, yes, I had many lovely gowns.' And indeed she had. Her father, who had ignored her as an inconvenient expense throughout her childhood, had proved unexpectedly generous when it had come to her first Season. He had gambled away most of her late mother's jewels, but from somewhere he had found the resources to dress her in the very latest and most flattering fashions when she had made her debut.

Almost paralysed with nerves at her first dance, Marissa had not realised she was under the scrutiny of the eligible, uncatchable Earl of Radwinter until he had asked for a dance. He had appeared to admire her for her stately beauty, for the dignity of her demeanour so unusual in a girl of just eighteen years. She had rapidly discovered, although her nervousness had diminished and she had soon felt at ease in Society, that her lord preferred her to retain an air of control and distance.

Innocent and sheltered, Marissa had not realised until much later how unusual Charles Southwood's courtship had been. He had never expressed affection, or even partiality. He had never touched her, except to take her hand in the dance or to assist her from the carriage. He had appeared to admire her, but almost as though she were an object, to be selected and purchased, not a woman with feelings and emotions to be engaged.

And if she had been taken aback by her father's urgency that she accept this very first proposal and that the marriage should swiftly follow, then her puzzlement had been swept aside in the hectic preparations for marriage.

'Marissa?' Nicci's voice broke through the memories.

Marissa smiled at her. 'I am sorry, Nicci. I was just reflecting that I am quite jealous of your freedom. I was engaged within weeks of my come-out, so I never really had the opportunity to enjoy myself as a single girl for long.' She leaned across and took Nicci's hand, looking urgently into the girl's blue eyes. 'Nicci…take your time. Do not feel you have to hasten into marriage. Enjoy yourself while you can.'

The girl's expression was first puzzled, then she laughed. 'You sound like Miss Venables! Do not worry, Marissa, I do not intend to find myself entangled.'

'Especially as your heart has still not recovered from Mr Ashforde,' Marissa replied slyly.

Chapter Nine

After dinner the ladies left Luc to his brandy and repaired to the drawing room, where the conversation soon turned to plans for the next day. Nicci demanded to know the names of all the most fashionable *modistes* and insisted that Marissa and Miss Venables accompany her to all of them as early as possible the next morning.

'No, no, dear,' Jane Venables protested. 'It will never do to patronise a *modiste* at random. We must consider who will best enhance your style and make gowns suitable for a debutante.'

'I have heard well of Madame Franchot,' Nicci said excitedly. 'Diane—our dear friend Madame de Rostan, who lived near us in Jamaica—patronises her when she comes to England, and Diane always wears the most stunning gowns.'

Marissa, a slight flush on her cheeks, said nothing. Miss Venables marked this and stored it away to puzzle over later. 'No, dear, that would not be a suitable choice. Madame Franchot does not specialise in gowns for debutantes; you will be able to shop at her establishment when you are married. But farther down Bruton Street there is an establishment owned by a dressmaker who previously worked for Madame Lavall, and I hear she produces the most charming, fresh gowns that will be quite your style.'

'Oh, yes! And then I will need shoes, and bonnets, and reticules and stockings…' The girl prattled on happily.

Miss Venables glanced at Marissa and was reassured to see she had regained her customary composure. She was laughing at Nicci's ambitious programme. 'We will need to plan our days like a military campaign, Nicci, if we are to get through it all!'

A floorboard creaked and Jane looked across to see Luc standing in the doorway, watching Marissa's laughing profile. Now *that* would be a suitable match, she thought. Entirely appropriate for her dear Marissa, and who knows? Perhaps his lordship could lift the mysterious shadow from her heart. However close, however intimate she grew with Marissa, Jane Venables had never been able to pinpoint the source of this deep and secret sadness in her cousin.

The Earl walked into the drawing room, a wicked smile on his lips, his tall figure immaculate in evening dress. 'Nicci, I am sorry to disappoint you, but Marissa is coming shopping with me tomorrow.'

Marissa looked up, startled, then sent him a reproving frown for teasing his sister.

'Luc, don't be a beast,' Nicci protested. 'And Marissa can't go shopping with you. It would not be proper for her to go to tailors and bootmakers! Even I know that.'

'Oh, I was not intending to buy clothes, sister dear. No, we have something far more important to engage us. Marissa is going to assist me in redecorating this house.'

Nicci was immediately diverted. 'How wonderful— I knew Marissa could not really like this chilly place, although naturally I would not say so! Now, for my room I want a pink silk tented ceiling and gauze bed curtains, and a shell-shaped bath in my dressing room…'

'Tell me, little sister, how have you managed to imagine a room better suited to a class of lady I devoutly hope you will never encounter?'

'My lord,' Miss Venables cautioned, but Nicci simply pouted at her brother.

'Stuffy man! I saw it illustrated in the *Lady's Intelligencer* last month. It was *beautiful*.'

'Well, I have no intention of redecorating your room, whatever your journals say. It will soon be buried under piles of shopping in any case. No, we will begin with the hall and the Salon. Marissa, at what hour tomorrow would it be convenient for you to accompany me to Schomberg House? Harding, Howell and Company are reputed to have the latest styles in furniture.'

The thought of spending an intimate day in Luc's company choosing furnishings like a married couple was dangerously attractive. Marissa dropped her eyes demurely and replied, 'I regret that I will be unable to give any attention to furnishings until we have ordered our gowns, my lord. Surely you would not have the house redecorated but none of us fit to entertain in it?'

Luc crossed one leg over another and looked at her steadily. 'Come, Marissa, you are reneging on our agreement.'

'Not at all. I am more than willing to assist you,' she replied with spirit. 'But all in good time: I had not realised that you were in quite such a hurry, my lord.'

'I know what it is,' Nicci teased. 'Luc is going to catch a wife and he wants the house to be in the mode to impress the ladies! Is that not so, brother? Deny it if you dare!'

There was a silence before Luc replied, 'Of course. And I must be sure that the house will reflect the taste of the lady I would marry.'

'Aha!' Nicci said triumphantly. 'Hoist by your own petard! You cannot be in a hurry, for how can you redecorate until you have found the lady and discovered her taste?'

Luc laughed. '*Touché,* little sister. Very well, I release Marissa for your orgy of shopping, but I reserve the right to claim her later.'

Marissa's eyes flew to his face and her heart thudded. What a thing to say. What a wonderful thought! It appeared he was still bent on marrying her, but she would not, could not fall in with his plans for her to be the new Countess of Radwinter. The realities of marriage would be far worse this time, for she loved Luc; she knew that now. She could not bear to have that love destroyed by marriage, when he would realise she could never be a true wife to him.

Miss Venables's sharp eyes moved from one face to another. What was going on—and why did Marissa seem so discomfited? She spoke firmly to break the mood. 'If we are to make an early start tomorrow we should retire. Nicci, if you do not go to bed this instant, I can promise that you will have black circles under your eyes! Come along now, say goodnight to your brother and Marissa.'

Left alone, neither Marissa nor Luc spoke. She because she could not, he because he seemed quite at his ease simply sitting and regarding the flames of the small fire flickering in the grate.

At last the silence became so oppressive, and the tension of waiting for him to speak so great, that Marissa blurted out, 'May I take the barouche…?'

Luc spoke at the same moment. 'Would you like to take the barouche tomorrow morning?' He laughed as their words collided. 'We appear to think as one.'

'On that matter, sir, yes,' she responded, as repressively as she could. 'I would be grateful for the carriage, and if I may I will take James: I suspect that the groom will find the number of packages too many for him to manage alone.'

'Take all the footmen; you will probably need them if my little sister has her way. I think I had better go and speak to my banker tomorrow: I will likely have to sell out of Government stocks to pay for this come-out!'

Marissa looked anxious. 'Perhaps you should let me

know what limit you would set on Nicci's expenditure and then I can ensure she remains within it.'

'No, let her have what you feel is suitable. There is nobody whose taste and judgement I trust more than yours, Marissa. But do not let her monopolise all your time—you have your own plans, I know. And,' he added, his eyes warm on her face, 'I look forward to seeing you out of mourning.'

Marissa flushed at both compliments and rose. Luc got to his feet in response. 'Jane is quite right, as usual. I will retire,' she said. 'We have all had a fatiguing day, with the prospect of another tomorrow. Goodnight, Luc.'

She smiled and turned to leave, but he came and took her hand in his, brushing his lips lightly over her knuckles in a formal salute. 'Goodnight, Marissa.'

He continued to stand after she had left, gazing thoughtfully at where she had sat. Marissa was an enigma to him, behind the perfect façade of control and elegance was a laughing, passionate, instinctive young woman. And yet the passion seemed to go only so far and was strangely innocent, at variance with her previously married state. It was almost as if it was curbed by something. He searched his mind for the word, but only 'fear' came to mind. That was too preposterous. He shook his head in denial and went to pour himself another brandy from the decanter. What in the world could Marissa have to be afraid of?

'Oh, Marissa, may I really have the figured silk?' Nicci breathed. 'It is so lovely.' She twisted and turned in front of the cheval glass, holding her hands away from the white fabric as though afraid to touch it.

'Yes, I think it will be perfect as your best ball-gown. But, *madame,* it must be cut a little higher in the bodice, and I am not certain about the silver floss at the hem. Jane, what do you think?'

Miss Venables turned from her scrutiny of several bolts of muslin and considered the gown. 'I agree, dear. It is too fussy for Miss Southwood: I always believe that understatement is better on a young girl.'

'Might I suggest a pearl beading, as we have on this gown?' Madame Lefevre crooked a finger and an assistant scurried forward with a sample.

'Yes, very pretty, and if that could be repeated on the puff sleeves along the line of the lace…'

'But, yes!' the *modiste* exclaimed. 'Your ladyship has impeccable taste. May I show Miss Southwood any other gowns?'

The little assistant, who seemed scarcely older than Nicole, brought the ladies glasses of orgeat and almond wafer biscuits and they reviewed their purchases.

'Now, we have the white silk ballgown for best, the pale green for less formal parties, the fawn walking dress with the chocolate-brown pelisse…' Miss Venables ticked off on her fingers. 'Your riding habit we will have tailored—your country one will do for the meantime. What you are lacking are simple day dresses. I suggest we visit some of the linen drapers

and select some dress lengths for Mary to make up
for you.'

Nicci clapped her hands with sheer pleasure. 'More
dresses! Oh, yes please!'

They arranged for the delivery of the new gowns
as soon as possible and made their way out to the
waiting barouche. Nicci's dread of being seen in an
open carriage in a dress of less than fashionable cut
had been forgotten in the excitement of driving behind
her brother's newly acquired matched bays with a liv-
eried coachman on the box and two footmen standing
behind.

'Shoes next, I think,' Marissa remarked, consulting
her notebook. 'Then Grafton House for dress lengths,
and we will end at Dickens and Smith for stockings
and trimmings. Bond Street, please, Henry,' she ordered the coachman. 'Seymour's shoe shop.'

The shoe shop was more a boudoir than a shop. Its
curtains were of silk, the patrons were seated upon
divans arranged tastefully around the room, and despite the sunshine outside the interior was lit by discreet lamps of fashionable design.

There was one other customer already seated, an
assistant kneeling at her feet gently slipping a daring
scarlet kid slipper onto her foot. She looked up and
cried out in pleasure when she saw who had entered.

'My dear Lady Southwood! How well you look,
and what a pleasure it is to see you back in Society
again.'

'Lady Valentine,' Marissa responded, moving forward to take the other woman's proffered hand. 'May

I make known to you my companion, Miss Venables, and my cousin, Miss Southwood? Jane, Nicole: Lady Valentine.'

The older woman cast an openly appraising glance over Nicole. 'So, you are the new Earl's sister from the West Indies, are you not?'

'Yes, ma'am,' Nicci said, bobbing a curtsey but looking from under her lashes at the young man in uniform who was lounging negligently against the wall, apparently waiting for her ladyship.

Lady Valentine caught the look and waved the young man forward. 'I had quite forgot you were there, Andrew. Lady Southwood, ladies, may I make known to you Captain Andrew Cross of the Seventh Light Dragoons. Andrew: Lady Southwood, Miss Southwood, Miss Venables.'

The Captain swept the ladies a bow, his cropped dark hair gleaming in the subdued light. Nicci batted her eyelashes, admiring his red jacket, gold braid and highly polished boots.

'Sit here beside me, all of you,' Lady Valentine suggested, patting the seat. 'Are you all here to buy shoes?'

'For Miss Southwood only this morning,' Marissa said coolly, nodding to the assistant who was hovering in the background. The young woman hastened forward and listened attentively as Marissa outlined the types of shoes they were looking for.

Lady Valentine extended one foot, drawing up the hem of her jade-green walking dress to expose an elegant ankle and turning her foot in one direction then

the other. 'Andrew, what do you think of these? Will
they do?'

Miss Venables drew in her breath sharply at the
impropriety, and glared at Nicole, who was openly
staring at the older woman.

'Very nice, Susan,' Captain Cross drawled, his eyes
lingering on the blatantly exposed ankle.

Fortunately at that moment the assistant returned
with some walking shoes and Nicci was distracted.
Unable to resist it, Marissa enquired sweetly, 'And
how is Sir Michael, and your three dear little boys?'

'Oh, well enough, I suppose. I am sure Sir Michael
would write if anything were amiss. They are still at
home in Bedfordshire. Sir Michael finds Town such a
bore: I always tell him not to disturb himself, coming
up on my account.'

Marissa repressed a smile at Miss Venables's snort
of disapproval and added maliciously, 'But your dear
sons, how could you bear to leave them?'

'Oh, the country air is better for them,' Lady Valentine responded, with a toss of her head which sent
her luxuriant dark curls bouncing. 'Besides, there is
very little for them to do in Town.'

Captain Cross had wandered off, scarcely bothering
to conceal his boredom at this talk of domestic circumstances, but now he reappeared, a dashing half-
boot in his hand. 'Try this, Susan.' He dropped to one
knee and eased the scarlet slipper from her foot, his
finger lingering at her ankle. Marissa became aware
of Nicci's dropped jaw and astounded expression and
jabbed her briskly in the ribs.

'Pay attention, Nicole, does the shoe chafe your toes? The colour is perfect for your new walking dress, do you not agree, Miss Venables?'

But even Miss Venables was distracted by the outrageous behaviour of Lady Valentine and her male companion. He was buttoning the half-boot with fingers which strayed frequently to the skin above.

'Andrew, behave,' Lady Valentine admonished indulgently, bending down to pat away his questing fingers. 'Yes, I will take those too.' She gestured for the assistant and while her purchases were being packed enquired of Marissa, 'Do you make a long stay in Town?'

'We are here for the Season; Miss Southwood is making her come-out.'

'I shall see you again, then.' As she passed Lady Valentine touched Nicci's cheek. 'Charming, so fresh. Andrew, stop staring and come along. Good afternoon!'

It was as much as Marissa could do to keep Nicci quiet until they reached their carriage. 'Well,' the girl burst out. 'Showing so much ankle—and letting Captain Cross put her shoe on like that! How very fast she was! The Captain is extremely handsome, but surely quite a bit younger than she is? And does her husband not mind?'

Miss Venables twitched her pelisse straight and fixed Nicci with a gimlet eye. 'That is what happens when a lady allows herself to behave in a fast and indecorous manner. Let that be a lesson to you, my girl.'

'You mean I would attract handsome army captains and wear beautiful scarlet shoes?' Nicole asked, wide-eyed.

'Do not be pert, Nicole, this conversation is at an end. I think we have had quite a surfeit of shopping today and I am in need of a cup of tea. Marissa, shall we return to Grosvenor Square?'

Chastened, Nicole refrained from sulking, and the three ladies were soon wearily ascending the front steps where Matthews held the door wide.

Their energies returned the next day, however, and a prolonged expedition saw Nicci's muslins, stockings, ribbons and laces purchased. An early start enabled them to scour the shops before the crowds grew too great, and Marissa then indulged herself with a lengthy consultation at Madame Lavall's. Miss Venables displayed an unexpected interest in evening gowns herself, and it was three very tired, but very excited ladies who finally returned home for tea.

'Is my brother at home, Matthews?' Nicci enquired as the under-butler held the door open for the laden footmen to stagger in under their burden of hat boxes, packages and parcels.

'I believe he has just gone out, Miss Southwood. Shall I have tea sent to the Blue Salon?'

'No, to my room, please. Marissa, Miss Venables— let us take tea upstairs and unpack all our purchases. I have quite forgotten what I have bought, we visited so many shops!'

The ladies spent a very agreeable and thoroughly frivolous hour re-examining every item, spreading the muslins out for Mary to see and thoroughly confusing the maid by disagreeing over which pattern in the *Mirror of Fashion* she should use for which fabric.

Miss Venables had invested in a pair of long buttoned kid evening gloves with silver embroidery. Now she was having second thoughts. 'Are they a little much, my dear?' she asked Marissa anxiously. 'I normally wear much plainer gloves, but these are such beautiful work I could not resist.'

'They are very fine, Jane. I agree you have nothing suitable to wear with them, but just think of that lovely cream silk shot through with silver we saw in Debenham's. You could have that made up in a simple, elegant style for evening and that would quite set off the gloves.'

'I do declare, Marissa, you are too extravagant. To buy gloves and then have a gown made to match is quite the wrong way round—I do not know what has come over me!'

Marissa jumped up. 'I know, the gauze scarf I brought with me would be perfect with such an ensemble. Let me fetch it and we will try it out with the gloves.'

She darted out of the door, leaving it ajar, and ran lightly down the corridor. Behind her she heard Jane call, 'Marissa, come back. This is really too frivolous for me!'

She spun round and called back, laughing, 'Nonsense, Jane, it will be just the thing, you will see!' Turning back, she stumbled and found herself colliding with a strong, warm male body. 'Oh! Oh, Luc—I thought you had gone out.'

'Did you?' he asked gently. 'What have you been up to?' He looked down into her flushed, laughing face, noting the sparkle in her eyes. 'Mischief, by the look of you. I like that gown.' His words were warm, his gaze appreciative as he took in her dress of jonquil twill, which moulded the soft curve of her breast and emphasised her slender waist.

Marissa's heart beat like a captive bird inside her ribcage, her breathing constricted by a strange excitement and an overwhelming desire to press herself against him, drink him in in a kiss that would bind him to her in the passion they had shared on the beach.

Something of her desire must have reached him, for he went very still, his blue gaze intent on her hot face as the laughter faded, leaving her staring up at him, wide-eyed and beseeching.

'No...not mischief. Shopping with my minx of a sister,' he said softly, the look in his eyes at odds with the light words. 'I like you like this. I wish I too could make you laugh.' His fingertip traced the curve of her cheek, down the fine line of her jaw, then up to her lips. He let it rest there on the full softness until Marissa let them part. Slowly, almost of its own volition, the tip of her tongue crept out to touch the pad of his fingertip.

A sharp intake of breath was his first response, but then he swept his arms around her, pulled her to his body and bent to kiss her. Behind them the sound of footsteps ascending the staircase made them both freeze, then Luc stooped, swept Marissa up into his arms and shouldered open her bedroom door.

She surrendered to his strong clasp, trying to believe that it would be different this time, that she could give herself to him completely. And then she could accept his offer of marriage…even if he did not love her it would be enough if she could give him everything…

Luc kicked the door shut behind him and made for the bed. For one giddy moment the passion swept her along, then, despite her desire for him, instinct froze her, made her limbs rigid, the breath catch in her throat. Luc stopped and looked down at her questioningly before turning to the chaise and sitting down, holding her on his lap.

To her great surprise he did not kiss her, instead he held her against his chest, stroked her hair and waited until she relaxed a little.

'Now, what was that about?'

'What do you mean?' she asked, her voice shaking.

'Just now you wanted me to kiss you, you would have met and answered my embraces, yet you froze in my arms. And on the beach you were the same. Tell me what is wrong, Marissa.'

In that instant she wanted to pour out everything to him. How she loved him, how she wanted him. He had shown her it was possible for a man to give pleasure to a woman, but that was only before the act itself. But two years with Charles had destroyed her ability to give herself, even to a man she loved. If Luc took her to his bed she would either freeze again or break down—and no man, however understanding, would tolerate that from his wife.

Luc waited patiently as she struggled for the words to describe to him something so intimate she could hardly even allude to it to a female companion, never mind a man! His fingers lifted the soft curls at the nape of her neck and stroked the sensitive skin beneath with mesmeric slowness.

No, it was impossible. She could find no way to explain to him that she could never respond to his lovemaking, that the very act was so abhorrent to her that, even loving Luc as she did, it would solve nothing. The words, when she finally spoke them, were true, but not the whole truth.

'Charles…you look so like Charles it is a constant reminder…' She struggled, but failed, to speak aloud the words in her head. *He treated me so coldly, used me so badly, that I can never give myself to you as I crave to.*

Luc became very still, his fingers arrested on her skin. When he spoke his voice was dry. 'I understand. You are trying to tell me that you are still in love with your husband. I am sorry that my attentions give you so much pain. I am afraid I can do nothing to alter my outward appearance, but believe me, I shall no longer press my attentions upon you.'

Marissa gave a little sob, burying her face against the lapels of his coat. Luc gritted his teeth and resisted the temptation to kiss away her tears. Of all the damnable luck: no wonder she responded at first to his lovemaking! She had fallen into his arms seeking the husband she had lost. Well, that was a salutary lesson to his pride—he was a poor substitute for Charles, and if he had not looked so like his cousin Marissa would not have given him a second glance, let alone let him glimpse the passion that burned within her.

'Marissa! Marissa, dear, where are you?' There was a tap on the door and without waiting Miss Venables bustled in. 'Have you lost that scarf? I thought I saw it—' She broke off, her face scarlet with embarrassment.

Marissa scrambled to her feet, equally flushed. 'Jane…er, his lordship was just…'

'Quite…er, that is…I will go back to Nicci. Oh, dear…' Miss Venables could be heard retreating along the landing, muttering, 'Oh, dear…oh, dear…' in very agitated tones.

It broke the tension between them. Luc caught Marissa's eye and broke out laughing. 'Poor Miss Venables! Will she ever recover?'

'It is no laughing matter, my lord,' Marissa reproved, but she too could see the humour in the scene. 'She will think me quite beyond redemption. I will tell her that we… Oh, dear, I cannot think of anything to tell her that is not thoroughly improper!'

Luc got easily to his feet, the laughter dying out of his face to be replaced with a rueful gentleness. 'Forgive me, Marissa, I would not have embarrassed you for the world. Tell Miss Venables what you will. I promise I will stand any amount of lecturing from her on the subject of my morals!' He smiled at her and left.

As she entered Nicci's room, carefully avoiding Jane's eye, Marissa thought, I do *like* Luc: he is so very kind, and he does make me laugh. It had never occurred to her that she could have that sort of friendship with a man, least of all one she was in love with. Perhaps she could learn to accept that friendship and keep her other thoughts, her love for him, secret always.

'Marissa, you have forgotten the scarf,' Nicci observed. 'And what have you been doing? You are quite pink in the face and your hair is disarrayed.'

'Oh, is it? Well, I thought the scarf might have dropped down behind the clothes press so I leaned over to look. I expect that made the blood rush to my face.'

Miss Venables cleared her throat reprovingly and stared out of the window. Much as she liked Luc, and considered him a highly eligible candidate for Marissa's hand, she was shocked to the core to have found them in such a compromising situation. And for Marissa to add an untruth to immoral behaviour…well, she would have to speak to her later, when they were alone.

Marissa, however, was unconscious of her companion's disapproving thoughts, her mind still on Luc, her hand touching her nape where his fingers had rested, her memory storing away each word, each gesture.

A discreet tap at the door, answered by Nicci, revealed Jackson, a broad smile on his face. 'Miss Nicci, Madame Diane has arrived.'

'Diane—here in London?' Nicci jumped up in a

shower of paper patterns, her eyes sparkling. 'But we did not look to see her for several weeks, I thought.'

'The winds from Jamaica were good, I understand,' the butler responded, still grinning.

'But where is she staying? Has she opened up the London house?' Nicci demanded. 'She must come to dinner…'

'You can ask her yourself, Miss Nicci—she is below in the hall. I must find his lordship—have you seen him recently?'

Miss Venables cleared her throat again, and Marissa said hastily, 'No. Perhaps he is in his study, Jackson.'

Led by Nicci, the ladies crossed the landing to where the sweep of banisters gave a view of the hall below and the lady who waited there. From above Marissa gained the impression of extreme elegance, of superbly coiffed honey-blonde hair just visible under the brim of a hat in the very latest mode, and of a woman no longer in her first youth but with a mature beauty that was still dazzling.

Then Luc's footsteps sounded on the marble floor and the woman swung round, threw her arms wide, sending furs and parasol flying across the hall, and was swept up into the bear-hug of Luc's embrace. Marissa stood stunned as he kissed Madame de Rostan full on the lips without restraint. And the embrace he received in return was just as uninhibited and generous. So Nicci had been right: this woman had been— still was—Luc's mistress.

'*Chéri*, I have missed you so much!' Diane cried when, after what seemed like minutes, they broke the kiss. 'You look so handsome, Luc—I thought you would have become all pale and uninteresting after a few months in this soggy country!' She ran a proprietorial hand down his lapels and across his chest.

Luc caught her hand in his, laughing down into her face. 'Behave, Diane, we are not alone,' he said huskily. The low-voiced words, caught by the acoustics of the hall, seemed to stab Marissa in the heart. Thank goodness she had not succumbed to the desire to tell him everything, especially how much she loved him.

Nicci, never one for subtleties, ran down the stairs, crying, 'Diane! Diane!' and threw herself into the Frenchwoman's arms. 'I have missed you so much! Are you well? Was the voyage dreadful? But you look *beautiful*, so you cannot have been seasick…'

Diane patted Nicci's flushed cheek with one gloved hand. 'You are prettier than ever, *ma petite*, but I regret to see that your manners have not improved one jot! You must introduce me to these ladies.'

Marissa reached the bottom of the stairs and found herself caught in the warmth of the Frenchwoman's personality. Smiling, deep blue eyes regarded her from a face lightly coloured by the sun but virtually unlined, even after reaching the age of thirty-nine in a tropical climate.

Luc stepped forward, a trace of colour on his cheekbones. 'Lady Southwood, may I make known to you Madame Diane de Rostan of Jamaica, an old friend of the family? Diane—the Dowager Countess of Radwinter, my cousin, who has graciously consented to act as hostess for me and help bring Nicci out this

Season. Miss Venables—Madame de Rostan; Diane—
Miss Venables, Lady Southwood's companion.'

The ladies exchanged polite bows and the entire
party moved into the drawing room, followed by Jackson and a footman with a tray of refreshments. Luc
conducted Diane to the sofa and waited while the
other ladies settled themselves before moving to stand,
one foot on the fender, his arm resting lightly on the
mantelshelf.

Marissa studied Diane while the footman handed
out glasses of ratafia and almond biscuits. Madame de
Rostan was tall, almost willowy, but with a full and
voluptuous bosom which the high-waisted fashionable
afternoon dress showed off to perfection. The fine
wool cloth was a soft, deep blue, the colour of peri-
winkles, in the highest kick of fashion and unmistak-
ably French-cut. The overall effect was to make Marissa feel washed-out and almost provincial in the
jonquil twill which had pleased her so much that
morning when she had donned it.

For a tall woman Diane had delicate hands,
sheathed in fine kid gloves just a shade paler than the
blue of her gown. Below the braided hem of her gown
peeped fine blue kid slippers. Sipping her ratafia and
maintaining a polite flow of conversation, Marissa
struggled with the unworthy feeling that she disliked
this woman on sight.

Nicci was chattering on, demanding news of mutual
friends and of old servants. Marissa let her attention
wander until she suddenly realised that from across
the room Luc was watching her intently. Bringing her

eyes up, she met the look with one of bland but polite indifference.

Madame de Rostan broke off from a description of someone's new plantation house to say, 'But, Nicci, you must stop asking me about Jamaica. We are discussing matters and people that are of no interest to Lady Southwood and Miss Venables.' Nicci instantly obeyed, apologising prettily to Miss Venables and Marissa.

Marissa was piqued by this instant obedience from Nicci, so much in contrast to her wilful behaviour when in Marissa's charge. She felt her brows drawing together into a frown and hastily rearranged her expression, feeling ashamed of herself. She was jealous of Diane de Rostan, jealous not only because she was Luc's mistress but also because she was so beautiful and Nicci held her in such affection.

It was a thoroughly unworthy emotion, Marissa chided herself, but she could not shake from her memory the passion with which Luc and Diane had clung together in the hall, the history of past passion that had shown in that embrace.

Marissa suddenly felt a great weariness, as if all her vitality had drained away. So much for her hope that she and Luc could be friends, that she could still be part of his life even if she could not marry him. Now he had Diane, who would doubtless take a discreet step back when he found a wife, but for now seemed more than ready to resume her former role as his mistress. With her and with his sister for female companionship Luc would not need Marissa and her tiresome emotions.

Suddenly she could not bear to sit there any longer.

'Madame, I do hope you will join us for dinner this evening? If you will all excuse me I must leave you: I had promised I would call on Lady Valentine this afternoon. I look forward to seeing you later.'

As she left she heard Nicci remark with her usual tactlessness, 'That is strange, I was not aware that Marissa had an engagement this afternoon, were you, Jane?'

The door closed behind her, leaving Jane to catch up the thread of the conversation and cover her gauche behaviour. Madame de Rostan glanced down into her ratafia glass. *Alors!* London was going to prove more interesting than she had thought.

Chapter Ten

Marissa came down to breakfast at eight, expecting to have the room to herself. Normally Miss Venables would have partaken of a slice of bread and butter and a cup of tea early and gone out for her daily constitutional in the gardens in the centre of the Square. Nicci never rose before ten and habitually took breakfast in her room. Luc, who had still not shaken the habit of rising early in order to take advantage of the cool of the morning in Jamaica, would have breakfasted by half past seven and be dealing with the day's business in his study.

To her surprise, however, they were all three at the table, deep in animated conversation. They broke off politely as she entered. Luc rose, but the moment she was seated and they had exchanged good mornings they carried on their conversation around her. After last night's dinner, where Diane had been very much the centre of attention, Marissa was feeling in need of reassurance. Diane had been stylish and effortlessly charming, the room illuminated by her personality. To

Marissa it had seemed that the Frenchwoman had broken into the circle of friendship and intimacy which had begun in Norfolk and had flourished in the family atmosphere of the Grosvenor Square house.

Diane had been charming to her, and had been at pains to include Marissa in all the dialogue over dinner, but none the less she had felt excluded and lonely, as though she were no longer the hostess. Miss Venables had revealed a fascination for the flora of the West Indies and had been delighted to discover that Madame de Rostan was a passionate gardener who had designed a large garden on the island. With Jane constantly asking questions, everyone except Marissa had been drawn into the discussion of the great houses and estates of Jamaica.

'Would you pass the chocolate, Jane, please?' Marissa prompted as her companion, deep in conversation with Luc, had failed to notice she was waiting for it. 'What shall we do today?' she asked, with a brightness she did not feel, once she had their attention.

'I am going shopping with Diane,' Nicci enthused. 'She has promised to take me to her glove-maker and to buy me a pair to go with my evening dress. My very first pair of long kid gloves!'

'But I thought we had agreed that we would buy your gloves at Schomberg House,' Marissa said, surprised.

'But *anyone* can buy gloves at Schomberg House,' Nicci protested. 'Diane knows a French glove-maker—very exclusive.'

Marissa waited for an invitation to join the shopping party, but it did not come and she did not care to invite herself. The lid of the chocolate pot rattled slightly as she put it down on the table. 'Well, that sounds very nice, Nicci: do not forget to take a sample of the dress fabric with you. Jane—shall we go to Hatchard's this morning? I believe they have a recent book by the author of *Waverley*—it is called *Guy Mannering*. I recall you saying how much you enjoyed *Waverley* when it came out three years ago.'

'Oh, did I not say last night, dear? Madame de Rostan has offered me an introduction to an old friend of hers who is an expert on the flora of the West Indies and has the most wonderful collection of native species in his conservatory here in London. Madame de Rostan promised to drop me off to visit Sir Frederick Collier and his sister this morning, on her way to the shops with Nicci.'

'I see,' Marissa said shortly, stung that everyone appeared to have their morning well planned without any thought of her. She turned to Luc and said, with a forced smile, 'Well, it seems there is absolutely no call on my time this morning. Shall we venture forth to those furniture warehouses you were speaking of and look for suitable items for the dining room and salon?'

There was a silence, broken only by the clink of cutlery as Luc's long fingers played with his knife and fork on his now empty plate. 'Please, do not be troubled with that: I was being very selfish asking you to give up your time in that way when you must have so much to do and so many friends to visit. Besides,' he added fatally, 'Diane has already offered to assist me.'

'She has wonderful taste,' Nicci enthused tactlessly. 'She chose all the draperies for our house at White Horse Cay.'

I am sure she did, Marissa thought acidly, unreasonable anger burning within her. Diane had been so pleasant to her, yet she found herself disliking her more and more. And the knowledge that this was entirely unworthy and due to jealousy did nothing to improve her mood.

She retreated to her chamber before Madame de Rostan arrived to collect Jane and Nicci, but she could not resist watching from behind the drapes as the stylish barouche drew up. The sun was shining from a vivid blue sky, gleaming on the railings around the formal central gardens and causing ladies on foot to raise their parasols like so many bobbing flowers. From above all she could see of Diane de Rostan was a dashing plumed hat in chip straw worn with a costume of eau-de-nil. Marissa craned to see details but could make none out, and withdrew hastily when Nicci and Jane came down the steps and were handed into the carriage by the attentive groom.

Marissa paced restlessly. There were many things she *could* do on such a lovely morning: she could walk to Hyde Park, order her carriage to take her for a drive in Green Park or to visit Hatchard's to buy *Guy Mannering*. She could call on Lady Valentine, but her languid manner and the presence of ever-attentive Captain Cross would only irk her in her present mood.

And it was all very well for Luc to suggest she visit friends when all she had was casual acquaintances. Her father had never brought her up to London before her come-out, she had been educated by a governess so had no schoolfriends, and after her swift marriage to Charles her husband had made it plain that close companions were unacceptable to him. 'After all,' he had said, 'you have your duties as my wife. What more should you require?'

But at least Charles had left her financially well-provided-for. Marissa knew it was shallow, and showed a weakness in character, but the only occupation that appealed to her that morning was to go shopping—and as extravagantly as possible. Diane had succeeded in a very short space of time in making her feel colourless and provincial. She rang the bell for Mary. 'Please arrange for Mr Hall to call tomorrow to give me a new crop,' she instructed. 'I really cannot be seen with this mass of hair; it is quite unfashionable.'

Mary looked shocked. 'Oh, but, ma'am, you have such lovely hair, so thick and curly. It's a crime to cut it off!'

'Nonsense! Now, get ready to accompany me, and order the carriage for half-past. I am going shopping.'

Marissa was just drawing on her gloves when the knocker sounded and she heard masculine tones in the hall. Matthews entered. 'Sir George Kempe, my lady.'

'My father! But, Matthews, I am not at ho—' But

it was too late. Her father was striding into the room on the under-butler's heels.

'Not at home! Nonsense, you cannot deny your own father! Come, kiss me, child.'

Marissa stepped forward and kissed him on the cheek with as much self-assurance as she could muster. She sat, pulling off her gloves, and said coolly, 'Please sit, Papa. May I offer you refreshment? Matthews—the decanters, if you please.'

It was three years since she had seen her father and she was shocked by the change in him. Sir George was tall, heavily built, and when she had last seen him his tight crop of curls had still been black. Now it was iron-grey, his face lined and reddened with pouches and broken veins. His figure had thickened to corpulence, making his fashionable trousers strain across the tops of his thighs. His eyes, despite his show of bonhomie, were cold and assessing beneath the shaggy grey brows, and Marissa could detect no sign of pleasure at seeing his only child again after so long.

'You are well, Papa?' she enquired dutifully and to break the silence. 'It is a long time since I have seen you.'

'Hah!' He barked. 'And whose fault was that? Denied the right to see my own daughter by that cold fish of a husband of yours! Much good it did him, all those high and mighty airs—in his grave at forty-five!'

'You did not come to the funeral,' she said quietly.

'What would have been the point of that? All the expense of posting up from Hampshire and not a chance the tight cove would have left me so much as a guinea in his will.'

'The hope of gain should not be the motive for attending the funeral of your son-in-law!' Marissa retorted stiffly.

'Spare me the moralising. You are as bad as your mother ever was.' Sir George removed his snuffbox with some difficulty from his waistcoat pocket and helped himself to a large pinch. 'He showed me no respect as his father-in-law, why should I pretend any for him?'

Marissa fought down the revulsion that came flooding back at the memory of the awful scenes between her father and her husband. In the end Charles had thrown Sir George off the estate with the threat that he would cut off even the small allowance he had agreed to pay his father-in-law if he showed his face again in either Norfolk or Grosvenor Square.

'He paid you an allowance; you had no cause for complaint.' It was hard for Marissa to keep calm, not to crumble in the face of this blustering man who had neglected her all her young life then thrust her into marriage with unseemly haste.

Matthews came in with the decanters, pouring a large brandy to Sir George's instructions. The baronet tossed it back as if it were water and thrust out the glass again. Expressionless, the butler replenished it. 'Will there be anything else, my lady?' he enquired pointedly, his eyes anxious on her face. It seemed to him that he had made a mistake in admitting her ladyship's father without asking first: he did not like the look of the man and her ladyship seemed none too pleased to see him.

'Thank you, Matthews, that will be all.' He bowed, and was closing the door behind him when he heard her say, 'Why are you here, Father?' Well, that did it—he was going to have a word with Mr Jackson. He would know what to do.

'Why do you think, you ungrateful child? Why have I heard nothing about my allowance being increased and the man's been dead over a year? I always thought that lawyer of yours was a slow dog.'

'Why should you expect to hear anything?' Marissa raised a haughty brow. Even a year ago her father would have browbeaten her; now, a year of independence had stiffened her resolve and given her the confidence to withstand his bullying manner. 'The allowance continues as before.'

'But does not increase?' he blustered. 'Now that arrogant husband of yours is gone, I expect a dutiful daughter to consider what a man needs to live on.'

All her life her father had been in debt, spending on racing, gambling and loose women. The colour rose in her cheeks. 'If you did not spend it on drinking and cards and paid attention to the estate you would have a very fine income, Father.'

'What do you know about affairs?' He heaved himself to his feet and poured another brandy, the neck of the decanter rattling against his glass. The blood vessels in his neck were beginning to swell and Marissa, inwardly trembling, recognised the signs of one of his frequent rages developing. He tossed back the brandy and began to pace the carpet in front of the fire. 'I haven't come here for a sermon; I have come here for you to tell that lawyer of yours to increase my allowance.'

Marissa gripped her hands together in her lap, the knuckles showing white, but she kept her voice steady. 'Charles would not have wished that.'

'Charles would not have wished,' he mocked, coming to a halt in front of her. 'Very dutiful, I'm sure, for a silly little ninny who was bought for five thousand guineas!'

'Bought? What can you mean?' Her hands moved to clutch the sides of her chair as the room tilted.

'The damn fool wanted you so much that he was prepared to pay off my gambling debts and forgo a dowry to get his hands on you.'

Shocked though she was, Marissa felt a sudden stab of amazement: Charles must have truly loved her at the beginning after all—what had gone wrong?

Her father saw the play of emotion on her face and pounced. 'Oh, don't think he was in love with you,' he sneered. 'He was quite frank with me: he wanted a well-bred girl who was young enough to be moulded to his...ways. And you happened to be the youngest and the prettiest that was available. I wanted to hold out for more, but I'll give him his due: he was a cunning bastard. Told me that if I did not sell you to him he would make damn sure your reputation was sullied and you would marry no one.'

'I do not believe you. You are lying,' she stammered, the blood draining from her face.

'Did he ever say he loved you? Did he ever show you any sign of affection? I would doubt it, knowing his reputation!'

'Reputation?' Could it be that Charles's cruelty and coolness were more widely known than she had realised? 'How could you do that to me, if you knew what kind of man he was?' she cried, starting to her feet, her hands clenched by her sides, wanting to hit out at that smirking red face.

'You are my daughter. Mine to dispose of as I saw fit. Girls are no good for anything else but marriage.'

'You are despicable. I hate you,' she choked out. 'You will not get another farthing from me. I shall stop your allowance today—'

He snatched at her wrist, pulling her towards him with some force. They were so close she could smell the brandy on his breath, see the broken veins in his cheeks. 'Tread very carefully, Marissa. There are things I could make known about your *esteemed* late husband that would ruin you and create a scandal that would blight the Southwood name.'

Behind them neither heard the door open until Luc spoke. 'Good morning.'

Sir George spun round, his fingers still clamped round Marissa's wrist, fury etching his features. 'Who the hell are you?'

'Lucian Southwood. Would you do me the favour of unhanding Lady Southwood?' It was not a request.

The baronet's face darkened to a damson-red, but he did not relinquish his grasp. 'What's it got to do with you? I am talking to my daughter.'

'You are hurting your daughter.' The words were quiet, but full of menace. 'I shall not tell you again.' Luc stalked forward, his eyes cold and narrowed on the other man's face.

Sir George released Marissa's wrist. Luc took it, his thumb gently massaging the white marks on the fragile skin, his eyes still locked with the baronet's. 'Get out of my house, and do not come back unless her ladyship asks for you.'

Marissa realised that her father was more likely to raise a fist to Luc than to obey. 'Papa, go now, please, and I will say nothing more about the matter of the allowance.' She realised that Jackson had joined them and was standing, just inside the doors, his muscular arms folded across his broad chest.

'Jackson—see this…person off the premises. He is not to be re-admitted except with her ladyship's express permission.' Luc turned his back contemptuously on the older man.

It was Jackson who saw Sir George lunge forward, Jackson who grabbed him before the blow could fall. But it took both men to wrestle the enraged baronet down the stairs and out of the front door.

Marissa stood in the middle of the room, frozen with shock, her fingers rubbing her bruised wrist. The front door slammed and then the knocker was pounded furiously for several seconds. Finally, with a great roar of anger, her father gave up and there was silence.

She heard Luc and Jackson clattering back up the stairs, their voices animated. They entered together, both men flushed and triumphant, somehow larger than life, Jackson massaging his knuckles. They stopped abruptly at the sight of Marissa's pale face and shivering form.

'Shall I call your maid, my lady?' Jackson was immediately the perfect butler once again.

'No…no, thank you, Jackson.'

Luc poured a glass of brandy and pressed it into her hand before leading her to the sofa. 'Drink this; it will help to calm your nerves. Jackson, send for Dr Lavery: her ladyship's wrist is badly bruised.'

'No, please do not! How could we explain how it occurred?' Marissa exclaimed. 'Witch hazel will soothe it; please do not concern yourselves.' She took a sip of the brandy and coughed as it burned its way down her throat. She tried to hand the glass back to Luc, but he urged her to take another sip.

As the door shut behind Jackson, Marissa raised her face to Luc. 'I am so sorry, Luc. I apologise for my father's disgraceful behaviour. I would not have admitted him, but Matthews was unaware of my lord's orders forbidding Sir George the house, and by the time I had realised it was he it was too late. Goodness knows what the neighbours will make of the hubbub in the street.'

Luc suppressed the urge to gather her into his arms and kiss her until the pain and humiliation had disappeared from her hazel eyes. 'Then this incontinent behaviour is not a new phenomenon?'

'I wish I could say yes, but sadly I have never known him be anything but domineering and given to frequent rages when crossed. I believe that strong drink aggravates his natural choler. My lord tolerated him until we were wed, but his constant demands for money and his drunkenness so disgusted Charles that he forbade him the house. He made him a small allowance, which of course I have continued.'

It was so humiliating to have to recount her father's weaknesses of character in front of a man she loved and respected. What must he think of her now that he had seen her parent at his very worst?

Luc got to his feet and stood at the window looking out across the Square. 'You should not have to deal with him. I will speak to Mr Hope and have him offer your father a single—final—payment in return for the ending of his pension and on condition that he never troubles you again.'

'No!' The syllable rang out across the room.

'But why not? Better to get rid of him now than to have him constantly dogging your footsteps.'

Marissa stared at him, white-faced, her mind able to comprehend nothing but the fact that Charles had paid five thousand guineas for her hand—no, for her body. The thought of Luc following in her husband's footsteps, however unwittingly, to buy off her father for a second time was too abhorrent to contemplate.

It was on the tip of Luc's tongue to ask if her father was attempting to blackmail Marissa. He had heard the tail-end of Sir George's menacing threat to 'create a scandal that would blight the Southwood name.' He knew that Marissa's loyalty and pride would force her to do whatever lay in her power to prevent such a disclosure—whatever it was. Yet if she would not confide in him, how could he ask? He felt the same frustration he had felt so often before with Marissa: the feeling that at the core of her was another, secret woman he could not reach.

'You do not know him like I do,' she was explaining. Luc jerked his attention back to the present. 'My father would spend whatever you gave him in a matter of months—gamble it away, drink it away, spend it on…' she hesitated, biting her lip '…loose women. And he would still come back for more. The only hope is to continue to pay his pension, for he would be reluctant to lose that.'

'Then *I* will pay it so he will have no excuse to approach you in the future.'

'No! He is my father; it is my responsibility.'

'But *you* are my responsibility now, Marissa,' he said quietly. Luc came over to her, took her chin gently in his warm palm and tipped up her troubled face. For a long moment each gazed into the other's eyes, then Luc said, 'You are my cousin, after all,' and dropped a chaste and cousinly kiss on her flushed cheek.

'Oh!' Marissa did not know what to say, or do. She was overwhelmed by his closeness, by the warmth of his body, by the scent of his cologne. Whatever else she wanted to be, it was not his cousin. With an effort she banished her thoughts from her face and said calmly, 'Thank you, Luc. I would be glad to be rid of the responsibility, I must admit. I am happy to abide by whatever you and Mr Hope decide is for the best.

Now, if you will forgive me, I think I will go and lie down.'

In her room Marissa found Mary tidying drawers, and sent the concerned maid off for witch hazel and lint to bind her bruised wrist. The girl wanted to make a soothing tisane and help her mistress into bed, but, despite her excuse to Luc, Marissa was determined not to give in to her nerves. Fresh air and sunshine were what she needed, not moping inside letting her mind run endlessly over her father's cruel words, the realisation that her husband had effectively bought her.

A new primrose-yellow pelisse with wide cuffs hid the bandage around her wrist, and a deep-brimmed cottager bonnet shaded her pale face from scrutiny. Marissa picked up her gloves and reticule and descended to the carriage waiting at the front door. The under-footman swung up behind, jammed his cocked hat down firmly on his curled wig, and hung on as the coachman took the corner into Grosvenor Street at a stylish clip.

Luc had sent down his matched Cleveland bays for the barouche, and Marissa was human enough to be well pleased with the fine picture the equipage presented. Once into the street the coachman was forced to rein back the spirited team, but the slower pace gave Marissa the opportunity to bow to acquaintances as the open carriage passed others out for jaunts or on shopping expeditions in the warm sunshine.

Marissa found, despite her recent shock, that the expedition was raising her spirits. It would be hard to remain indifferent to the colour and bustle of the streets as they drove through them, occasionally coming to a complete halt as a heavy wagon loaded with coal manoeuvred around a corner or a hackney carriage plying for trade created a temporary jam outside a fashionable establishment.

Street traders cried their wares: 'Pots mended… Chairs caned, chairs caned… Fresh milk, straight from the cow… Ribbons and laces, French laces… Knives sharpened. Bring me your knives… Latest broadsheets! Read about the hanging of Black Jack the Highwayman…!'

New Bond Street gave way to Old Bond Street and they turned left into Piccadilly, past the front of Burlington House. Marissa had dutifully accompanied her husband to view the Elgin Marbles when they had been exhibited there, but had not admired their cool beauty. The Earl of Radwinter, on the other hand, had been deeply impressed and, Marissa had suspected, not a little put out that Lord Elgin and not himself had acquired them.

The memory of Charles was uncomfortable, and Marissa metaphorically shook herself as they approached Hatchard's. The coachman skilfully pulled into a space right outside the double windows of the bookshop and the footman jumped down to lower the steps and open the door of the carriage. Marissa took his arm and stepped lightly down, making her way past the bench where footmen in livery chatted and gossiped while their masters and mistresses browsed inside.

Mr Hatchard himself hastened forward to attend

personally to such a distinguished customer, and led
her to a table where the anonymous writer's latest *oeu-
vre* was set out. 'The set in half-calf, my lady, or the
blue tooled leather? A very handsome set in that bind-
ing, but perhaps a little masculine…?'

Ashamed of her mood at breakfast time, Marissa
purchased the half-calf edition of *Guy Mannering* for
Miss Venables, and then browsed happily. It was
pleasant buying gifts: Marissa found some thoroughly
frivolous love poems for Nicci, and Southey's stirring
Life of Nelson for Luc.

Finally reseated in the barouche, with her parcels
piled on the seat beside her, Marissa ordered the
coachman to return to Grosvenor Square through
Hyde Park. The sunshine was so bright that she raised
her sunshade, a new acquisition in amber silk that cast
a flattering glow over her pale complexion. The Park
was green and verdant and, despite the fact that it was
early for the truly fashionable promenade hour, many
members of London Society were taking the air on
horseback, in open carriages or on foot. The coachman
was called upon to pull up several times, for Marissa
to exchange greetings with acquaintances or simply
because the press of phaetons, curricles and barouches
slowed the traffic to walking pace.

After half an hour their circle through the Park had
brought them almost to Grosvenor Gate Lodge and
their exit into the top of King Street. The footman
leaned over and said, 'Excuse me, my lady, but I do
believe that is Madame de Rostan waving to you.'

'Pull up, please, Morton,' Marissa ordered, firmly

quelling a desire to pretend she had not seen the other woman. To her surprise, Diane was alone and on foot and there was no sign of Nicci. 'Good morning, *madame*,' Marissa greeted her politely. 'Has Nicci returned to Grosvenor Square already?'

'Indeed, no,' the older woman laughed. 'She met the Misses Richardson in the linen drapers and they invited her to luncheon. I let them take my carriage— and of course my maid is with them and will ensure Nicci comes directly home afterwards. I do hope you have no objection?'

'Indeed, no. How could I?' Marissa rejoined rather coolly. 'Nicci is not my ward, nor do I have power to control her doings. I am sure her brother would have no objection to any decision such an old friend as yourself might make.'

As soon as she said it Marissa regretted the words and the cool tone. A slight shadow crossed the Frenchwoman's beautiful face, but she smiled and said merely, 'Would you join me in a short stroll, Lady Southwood? The shade under the limes is very pleasant.'

Marissa descended and they strolled in silence for a few minutes, the footman bringing up the rear, discreetly out of earshot. After a while Madame de Rostan broke the slightly prickly silence. 'I think you may underestimate the influence you have over young Nicole, Lady Southwood. She holds you in high regard and affection.'

'She is a very charming child,' Marissa replied neutrally.

'And I must say that a year in your company has greatly improved her demeanour. She always was a sweet child, but a sad romp, and our easy ways in Jamaica are not appropriate for London Society.'

'You are kind enough to say so, *madame,* but I must deny any influence. Any improvement in Nicci's behaviour must be put firmly at the door of Miss Venables, who has much experience as the preceptress of young people.'

Another silence ensued. Madame de Rostan unfurled her own parasol and under cover of that slight diversion sought for another conversational gambit. Despite her best efforts Diane was well aware that she had singularly failed to charm Marissa. In fact, it was not just that the younger woman appeared indifferent to her overtures of friendship, but that she seemed positively to dislike her. And Diane de Rostan was not used to being disliked by men or women. She suspected that she knew where the problem lay, but it was hardly a matter she could broach openly, even with a woman who had been married before.

'It is strange to see Nicci—and Luc, of course— away from Jamaica. Do you not find it odd when one encounters people out of the *milieu* one is accustomed to seeing them in?'

'I really could not say,' Marissa replied indifferently.

Diane gritted her teeth, but continued to smile as she tried again. 'I have known them both for such a long time…'

'So I believe.'

Yes, she was correct in her guess, Diane thought. There was undeniable frost in the young woman's tone now. She persevered. 'Of course in any relationship things change over the years. Feelings alter and mature, passions mute into friendships... I always think it is a wonderful thing when friendship survives when other, more intimate emotions wane.'

Marissa stopped abruptly and turned a surprised, yet candid look on the Frenchwoman, who smiled at her. 'You understand what I am saying to you?'

'I do—you are telling me that you are no longer Luc's mistress.' She could feel the colour stain her cheek at the frankness of her own words, but she continued, 'But I do not understand *why* you should tell me that.'

'Do you not?' The blue eyes sparkled quizzically. 'Well, perhaps this is not the time or place to say more. Let us just leave it that I thought things would be clearer between us—more comfortable, shall we say?'

Marissa blushed furiously. Were her feelings for Luc so transparent that in such a short space of time this woman—even though she had never set eyes on her before—should realise that she needed to be reassured? And if Diane, not knowing her, could see it, was it blindingly obvious to Nicci, to Jane—to Luc himself?

Diane smiled and patted her burning cheek. 'Do not upset yourself *chérie*. You are afraid you are being obvious, *non?* But you are not. Sometimes perhaps it takes an outsider to see what those who are close to us cannot.'

'You think I am in love with him!' Marissa protested hotly.

'Well?' The Frenchwoman raised an eyebrow. 'You are, are you not?'

'Certainly not! I am, after all, in mourning for the late Earl.' Marissa's fingers twisted the reticule in her agitation.

'Mourning?' Diane's eyes ran up and down the stylish primrose-yellow outfit, the frivolous bonnet and the jaunty parasol.

'Well, just out of mourning. And Luc is my late husband's cousin...'

'And that makes him no relation to you,' Diane interposed smoothly.

'I like him very well. He has been kind to me during a very difficult period in my life.'

'Kind?' Diane seemed to be considering the word. 'So that is how he strikes you? Well, if I have misinterpreted the situation, please accept my apologies, Lady Southwood.'

Marissa turned and began to walk back to the barouche. When they had passed the waiting footman and were safely out of earshot again she said, 'Indeed, you have misinterpreted my feelings. I do hope I can rely on your discretion to say nothing of this conversation to the Earl of Radwinter?'

They reached the carriage and Diane waited until the door was closed and Marissa seated. 'I would never gossip to Luc.' She smiled. 'Goodbye, Lady Southwood. I have enjoyed our little chat.'

As the carriage drove out of the Park and into King Street Marissa reflected uncomfortably that Diane's parting words had hardly been the reassurance she had requested.

Chapter Eleven

By the time she reached Grosvenor Square Marissa's unease had turned into a strong suspicion that Diane had been laughing at her for being naive. The entire conversation had been shocking and improper: Diane was obviously fast, Marissa concluded, and must have taken delight in scandalising someone she saw as a prim and proper dowager.

Sweeping across the hall, untying the ribbons of her bonnet as she went, she had one foot on the bottom stair when she heard the study door open and Luc demand, 'Where have you been? I thought you were resting in your room.' Marissa spun round, her already warm cheeks flaming in embarrassment at seeing him so soon after Diane's improper references to him. 'Look at you!' he exclaimed, seeing her heightened colour and bright eyes. 'Are you sure you are not running a fever?'

Luc took a hasty step towards her and Marissa's temper snapped. 'No, my lord, I am not running a fever! And I was not aware that I had to seek your permission before going out. I am, naturally, extremely grateful for your assistance this morning, but that does *not* give you the right to order my comings and goings!' Jackson, who, hearing voices, had emerged through the green baize door, hastily withdrew again. 'I am not your sister, my lord!'

'For heaven's sake, Marissa, come into the study— the whole household can hear you!' Luc took her hand to lead her into the room and inadvertently touched her bandaged wrist.

'Ouch! There is no need to manhandle me, my lord!'

Gently, but firmly, Luc propelled her through the study door and closed it behind them. 'What is the matter with you, Marissa? And, please—' as she opened her mouth '—will you stop calling me "my lord" every second sentence?'

Marissa paced agitatedly across the Turkey rug before Luc's desk. She could hardly tell him that the source of her irritation was a conversation she had newly had with his mistress—or, if Madame de Rostan was to be believed, his ex-mistress. 'Oh, I do not know! It has been a horrid day. No one wants my company; you all have something better to do. And then my father arrives, and now you are shouting at me! I think I will go home to Norfolk,' she almost wailed, managing to sound just as young and silly as Nicci in one of her tantrums.

The next moment she was in Luc's arms. He was laughing down into her face, amused by her outburst, his blue eyes sparkling like the sun on the waves.

'You are laughing at me!' she said indignantly. If she had had any space to do so she would have stamped her foot, but he was so close, holding her so tightly, that she could not. 'Luc, that is not fair. I feel so miserable…' And she gave up struggling and buried her face in the fine wool of his jacket. It was so very comforting, being held against his chest: warm and reassuring, yet with a hard strength that excited her strangely.

He had stopped laughing, and his breath stirred the fine hair at her temple. 'Poor Marissa. Poor darling.' Her heart leapt at the endearment. 'You are having a miserable time, are you not?'

'I am all right,' she said faintly. 'I am just being silly…'

'No, I keep forgetting that you must feel so alone. You have been used to being protected and cherished by Charles.' She was so close that the words seemed to echo in his chest. Was she imagining it, the constraint in his voice as he spoke of her late husband? If only he knew the truth. But she could never tell him.

Marissa put her hands on Luc's chest and pushed him away slightly. 'That part of my life is gone. I must put it behind me, stop dwelling on it. I was being foolish just now. I am tired and my father upset me. You were right; I should not have gone out.'

Luc looked down at her bowed head. If she meant it, if she really thought she could put her feelings for his cousin behind her, perhaps she would consider a proposal of marriage from him now. There had been a long enough interval between the offer he had made in the wake of their passionate encounter on the beach: she had had time to put the confusion and embarrassment of that tumultuous meeting behind her. And, despite his scruples about her love for the late Earl, perhaps it was his duty to make the offer again. She needed protecting, looking after.

'Marissa, look at me.' She did as she was bid, lifting shadowed eyes obediently. 'Marissa, if you mean it, if you can put the past behind you, will you make a future with me? Marry me, Marissa.'

For one long moment she looked at him, unable to speak, overwhelmed by the rush of love for him, by the sensation of joy that he too might love her. But, no, she could not do it, could not promise herself in marriage when she could not be a proper wife to him.

The doubt chased across her face and Luc, seeing it, hastened to reassure her. 'It would be an entirely suitable match—you are young, beautiful, educated. You are already the perfect chatelaine for Southwood Hall; you have proved that. My cousin made a wise choice!' Marissa threw up one hand as if to ward off the words. 'No, wait, Marissa, do not dismiss the suggestion too hastily! There are great benefits for both of us in this suggestion.'

'You do me great honour, my lord, but I cannot agree to marry you—as I told you once before. Thank you for your flattering offer, but let us speak no more of it.' Marissa turned from him in agitation and took a hasty step towards the door, fighting down the impulse to throw herself into his arms and tell him how much she loved him and wanted to be his wife. But it was because she loved him that she could not assent, and blight his life by tying him to a woman who could not share his bed or bear his children.

If she thought her words would rebuff him she was wrong. 'Wait, Marissa—I will not take no for an answer unless you will tell me why. Surely we are good enough friends, you and I, for you to give me an explanation?'

Marissa turned, cornered. How could she explain, even if she could find the words for the fear and the pain she had always encountered whenever Charles demanded that she do her wifely duty? Marissa bit her lip, avoiding Luc's searching gaze as he stood patiently but implacably waiting. She could not give him a reason for saying no, so finally, bluntly she said, 'Yes, very well, if you insist. I will marry you, Luc.'

The coldness of her words seemed to take him aback and she saw the animation in his face freeze into formality. He took her hand and brushed his lips across her knuckles. 'Thank you, Marissa. I am honoured by your acceptance. I shall do everything in my power to make you happy. I know our friends will be delighted for us.'

'Oh, please, no, Luc, do not tell anyone, not yet. Can we not keep it our secret for a little while, at least until I have become more accustomed to the idea?'

'Of course, Marissa, if that is your wish. I am yours to command, as always. Now, will you not go and rest?' He made no move to touch her, let alone kiss her as she had both hoped and dreaded.

Without another word Marissa slipped out the door and hastened upstairs.

The next week was Derby week, and in the flurry of activity as the household prepared to move down to Epsom for the races Marissa managed to avoid being alone with Luc. She swung wildly between elation at the thought of marrying the man she loved and utter despair when she realised that she could not go through with it.

Unable to sleep, she paced her room into the small hours, frantically seeking for a way out. How could she have been so stupid to allow herself to be cornered into saying yes? Now she could think of a dozen reasons for turning him down: unfortunately all had eluded her at that critical moment when he had pressed her to be his wife. And whereas they were all perfectly acceptable reasons for turning him down in the first place, none of them were convincing excuses for going back on her word after the passage of several days. And the longer it went on, the more impossible it became.

Whenever she caught Luc's eye she saw a question in it, but would only smile and shake her head slightly. Heaven knows what he thought her reasons for wanting to keep their betrothal a secret were, but she made sure they were never alone for him to press the point. Her appetite waned until even Nicci, usually so preoccupied with her own concerns, noticed that she had lost weight. Pressed by Miss Venables to eat more, Marissa murmured vaguely about the heat and the noise of London, assuring her friend that all would be well in the peace of the countryside.

Luc had taken a lodge within five miles of Epsom racecourse for a week and they set out, Nicci in a high state of excitement, on the Wednesday morning. They intended to attend the Derby on the Thursday then spend the rest of the time rusticating before another flurry of balls and parties.

The grooms had gone ahead with the riding horses, the barouche and most of the luggage. The ladies would follow in the travelling carriage and Luc intended to drive himself down. He refused point-blank his sister's pleas, demands and cajoling to be allowed to ride in the curricle with him and take the reins once they were out of London.

'No, Nicci,' he said firmly for the fourth time as he handed the three ladies into the travelling carriage. 'And I do not care if any of your acquaintances are allowed to drive on the public highway—you are not. And that is an end to the subject.' He regarded his sister's mutinous countenance and added, 'And do not sulk and make Miss Venables and Lady Southwood regret that we did not leave you at home!'

'Now then, Nicci,' Miss Venables said firmly. 'Surely you do not wish to drive all that way on dusty roads, ruining your complexion? Why, you would end up sadly freckled, like Miss Richardson, and that would never do.'

The thought of the unfortunate Miss Richardson's complexion seemed to mollify the girl somewhat. She settled willingly enough in the seat opposite Miss

Venables and began to prattle about hats, wondering aloud if she would have the prettiest bonnet at the races or whether a last-minute shopping trip to the Epsom milliners would be necessary in the morning.

Luc took the opportunity to exchange a few words with Marissa, catching her hand to restrain her as she began to step up into the carriage. 'We have much to speak of, Marissa. We must find time to be alone at the Lodge.'

'Yes, indeed,' Marissa replied in a colourless tone, before settling in her seat and tucking her reticule safely beside her. Mary, her dresser, was waiting patiently to take her place beside Nicci, with their back to the horses, so Luc was forced to step aside and make no further attempt at conversation. Mary was almost beside herself with self-importance and excitement as she sat, straight-backed, her mistress's jewel case held tightly on her knees.

The journey was uneventful, if rather stuffy, as Nicci repeatedly pointed out. The latter half of May had been exceedingly warm and dry but the countryside was still green and burgeoning except where the chalk dust from the highway cloaked the leaves.

'Diane is taking her barouche down,' Nicci complained. 'And she will be able to have half the roof down and not be so stuffy. Why could we not have taken the barouche today, Marissa? This is such an unfashionable coach and I have the headache.'

'Then take some *sal volatile*,' Marissa said quite sharply. She did not want to discuss Diane de Rostan, whom she had not met since that encounter in Hyde

Park, nor did she want to be reminded that the other woman was staying with friends in Epsom and was sure to be much in evidence at the races. Luc's low-voiced comments about discussing their future filled her with unease. Sooner or later matters would come to a head, and she would either have to tell him the truth—which was impossible—or find a convincing excuse to cry off. To go through with the marriage was impossible.

The Lodge turned out to be a charming small house of only ten bedrooms, secluded from the road behind high beech hedges and with a delightful view of the Downs. The air was fresh, the house well aired, the servants installed, and everyone soon felt at home. The small party dined early, fatigued by their journey and in readiness for an early start on Derby Day.

After the ladies left Luc to his port, Marissa slipped out into the garden and began to wander along the grass paths. The garden, sloping away from the terrace which skirted the house, had been laid out with beds of fragrant roses underplanted with lavender. Now, in the very last days of May, they were in full bloom, their scent almost drugging in the still evening air.

As she strolled, twisting a rosebud between her fingers, Marissa felt soothed and calm. Away from London things seemed simpler: she must tell Luc that she had made a mistake and that she had decided to stay single for the rest of her days. There was no need to give him an explanation for that decision. It would be best to speak now, and, after all, only his pride, not his feelings would be hurt. He had never pretended to be in love with her, and it had formed no part of his declaration. Thank goodness she had not let him announce the engagement!

It cost her heartache to come to this conclusion, but Marissa knew, deep down, that any hope of happiness with Luc was doomed.

It all seemed perfectly clear and simple, if painful— until she came round one corner of the lawn and saw him leaning on the balustrade of the terrace, an unlit cigarillo between his fingers, his gaze fixed on the darkening Downs over the trees. The late sun glinted on his blond head, the dark blue superfine coat of his evening dress sat perfectly across his broad shoulders and his face was thoughtful and relaxed.

Marissa's heart leapt with love for him, and his name escaped her lips before she could step back behind the sheltering rose bushes.

His face lit up with pleasure when he saw her, and he tossed aside the cigarillo, vaulted the balustrade and with two strides was by her side. She was wearing the periwinkle-blue that suited her dark colouring so well. Her slender figure was set off by the high-waisted gown and the elegant sweep of her silver shawl caught up over her elbows. He stood for a moment, drinking in the picture she made, before gathering her in his arms and kissing her.

Every sensible resolution that Marissa had reached evaporated at the first touch of his lips. She melted into him, her nightly dreams becoming reality as she returned his kiss with ardour. If only, she thought hazily as his tongue parted her lips and teased the tip of her own, if only this was all there was to marriage. If it only stopped here, on this tide of sensation and pleasure, and went no further…if the only invasion was that of his tongue, the only violence the strength of his arms holding her to him.

It was Luc who finally broke the kiss. He spoke huskily into her hair, his hand running caressingly over her nape exposed by the low-cut gown. 'Thank heavens you are still of the same mind. I had thought you had changed your mind, grown cold towards me this past week. But that, my darling Marissa, was not cold…'

She shivered against him as he bent and began to feather soft kisses down the slope of her shoulder, his progress impeded only by the cap of her sleeve. His right hand slipped from her other shoulder and grazed subtly down the curve of her breast to stroke her peaked nipple through the silk of her gown. Marissa gasped and arched towards him. Encouraged, his fingers explored further under the fabric, both the silk and the fine cambric of her shift beneath.

'You are so beautiful,' he said against her neck. 'Ever since that night by the sea I have been haunted by the memory of your perfect white body in the moonlight, of the way you opened to me on the beach.' His voice was not quite steady, his breathing ragged. 'I cannot wait until our wedding night, when all of you will be mine…'

Marissa's ecstasy was chilled by the thought of that wedding night, of the pain and recrimination that would surely follow…

'Marissa!' It was Miss Venables's voice, approaching rapidly from the direction of the drawing room. 'Marissa, my dear, are you out here? You will catch your death of cold.'

Luc seized Marissa's hand, and, pushing through the door of the gazebo which stood at the end of the terrace, closed it swiftly behind them. They stood entwined in the wood-scented gloom until they saw Miss Venables pass by the leaded window and vanish around the corner of the house.

'Now, where were we?' Luc murmured, bending once more, catching her around the waist and imprisoning her in his embrace.

'No, Luc, stop…' Marissa protested shakily. 'I must go in—Jane will be worried about me. And we should not be doing this.'

'Why not?' he said, his voice smothered as he nibbled delicately at her earlobe. 'I fully intend doing this—and more—all the time when you are my wife.'

'Oh, yes…I mean, no, *stop it*. You make it so difficult,' she added weakly, pushing him away.

'You are right. The wooden floor of a gazebo is hardly the right place for the first time—any more than a sandy beach was.' He opened the door for her to slip through, adding, as she turned to run along the terrace, 'But do not make me wait too long for you, Marissa.'

Those words sounded almost threatening in her ears as she slowed to a sedate walk and re-entered the Salon through the long windows which opened down to the ground. Fortunately Nicci had retired, but Jane Venables was waiting anxiously for her.

'There you are, dear! I have been to look for you. I was worried you might get chilled—the evening air is so treacherous. Did you not hear me call?'

Remembering the circumstances under which she had heard Jane, Marissa blushed rosily. Miss Venables, after a searching look at Marissa's heightened colour and escaping hair, said sharply, 'Marissa! Have you been alone again with his lordship? Is there anything you wish to say to me?'

'Er…no.' Marissa felt like a naughty schoolroom miss caught kissing the music master. 'I just happened to meet Luc in the garden. The roses are most delightful; we must pick some for the breakfast table.'

Miss Venables had not been a governess for over ten years without being able to detect prevarication when she heard it. 'Really, Marissa, do you think I was born yesterday?' she demanded robustly. 'I am not lecturing you. Heaven knows I am not responsible for your morals. After all, you have been a married woman and are old enough to conduct your own affairs. But do consider the proprieties! I will say no more. I will retire and say goodnight.'

May 30th dawned clear and bright, and the ladies breakfasted in their rooms to hasten the business of getting ready. At ten o'clock Miss Venables, magnificent in bronze twill with an almost jaunty bonnet of moss silk and feathers, popped her head around Marissa's bedchamber door.

'Are you almost ready, my dear? Oh, now, that *is*

nice!' she said approvingly. 'I knew you were right to choose that simple fern-green jacconet cloth—it sets off the lines of your new pelisse to perfection. Understatement is the very essence of elegance, especially when one has the height and figure to carry it off, as you do.'

Marissa smiled her thanks at the compliment as she took her seat at the dressing table to allow Mary to set the dashing O'Neil hat, with its high crown and curving brim, on her head. She had heeded Luc's plea not to have her hair cropped, and the maid had piled up the luxuriant mass on her crown and allowed only the little curls around her hairline to peep out from under the arc of the brim.

'How very fashionable, dearest!' Miss Venables exclaimed. 'When did you buy that?'

'Last season, in Norwich. I could not resist it, even though I knew I could not wear it for some time. Is Nicci ready?'

'She was so excited last night I doubt she has been to bed, so she had better be! Her brother warned her that if she were not down by ten he would leave her behind—and I fear he was not speaking in jest.'

Marissa had pushed thoughts of Luc firmly to the back of her mind, determined that nothing should spoil her day at the races. She would face up to breaking her betrothal later that week. The fact that the evening before she had quite made up her mind on her course of action and it had only taken a second in his arms for her resolution to crumble utterly she conveniently ignored.

The clock struck ten and both ladies picked up their reticules and sunshades and stepped out onto the landing as Nicci's door opened.

For a moment both were speechless, then Miss Venables's cry of dismay echoed clearly round the landing. '*Nicole!* You cannot go out attired like that. Go and change immediately! Where did you get that hat?'

'It is a lovely hat and I am not going to get changed and I think this will be the most striking outfit on the course.' Nicci stamped her foot and refused to move.

Marissa's thunderstruck gaze travelled from deep purple pumps, up the length of what had begun as a simple white cambric gown but which was now transformed by an abundance of dark ribbons and braid, to Nicci's crowning glory, a bonnet of midnight-purple curled silk, edged, trimmed and lined in white satin, high in the crown with an abundance of white bows.

She finally found her voice. 'You bought that in London when Madame de Rostan left you with the Misses Richardson, did you not, Nicci? How you could have thought for a moment that this would be suitable for a young girl, a debutante…'

'What is going on?' Luc ran up the stairs. 'The carriage has been at the front door these last fifteen minutes and I do not care to keep my horses waiting… Good God, Nicci, you look like a magpie! Marissa, whatever possessed you to allow her to rig herself up like that?' Despite his words he sounded more amused than annoyed.

'My lord, I believe you may lay this unique outfit at the door of your friend Madame de Rostan: I can claim no credit for it. Nor do I intend to make any further comment—doubtless you can prevail upon your sister to change into something more suitable: it seems that neither Miss Venables nor I have that sort of influence any longer.'

Marissa swept downstairs with a faintly clucking Jane on her heels. She had surprised herself at the sudden wave of anger that had swept through her. In the carriage, listening to the raised voices issuing through the front door, she examined her mood. Annoyance with Nicci, of course, but also, maddeningly, annoyance with herself, that Luc's attention had been entirely on his sister's outrageous outfit and diverted from her own appearance. She had wanted to look good on his arm, to do him credit, to be seen and admired with him on this one day before she broke off the betrothal. And to be blamed for the effects of Diane de Rostan's influence was the very last straw.

Five minutes later Nicci swept triumphantly out of the door, her outfit intact. Luc, on her heels, caught Marissa's eye and shrugged resignedly. She returned the look frostily and averted her face.

Miss Venables was still protesting as the doors of the barouche were shut behind him and he took his seat. 'But, my lord, you cannot possibly permit Miss Southwood to appear in public in such an unsuitable outfit!'

'Why not?' he enquired laconically. 'Do you fear some gamekeeper will mistake her for a magpie and shoot her? Quite frankly, Miss Venables, I am just thankful that she is decently covered. And when people laugh at her she will soon learn her lesson.'

'Ha! Much you know about it,' his sister riposted. 'All eyes will be upon me.'

'Precisely,' Luc said drily, and looked out at the passing countryside.

Derby Day was one of the highlights of the Season and the *ton* was out in force. The racecourse was already a sea of colour from the fashionable gowns and parasols, the uniforms of many officers, the silks of the jockeys and the gay bunting on the pavilions. The barouche drew up alongside many other elegant conveyances and Miss Venables exclaimed with pleasure at the sight of many acquaintances.

Nicci was bouncing in her seat with excitement. 'Come on, come on, we are missing everything! Let us promenade.'

'Calm down, Nicole,' Miss Venables chided as the footman helped them to descend. 'Too much excitement is so unsophisticated—surely you do not wish to appear gauche?'

Effectively quelled, Nicci fell in beside the others and began to stroll meekly along, casting looks from under her bonnet-brim to see what effect her outfit was having.

Luc shepherded them through the entrance into the Royal Enclosure and found a place by the rail where they could assess the horses being led around the ring. He had acquired race cards for them all, and now described the runners and riders.

'There were fifty-one entries, but only eleven are

running: that is not unusual,' he explained, as Marissa tried to separate what seemed at first sight to be an indistinguishable crowd of horses. 'The favourite is Nectar, owned by Lord Cavendish—see, over there, the bay colt. He looks very well, does he not? And he has already won the Two Thousand Guineas.'

'It does look a very fine horse,' Miss Venables observed. 'What are the odds, my lord?'

'Ten to six: hardly worth putting money on at this stage, I would have thought. Let us choose horses with longer odds—it will be more exciting. How about Lord Stawell's chestnut, Pandour? It is from the same sire as the favourite, but it is at sixteen to one.'

Both Miss Venables and Nicci agreed to place a guinea each on Pandour, but Marissa was feeling perverse and was in no mood to take any advice from Luc that morning. 'Which is that?' she asked, pointing a gloved hand at a large bay as it passed them close by the rail.

Luc checked the colours against the race card. 'That is Prince Leopold. It is running in the colours of Mr Lake, the Duke of York's Master of Horse, but I believe it is owned by His Royal Highness himself. First time out, and the odds are long—twenty to one. With no form to go on, I would not hazard your guinea on him, Marissa.'

'A guinea? Why, nothing so paltry,' she declared with a toss of her head. 'I shall place ten guineas on Prince Leopold. Here.' She felt in her reticule and handed him ten coins. 'Will you place the bet for me, please, my lord?'

Luc looked down into her eyes, noting once again how green they sparkled when she was excited or emotional. In all the furore over Nicci's outfit he had not had the opportunity to tell her how beautiful she looked, and in that moment he wished the crowds a thousand miles away so he could take her in his arms and make love to her. 'You are an inveterate gambler, Lady Southwood! I had not suspected it.'

He collected the bets from the others and went to find a bookmaker while the ladies continued to view the parade of horses. Miss Venables now held the race card and pointed out the Duke of Grafton's horse, Alien, and Mr Blake's John of Paris. 'What a magnificent appellation,' Jane declared. 'Perhaps I should have put my guinea on him after all.'

'Good day, ladies.' They were greeted by Lady Valentine, who joined them at the rail. She was dashingly attired in fawn twill, her new scarlet half-boots peeping from under the hem. On her head she sported an outrageous toque of Ionian cork, cut like mosaic and adorned with scarlet tassels and plumes. Nicci's jaw dropped until she was jabbed sharply in the ribs by Miss Venables. 'My dear Lady Southwood. You do look…well,' she remarked, leaving everyone in no doubt that she considered Marissa's tasteful outfit to be dull. She merely raised an eyebrow at the sight of Nicci's magpie magnificence, commenting only that she thought her hat to be 'So droll.'

'Oh, I am forgetting myself. Let me make Mr Templeton known to you. Captain Cross you know already, of course.'

Mr Templeton bowed to the ladies as they were

introduced, but his attention was obviously all for Lady Valentine, who hung onto his arm possessively. He was a remarkably well-set-up young man, with broad shoulders, muscular thighs and a handsome profile under dark brows. Captain Cross gave the distinct impression of a man whose nose had been put out of joint, and he lost no time in making eyes at Nicci from behind the backs of her chaperons.

Lady Valentine's party took up position on the rails a few yards farther along and Nicci almost imperceptibly drifted along until she was in a position to chat with Captain Cross. Miss Venables, who would normally have spotted such a manoeuvre, had been diverted by the arrival of her new friend Sir Frederick Collier, with whom she had been visiting museums and galleries ever since Diane de Rostan had introduced them. The distinguished banker bowed gallantly over her hand and Marissa thought she had never seen Miss Venables look so handsome. Skilfully he drew her off to one side and Marissa found herself alone, fondly thinking that dear Jane might have found a little romance of her own in her middle years.

Marissa was smiling to herself when her mood was shattered by the sight of her father, pushing his way aggressively through the crowd towards her. Her heart sank, then rose as she saw Luc, Diane de Rostan on his arm, cross her father's path. There was a brief conversation of which she heard nothing, but she saw Sir George's florid features darken and he turned abruptly and stomped off.

Luc uttered a few words, obviously explaining the uncouth stranger to the Frenchwoman. To Marissa's relief Diane released Luc's arm, patted his cheek and made her own way off towards the pavilion.

'Well, here is your betting slip,' he greeted Marissa as he joined her at the rail. 'Put it safely in your reticule, although I doubt you will need it—the more I look at that horse of yours, the less I like it.'

Tension was growing as the horses lined up at the start. The starter dropped his flag and they were off. Nectar took the lead and stayed there, running strongly, the rest of the field bunched behind. Luc groaned at the performance of his choice, then gave a great yell as, a furlong and a half out, Pandour and Prince Leopold took up the challenge.

'Come on, come on, Prince Leopold!' Marissa screamed, her unladylike behaviour lost in the sea of noise all around them.

'Pandour!' Luc urged, but Nectar was holding them. Marissa found she was jumping up and down on the spot, her hand gripped tightly onto Luc's sleeve. Suddenly, with the winning post only five lengths away, Prince Leopold sprang forward, straining under his jockey's whip. They ran neck and neck for a few seconds, then, as they flashed past the post, Prince Leopold was seen to have taken the lead by half a length.

'He has won, he has won!' Marissa shrieked, and threw her arms round Luc, kissing him on the cheek. In response, hidden by the milling crowd of excited racegoers, all intent on the track, he bent his head and kissed her full on the lips. Instinctively she kissed him back, and suddenly it was as if they were alone in the garden again.

'God, I want you,' he groaned.

The thrill of winning after the tension of the race had left Marissa dizzy with reaction. All she knew was that she loved him and she wanted him too. Mutely she nodded.

Luc looked around, spotted Sir Frederick with Miss Venables, and, leaving Marissa by the rail, crossed to speak with them. 'Sir Frederick, may I beg a favour of you? Lady Southwood is quite overcome by the crowds and I must take her back to the Lodge. Could I ask you to escort Miss Southwood and Miss Venables for the rest of the day? Lady Southwood would be so distressed to think she had destroyed their pleasure.'

The baronet willingly agreed, took charge of the winning betting slip with a word of congratulation and could be heard soothing Miss Venables. 'No need to worry, my dear Miss Venables. Your friend is in the best of hands and would not wish to mar your day. Now, a little luncheon, some champagne, perhaps...'

Marissa felt dazed as Luc swept her out of the Enclosure into the press of other racegoers. 'How extraordinary... No, I must be mistaken. I thought I saw my father with Madame de Rostan,' she exclaimed.

Luc soon had her seated in the barouche. With a short word of explanation to the groom and coachman the carriage was soon wending its way slowly against the press of vehicles still flooding onto the course.

'Luc,' Marissa whispered. 'We should not be doing this...'

'Yes, we should,' he murmured back. 'I am going to make you mine—and then we will name the day.'

Chapter Twelve

The journey back to the Lodge seemed interminable to Luc, but frighteningly short to Marissa. She loved him, she wanted him—far too much to even think about impropriety. Yet she dreaded the moment he discovered that she could not respond to him as a lover, as his wife should do. But for the moment it was enough to be with him, and one corner of her mind told her that it was better he discovered the truth now rather than when they were married.

They sat close together, outwardly totally proper in the open carriage, the footman standing behind. But through the fabric of her skirts Marissa could feel the heat of his hard thigh pressed against hers. Her mouth still burned with the intensity of that last kiss, of the sweet invasion of his tongue. Despite her apprehensions she was tingling with anticipation and longing.

As the footman let down the folding steps Luc said, 'Take the rest of the day off, both of you.'

'But, my lord, all the servants are at the races—

only the watchman left in the gate cottage. Who will wait upon you?'

'Do not concern yourself; we will wait upon ourselves. Today is a festival—go and enjoy it.' He slipped a gold coin into each grateful hand and watched them take the barouche round to the stable.

'Now, my lady,' he said as he bent and effortlessly lifted her up into his arms, shouldering open the door and kicking it closed behind him. Marissa was conscious of the strength of him as he carried her up the stairs and into the master bedroom. She could hardly breathe as he laid her on the bed, hat, parasol and all. Crossing to the windows, he threw them open, then tugged the billowing white drapes closed, filtering the hot sunlight across the polished boards.

Shrugging off his jacket and tugging loose his neck-cloth, he stood looking down at her. For a long moment neither moved, then he tossed her reticule and parasol to one side and eased off her hat, releasing her hair to tumble down across the snowy white pillows. Marissa lay still and watched the man she loved gently unbutton, then push off her pelisse. His hands found the ribbons tying her kid pumps and his fingertips tickled her ankles as he untied each one and tossed the shoes off the bed.

Her heart was thudding so hard she could hardly breathe: she wanted him to hurry, and yet for every moment to last for ever. Now he raised her in his arms so he could reach the row of little buttons securing her gown, and with surprising skill he removed it, and the petticoats under it, to join the rest of her clothing on the floor. Left naked except for her stockings, tied by their ribbon garters above the knee, Marissa was swept by self-consciousness and tried to pull over the sheet to cover herself.

'No,' he said with gentle insistence, removing the sheet from her nerveless fingers. 'You have a beautiful body. Every night I have dreamed of seeing it in daylight.'

Obedient under his gaze, Marissa lay watching as he shrugged off his shirt impatiently. Then he joined her on the big bed and, bending over her, traced hot kisses from her mouth to the tip of her aching nipples, catching them between his lips and teasing, tantalising the swollen peaks.

She moaned, catching his head in her hands, pressing his mouth against her soft flesh. Her fingers tangled in his blond hair, tasting it with her fingertips, alive to every texture of his body.

Luc released her nipple, shifting against her to reach her mouth, kissing her slowly, deeply, marvellously. When she thought she would surely drown in sensation he broke the kiss to look down into her face. 'You taste of wine and strawberries—even better than the salt.'

The reference to their moonlight encounter brought the delicate colour flooding up under her skin. She buried her face in his shoulder, licking his satiny skin with the tip of her tongue, letting her fingertips trace the muscles under the smoothness of his back until they encountered the waistband of his trousers.

In response to her impatient fingers he groaned,

rolling over on his back to release the fastening and discard the final garment. Marissa gasped at the sight of him, naked and aroused, and shut her eyes as his weight came over her and the heat of him burned her aroused skin. His lips sought hers blindly, and he kissed her again, the invasive pressure of his tongue echoing the urging of his body. It was the moment she was dreading, and despite Luc's skilful lovemaking, his attention to her pleasure, she felt the paralysis creeping through her limbs, the fear rising in her breast.

It was enough to give him pause. 'Marissa? You do want this, do you not?'

Her eyes were very wide and green in the subdued light, and he experienced the uncanny feeling that it was not he that she saw. 'Don't hurt me. Please don't hurt me...'

He ran the back of his hand gently down the soft curve of her cheek. 'Hurt you? I would never hurt you, Marissa darling.'

The endearment gave her the courage to wrap her arms around his neck, pull his head down to hers and kiss him as she had never kissed him before. He groaned and entered her, too goaded by her enticement to realise until it was too late that the yielding, passionate woman had turned to stone in his arms.

When it was over he gathered her tenderly into his arms and stroked her quivering body until she stilled. He kissed her damp forehead and then her eyelids and realised that it was not passion that had made her quiver, but soft sobs.

'Marissa? Marissa—do not cry. You must tell me what is wrong. What have I done?' He sounded deeply troubled and her heart contracted with love for him. She hastened to reassure him.

'It is only that it has been such a long time, and I was shy… I am quite all right, Luc, believe me.'

But he could not. Luc Southwood had never taken an unwilling woman, nor would he ever. But although she had hidden it so much better than she had on the beach, hidden it to the point that he had, for the moment, been totally deceived, Marissa had been afraid at the moment he had taken her.

They lay together quietly, Luc nuzzling her hair, stroking the white slope of her shoulder until Marissa dozed. When he was sure she was settled he gently eased his encircling arm from under her and pulled the sheet over her body. Then he lay back on the pillows, hands behind his head, gazing up at the ceiling as though the chaste classical moulding could furnish him with a clue.

She had wanted him, had responded to him with an ardour and passion he had never experienced before. And the thought came to him again, as it had done after the night on the beach, that her responses had an edge of innocence which did not square with her married state. If he had not known better he would have sworn she had never been kissed before.

He shook his head as if to clear his thoughts. It was not his lovemaking that had frightened her, but the act of possession itself. She had begged him not to hurt her, but it was not her heart she feared for, but her body. What sort of man had his cousin been, for heaven's sake, to frighten his beautiful young wife so? He felt uneasy, remembering the odd hint he had picked up in the clubs that the late Earl had had…unusual tastes. He recalled the chilly perfection and discipline of Southwood Hall, the reticence of the staff and estate workers to say anything about their late master, good or bad.

Luc shifted restlessly. Could he talk to Marissa about this? He instantly dismissed the idea. If she was capable of speaking of it she would have done so—she had been so reluctant to allow him to make public their betrothal. No, he could not talk to Marissa, but he needed a woman's viewpoint. Miss Venables was obviously out of the question, but he could discuss anything with Diane. Friendship had always been more important to them than their physical affair.

He had just come to this conclusion when Marissa murmured and stirred. The she opened her eyes, and as soon as she saw Luc coloured and drew the sheet up to her chin. 'I must get dressed before the others get home and the servants return,' she stammered.

She was so obviously embarrassed he made no move to detain her, handing her his dressing gown and tactfully turning his back as she gathered up her scattered clothing and hastened quietly from the room.

It was a very thoughtful Earl of Radwinter who stood at the drawing room window as Sir Frederick's carriage brought Jane and Nicci home. He had heard Marissa moving around upstairs but had made no attempt to speak to her. The servants had returned an hour ago and were busy preparing the evening meal.

Luc went out onto the steps to greet the returning party, offering his hand to Miss Venables to assist her to alight. She thanked him frostily, turning to bow to Sir Frederick and thank him in a shaking voice for his kindness in conducting them back to the Lodge. Nicci, her face flushed under her ridiculous hat, bobbed a schoolgirl curtsey before scuttling into the house, her hot face averted from her brother's puzzled gaze.

Sir Frederick was still standing in the open carriage as Luc came down the steps to offer the baronet his thanks. 'Will you not come in and take a glass of wine? I am most obliged to you for escorting Miss Venables and my sister.'

'No trouble, old chap, a pleasure,' the banker replied with a twinkle. 'But I will not accept your kind offer—I rather think you will be glad to have no strangers in the house this evening.' And on that enigmatic note he sat down, resumed his hat and called out, 'Drive on, John!'

Luc was barely in the hall when the storm broke. Nicci was halfway up the stairs, Miss Venables at the foot. 'Come down here immediately, Nicole, and tell your brother how you have disgraced yourself.'

'No, I shan't!' Nicci sobbed, sitting down on the stair and putting her head in her hands.

'Oh, Lord!' Luc muttered under his breath, before stepping up to Miss Venables. 'Nicci, come down here. Marissa is not feeling well and I do not want her disturbed by you making a hullabaloo out here. Miss

Venables, let us go into the drawing room and you can tell me what has occurred.'

Nicci, descending reluctantly, stood sniffing while Miss Venables recounted how she had discovered her young charge. 'I can hardly bring myself to use the word, my lord, but there is no other way of putting it—she was in the embrace of a…man! An officer, and behind the pavilion! Anyone could have seen her! My lord, I am so sorry that I have failed in my duty as a chaperon…'

Luc cut across the anguished apology. 'But *did* anyone else see them?'

'Only Sir Frederick, and on his discretion I believe we may rely absolutely. As soon as I realised she was missing, during the second race, he accompanied me in search of her. Oh, I would never have believed she could behave so…' Miss Venables rummaged in her reticule until she found her smelling bottle and waved it wildly under her nose.

'Who was the man?' Luc enquired with dangerous calm. Damn Nicci, now he supposed he would have to come the heavy brother. Thank heavens Miss Venables had interrupted them, or he would have found himself calling the man out on top of all the other things he had to concern himself with at the moment! 'Nicci, stop snivelling, take that blasted hat off and answer me: who was it?' He had never spoken to her like that before, and his sister wrenched off the bonnet and cast it aside.

'Captain Cross,' she wailed.

'And who the devil is he? Don't tell me you just

picked up some uniformed whippersnapper on the racecourse,' he roared, incensed at the thought of his sister in the arms of a complete stranger.

'A friend of Lady Valentine's,' Miss Venables said grimly, as if that summed it all up.

'That trollop!' For once, Miss Venables did not wince at the word—she was inclined to agree.

'I fear,' she ventured, 'that Miss Southwood's attire may have misled the Captain into thinking she was older and more worldly-wise than she is.'

Luc regarded both ladies with a smouldering eye. 'And I suppose you are going to say it was all my fault for letting her out dressed like that?' He gestured furiously at Nicci's crumpled outfit.

Wisely Miss Venables did not respond to this question. She got to her feet and took Nicci's arm. 'Come along, Nicole, I think you had better take supper in your room tonight.'

Luc waited until the ladies had disappeared around the curve of the stairs before tugging the bell-pull to summon Jackson. 'My compliments to Lady South-wood, and I shall not be dining at home this evening.'

'Very good, my lord. Shall I say where you are going?'

'No. But should you have need of me I shall be at Madame de Rostan's.'

Minutes later Luc was cantering down the drive, gravel spurting from under his horse's hooves. Half an hour later he was entering the busy streets of Epsom, thronged with racegoers either flush with their winnings or drinking away their sorrows. Reining back to a trot, he entered the quiet street where Diane had borrowed a friend's house for the week.

Although he was not expected, he was swiftly admitted and was shown into the Salon. Despite having no guests for dinner, the Frenchwoman was as beautifully attired as ever in a simple cream silk gown, her hair in artfully arranged ringlets, her family diamonds gleaming at her throat.

'*Chéri!* What a surprise, but always a pleasure to see you.' She rose gracefully from the chaise and offered her cheek for his kiss. 'I must confess I had not looked to see you tonight. You will dine, of course?' She pulled the bell before resuming her seat.

Luc dropped into a chair, his long booted legs stretched out in front of him. He knew Diane so well that every nuance of her words was plain to him. 'Why so surprised to see me tonight? And, yes, if you will excuse my informal attire, I would like to dine here.'

The butler appeared, received his mistress's instructions and vanished discreetly after pouring his lordship a glass of Madeira.

Diane waited until the door closed behind him before replying, with a wicked curve of her lips, 'You forget, I saw you leave the racecourse this afternoon with Lady Southwood.'

'And?' Luc raised an eyebrow, not liking the implication that his intentions had been so transparent.

Diane laughed at him affectionately. 'My darling Luc, it is only I who would have realised the significance of you taking Marissa home in the early afternoon.' Again her lips curved, this time in remembrance. 'She really is a very charming young woman: I must congratulate you.'

'I am glad I have your blessing,' Luc said drily, sipping his dry wine. 'However, I fear it may be a little premature.'

'But if you have been making love to her you really must marry her, you know,' Diane teased, then, seeing his face darken, was suddenly serious. '*Chéri,* what is the matter?'

'I only wish I knew,' he confessed. 'Yes, we did make love…but there is something wrong. Diane, she responds to me with passion and fire, and yet…there is a part of her that remains untouched, for all the intensity of our lovemaking. It is almost as though she were afraid.' His blue eyes were puzzled as he looked at his former lover.

'But she was married—for two years, was it not?' Diane broke off as the butler entered.

'Dinner is served, *madame.*'

Both the butler and a footman were standing attentively by the high buffet, but Diane waved them away. 'Thank you, Henry, Monsieur le Comte will carve; we will serve ourselves.' As soon as they were alone she said, 'A little salmon, please, Luc, and if you will pass the dish of peas… Thank you, darling. Now, where were we?'

'You were asking how long Marissa had been married. It was just over two years, I believe; she wed very young. And yet… I find this difficult to believe,

Diane, but I could swear she had never been kissed until I kissed her.'

'Perhaps it is simply that she has not yet fully recovered from the loss of her husband? Would you pour me a glass of the Sancerre?'

Luc complied, absently passing her the glass. 'She can hardly bear to speak of him. I found her in tears in front of his portrait and she is always very formal when she speaks of him, as though she wants to keep me at a distance from the marriage. And, of course, my likeness to him is a constant reminder of what she has lost. Do you know, she fainted dead away the first time she saw me? She must have loved him very much.'

'Loved him...or hated him. They are two sides of the same coin, Luc.'

He put down his wine glass with great deliberation, his eyes fixed on her intelligent, concerned face. 'Hated him... But, Diane, that would explain a great deal. One day, soon after the funeral, I found her in the family chapel. She was standing by the mausoleum, and when she saw me she was terrified, as if I were his ghost. And her words... They struck me as strange at the time, but I put it down to the shock of her loss.'

'What did she say, Luc?' Diane's food lay untouched on her plate.

'She said, *"He has really gone, has he not? He will not be coming back?"* Naturally I assumed that her words were spoken in grief.'

'Oh, no.' Diane shook her head, making the ringlets

fall over her shoulder. 'Oh, no, she wanted to make
sure he was really dead. That is why she needed to
see the tomb, to make certain he was in it.' She forked
up a piece of salmon and chewed thoughtfully. 'Did
you see me speaking to her father? *Mon Dieu,* but that
man is a pig. How one such as he could have sired
Marissa, I cannot imagine! All the time he was talking
to me he was undressing me with his eyes, leering at
my bosom. Urgh!' She shivered and sipped her wine,
as if to wash away the thought of Sir George's lech-
erous behaviour.

'It is not like you to tolerate such a type: why did
you remain with him?'

'I was curious to know more of Marissa. The first
time I met her I could tell she was not happy, that she
was hiding something. And I tell you, that man would
sell his soul to the Devil, never mind his daughter, if
the money was right. That first marriage was all
wrong. Yet I can tell she is in love with you.' She
met his arrested gaze with a smile. 'Yes, she is in love
with you, you fool! How could you doubt it?'

Luc pushed his chair back and stalked over to the
buffet. But then he stopped, the carving knife and fork
in his hands, staring at the roast capon with unseeing
eyes. 'But if she loves me why was she so reluctant
to agree to marry me, and, when she finally did agree,
why did she insist we keep it a secret?' He hacked at
the chicken, producing a ragged lump of breast meat.

'And?' Diane prompted gently, knowing that something else was eating at him.

'And when I made love to her this afternoon, she wept.'

'Because she was happy?'

'No,' Luc said bleakly. 'Because she had forced herself to go through with it.'

'She was unwilling?' Diane asked incredulously.

Luc abandoned the capon and paced away, to stare down into the dark street below. 'Not at first. For God's sake, Diane, you know I would never force myself on a woman!'

'I know, *chéri,*' she said soothingly, recognising what all this was costing him.

'Then I thought she was shy—and, after all, it is over a year since her husband died…'

'But there is more,' the Frenchwoman stated.

'Yes. It is fear, Diane. I know fear when I see it, and she was afraid. How can that be?'

'Has it occurred to you that your highly respectable late cousin was not all he seemed? That perhaps he had tastes which, how shall we say, were unusual, that made his young bride afraid?'

Luc stared at her, aghast. *'What?'*

'Oh, for heaven's sake, Luc, you are a man of the world. You know there are other men who take pleasure in inflicting fear. She was a very young woman, a virgin, when she came—was sold—to the Earl. How was she to know it could be any other way?'

'And every time I made love to her…' He dropped into his chair and held his head in his hands. 'I would remind her of him every time she looked at me. She was waiting for me to be cruel to her as he had always been.' A vivid image of her reaction on the beach, when the moonlight must have increased the likeness even more, stabbed through him.

Eventually he raised troubled blue eyes to Diane's. 'But how can I confront her with this? How can I ask her to resurrect the humiliation of her marriage? Yet if I do not we could never be happy together; it will be doomed from the beginning.'

'But knowing you love her, she will come to trust you,' Diane said gently, then saw his face. 'You have told her, have you not?' None of the pain this conversation was causing her showed on her lovely face, yet inside it was as though she was being pierced by a thousand needles. She had loved Luc ever since she had known him, had allowed their *affaire* to dwindle into friendship because she knew that she was not the right woman for him. She was ten years older than he, and she had known from the beginning it could never last, but that did not make it any less painful.

'No: how could I speak of love when I thought she was still in love with Charles?'

Diane uttered a particularly unladylike word in French, jerking Luc out of his thoughts. 'Why are men so *stupide?*' she demanded. 'Tell her you love her, tell her you know that Charles was a beast and that you are not. Make love to her until she forgets he ever existed. And do not,' she added with a wicked twinkle, 'tell me you cannot do that!'

He smiled back warmly, sharing the memories for a moment. He stretched across the table and took her hands in his. 'Then I can only attribute it to my excellent teacher. Thank you, Diane, for all your love and warmth.'

'Foolish man!' She caressed his cheek affectionately. 'Now go. Do not waste time here. Go to your Marissa and tell her you love her.'

'Bless you.' He dropped a kiss on her cheek and was gone.

As the sound of the street door closing reached her, she whispered, 'But do not forget your loving friend.' Two fat tears trickled unheeded down her smooth cheeks and fell onto her plate.

The moon was high as Luc sent the bay gelding flying back along the road towards the Lodge. The air was warm and balmy, clouds of gnats danced above the thick hedgerows, and amongst the tangled banks of dog roses nightingales pierced the silence with their bubbling song.

All Luc could think about as the hooves thudded beneath him was that Marissa loved him and that they could be happy together.

His mind was so full of her that he was not surprised when he opened the door, stepped into the hall and she ran headlong down the stairs and cast herself into his arms. For a moment he was so overwhelmed to find himself holding her warm, urgent form, clad only in her nightgown and peignoir, that he held her close, his mouth in her hair, drinking in the scent of her.

Then he looked up into the reddened eyes of Miss Venables, at Jackson standing behind her, looking grave and concerned. Luc cast round and realised the hall was full of people—both footmen, a weeping lady's maid and even Cook, tangling her hands in her apron.

Gently he released Marissa's grip on his body and, keeping one arm protectively around her shoulders, asked Jackson, 'What the Devil is going on?'

'If you would take the ladies into the drawing room, my lord,' the butler said repressively, 'I will join you directly. Thomson, take the rest of the staff back below stairs. Cook, please send up tea.'

Luc, baffled, conducted Marissa into the drawing room while Jackson helped a weeping Miss Venables to an armchair. When the door had closed Luc demanded, 'Now, will someone please tell me what is amiss?'

'Oh, Luc,' Marissa began. 'I am so thankful…'

'No, let me tell him; it is all my fault,' Miss Venables wailed, but then could get no further, tears overcoming her again.

It was this, the sight of the redoubtable Jane Venables sobbing into her handkerchief, that convinced Luc that this was more than the usual domestic upset.

'Perhaps, my lord, I could be permitted to explain,' Jackson said stolidly as Marissa slipped out of the room, closing the door behind her.

'I wish you would,' Luc replied grimly. 'Sit down, man.'

The big man dropped into an armchair opposite his master, and it was as if the crisis had transported them back to their old, informal relationship in the West Indies. 'It's Miss Nicci, Luc. She's gone—off with that Captain Cross, if I read her letter aright. I was about to take the curricle out after her when you came back.'

'Bloody hell!' Luc swore, getting to his feet, raking his fingers through his wind-disordered hair. 'Stupid little fool!' He paced the carpet, then turned to face his old friend. 'You're sure she's with Cross? There can be no doubt?'

In reply, Jackson handed Luc a sheet of writing paper, crumpled and tear-stained.

I have gone to Andrew, because you are all so beastly to me. And he says I would make a wonderful army wife and would enjoy all the balls and parties that the Regiment holds. I shall marry him and then you will be sorry you were so unkind. Do not follow me, for I shall never return willingly.

'Stupid child! Even that milksop curate would have been better than this! Jackson—do we know where this Captain Cross lodges?'

'No, Luc.' Jackson shook his head. 'From what Lady Southwood remembers of his uniform, the regiment is one of those based down in Brighton: he obviously came up for the races this week.'

Miss Venables blew her nose and peered over the handkerchief, red-eyed, but finally in control of herself. 'My lord, I think I may be able to throw some light on this. While I was with Sir Frederick Collier this afternoon we encountered an old friend of his,

Colonel Seymour. He is the officer in command of Captain Cross's regiment, for he mentioned that he and several of his officers had taken lodgings in Epsom for the races.'

'Do you know where?'

'No, but Sir Frederick will, for they dined together last night.'

Ten minutes later the curricle was at the front door, Jackson already in the seat. As Luc gathered up the reins Marissa appeared on the doorstep, fully dressed, a cloak around her shoulders. 'Luc!' she cried. 'What are you going to do?'

'Call on Sir Frederick, find the Colonel, get Captain Cross's direction—and kill him,' he replied grimly.

'Take me with you! She is going to be in such distress, and if we are seen my presence may help reduce any scandal.'

'It makes sense, Luc,' Jackson murmured, swinging out of his seat to sit on the Tiger's perch behind.

'Very well, then.' Luc stretched down a hand and almost pulled Marissa up beside him. 'Hold tight,' he warned, laying the whip across the bays with a snap.

If Sir Frederick Collier was surprised to be interrupted as he sat reading in his study, he was too well mannered to show it. He urged Marissa and Luc into the room and listened gravely to Luc's frank explanation of why they were there. He crossed to his desk and wrote an address on a slip of paper. 'Here, this is Colonel Seymour's direction. You may rely on my total discretion. Now, hurry.'

The Colonel, fetched from a game of cards by his

batman, was less phlegmatic. His florid complexion darkened dangerously, but he checked the oath that rose to his lips in deference to Marissa. None the less Luc had the distinct impression that the Colonel would be exacting his own price for the Captain's behaviour. 'I will come with you, my lord. Ma'am, perhaps you would be more comfortable here: I will ask my wife to come down to wait with you.'

'Thank you, no. The fewer people involved the better, I feel, and Lady Southwood may be able to lend some countenance to my sister if she is seen leaving this man's lodgings.'

The Captain's lodgings, ten minutes away on the edge of town, were in darkness save for lights on the first floor. Luc, thankful that the house seemed a respectable one, tugged at the bell-pull impatiently, and when a manservant answered shouldered past him. Jackson followed, his hand on Marissa's elbow.

'Stand aside, my man, and do not raise a noise if you know what's good for you. Better wait down here, my lady,' he added, as the sound of Luc hammering at an upstairs door echoed through the house.

'No! Who is to say what will happen if I am not there? Come on, Jackson.' She hurried in his wake up the stairs, her heart in her mouth. From the moment the note had been found her thoughts had all been for Nicci: how she would ruin her life for this single moment of childish defiance. For she doubted that Nicci understood the enormity of what she was doing, or the danger she had placed herself in.

But when Luc had returned her joy and relief at

seeing him had turned to cold fear that either he would kill the Captain, and have to flee the country, or that he himself would be injured in the duel that he would surely force.

The scene that confronted them as they entered the room close on Luc's heels would have been comic if it had not been so serious. Nicci, whose riding habit at least explained how she had arrived there, sat by the fire, her pretty face a picture of indignation. The gallant Captain seemed determined to put as much distance between them as he could, for he was backed into a corner, a hunted look on his face.

'Thank God you have come, my lord!' the young man exclaimed at the sight of the Earl of Radwinter.

It gave Luc pause and he stopped, his eyes narrowed as he looked from one to the other.

'I did not ask her to come here, believe me, my lord,' the Captain said with feeling. 'I have never been so glad to see anyone in my life as I am to see you.'

'Andrew! How could you?' Nicci cried, her cheeks burning with humiliation. 'After all the things you said to me…'

'What things, Captain?' Luc enquired dangerously.

Marissa pushed past the men and gathered Nicci in her arms. 'Oh, do be quiet, both of you! There, there, Nicci. We have come to take you home. You are quite safe now.'

'She was quite safe before, let me assure you!' the Captain interjected indignantly. 'Kiss a girl at the races, and the next thing you know she turns up on the doorstep without a handkerchief to her name!'

Luc looked hard at the defiant young officer, a sneaking sympathy growing on him, although he allowed no hint of it to show on his stern face. 'Well, Captain Cross, this is a pretty pass: when *are* you intending to marry my sister? I am sure we can obtain a special licence: I believe I saw the Bishop of Chichester at the races yesterday. He will doubtless be happy to expedite matters.'

'Marry her!' the unfortunate Captain squawked. He was appalled, and it showed on his handsome face, sending Nicci into fresh sobs. 'Damn it, my lord, I never intended to marry her!' He saw the darkening look on Luc's face and hastened into speech again. 'I did not ask her to come here—I admit I was flirting, stole a kiss, but that is all, I swear it.' He was now becoming desperate, beads of sweat standing on his forehead.

Luc was beginning to enjoy himself. He felt the tension uncoiling from his muscles. He was certain that Captain Cross was as innocent of any attempt at seduction as he claimed, and that any blame could be laid firmly at the door of his silly, impetuous sister.

Marissa watched with her heart in her mouth as Luc strolled across the room to stand in front of the quaking Captain. 'You have had a very narrow escape, my friend,' he drawled, the Caribbean lilt suddenly strong in his voice.

'You…you aren't going to call me out?'

'No, although that was not what I meant. You have had a very narrow escape from finding yourself yoked to probably the silliest girl in England. She would have led you a merry dance, and you would have soon found that kisses come very expensive.'

Marissa, her arm around Nicci, let out her breath in a shuddering sigh of relief. Luc was not going to challenge him; the man she loved was not going to hazard his life in a pointless duel.

Leaving the Captain wilting visibly, Luc ushered them downstairs, leaving Jackson to locate Nicci's horse and ride it back to the Lodge. The journey was silent, broken only by Nicci's hiccuping sobs of mingled relief, humiliation and fury at her brother and Marissa's murmured words of comfort.

A relieved and furious Jane Venables swept Nicci up to bed, leaving Marissa and Luc alone. 'Oh, Luc, I have never been so glad to see anyone as I was to see you when you came home this evening!'

Luc looked across at her pale face, her eyes huge with worry and tiredness. 'Marissa, darling, there is something I must tell you,' he began, walking towards her, meaning to take her in his arms and tell her how much he loved her.

But Marissa was still too wrapped up in the events of the evening to take in his words. 'Where were you?' she continued. 'Jackson said you were not dining at home, but he was so vague...'

Without thinking, intent only on the declaration of love he was about to make, Luc said, 'I was with Diane.'

Marissa froze, her face becoming set. So, unable to find satisfaction in her arms, he had sought it in the bed of his mistress. Had he told Diane how cold she was, how unresponsive? Had the other woman smiled secretly to herself at the thought of Marissa's failings?

'Marissa,' he persisted, 'there is something I must tell you…'

'I do not want to hear it, my lord. But here is something *I* must tell *you:* you may consider our betrothal at an end.' And she turned on her heel and swept up the stairs.

Chapter Thirteen

It was a silent and subdued party which arrived back in Town, three days ahead of schedule. Miss Venables, still inclined to blame herself for Nicci's appalling behaviour, found that she was missing the congenial company of Sir Frederick Collier. He had sent round to her a warm note in response to her own message apologising for missing their planned picnic on the Downs and thanking him for his help and discretion.

Luc, brooding darkly over Marissa, spent most of the journey back fixing his sister with a look of such glacial indifference that Nicci was firmly convinced he was planning to send her back to Southwood Hall in disgrace.

For her part Marissa was in a state of despair. She had believed that when he made love to her she had disguised her fears: but she must have failed—again— if he could not wait to go straight from her arms to those of his charming and practised mistress. Why, she thought, plunging herself even further into gloom, should a man like Luc want to marry her when he could have a wife who would return him passion for passion?

And, indeed, there was no reason why any other woman would not respond to him, for her instincts had been correct. Luc might bear an uncanny resemblance to his cousin Charles, but there the similarity ended. It seemed, after all, that not all men were as her late husband—cold, cruel, controlling.

The next morning Marissa was breakfasting in her own chamber when she heard the sound of the doorknocker and, looking out, saw Sir Frederick Collier's carriage at the kerb. Hastily she dabbed her lips with a napkin and hurried downstairs.

Jackson was standing in the hall, in the act of placing Sir Frederick's hat and cane on the mahogany chest. 'Good morning, my lady.'

'Good morning, Jackson. Which room have you shown Sir Frederick to?'

'The Blue Salon, my lady. But,' he added as she turned towards the door, 'Miss Venables is already there.'

'Yes?' Marissa raised a dark brow, puzzled at his tone.

'I believe, my lady, that Sir Frederick was desirous of seeing Miss Venables alone.'

Marissa stared at the butler in wild surmise. 'You mean he…? My goodness Jackson, why have I not noticed? She is my dearest friend…'

'You have had one or two other things on your

mind, my lady,' Jackson supplied drily, his eyes lifting in the direction of Nicci's chamber above.

Marissa entered the morning room to wait for the suitor to emerge. She sat down, picked up a book, then tossed it onto the sofa and wandered over to a small table to fiddle with the flower arrangement on it. Having effectively wrecked Jackson's floral scheme, she fidgeted over to the window and was rewarded by the sight of Luc descending the steps and striding away across the Square in the direction of Ryder Street and his club.

She stood watching his broad shoulders in the dark blue jacket, the long line of his legs as he strode down the street in the warm sunshine. At the corner he paused, doffing his hat to a passing lady, and Marissa caught a glimpse of his face, paler than of late and, she thought, thinner.

Her heart turned over with love for him: the worry over Nicci must be taking its toll on him, and Madame de Rostan was not yet back in Town for him to seek solace with.

Marissa's fingers tightened heedlessly, crushing the pale primrose drapes. Oh, what a mess they had got themselves into! She loved him, and he at least wished to marry her, but how could she when her failure to be a true wife to him would always send him back to the arms of Diane and whoever succeeded her? Looking back now, Marissa realised that the one saving grace in her marriage to Charles had been that she had not loved him, and therefore his capacity to hurt her had been that much reduced.

Sounds in the hallway distracted her. The front door opened and Sir Frederick stepped out, his face alight. He turned as he was about to get into his carriage and waved, and Marissa realised that Jane must be in the doorway.

Thank goodness her dear Jane had found happiness! Marissa told herself she must have been blind not to have seen the growing affection between the retired banker and her friend. Before she could go out to her the door opened and Jane almost flew in. Her normally sallow complexion was rosy with colour, her eyes sparkled and she looked almost pretty.

'My dear! I am so happy for you.' There could be no doubting Jane's good news. Marissa embraced her cousin warmly, feeling the tears running down her cheeks in mingled happiness for Jane and regret at her own circumstances.

Fortunately Jane was too happy to notice any ambiguity in Marissa's response, and for a long moment the two women hugged each other wordlessly.

At last Jane broke free and sank onto the sofa as though her legs would no longer support her. 'Marissa, I was never so surprised as when he declared himself! I had believed at my age I was past all such hopes of happiness.'

'But you have so much in common, so many shared interests, and he is a truly kind man.' And he loves you, she thought wistfully, remembering Sir Frederick's face as he turned to wave. 'And when will you be married?'

Jane's face creased with a sudden worry. 'I told

Frederick that I could not think of it at the moment because of Nicole. She needs close supervision.'

'I will take care of Nicci,' Marissa said firmly. 'You must place your own happiness first, Jane—for once in your life!' And after all, Marissa thought, what else is there for me to do with my time?

'Oh, dear, look at the time!' Jane jumped to her feet. 'Cook had asked me to look at the week's menus—she is in such a taking with us arriving back early that I really must spend some time with her or we will be eating cold cuts all week.' Jane bustled out, leaving Marissa feeling breathless.

The square outside was bustling with activity as the Quality took advantage of the lovely weather to drive and ride out. Marissa, suddenly decisive, got to her feet. She would not sit moping; it would change nothing. She would order the barouche with the top down and go and buy Jane a present. She had so admired a beautiful ivory silk shawl they had seen whilst shopping in the Burlington Arcade, but had dismissed it out of hand as too expensive and quite unsuited to her lifestyle.

As the wife of a distinguished public figure dear Jane would find many opportunities to wear it, and Marissa was pleased with her inspiration as she called for Matthews.

The under-butler sent orders for the carriage, then apologised for the absence of footmen to accompany his mistress. 'I am sorry, my lady, but they are all out on errands: will it be acceptable if I accompany you instead?'

'Yes, of course, Matthews. Thank you. Tell the coachman I wish to go to the Burlington Arcade, if you please.'

Marissa strolled through the Arcade, Matthews behind her, already carrying an awkward collection of parcels which, in addition to Jane's scarf, included a pink-lined parasol, some rose water, a pair of embroidered slippers and a length of linen for a chair-cover Marissa had decided to embroider.

The beadle, on duty to curb the excesses of any unruly children and to uphold the rules of the Arcade, touched his hat as she passed and re-emerged into a sunlit Piccadilly. 'I will just stroll over to Fortnum's and see if they have that blend of tea in that his lordship particularly likes, and then I will go into Hatchard's. Please have the barouche wait, Matthews.'

Luc meanwhile was still in his club. He had chosen a quiet corner in Brooks's to sit and think through the coil he found himself in. Despite what his sister thought, she did not feature in his musings at all. He knew her too well to think that she would repeat her escapade; equally he knew something—or someone—else would happen to take her mind off Captain Cross. Sooner or later his little sister would grow up and the right man would come along...

No, it was Marissa who filled his thoughts. Thanks to his conversation with Diane, he now realised that whatever Charles had done had scarred Marissa deeply: she had not been mourning for her husband; she had been having nightmares about him.

Luc had gone from being jealous of the man he had

believed she still loved to wishing the man was not
already dead so he could strangle him himself. How
could he ever overturn the legacy of that marriage?
Convince Marissa that with him she could forget two
years of hell? How could he convince a woman who
had been badly hurt that he would never hurt her?

His dark, brooding face convinced many acquaintances who saw him across the room that he had either
had a heavy night on the tiles and was suffering as a
result or had had major losses at the races. It did not,
however, deter Sir Frederick Collier.

The baronet, full of the joys of spring, had come
directly to his club from his successful meeting with
Jane Venables, soon to be Lady Collier. His spinster
sister would be delighted at the news, but she would
fuss too, and he needed time to contemplate and reflect on his happiness alone in this male preserve.

The clubs of St James's—Boodles, Brooks's,
White's and many other lesser sanctuaries—provided
havens for the gentlemen of the *ton,* for no lady could
cross the threshold, nor even be seen driving down St
James's itself.

Shaking his head at an invitation to join an early
game of whist, and deflecting a suggestion that he dine
that night with a group set on finishing the evening at
a cocking pit, Sir Frederick strolled through to the
library.

He thought himself alone, then saw in the farthest
window embrasure the long-legged figure of the Earl
of Radwinter. Luc was sitting, legs outstretched, hands

thrust deep into his pockets, chin dropped on his chest in thought.

Usually a sensitive man, Sir Frederick was too buoyed up with happiness to notice the mood of the other man, and strode over to greet him. 'My lord! I am so glad to have seen you. May I share with you, in confidence, my happy news?'

Luc looked up and said drily, 'I would appreciate happy news.' After all, he could see that Sir Frederick was going to tell him anyway.

Sir Frederick pulled up another leather wing chair and said, 'It will be announced next week, but I am delighted to tell you that Miss Venables has done me the honour of agreeing to become my wife.'

'Good God!' Luc was startled out of good manners. 'My dear fellow, I do apologise, but this is a shock to me—I have obviously been most unobservant. You have my heartiest congratulations: Miss Venables is an admirable woman, and will make you very happy. My sister Nicole will miss her very much.'

Sir Frederick tugged the bell-pull and when the footman appeared, ordered Madeira. 'And my dear Jane will miss Miss Southwood greatly: it is something which concerns her, and is frankly making her reluctant to set the date.'

'I am surprised, after my little sister's last escapade, that Miss Venables does not seize with delight on the prospect of being free of her!' He looked at the other man wryly and sipped his wine. 'And I must thank you again for your help and discretion in the matter…'

The men fell silent for a moment, then Sir Frederick

ventured, 'I do hope that Lady Southwood was not too distressed by that evening's events. I thought at the races that she looked happier than I had ever seen her: I would be sorry to think that her new-found freedom should be marred by any anxiety.'

'Freedom?' Luc queried sharply.

'Ah.' Sir Frederick winced. 'Forgive me, my lord, for speaking out of turn. Please, ignore my tactlessness.'

'No, please, you interest me. I know little of Lady Southwood's history. You must know this is not something I would normally speak of, but I have a specific reason to ask and I know I can trust your discretion.'

The baronet got to his feet and checked that the other window bays in the quiet room were empty before resuming his seat. 'Indeed you may. What is it that you wish to know? I had forgotten that you have been living abroad.'

'Tell me about my cousin Charles,' Luc asked quietly. 'What manner of man was he?'

'I assume you do not need me to tell you that he was a patron of the arts, a man of highly refined artistic taste and the most rigorous standards?'

'No, you assume correctly. I need to know what manner of man, what manner of…husband he was.'

'My lord, what I am about to tell you is well known in certain circles, but never spoken of. The late Earl had certain very discreet tastes. You will have observed the strict discipline of his household affairs: I believe he took a similar approach to his amatory affairs. Not every woman is prepared to tolerate such demands: a very young, very innocent wife may be cowed into it. And, of course, if you know where to purchase them, these pleasures may always be bought.'

'The bastard,' hissed Luc. He had gone white and his fingers clenched tightly on the stem of his wine glass. He had expected to hear that Charles was unkind, uncaring, demanding the highest standards in his self-centred existence, but not this.

'Indeed,' the baronet concurred.

Suddenly Luc needed to know more, to understand the full depths of his cousin's character. 'And can you put a name to an establishment he patronised?'

Sir Frederick picked a sheet of notepaper from a rack by his side and dipped the quill pen in the standish. He scratched a few lines, dusted it with sand and folded the note. 'Here.' He passed it over. 'If you really have the stomach for it.'

Luc glanced at it, then tucked it into his pocketbook. 'Thank you. If you, and others, knew of this, how could it be that her father did not?'

Sir Frederick got to his feet. 'Oh, he knew all right. But Sir George would never let a detail like that worry him if he saw the chance to sell his daughter and finance his own dissolute life.'

Luc walked slowly into the hall and waited while the doorman found his hat and cane. He did not want to visit Madam Hall's establishment, but he had to; he urgently needed to understand exactly what the woman he loved had endured. Only then could he seek to heal her. Only then could he teach her to trust again.

Ignoring the passing hackney carriages, he struck off on foot along King Street and across St James's Square, into Charles Street towards the Haymarket, and thence Panton Street.

As he entered the Haymarket Marissa was climbing into the barouche outside Hatchard's. 'Matthews, can you recall where that art gallery was that Lady Smithson recommended when she called the other day? I think you were in the room serving tea when we were discussing it. I must think of a wedding present for Miss Venables, and Lady Smithson said they had some interesting Italian Renaissance canvases which might appeal.'

'Oxendon Street, I believe, my lady. It is just off the Haymarket. Shall I direct the coachman to take you now?'

'Yes, please.' Marissa settled back against the silk upholstery and let her thoughts stray as they made their way along the crowded thoroughfare. As usual, they strayed to Luc, and a little smile curved her lips as she thought of him. The warmth of the sunshine soothed her, the bustle of the street surrounded her with life and vitality, and her spirits rose. Could there be some way for them to be happy together? She could not deny her love for him, her response when he kissed her. And he desired her, liked to be in her company, was a friend to her...

Without any plan, without any clear idea of what she could do to get out of this coil, still Marissa felt suddenly optimistic, almost happy. He was a good man, a kind man…there must be a way for them…

As she thought it the carriage turned into Panton Street and there he was in front of her, on the right-hand pavement, just turning to ascend the short flight of steps to a glossily painted front door. 'Matthews! There is his lordship! Coachman, pull up!'

'Drive on!' Matthews commanded with uncharacteristic sharpness, and the startled coachman flicked his whip over the bays' rumps. The horses broke into a canter and the barouche was past the house before Luc's hand dropped from the knocker.

'Matthews!' Marissa twisted round in her seat to glare at the under-butler, perched up behind on the footman's seat. 'How dare you? I had expressly asked the coachman to pull up!'

'I am sorry, my lady,' the man stammered, red to his hairline. 'I think you were mistaken and that was not his lordship… I wished to save any embarrassment caused by you greeting a perfect stranger.'

It *had* been Luc, and Matthews was so obviously lying that Marissa was momentarily speechless. When she recovered herself she realised she could hardly pursue the subject in an open carriage. The driver was doubtless agog over the exchange as it was.

'Drive home, please,' she ordered stiffly.

Inside Madam Hall's discreetly painted front door, Luc found himself in a dark, heavily panelled front hall. There were a few white marble statues which reminded him, with a shiver, of Southwood Hall. The butler, a saturnine individual, bowed and enquired his business.

Luc experienced a momentary doubt about the information Sir Frederick had given him. In his youth in Jamaica he had visited as many houses of ill repute as the average young buck out with a party of high-drinking friends, but nothing like this.

He looked round at the heavy drapery and subdued lighting and the many doors that opened off the hallway. 'I would like to speak to Madam Hall.'

'Do you have an appointment, my lord?' Luc realised that the butler must have recognised him, although he had not offered his card. Given that he had spent so little time in London, the man could only know him from his resemblance to his late cousin. Perhaps Sir Frederick was correct after all.

'I am not expected.'

'Then I will enquire if madam is at home.' The man bowed and disappeared upstairs, leaving Luc standing in the hall. Luc, spurred by curiosity and unease, tried one of the doorhandles, but it was locked, as were all the others he turned before he heard the sound of the butler's return.

'This way, my lord. Madam Hall will see you now.'

Luc followed the man up the curving staircase, along a heavily draped corridor and up to a pair of imposing double doors. The silence in the house was eerie, oppressive, as though the building was smothered in cloth.

'The Earl of Radwinter, madam,' the butler announced, before closing the doors to leave Luc alone in the Salon.

The woman who rose as he entered was tall, brown-haired, modestly attired and almost motherly in appearance, until he looked into her hard brown eyes. Whatever he had been expecting it was not this woman, dressed in a plain but beautifully tailored gown without a single item of jewellery.

'Please be seated, my lord.' She waved him to a seat and resumed her own beside a low table.

'You appear to know my name, madam, although I did not send in my card. Can I assume it is because you were acquainted with my late cousin?' He was in no mood for small-talk and pretend niceties. The hair on the back of his neck prickled and he wanted nothing more than to be out of this house.

'Indeed. The resemblance is very great.' Her voice was accentless and flat, without any emotional colour.

'In outward appearance only, I can assure you, madam.'

She smiled slightly and without warmth. She was fiddling with something on the table beside her, but he found himself held, both fascinated and repelled, by that hard brown gaze. 'To what do I owe the honour of your visit, my lord?'

'Some answers. What is the nature of this house?'

'You are very blunt. This house exists for gentlemen who have an interest in…shall we say, the arts of discipline?'

'In giving it or receiving it?'

'Both, my lord,' she replied calmly. 'In which direction does your own interest lie?'

'In neither.' He just managed to keep the fury out of his voice. 'And my cousin?'

'Oh, in giving it, undoubtedly.' Her fingers continued to toy with the object on the table. 'His lordship's tastes were very clear.'

Luc dropped his eyes to her hand and saw with a frisson of distaste that what she was touching was a riding crop, a beautifully made piece of plaited leather with an ivory handle. His appalled gaze came back to hers and she smiled tightly. 'Exactly so, my lord,' she said, as though in reply to an unasked question.

Suddenly Luc could see nothing but the image of Marissa's stricken face on the day he had lost his temper with Nicci over her dalliance with Mr Ashforde. He had been holding his riding crop, had brought it down onto the polished table-top with a crash…

He felt ill at the memory, repulsed by the thought of what it had represented to poor Marissa, and filled with the overwhelming desire to lock his hands around this creature's neck and choke the poisonous life out of her.

He got abruptly to his feet: the atmosphere of the bordello seemed to be invading his pores, seeping into the fabric of his clothing. He had to get out. 'Madam.' Without waiting for her to ring he wrenched open the doors and ran down the stairs into the clean fresh air and daylight of the street.

Marissa, uncharacteristically furious, bottled up her temper until she was home once again. Matthews, still flushed at his temerity, stood before her in the Salon, not meeting her eyes. 'Well, Matthews. I hope you have a good explanation for gainsaying my instructions in such a manner.'

The under-butler met her sparkling green angry eyes and sought for the words. 'I did not think it was his lordship…'

'Rubbish! Tell me the truth, man.'

'Well,' he improvised wildly, 'it is not a very salubrious area. I did not think we should stop…'

'Nonsense! It was nothing to do with the street… It was the house, was it not? Tell me, what is that house?'

'I have no idea, my lady.' But it was unconvincing, even to his own ears. Matthews was not used to lying, and was not good at it.

'Matthews,' Marissa began, dangerously quiet, 'if you do not tell me the truth, I shall go out, find a hackney carriage and go there myself.' Normally it would have never crossed her mind to wonder what Luc was about. But Matthews's reaction had been so extreme she could not leave it now.

'No, my lady, you cannot do that!' He was obviously appalled.

'Well, then…' She was implacable.

Matthews went even redder, shuffled his feet and blurted out, 'It is a house of ill repute, my lady.'

'Oh.' Marissa was taken aback. She did not like the idea of Luc visiting such a place, but she was realist enough to know that men did these things—and he

owed her no loyalty now she had broken the engagement. She looked at the under-butler again and saw
that he was looking almost shiftily relieved. There was
more to it than a simple bawdy house: if that was all
it was even Matthews could have come up with a convincing response. A gentleman's club…a gaming
house, my lady, was all he would have needed to say
and she would have dropped the subject instantly.

'I warn you, Matthews, I know there is more to it.
Tell me, or I shall go there.'

'It's a bordello for men who like—oh, gawd, my
lady!—different things…er, whips…oh, please, my
lady, don't ask me any more.'

Her knees gave way and she sank down on the sofa,
but she kept her voice hard. 'How do you know, Matthews?'

'His late lordship…' The man's voice trailed off
miserably.

'Thank you, Matthews. You may go.'

The ice seemed to be spreading up her body from
her toes to the top of her head. It was like doing a
puzzle, and suddenly the last few clues fell into place.
That was why when they had come up to London
Charles had never troubled her: he had had this place
to go to, to satisfy his depraved tastes. And now
Luc…was it in the blood? She could not bear to think
about it, could not bear to think that he too had this
taint. She loved him; now she could not bear the
thought of seeing him again. Marissa shuddered at the
thought of how close she had been to once more placing herself in the power of a man: wives had no choice

but to obey. But she was free, and at least she could run.

Marissa got to her feet, hardly able to feel her limbs, but somehow they responded. She tugged the bell-pull and when the footman came ordered, 'Send Mary to my room and fetch down two of my travelling cases and my dressing case.' As the man turned to obey she added, 'And send to the mews for the light travelling coach to be ready as soon as possible.'

Within the hour all was prepared, the few cases loaded, and, accompanied by a bemused Mary, Marissa was on the road heading for Norfolk and sanctuary.

If Jackson had been on duty doubtless he would have found a way to delay her, but he had had the morning off and strolled back into the butler's pantry over an hour after Marissa's departure to find his assistant sitting, head in hands, and muttering, 'Oh, gawd,' monotonously.

By the time Luc returned ten minutes later Jackson was extracting every detail of that morning's shopping expedition. He hastened upstairs to find his master pulling off his shirt and calling for hot water. 'Damn it, Ned, I feel as though I'm never going to be clean again. I've been—'

'I know where you've been, Luc—and so does she.' Jackson had no need to say who *she* was; his expression said it all.

'How the blazes…?'

'She saw you. She made Matthews tell her what that place is.'

'How the devil does Matthews know?' Luc's head was whirling, but he snatched up a clean shirt and began to fasten it.

'All the servants knew what your late cousin was,' Jackson said darkly.

'Oh, my God…I must go to her. What she must be thinking… What hell is she going through if she thinks I am like him?'

'You can't talk to her, Luc, she's gone. Two hours since.'

'Where?' he demanded, raking his hand through his already disordered hair.

'Back to the Hall. One of the footmen overheard her orders to the coachman.'

'No, she would never go back there. But she will go back to the Dower House: it is the only place where she has no memories of him.' Luc stopped, thinking. 'Pack a saddlebag and send to the stables for the new bay stallion: it is fresh enough to get me a good distance before I have to change.'

'Yes, Luc, but I'm coming with you.' Jackson tugged the bell-pull with such force that three footmen arrived simultaneously and were sent off at the run to obey his orders.

It was dark when Luc and Jackson, stiff, tired and travel-stained, trotted into Newmarket and reined in in the yard of the Three Crowns. 'Look, Luc.' Jackson pointed to the travelling carriage, standing, its empty shafts on the cobbles.

'Thank goodness. This is a respectable house; she will be all right here tonight.'

'But aren't you going in to talk to her?' Jackson furrowed his brow in perplexity as Luc dug his heels in and trotted out of the yard.

'Not here, man! This is hardly the place for the sort of conversation we are going to be having! Here is the King's Head; let's hope they have beds for the night.'

The following morning Luc played a waiting game, eating his breakfast by the window of the inn until he saw the travelling coach, with his own coat of arms on the door, clatter past over the cobbles. He and Jackson followed at a discreet distance, letting the coach go out of sight in case they were seen and the driver thought he was being followed by highwaymen.

It was a long day, but Marissa insisted that her coachman keep going, changing horses whenever he saw fit, but she refused his pleas to stop and rest for the night. Even though it was June the sun had set before the Hall came in sight. Marissa averted her gaze and waited, with sudden impatience, for the Dower House to appear.

For the long journey she had sat silent, frozen and almost immobile, responding automatically to Mary's worried attempts at conversation until the girl had finally given up and fallen silent. She supposed she had had something to eat the night before, but could not remember what. Nor could she remember sleeping, although there seemed to have been moments of unconsciousness.

Lights were twinkling as though in welcome in the windows of the old house. At the sound of carriage wheels on gravel Whiting threw open the front door, and at the sight of his familiar, kind face Marissa felt the ice that had been covering her break. Life, and with it pain, flowed back into her limbs and mind. Seconds later Mrs Whiting appeared at her husband's side, exclaiming with mixed worry and delight at the sight of her mistress.

Marissa half tumbled from the carriage into the housekeeper's arms, hugging her convulsively, determined not to cry.

'It is all right,' she was explaining. 'I have not been very well—London is so hot and noisy. I just need to be back in the country for a while.'

The Whitings broke off from their worried greetings as the sound of hooves travelled clearly on the still night air.

'Who can that be at this time?' Whiting asked, then his jaw dropped at the sight of the two riders.

'Marissa!' Luc's voice reached her clearly through the twilight.

She took to her heels and ran, through the hall, up the stairs and into her chamber, slamming the door and locking it behind her.

Chapter Fourteen

Marissa twisted the key in the lock and leaned back against the panels, her bosom rising and falling with her panting breaths.

What was Luc doing here? How had he managed to follow her so closely—and what did he want with her? She braced herself for the sound of pursuing footsteps, expecting at any moment that he would pound on the door, demand that she come out.

It was not that she feared him: even after yesterday's awful revelation that he was visiting the same house of ill repute as her husband had she knew in her heart that Luc would never raise a finger to her. A sob rose in her throat and Marissa stumbled away from the door to throw herself across the four-poster bed. If only she could make any sense of it! Luc had always been so kind, so patient, so considerate to her. In his dealings with his sister he was loving and indulgent, and even after her worse excesses in Epsom he had not punished her in any way.

All this, and her instinctive love for him, was totally

at odds with the sort of man who frequented *that* sort of place. Marissa stiffened as the sound of muted voices reached her through the heavy door, then there was the scrape of moving furniture. Puzzled, she sat up, scrubbing her hand across her wet eyes, but all was once more silent.

How long she lay curled up on the bed, fully dressed, before she fell asleep she did not know, but she was woken by the chorus of dawn birdsong and fitful sunshine through the undraped east window.

Marissa swung her legs off the bed and stood up stiffly. What time was it? She rubbed her eyes and looked around the room, all the while listening for sounds that the servants were up and about their business.

All was still, but on the washstand stood a jug of cold water, and soaps and towels were laid out ready. Pulling off her travel-stained clothing, Marissa washed swiftly, wincing at the chilly caress of the water, but grateful to feel clean and fresh once more. She pulled the remaining pins out of her tangled hair and brushed it hard until the dust was gone and it clouded out from her head in a dark mass.

All her clothes were still in the travelling cases, presumably in the hall. Marissa pulled open drawers in the dresser and found a nightgown and peignoir of pale biscuit-coloured lawn. Clean and clothed, she climbed back into bed and prepared to wait patiently until the servants were up and about.

There was no chance she would fall asleep again: her head, now she was properly awake, was spinning with thoughts of Luc. Where was he? Presumably he had gone back to the Hall to spend the night, but she had no doubt that he would be back at the Dower House soon after breakfast to demand an explanation for her precipitate flight. And what could she possibly say to him? *I love you, but I know you patronise a house where...* No, she could not even think the words, let alone say them.

If she had not seen Luc with her own eyes she would never have believed he could share any of her late husband's tastes, for Charles had been a cold, cruel man in thought as well as deed. But Luc...Luc was warm, loving... She shivered pleasurably at the recollection of his lovemaking, of his eagerness to pleasure her before himself. No, that did not sit with the picture of a man who indulged in secret vices, closet cruelties.

A realisation that she might have been too hasty in her conclusion was dawning on Marissa. She caught her breath, sitting up, her heart racing with sudden hope. Could there be another explanation for his presence on that doorstep on Panton Street? And, that being the case, did she not owe it to the man she loved to ask him what it could be?

Seized with hope and optimism, Marissa felt her stomach growl, and for the first time in what seemed like days giggled. How ridiculous, after all this heartbreak and drama, to feel something as mundane as hunger. But she was starving. The sound of the hall clock striking five came faintly through the panels: it was no good sitting here waiting for another hour. She decided to make a foray to the kitchen to see what the larder held.

Marissa climbed out of bed and padded silently to the door. She did not want either Mary or Mrs Whiting fussing over her, or feeling that they should get up and attend to her needs. Using both hands, she eased the key round in the lock, starting as it clicked. Then she opened the door and stepped out onto the shadowed landing, her eyes fixed on the corridor to her left where the servants' wing lay.

All was still and silent so she turned towards the stairs—and almost cried out in alarm. A heavy carved armchair had been pulled up and blocked her way. It was occupied by the sprawled, sleeping figure of Luc. Jacket off, cravat loose at his neck, boots discarded by his side, he slept deeply.

Marissa found her hands had flown instinctively to her chest, to still her thudding heart, but he did not wake. She gazed down at him, at the relaxed, stubble-shaded face, the thick dark eyelashes fanning his cheekbones, at the firm mouth now faintly smiling, perhaps at some dream. Instead of spending the night in his own comfortable bed he had been here all the time, sleeping across her threshold as if guarding her.

A wave of love swept through Marissa and her hand crept, as if of its own volition, to stroke his tanned face. But before she could touch him his eyes opened, wide and blue, and he smiled at her. 'I was dreaming about you,' was all he said as he stood to sweep her into his arms.

Kicking open the bedroom door, Luc strode to the

bed and laid Marissa down against the pillows. For a long moment he stood looking down at her, as if deciding something, then to Marissa's surprise he crossed to shut the door, twisting the key in the lock. Carrying the key across, he dropped it on the bedside cabinet by her hand then went to sit on the window seat.

Marissa met the steady, grave look he fixed on her face. 'You spent all night out there on the landing?' she asked, almost in disbelief. 'Why?'

'I was worried about you,' he replied simply. 'You ran away from me.'

She flushed, biting her lip, and for a moment could not meet his eyes. But Luc did not help her out. Marissa realised that this was the turning point: she could be honest, trust him, tell him what she knew and had feared, or she could prevaricate and send him away. If she trusted her instincts and she was wrong about him, then they had no future together—but if she did not grasp this nettle they had no future anyway, and she wanted a future with Luc.

'I saw you going into a house. One that Matthews told me Charles used to visit…'

'Yes.' The single syllable was like a blow: one part of her mind had been clinging to the hope that Matthews had been wrong, or that it had not been the right house.

'You don't deny it?' she almost whispered, her hands creeping to her throat.

'No, I don't deny it—but why do you think I went

there?' His voice was even, but she could see the pulse beating in his throat and his body was tense.

'At first I was shocked. I thought you were going there for the same reason as Charles had always done. I was devastated that I could have been so wrong about you. That was why I ran, because I could not bear to be close to you if that was the truth.'

'At first?' he queried. 'What do you think now, Marissa? What do you believe?'

'I believe I was wrong.' Her eyes were huge in the early-morning light and he could see how much it was costing her to speak so frankly. 'Lov...knowing you as I do, once the shock wore off, I knew there had to be another explanation.'

Luc stood and walked slowly to the foot of the bed, his eyes fixed on her face. 'There is another explanation. You have been very discreet about Charles, very loyal—but I knew he had hurt you very badly, had frightened you to the point where I feared you could never love me.' Marissa caught her breath: did it matter, then, that she loved him? He smiled at her and carried on speaking gently. 'I had heard something of my late cousin's tastes...I decided to seek out the truth for myself.'

'But why? Why does it matter to you? He is dead.'

'But his shadow still lies over you, and, loving you as I do, I want you to be free.'

'You love me?' Marissa breathed, afraid to believe her own ears.

Luc came and sat beside her, gathering her hands in his, a rueful smile on his lips. 'It has taken me a long time to say it, but I think I must have loved you from the moment I saw you. For a long time I believed you were grieving for Charles, that you could never love anyone else, especially someone who reminded you so painfully of what you had lost.'

'*Lost!* I lost only fear and cruelty. You taught me that not all men are like that, that I could love, and trust a man not to hurt me…'

Marissa's voice broke and she shut her eyes against the tears that threatened to fall. She found herself gathered in Luc's arms, held so tightly against his chest she could hardly breathe. 'The bastard!' he ground out, before covering her face in kisses.

When she emerged, breathless, she saw he was searching her face, a touch of doubt in his eyes. 'You do love me, Marissa? When we made love I could sense your reserve.'

'Yes, I do love you. I knew I loved you when you went back to Jamaica and I ached for you, lived for your letters to Nicci.'

'Then why would you not marry me?' His hands were straying down her shoulders, stroking through the lace, tangling as his fingers sought the ribbons tying her peignoir.

'I believed I could never be a true wife to you, that Charles had so affected me that I could never give you everything. And I believed that you would turn to Diane for comfort. Loving you as I do, I could not bear to share you.'

'Diane? It has been all over between us for a long time…before I left Jamaica to come to London just before Charles's accident. She has been a true friend to me, and,' he added in gentle admonishment, 'to you too. It was she who made me see that there must be a reason why you could not surrender to me completely.'

His fingers had now found their way beneath the fine cotton lawn and were stroking the swell of her breasts. It made it difficult to think, to speak, to do anything but give in. 'But, Luc, I do not know if I can,' she said in a despairing tone. 'I do not know if I will ever be able to love you as I want to.'

To her shock he stopped caressing her and sat back, watching her with smiling eyes. 'Then now is the time to find out. Make love to me, Marissa: you take control; you do what you want.'

He was shrugging off his shirt and breeches as he spoke. Marissa's eyes were wide with shock. 'But…I don't know…I mean, I've never…Luc, what do you want me to do?'

Luc threw himself on the bed beside her and with a deft twist of his arm caught her up, stripping off the peignoir and nightdress and throwing them across the room. 'Right.' He lay back against the pillows, pulling her on top of his aroused body. 'Now, Marissa, you are in charge.'

Suddenly liberated, fearless, Marissa took his face in his hands and kissed him deeply, exploring the taste of him with her tongue before pulling back to look down into his face. Something in the quality of the light—or was it his obvious delight and love for her?—made him look only like Luc, not in the slightest like his cousin.

She nibbled his earlobe and he gasped as her lips moved relentlessly down the hard planes of his chest, teasing his nipple before, daringly, exploring further. His skin was satiny, hot with his desire for her, yet she could sense his restraint as he let her set the pace.

It served only to incite her. Impatient with his patience, she twisted round, pulling his glorious weight on top of her, opening her body to him. 'Luc,' she managed to say, 'I cannot wait any longer. Make love to me, *please.*''

And he did, gently at first, but he too was beyond restraint, swept along with the passion of her surrender which when it came shocked and delighted them both.

It seemed hours before they stirred, then Marissa opened her eyes to find him looking into hers with such love that she was almost unable to say, 'Is that how it is meant to be, my love?'

Luc's voice was shaky as he replied. 'I have no idea. I have never experienced anything like it. But...' he smoothed her damp hair back from her forehead '...I suggest we spend the rest of our lives finding out.'

Half an hour later Mrs Whiting with a tea tray and Mary with a ewer of hot water met outside the bedchamber door. Their eyes fell on the empty carved chair, then the firmly closed door. Without a word they turned and made their way downstairs.

*   *   *   *   *

MASTER OF TAMASEE
by
Helen Dickson

Helen Dickson was born and still lives in south Yorkshire, with her husband, on a busy arable farm where she combines writing with keeping a chaotic farmhouse. An incurable romantic, she writes for pleasure, owing much of her inspiration to the beauty of the surrounding countryside. She enjoys reading and music. History has always captivated her, and she likes travel and visiting ancient buildings.

Also by Helen Dickson
in Mills & Boon Historical Romance™:

LORD FOX'S PLEASURE
JEWEL OF THE NIGHT
HIGHWAYMAN HUSBAND
THE PIRATE'S DAUGHTER

Look for
BELHAVEN BRIDE
Coming September 2004

CHAPTER ONE

THE Milton carriage was only one of a glittering array that rattled and streamed through the Portland stone gateway of Holland House, and Clarissa, seated beside Betsy, her companion, and across from her father, Harry Milton, was trying hard not to think about the long night ahead. How she hated these frequent dinner parties which they were invited to attend while in London. She sighed, wishing she were back at Ashton Park in Kent with her brother, Richard.

Amid the shouting of coachmen and the jingle of harness the carriage came to a halt, waiting for the ones in front to discharge their occupants at the foot of the steps of Holland House. Slowly their carriage edged its way along, and Clarissa leaned her head against the soft upholstery, thinking with longing of the quiet solitude and leafy green meadows of home. She closed her eyes and, as so often of late, the image of Edward's handsome, laughing face flashed before her. They would have been married now had he not been killed, along with her brother, Simon, at the battle of Albuera in Spain with Wellington's army in May, seven months earlier.

She would never forget the day when the tragic news had come to them at Ashton Park and all the pain that had come with it. The only pain she had ever experienced in her twenty-one years had been when her mother had died two years ago after a long illness. Then, that had been terrible, but it had not been like the pain and desolation she had felt over the deaths of her betrothed and older brother. Never had she

believed she could feel such pain, such anguish that
went deep – deeper than anything she had ever known.
She had continued to carry on but, determined never
again to feel for any man the way she had for Edward,
that no man could ever take his place, she had hardened her heart, built an emotional wall around herself,
resolved that no man would ever breach it.

Followed by Betsy, she stepped out of the carriage
and, escorted by her father, climbed the steps to the
splendour and opulence of Holland House, ablaze with
lights shining from every window. From somewhere
inside the musicians began to play, their music filling
the rooms, dipping and rising, sweet and sublime,
which at any other time she would have found soothing.
But not tonight. The strains of the violins matched her
nerves, which were as taut as their strings. As she
entered the glittering world of fashionable London
society where chandeliers blazed and baskets full of
flowers scented the air with a lovely delicious fragrance,
she thought, wistfully, how different it would be if
Edward were here to share it with her.

They were greeted by Lady Holland, brimming over
with her usual exuberance. She was one of the most
popular hostesses at this time – in fact, probably one
of the most favoured in London society – giving the
most elaborate and brilliant parties, surpassed only by
those given by the Prince Regent at Carlton House.
Invitations were only sent out to those with a particular
social standing.

Clarissa liked Lady Holland. She had been a good
friend of her father's for many years and was a clever,
astute woman with an amazing wit. If somewhat domineering and bossy, she was no fool, and her guests
could always be assured of some high-level, interesting
conversation covering a wide range of topics at her
crowded dinner table. Over the years Holland House

had become the social centre of many Whig politicians and literary men.

'Why, Clarissa,' said Lady Holland, taking her gloved hand in her own and squeezing it with genuine affection. 'How lovely you look. I'm so glad you were able to come,' and to her father, poking his portly frame good-humouredly with her folded fan, 'You must be proud of your daughter, Harry. Clarissa does you credit. Now – off you go, my dear, while I talk to your father,' she said, giving Clarissa a knowing smile. 'Letty Davenport was looking for you earlier. She's just dying to tell you about her visit to Brighton. We'll have a chat later on.'

Clarissa smiled gratefully, knowing Lady Holland was well aware of her father's over-indulgence where both alcohol and gambling were concerned and would be sure to keep a watchful eye on him while he was under her roof. She turned and went in search of Letty, moving through richly furnished and carpeted rooms, swarming with nobility and gentry alike. Anyone who could lay claim to wealth and position was here. This was supposed to be an even grander affair than usual, given in honour of the Prince Regent, but Clarissa didn't particularly care. All she was concerned about was getting through it and making sure her father didn't drink too much or gamble away any more of his wealth at Faro or Whist.

Betsy paused to talk to an acquaintance and Clarissa moved on alone, searching for Letty. As she made her way down the long gallery she did not notice the man standing apart from the rest, leaning casually against an over-large statue with a calm but bored expression on his darkly handsome face. But then he saw Clarissa, and for the first time since arriving in London from America two days ago he became alert, amazed at having found so soon what he had crossed the Atlantic for.

He watched her move with a serene grace along the gallery, her figure swaying slightly as she walked, and he stared, suddenly transfixed. She was quite tall and breathtakingly beautiful in a slim, high-waisted dress of shimmering lavender silk, beneath which he could discern all her alluring curves and imagine all the hidden delights of her slender body.

The effect was stunning. She aroused envy in almost every woman present and admiration in the eyes of the men, although none could have said whether it was given to the proud beauty of her face, with her thick pale gold hair coiled expertly about her head, or to the exquisite perfection of her body – or to the lustre of the Milton pearls resting on the creamy swell of her breasts.

Christopher watched her smile and offer words of greeting to people she passed, but her smile was as if pinned to her face and her actions mechanical – a façade. She appeared remote and detached, totally uninterested in everything that was going on around her, which aroused all his curiosity.

Sensing his gaze, Clarissa paused and turned, seeing the stranger immediately and fixing him with a cool, indifferent stare. He was dressed in black with a white cravat and silk stockings. There was no fuss to his dress and yet there was no denying that he had exquisite style. Only once had she seen a man so soberly dressed and that was George Brummell, the good friend of the Prince Regent and also the dictator of men's fashion.

This man possessed a commanding presence and was tall, taller than any man present, and built with all the virility of an ancient Greek athlete, with long limbs and powerful, broad shoulders. His features were dark and handsome, his hair thick and black, taken back from a pronounced peak. His presence formed a stark contrast to all the other gentlemen present who seemed to fade into insignificance beside him. There was an air of complete assurance about him and he seemed curiously out of place among all this gentility, the fine dandies and frills and flounces of Lady Holland's party. He seemed to belong to another world, one where the wind and sun had turned his skin the colour of bronze, one that was wild and exciting and far removed from Holland House.

There was a cool recklessness about his swarthy face, and his stare was bold – as bold as that of someone appraising a horse, she thought indignantly, dragging her eyes from his and turning away immediately, feeling insulted by his look, considering it the height of bad manners for a gentleman – if he could be called that – to stare quite so openly at a lady, and in public too. But for the first time since Edward's death there was a delicate flush mantling her cheeks. It had been a long time since a man had aroused any kind of emotion in her.

Christopher whistled softly under his breath as she turned away. My God, he thought, what a glorious creature she is, and before she had disappeared at the end of the hundred-foot-long gallery he had already made up his mind to make her acquaintance before the night was over.

Clarissa soon found Letty, her real name being Letitia Davenport. They had become firm friends some years ago when they had both attended Lady Margaret's Academy for Young Ladies here in London. Letty had been the one good thing about coming up to London. She was small with an abundance of glossy auburn hair, which her hairdresser had arranged into fashionable Grecian curls. Lively green eyes danced in her small, elfin face with a smattering

of pale gold freckles over her nose. She was generous
and warm-hearted and had been a great comfort when
Edward was killed, but she was also vivacious and a
terrible flirt, constantly surrounded by a lively circle of
friends – especially masculine friends, whom she not
only encouraged but also seemed to thrive on their
attention. Clarissa was glad of her company tonight
and that they were placed near each other at dinner
along with Betsy.

Betsy was a distant cousin of Clarissa's who, after
the death of her parents, had found herself quite
destitute. On hearing of her sad plight and wanting to
help, Clarissa's mother had suggested that she come
and live with them to be Clarissa's companion. Suitably
grateful, Betsy had readily accepted. She was eight
years older than Clarissa and had been with her for five
years now, having become more like an older sister
than a companion.

While they were waiting for the first course Clarissa
glanced up the table, loaded with long-stemmed crystal
glasses and gold and silver plate and wine. Her father
was seated next to the opulent Lady Melbourne, the
two already engaged in lively conversation. Clarissa's
heart sank despairingly, for his wig was already askew
and his over-bloated face flushed crimson from drinking too much wine. She tore her eyes away from them,
praying he wouldn't drink much more, but she knew
this was futile. He would be well and truly drunk when
they left. She became desperately anxious for the night
to end.

Looking in the opposite direction, she noticed the
increasingly popular young poet Lord Byron, his face
pale and surrounded by a riot of chestnut curls, his
whole attitude tonight being one of disdain. She let her
eyes wander to the lady seated beside him, recognising
her immediately as being the outrageous Lady Caroline

Lamb, whose scandalous behaviour and indiscreet affairs had made her the most notorious, talked-about woman in London, to which she didn't object in the slightest – in fact, she adored being the centre of attention, positively thriving on it.

But then Clarissa froze, for sitting right next to her was the stranger she had seen earlier in the gallery, and again he was looking directly at her, the look in his dark eyes unnerving. A crooked smile curved his lips and she noticed his long and slender hands toying with his napkin on the table.

Immediately she dropped her gaze and tried not to look in his direction again. All through the first course of turtle soup she fought to ignore him, uncomfortably conscious of his eyes on her constantly, burning into her flesh, but during the second course of saddle of mutton her curiosity got the better of her and she spoke quietly to Letty.

'Who's that man, Letty? The one at the end of the table – seated next to Lady Caroline Lamb?'

Letty glanced down the table, knowing immediately who she meant. 'Oh – you mean the one who keeps looking at you.' she said quite candidly.

Clarissa nearly choked on a piece of meat at the directness of her reply.

Letty smiled mischievously, her green eyes dancing merrily. 'Come on, love. He hasn't taken his eyes off you all night. And you mean to say you don't know who he is? Why, you must be the only person here who doesn't. That's Christopher Cordell – Lord Buckley's nephew, recently come over from America. He's devilishly attractive, isn't he? And he owns one of those huge plantations in South Carolina and grows cotton.' She leaned closer to Clarissa, whispering confidentially, 'Rumour has it that he's here to look for a wife,' and, looking down the table, she shamelessly flashed him a dazzling smile. 'Isn't he wonderfully virile – despite that polite exterior? I wouldn't mind if he chose me, I can tell you,' she sighed dreamily. 'He's as handsome as Narcissus and, I've heard, as rich as King Midas.'

'And we all know what happened to them,' quipped Clarissa drily. 'Narcissus was so vain that on gazing into a pool he fell hopelessly in love with his own reflection and, being unable to endure to possess and yet not possess himself, he plunged a dagger into his heart. And as for King Midas, his end was little better. After nearly starving to death because everything he touched turned to gold – including his food – and then being given ass's ears, unable to live with the disgrace, he died miserably. No, Letty. I wouldn't liken this Christopher Cordell to either of them.'

'Perhaps not – but you can't blame me for wondering what could happen if he were looking at me instead of you. Oh, Clarissa – don't you ever dream that one day——?'

'No,' cut in Clarissa crossly, her expression hard, suspecting that Letty was about to embark on one of her daydreams about love and romance. 'I don't dream any more, Letty. I stopped dreaming of romance when Edward died. He took my heart with him to the grave and there it will remain.'

Letty's eyes filled with remorse and she silently cursed herself for her careless, thoughtless words – although she had never shared Clarissa's admiration for Edward Montgomery, thinking it wise to keep her opinion of him to herself. Reaching out, she squeezed Clarissa's hand. 'I'm sorry, love – truly. I didn't mean to hurt you. It was unforgivable of me.'

Clarissa sighed and smiled weakly, placing her free hand over Letty's. 'It's all right, Letty. It's not your fault that I'm so edgy tonight, but – well – it's not just thinking of Edward that hurts – it's Father.' She glanced in his direction just in time to see him pour another glass of wine down his throat.

When dinner ended it was with relief that Clarissa saw nothing more of the American, and at two o'clock in the morning she went in search of her father, knowing where he would be and making straight for the gaming-room. She passed a long mirror and caught her reflection, pausing for just a moment to gaze at the shimmering apparition she presented in her lavender dress, enhanced by the candle-light. She looked lovely, she knew, but her beauty gave her no joy. What was the use of it when Edward was not here to see it? The eyes staring out of the glass were the cold blue eyes of a stranger and bore no resemblance to how they had looked all those months ago when they had sparkled and been filled with love, when her tender heart had beat with all the passions of being in love and which held nothing now but emptiness.

She sighed and turned away, moving towards the gaming-room, wondering what was to become of them all because of her father's drinking and gambling, and she was filled with a terrible deep sadness when she remembered how different things had once been. But she was also filled with a new kind of fear that was gnawing away at her inside, fear of the unknown if they were to suddenly find themselves penniless and without a roof over their heads.

While ever there was hope she had refused to see the truth staring her in the face, but now it was no longer possible for her to deny what was happening. In his grief over the death of his eldest son her father had sought solace in drink. He was seldom sober any more, and when he wasn't drinking he was silent and morose. Heaven knew, he had always gambled, but now he did it to excess, especially since coming up to London. It was as if he didn't care any more, as if he wanted rid of Ashton Park and all its memories.

On many occasions he wouldn't come home from Brook's or White's – just two of the gentlemen's clubs he frequented, where women were forbidden – until daybreak. Somehow he would manage to make it up to his room, sodden with drink and often thousands of pounds poorer, where his valet would put him to bed. Clarissa had seen men lose up to twenty thousand pounds in one night at the tables, and often the shake of a dice would decide the fate of some of England's most noble country estates.

She wanted to rage at him when the debts began to mount and when she saw how unkempt he was becoming, with his bloodshot eyes staring out from beneath heavy lids, but nothing she said could penetrate his fuddled mind. He was bringing shame on them all but he couldn't see it, and he could not afford to lose any more money. Already most of the Milton jewels were gone and, fingering the pearls at her throat, she wondered how long it would be before they too met the same fate.

Clarissa refused to sit back and wait for the final insult – for the time when Ashton Park had gone too – and so she squared her shoulders, determined that they would not go under, refusing to let him bring ruin and disgrace upon the family because of his irresponsibility. Ashton Park was Richard's now and it was only right that he should inherit. Besides, he loved the old family home in a way that Simon never had. All his life Richard had lived in the shadow of his older brother, always aware that his father did not possess for him that same fierce pride he did for Simon. He had never made any secret of his preference for his eldest son, who was so much like himself, his life dominated by the pleasure principle, preferring to spend his time in

London, where he could indulge his expensive passion of socialising and gambling, whereas Richard was serious and quiet, like Clarissa and their mother, and was content to remain at Ashton Park.

Whatever sacrifice Clarissa had to make, and if it killed her, she would see to it that Richard got what was his by right, but she was also doing it for herself. The world that she had known and loved had fallen apart. Everything she had cherished had gone except for Ashton Park. She would not lose that too.

She entered the gaming-room, the air thick with tobacco smoke. Glancing quickly about the room, she saw her father seated at one of the card tables, the all too familiar glass of liquor at hand, ready to be refilled by a hovering waiter.

Why does he have to drink so much? she thought angrily. If he has to gamble then why can't he do it with a clear head? At least then he might stand a better chance of winning some of his money back. But she was relieved to see that he was not as drunk as he usually was on these occasions, and with any luck she would get him home without his making too much of a fool of himself.

His fellow players were sprawled around the green baize table, temporarily out of the game, watching with intensity the one that was taking place between her father and his partner. Somehow it came as no surprise to her that that partner should be Christopher Cordell, the American, and she was not in the least surprised either to see that, unlike her father, he had no drink beside him. His presence contrasted sharply with the pink-faced, over-dressed fops and aristocratic land-owners around the table.

As Clarissa came to stand behind Lord Milton she caught all of Christopher's attention. She appeared like a beautiful pale vision, and his breath caught in his throat. Close to she was even more lovely, her skin smooth and flawless with delectable soft lips. Her eyes were as bright as jewels. But there was no inner warmth in them – they were charged with mystery, and this aroused his curiosity about her even further. Her beauty was ice-cold and it seemed that nothing could penetrate that frozen exterior. It was as if she were made of stone. What could have happened to make her like this? But despite her air of aloofness he felt a defencelessness about her, a fragility that disturbed him, and he believed that behind that cold façade there beat the heart of a warm and passionate woman.

Clarissa moved to stand by her father's chair at the same time as the game ended, and she sensed, by the slump of his shoulders and the beads of perspiration on his brow, and also by the subdued murmur of his fellow players and the shake of their heads, that he had lost heavily. Everyone but the American and her father moved away from the table, and before he had the chance to become immersed in another game she placed a hand gently but firmly on his shoulder and spoke softly.

'Come, Father. It's late. I think it's time we left.'

Only then did he become aware of her presence and he scowled up at her, his red eyes full of displeasure and annoyance by her presence here in the gaming-room. Did her meddling know no bounds? Since coming to London she had given him no peace. Should've stayed behind at Ashton Park. Lord knew, he was fond of the girl, but it was high time she was married. Pity about young Montgomery. If he hadn't been killed in Spain they'd be married by now and she'd be off his hands and living in Bedfordshire.

'Go?' he growled, slurring his words. 'I can't leave yet, and the hour is not late. Besides – I must try to win back some of my money.' Time held no meaning when he was absorbed in a game of cards.

'Perhaps tomorrow,' persisted Clarissa, braving his wrath.

'No. And I will not be dictated to by you, Clarissa. Now run along if you must. I'll be home later.'

Obstinately Clarissa stood her ground, and it was the anger he saw spark in her eyes that prompted the American to rise to his feet, realising for the first time that this delightful creature must be the daughter of Harry Milton, the man who had just lost one thousand guineas to him. He cursed himself for allowing himself to be drawn into a game with this man. Had he known from the outset who she was he would have refused, for one thing was certain – the fact that he had taken money off her father would not endear him to her in the least. However, at last he had the opportunity of making her acquaintance and he was determined to make the most of it. When he spoke his words were directed at Lord Milton, but his eyes were fixed firmly on Clarissa.

'Will you not introduce me to your daughter, Lord Milton?'

Harry looked at him, a trifle nonplussed. 'Humph— — Oh – of course – forgive me. This is my daughter, Clarissa. Clarissa – Mr Christopher Cordell, recently come from America. Lord Buckley's nephew.'

Christopher bowed his head slightly but without taking his eyes from hers. 'Your servant, Miss Milton.'

His voice was deep and incredibly seductive, as smooth as silk, and he exuded a potent masculine allure that was almost impossible to ignore, and, however much Clarissa told herself she was immune to it and despite all her efforts, she could not prevent the colour from tinting her cheeks.

Christopher noticed and one corner of his mouth lifted in a little smile, which Clarissa found infuriating.

'I think your daughter is right, Lord Milton. The hour is late and I too must be leaving.'

'Nonsense. There are a good few hours left yet.'

'Not for me, I'm afraid.'

Glancing around the emptying room, Harry reluctantly, and with some difficulty, rose from the table. 'Oh, very well,' he said grumpily, 'but tomorrow night you'll find me at Brook's. Come along, won't you? Give me the opportunity to win back the thousand guineas you've just taken from me.'

Christopher smiled and did not reply immediately. Instead he looked again at Clarissa, who had blanched at the mention of the enormous sum, and anger was sparking from her eyes. He was not in the least discouraged.

'We shall see. Now if you will permit me I will escort you to your carriage.'

Good manners obliged Clarissa to allow him to lead them out of the room but, walking beside him, she struggled with a helpless rage welling up inside her. Rage against him and his cool self-assurance. He had just taken one thousand guineas from her father and yet he behaved as if it were a mere twopence. Before they reached the doorway, where Lady Holland was bidding her guests goodnight and where Betsy was waiting for her, she had already placed him in the category along with all the others to whom her father had lost his money – architects who were responsible for all her wretchedness.

'Ah, Harry,' said Lady Holland, her face flushed with pleasure. 'I see you're leaving and that you've met our American.'

'Yes. Just taken a thousand guineas off me, the young rascal,' and he turned to Christopher before going down the steps. 'Tomorrow night at Brook's, young man. Don't forget. Oh,' he said as an after-thought as he was about to turn away, 'and give my regards to your uncle when you see him, will you?'

'Of course. Goodnight, sir.'

Clarissa would have liked to follow him as he went down the steps accompanied by Betsy, but the tall figure of Christopher Cordell barred her way. She turned to Lady Holland. 'Goodnight, Lady Holland, and thank you for a lovely evening.'

'Lovely?' she said not unkindly, reaching out and touching her arm in an affectionate gesture. 'I think not, Clarissa. At least not for you. I know just how painful these parties are for you – having to watch Harry throw more of his money away while all the time your heart is pining to be back at Ashton Park. Harry has a hopeless passion for gambling,' she said to Christopher, 'and if Clarissa weren't here to keep an eye on him then he'd soon have nothing left. But – anyway,' she said, glancing sharply from one to the other, 'I'm glad you two have met. Might put a sparkle back into her eyes, Christopher. Clarissa has too many worries for one so young. It's not good for her. By the way,' she said, eyeing him quizzically, seeming reluc-tant to let either of them go, 'what are you doing here in London? Aren't we supposed to be at war with America?'

'No – not yet, and let us hope it doesn't come to that. I am here because I have business to attend to.'

'Cotton business, I don't doubt.'

'But of course. What else?'

Lady Holland's eyes twinkled mischievously. 'What else, indeed?' she chuckled meaningfully. 'And you're still not wed?'

He laughed. 'No – I have not put my mind to the matter yet. But I shall.'

'Yes – you should – and soon. If you run true to
form, with your looks, you shouldn't have any difficulty
finding a wife. If my memory serves me correctly,
women never used to be a problem. Rumour has it that
this is the reason why you're here – to look for one.'

'No. That is only one of the reasons.'

Lady Holland gave an exaggerated sigh and looked
at Clarissa. 'If only I were younger, Clarissa, and not
already married to Henry – but you,' she said, smiling,
a mischievous twinkle dancing in her shrewd eyes, 'now
you would make someone like Christopher an excellent
wife.'

'But perhaps Miss Milton does not wish to marry
anyone,' said Christopher, his smile challenging and
his brown eyes darkening so they were almost black,
resting on Clarissa's tight face.

Clarissa had listened to the brief interchange
between them and was neither shocked nor surprised.
She was not at all disconcerted by Lady Holland's
words, whose laughter made light of them. But Clarissa
was no fool and knew what lay behind them, that Lady
Holland thought it high time she stopped thinking of
Edward and what might have been and began looking
to the future. Perhaps she was right. Again she looked
directly at the American, at the merry gleam dancing
in his brown eyes, one of his winged brows arched as
he waited expectantly for her reply. She looked at him
with new interest and found herself remembering
Letty's words and her reference to King Midas, and
wondered if he really was that rich. She told herself to
stop it, not to think like this, but she couldn't help it
and the reply was already on her lips before she realised
what she was saying.

'Sir,' she said coolly, 'I would marry the devil himself
if he would settle the debts on Ashton Park.' She saw
the startled look that appeared on his face, quickly

followed by a thin smile curving his lips, and she caught a glimpse of very white teeth. 'Now, if you will excuse me, I will bid you goodnight,' and without further ado she turned, following her father down the steps to the waiting carriage.

'Well, now,' said Lady Holland, a smile of approval for the way Clarissa had responded to their teasing curving her lips. 'There's a challenge if ever there was. A challenge not to be ignored, I'd say.'

Watching the Milton carriage drive away, Christopher nodded thoughtfully. Her reply had been brief but to the point, and it had certainly given him food for thought. It was as if she had thrown down a gauntlet and he was forced to pick it up.

'You're right, Lady Holland. I have no intention of ignoring it. Ashton Park, I take it, is her family seat?'

'That's correct. In the heart of Kent – although if Harry doesn't watch himself I'm afraid it will have to be sold to cover his debts.'

CHAPTER TWO

IT WAS on the following day that Christopher joined his uncle in the gloomy comfort of his club in St James's Street. They sat surrounded by heavily carved mahogany furniture with dark red upholstery. The atmosphere was heavy, the aroma of tobacco lingering in the air. They were seated in his favourite corner, where he always sat to savour his port and read his newspaper and indulge in conversation with his companions.

Christopher had come to know and be extremely fond of his uncle, his mother's brother, when he had come to London to study law at the Inns of Court several years ago. His hair was fine and white and he was tall and lean, holding himself extremely erect for all his sixty years. His grey eyes were shrewd and steady and had lost none of their youthful sparkle. He gave the impression of superiority with his quick, penetrating mind.

They had discussed at length the growing discord between the United States and Britain, and Christopher was only here now because, for the first time in almost four years, peace, of a sort, had been restored between the two countries, albeit an uneasy one.

Ever since England and France had been at war both countries had been dependent upon the United States and were able to manipulate her trade and use it as a weapon against the other. England had ordered that no neutral ship could trade with France or her allies, and France had issued orders that no neutral ship could

22

trade with England. American ships had tried to break the blockade and, as a result, hundreds were captured. Almost four years ago the then President of the United States, Thomas Jefferson, in his economic thinking, instead of taking sides with one or the other, had chosen to withdraw. After obtaining an embargo from Congress, prohibiting the exportation of any goods whatever from the United States, for a time virtually cutting off all American trade with Europe, he had hoped to starve England into a change of policy. For fifty years Britain had depended upon America to feed and clothe her people, but now, with the European continent closed to her because of the Emperor Napoleon's blockade, the embargo had cut off the supply at the source, and through privation America had hoped to bring her to heel. But the embargo had also struck a deadly blow at America's national industry, prohibiting the departure of any vessel from American ports to any foreign port, especially those dependent on the British market.

During the embargo Christopher had been forced to store his cotton in warehouses and sold as much as he could to merchants in the north, in New England, for whatever they would pay, and, like many more southern planters whose whole existence depended upon the sea as a safe highway for exporting their raw cotton to the hungry mills of England, he had uttered a sigh of relief when it was lifted; taking advantage of this, he had come to England both on business and to see his uncle concerning the death of his mother, for while tempers were still running high among the inhabitants of America against Britain there was no telling how long it would last.

But business was not his only reason for coming to England; there was another, more pressing reason, and Lady Holland had been correct when she had said it

was to look for a wife – although his masculine pride
had prevented him from admitting just how important
it was that he find one – and soon, for since the death
of his mother six months ago Tamasee desperately
needed a mistress and he a wife. Leaving the plantation
in the capable hands of his main overseer, Ralph
Benton, he had booked a passage on a ship bound for
England.

A silence had fallen between Christopher and his
uncle. Lord Buckley observed his nephew fondly,
remembering those few short years during which he
had come to know him, when, as a young man,
Christopher, full of enthusiasm for all life had to offer,
had left his beloved America to take up his studies in
London, secure in the knowledge that Tamasee was
being well taken care of by his father and older brother,
Andrew. Having no immediate family of his own, never
having married, Lord Buckley had been delighted
when Christopher had come to stay with him. His
refreshing, exhilarating company had knocked years
off his age, reminding him so very much of his own
youth, when he too had studied at the Inns of Court.

But then Christopher had been devastated when,
shortly after he had passed the bar, his mother had
written, telling him of the deaths of both his father and
brother in a tragic river-boat accident, and the enormous task of running Tamasee had suddenly been
thrust upon him. Lord Buckley had no doubt that if
this had not happened, being confident and ambitious
for his country, Christopher would have gone far in the
politics of America.

Looking at him now, after ten years, he realised just
how much of a man he had become, no more the young
student all set to put the world and its problems to
rights. His build and his features were those of his
father, but there was that about his bearing which

reminded him so very much of his dear, departed sister, and he wondered, because of the tragic circumstances that had forced him to abandon his dreams of a political future, when he had found out that life was no simple thing, how often he had been obliged to look into himself and realise the bitterness of his situation.

'I have a distinct feeling that there are other things you wish to discuss that have nothing to do with the price of cotton, Christopher.'

Christopher sighed and relaxed into his chair, his long booted legs stretched out in front of him. 'Yes, there is something else I would like to ask you. What can you tell me about Lord Milton's daughter?'

Surprise registered in his uncle's eyes. 'Clarissa?'

He nodded. 'Yes.'

'You've met her, I take it?'

'Yes, last night at Lady Holland's dinner party.'

'Then what do you wish to know?'

'What she's really like.'

'You've seen her. Surely that should speak for itself.'

'I know, and she's a beauty – there's no denying. But – I want to know what she's like beneath that.'

Lord Buckley smiled slowly. 'This is not just a passing interest?'

'No. She impressed me a great deal and I wish to know more about her.'

'Well, I will tell you all I can, and will begin by telling you that she is not like her father – whom I have known personally for a good many years – or her brother, Simon – the one who was killed in Spain. No, she is more like her mother and young Richard. Simon, like his father, was a notorious lover of pleasure. Hated being at Ashton Park – that's their family home in Kent. Beautiful place it is, but he preferred to live here in London. He existed for the army, too. His father didn't want him to go to Spain, being the oldest son and all that, but he was set on it. Unlike them, Clarissa deplores London and likes nothing better than to bury herself in the country with her horses and dogs. She is quite extraordinary, enduringly devoted to those she cares about. A highly intelligent young lady with a certain wilfulness about her – a certain headstrong quality. She was to have married Lord Montgomery's son, Edward. Known each other for years, and devoted to him she was – although I never cared much for him myself. Too much of a gad about town for my liking, like her brother, Simon. He was reported killed at Albuera, along with Simon. It's hit her hard. Some say she'll never get over it.'

So that was it, thought Christopher, understanding at last the reason why Clarissa looked so distant, a mournful solemnity in her lovely eyes. She was suffering from a broken heart. But he had no intention of being deterred by this and believed that time would heal her wounds. She had built up a resistance around her inner core, and he had every intention of breaking it down. However long it took, he believed it would be worth it.

'Nevertheless, Uncle, young Montgomery must have been someone quite exceptional to have inspired such love. One only has to look at her to see her suffering. But what did you mean when you said he was reported killed?'

'His body was never found. So many were killed at Albuera – a blood-bath it was, and eye-witnesses have reported seeing him shot down. His father received a letter from his commanding officer, informing him that Edward had fallen on the field of battle – seen it himself. Unfortunately it could not be ascertained whether or not his body had been buried along with many others who had fallen, nor was his name on the list of prisoners.'

'I see,' said Christopher calmly. 'Then is there any possibility that he might not be dead – that he might have been picked up by peasants or the partisans?'

Lord Buckley nodded. 'There is that possibility, but I doubt it. After Albuera, reports were confused, but I believe something would have been heard before now.'

'Then tell me – why does Clarissa come to London if she dislikes it so much?'

'Because if she didn't keep an eye on Harry and his gambling they'd have nothing left and, if rumour is correct, she has cause to be worried. He loses staggering amounts at the tables nightly. They're heavily in debt. Since the death of her mother two years ago Clarissa has had nothing but heartache, and to add to her worries she now has poverty staring her in the face. But – if my judgement of her is correct – she will fight tooth and nail to keep Ashton Park because if that goes it will break her heart. No – I feel nothing but admiration for the way she has coped with the arduous task of Harry and his gambling. I am sure she'll come through in the end. She is a very resilient young lady.' He paused and studied Christopher's face. 'There is a great deal more to this than just a casual interest in Clarissa Milton, isn't there, Christopher?'

'Yes,' he said, trying to sound casual, but Lord Buckley could tell that she had caught more than his eye.

'And I am correct when I say that you are here to look for a wife?'

'It is one of the reasons. I must admit that since Mother died I do need someone to manage the house and servants. I have my work cut out running the plantation.'

'And what about the young lady whose company you have been keeping for the past two years – the one in

Charleston?' asked his uncle, glancing sideways at him, a meaningful, mischievous look in his half-closed eyes.

Christopher grinned. 'There's not much that escapes you, is there, Uncle?' and into his mind flashed a picture of voluptuous, lovely raven-haired Marie, untamed, like a cat, but possessing all the softness – and the claws. Unlike Clarissa, whose beauty was delicate and passive and so spiritually passionate, Marie's was of the devil's kind, with a strong seductive power, whose every look offered men pleasure. He remembered the warmth and pleasure he derived from her and how she twined her naked body about him – but not his heart. 'Men do not marry women like Marie, Uncle. As a mistress she is perfect, but as my wife – no. She has none of the qualities and virtues I would wish my wife to have, and, anyway, our relationship ended before I left for England.'

'But surely there are countless southern ladies who would meet your requirements and leap at the chance of becoming your wife and mistress of Tamasee? Women who would fit into plantation life perfectly. More so than one from England who will find your way of life strange and different – not to mention that infernal climate of yours she will be forced to endure.'

'Yes,' replied Christopher wryly, 'that's just the trouble. There are too many. Over the months there has been a constant procession of young ladies – empty-headed, most of them – and all have been paraded before me by scheming, ambitious mothers.' He sighed. 'I want none of them, Uncle, and I will not marry just anyone. Tamasee deserves better than that,' he said quietly. 'So – I thought that while I was here I would look for a wife. Don't forget that my father did exactly the same. He came to England and he found an ideal wife.'

'Ah, but if I remember correctly my sister – God rest

her soul – had already caught his eye months before he actually proposed. It was no sudden decision. Theirs was a match made in heaven. Never were two people more ideally suited. It may be a long time before you find anyone quite like your mother, Christopher.'

Christopher shook his head slowly, his voice low and serious when he spoke. 'I'm not looking for a woman like her – but I do believe I have found the one I want. As you know, I am the last of the Cordells and I don't want any ordinary woman to be my wife. You see, she will not only be my wife but also the mother of my children. I want someone who will be able to teach them the finer things of life that I can't teach them. America is still new, still being built and the opportunities greater now than when my great-grandfather, Jonathan Cordell, went out there. I want my sons to have a part in the building of America. Whether they be planters or statesmen, whatever power and influence they may rise to they will choose, but I want to make sure I give them that chance, and to do that I must marry the right woman.'

His uncle nodded, understanding, knowing Christopher well enough to be sure that he must have thought about this seriously, and he certainly approved of his choice. 'Then, if she'll have you, marry her, Christopher. You'll not regret it. She may be nursing the hurt of young Montgomery's death, but she's young, she'll get over it, and if I know anything you're just the man to make her forget. It may cost you a pretty penny, but you can afford it. Yes – it will be a perfect match. Whoever gets Clarissa Milton will be a lucky man.'

From the moment the maid had shown Mr Palmer, the family lawyer, into the drawing-room, where Clarissa received him with her father, an icy hand had gripped her heart, and her feeling of dread deepened as immediately she feared the worst. When he finally went away he left her staring at the closed door in a state of shock. She remembered very little of the conversation but she had retained a confused impression of what Mr Palmer had said. She had a vague recollection that she had deliberately tried to close her mind to what he was saying by pretending that if she didn't hear him then it couldn't be true. It could not be true that he was telling them that the whole estate would have to be sold. Even this fine, fashionable house in St James's Square would have to go. It was the only possible way they could hope to pay off their enormous debts.

Clarissa was aware of a deadening of her senses, and her heart was pounding so hard that she could scarcely breathe. All around them the house was silent. When she looked at her father a bitter taste filled her mouth and she wanted to shout hurtful words at him for bringing them to this, this state of ruin and degredation. But when she saw the look on his face her conscience smote her and the cruel words died on her lips. What could she say, anyway, that would hurt him? He knew only too well what he had done and it was killing him.

Like a sleep-walker, Lord Milton moved towards a chair, supporting himself with trembling hands on the cushioned arms as he slowly lowered himself into it, a stunned, dazed expression on his face. It was as if he had lived through the past few months in a nightmare and had just woken up to reality. He was silent for a long time before he finally spoke, his voice full of anguish and self-castigation, his eyes awash with fear more profound than anything Clarissa had ever known. He stared at his daughter, her eyes enormous in her stricken face.

'Clarissa – oh, Clarissa. What have I done? That I should have brought us to this.'

Slowly he began to shake his head, his shoulders sagging as his head sank on to his chest. Clarissa couldn't move; she could only stand and stare at him as suddenly he seemed to shrink and become old before her eyes, his usually florid complexion the colour of parchment. He was defenceless, a beaten old man. There was a pain somewhere in the region of her heart as slowly she moved towards him, dropping to her knees beside his chair and gripping his arm to try to still the trembling. The emptiness and despair that engulfed him smote her heart and the Milton pride that had always been so much a part of him had gone forever.

'Don't distress yourself, Father. It may not be as bad as Mr Palmer has led us to believe.'

'Nay, Clarissa. Let us not deceive ourselves. 'Tis worse – far worse. I never imagined it was so bad, and I thank God your mother isn't here to see what I've done.' He lifted his head and looked at her, his face marked with sorrow. 'I have no excuse for what I've done. In my blind stupidity I believed I could go on and on – like a fool, thinking nothing meant anything to me any more – but I was wrong. In trying to obliterate the misery Simon's death caused me I have betrayed that which was most dear: my family – you and Richard – and your trust.'

Clarissa's heart went out to him. 'Don't – you mustn't say that. We'll come through, Father, you'll see. There must be somewhere we can get the money to pay off the debts – something to sell. We still have some of the Milton jewels.'

Her father shook his head. 'No – it's gone too far for that, and you and Richard must keep what is left of the jewels now that Simon's gone. He was very dear to me,

Clarissa – you know that – and I mourn him. We were so much alike. When he died I tried so hard to forget, and it was only when I was at the tables and out of my mind with drink that I was able to. I never stopped to think of what I must be doing to you and Richard – how you, too, must be suffering. Especially you, because your loss was double my own. A brother and your betrothed. Ah, Clarissa – what a terrible burden this is to bear.'

'But a burden we can share,' she said, trying to infuse some hope into him – although she had none herself. 'Oh, Father, we'll manage – you'll see. Somehow we'll find a way to come out of this. You've always been so strong——'

He shook his head resignedly. 'No, not any more. My strength went with your mother.'

He fell silent and with a deep sigh got to his feet. Still on her knees, Clarissa watched him move slowly towards the door, where he stopped, and for a moment there was some semblance of the man he had once been as he straightened his back and lifted his head, assuming an air of dignity she had not seen in him since he had played host at Ashton Park when she had been a little girl. He turned back to her, a strange look on his face. For the first time in months his eyes were clear – as if a veil had been lifted from them, but when he spoke his voice seemed far away.

'It's as if I've been dead for a long time and now I am alive, only to see how cruel life can be – because now I know I cannot live with what I have done. Forgive me, Clarissa.'

He turned and went out, leaving Clarissa staring after him with burning eyes, weighted down with despair, wondering at his words and what he had meant. A hard lump had risen in her throat, which she swallowed down angrily. She wouldn't cry – she mustn't. Now was not the time, and, anyway, what good would it do – it would only weaken her and make her feel worse. No, she must accept what Mr Palmer had told them without tears or emotion and do all in her power to find a way of keeping Ashton Park. It was up to her now and she would not recognise defeat. With that she took a deep breath and, getting to her feet, squared her shoulders. She paced the room, desperately trying to sort out in her mind what she could do. There must be someone who would lend them the money. But then, if someone did lend them the money, how could they ever hope to repay it?

In the dim grey light of the drawing-room she paused by the window and gazed out at the spacious simplicity of the square, letting her eyes linger on the bronze statue of King William III astride his horse with the last rays of the afternoon sun glinting on it. Over and over, again and again she asked herself what she could do, where she could turn. What was to become of them and where would they live? Mr Palmer had tactfully suggested that perhaps she and Richard could go and live with their aunt Celia in Buckinghamshire. This suggestion she had fiercely rejected. No – never would they go and live on Aunt Celia's charity, nor that of anyone else in the family, like poor relations. Never. Not while there was breath in her body.

It was then – like a thunderbolt – that she remembered what Letty had told her, and for the first time since that moment when Mr Palmer had told them just how serious their situation was she felt a faint dawning of hope. If what Letty had said was true then she knew only one man in the whole of London who was rich enough to lend them the money – Christopher Cordell.

When she thought of him and their brief meeting at Lady Holland's party she recalled the way he had looked at her, his smouldering brown eyes boldly appraising, and at the memory a strange tingling swept over her and a soft flush tinted her cheeks. Yes – she believed he would lend them the money, but at what price to herself? And then an idea entered her mind which she considered with cold, practical logic. Lady Holland had said he was here to look for a wife, and if that was true and he wanted her then she would marry him. After all, she had nothing to lose but everything to gain. Yes, marriage to the American would benefit them all.

For one brief moment she tried to imagine what it would be like married to a man like Christopher Cordell, what he would expect of her, but when the memory of Edward flashed into her mind and how appalled he would be at a match between herself and this strange, savage American she thrust all intimate thoughts like that away.

But the awful feeling of guilt and betrayal disappeared when she thought in cold desperation that Edward was dead and she must go on, and that if marrying Christopher Cordell would ensure that she could go to bed at night and sleep peacefully without having to worry about money, knowing both Richard and Ashton Park were safe, then she would do it.

But then a sickening chill crept over her as something else occurred to her. Christopher Cordell was no fool, and he would already know what desparate straits they were in. Knowing this, he might not want to marry her, and then what would they do?

It was much later and the many candles in gilt sconces had been lit in the Milton household when the maid knocked on Clarissa's bedroom door and told her that Mr Cordell was downstairs asking to see her. It took Clarissa several moments before she could bring herself to reply and tell her to show him into the drawing-room, that she would be down shortly, but strangely it came as no surprise to her that the American had come. Deep down she had expected him – although perhaps not quite so soon.

Casting all melancholy thoughts aside, she went down the stairs with a firm resolve inside her – to face Christopher Cordell and what he had to offer squarely. Whatever price she had to pay, she would pay it to get the money to secure Ashton Park.

She entered the drawing-room quietly and, although the candles had been lit, the heavy curtains were not yet drawn, and Christopher was staring out at the deserted square, his hands joined loosely behind his back. The soft rustle of her deep pink silk dress betrayed her presence and he turned sharply. For all the room was large and high-ceilinged, his tall, broad-shouldered frame appeared to make it smaller. He was as immaculately dressed as he had been at Lady Holland's party with the exception that his long, muscular legs were now encased in polished black knee-boots. In the candle-light his tanned, strikingly handsome face had taken on a curiously softer look than she remembered of the night before. But despite this and his polite, correct manner Clarissa sensed something purposeful and intent about him which troubled her and made her feel uneasy.

As she glided almost soundlessly over the thick-piled carpet towards him, slender and long-limbed, Christopher was enchanted by her and gave a slight bow, his brown eyes making an instant appraisal. His breath caught sharply in his throat. Never had he seen a woman with so much beauty – an ethereal beauty – and it was as if he were seeing it for the first time in his life. She was different from any other woman he had ever known and he could not take his eyes off her, but today the smooth skin of her face was marred by mauve shadows circling her eyes, which, he suspected, were the result of worry and a sleepless night.

But one thing had not changed about her and at this he felt a pang of dismay: there was still no warmth in those glorious blue eyes, which stared out of her pale face with a solemnity that touched him. But instinctively he knew that no matter how sad she was her sorrow only enhanced her magical power, and that if he was not careful it would enslave him forever.

When she was close there came to him the faint, heady scent of crushed rose petals, a scent he would forever more associate with her. They looked at each other steadily for a long moment before Clarissa spoke, seeming ill at ease, and Christopher had an animal instinct for sensing that all was far from well with her. Seeing her again, he knew last night had been no illusion. He wanted her more than he had ever wanted any other woman and he meant to have her, but more important was the fact that he wanted her to want him, and if he hoped to win her affections then he was going to have to hold his emotions under restraint – which would be no simple matter.

'Why, Mr Cordell – this is a surprise,' said Clarissa with a cool composure she was far from feeling. 'If you wish to see my father I'm afraid he is indisposed.'

'It isn't your father I've come to see,' he said in his deep, lazy voice. 'It's you.'

'Oh?'

'Yes, and I wouldn't have blamed you in the slightest if you had refused to see me.'

'Why should I do that?' she enquired, remembering their conversation of the previous evening and hoping he was too much of a gentleman to mention it, but she need not have worried.

'A matter of a thousand guineas,' he replied, having no intention of making any reference to her parting words regarding Ashton Park. Perhaps later, when they knew each other better and he had gained her confidence.

'That is between you and my father. It is not my concern,' she said firmly, conveying by the tone of her voice and the look in her eyes that she did not wish to discuss the matter further.

Christopher understood and was full of admiration for her steadfast loyalty to the man who had brought her to near ruin. But he was her father, and whatever he was guilty of she would cloak his sins and utter no words that would dishonour him in any way.

'Nevertheless, please believe me when I say that I regret the circumstances of our meeting and it would give me great pleasure if you would permit me to make amends.' He would have liked to offer to return the thousand guineas but he knew she would be offended by the gesture and too proud to accept it and, besides, their debts were too numerous now for it to make any difference. 'Tell me – have you eaten?'

'No,' she said, slightly nonplussed.

'Then if your father is indisposed perhaps you would consider having supper with me.'

Clarissa stared at him in amazement. What he had suggested was quite unexpected. Supper? Never had she been out to supper with a gentleman alone in her life before – not even Edward. Thoughts of Edward stirred powerful, painful memories and emotions, emotions she would rather have left in the past – especially now while in the presence of this American, who she hoped would provide the solution to all her worries and when it was imperative that she keep all her wits about her.

'Why, Mr Cordell – I hardly think I know you well enough for that.'

At her reaction he smiled, a long, slow smile, not in

the least discouraged. 'Then I think we should remedy that, and why don't we start by you calling me Christopher? No doubt you consider what I have suggested highly improper. I merely came to apologise for last night, but now I'm here I can think of nothing that would give me greater pleasure than for you to accept my invitation – and, besides, I do so hate dining alone.'

A serious note had entered his voice and he wasn't smiling any more as his eyes held hers. Startled by his frankness, curiously Clarissa felt her nervousness subsiding, and she wasn't at all displeased by his suggestion that they have supper together. And why should she be? she thought wryly. Wasn't this just what she wanted – an opportunity for them to get to know each other better? But it was out of the question. It would be highly improper for her to have supper alone with him.

'Won't you agree to have supper with me – or is it that you have a prior engagement?'

'Oh, no – it isn't that, only. . .' she faltered, unable to go on. Last night in the midst of Lady Holland's guests she had felt protected and full of a cool self-assurance, but here, in the intimate privacy of the drawing-room, where the only sounds to be heard were the clatter of carriage wheels out in the square and the somnolent tick of the clock on the mantelpiece, she was uncomfortably conscious of the overwhelming presence of this man who had come so suddenly into her life and at a time when she was lonely and so very vulnerable, when her spirits had sunk to such a low ebb that it would be so easy for her to turn to anyone who offered comfort.

At her hesitation he laughed, a soft, velvety sound. 'You're not afraid of having supper alone with me, are you?' he asked, his eyes and voice challenging.

Clarissa looked at him steadily for a long moment, at his darkly handsome face, conscious of the fact that if she did indeed agree to have supper with him then there would be no going back. Fate was moving quicker than she had anticipated. 'No, I'm not afraid of you,' she said steadily.

'Then perhaps you hesitate because it is not the way it's done over here. Is that it?'

She sighed, her manner relaxing, and the ghost of a smile hovered on her lips. 'Yes.'

He grinned broadly with mischievous delight. 'I'm an American, Clarissa, and we do things differently over there. We do not stand on ceremony like you English. Now – I have a carriage waiting outside and I know a very select little eating house not far from here where the food is exquisite.'

Looking deep into his eyes, she saw he was sincere and, unable to resist his charm, she melted just a little and her smile widened, revealing her small white teeth.

'You know,' said Christopher, frowning, a serious note entering his voice, 'you really should smile more often.'

She flushed, lowering her eyes beneath his intense gaze. 'I've had very little to smile about of late.'

'Then all the more reason why you should have supper with me,' he said softly.

'You are extremely persuasive, sir. But – you were right. It would be highly improper for me to dine alone with you, so instead will you join my companion, Betsy, and me for supper here? We shall be dining shortly and you are most welcome.'

Disappointment flickered in Christopher's eyes and he frowned at the thought of her companion being present at what he had hoped would be a private, intimate supper for two, but, determined to retain her company a little longer, he smiled. 'Thank you. It will be a pleasure.' His eyes darkened and he looked at her intently. 'Tomorrow I leave for Portsmouth, Clarissa. I'm not sure how long I shall be away but it was very important to me that I saw you before I left. I'm glad you didn't deny me that. Please forgive my haste but no power on earth would have prevented me from seeing you today.'

There was a moment of silence between them, the implication of his words all too clear. Clarissa lowered her eyes as she was seized by panic and also an indescribable fear that the situation developing between them, between herself and this man whose existence she had not been aware of until yesterday, was becoming all too real.

Noticing the confusion his words had caused her, Christopher laughed softly, wanting so much to put her at ease, but before he could say anything further the door opened and Betsy came in to tell them supper was ready.

CHAPTER THREE

THE dining-room at the Milton house in St James's Square glittered with light from a single crystal chandelier, the hundreds of tiny prisms shimmering, catching and holding the light from the many candles. Clarissa, Betsy and Christopher were seated at a table in the centre of which was a china bowl full of pink roses, each one soft and velvety and perfect, giving off the most gentle, heavenly perfume. Christopher was both polite and attentive throughout the meal, keeping the conversation impersonal. The more Clarissa relaxed, the more she looked at him, letting her gaze linger, which did not go unnoticed by Betsy, who was full of curiosity about Christopher Cordell. It was a long time since a gentleman had come calling on Clarissa – too long, she thought – and never one quite so handsome. No – not even Edward Montgomery.

Clarissa was beginning to feel all the power of Christopher's gaze and, although she had sworn never to become romantically involved with any man again, the memory of Edward still too painful, she was not immune to his dazzling good looks. But she did ask herself if she would have been quite so eager to invite him to supper if it were not for his wealth.

After the meal Betsy tactfully took up her sewing close to a lamp away from them, hoping that this would be the first of many visits from this handsome American who was obviously attracted by Clarissa, who hadn't looked so happy or relaxed for a long time.

Clarissa relaxed for the first time in weeks as she seated herself opposite Christopher by the fire. Worry

41

and nervousness were forgotten as she slowly stirred her coffee. Christopher watched her, a half-smile curving his firm lips as he swirled his brandy around the bowl of his glass. Clarissa asked him about his visit to Portsmouth, curious to know more about him.

'I'm going to stay with a friend of mine and his family. He is someone I was at law school with, here in London. Many years ago now, it seems.'

'You are a lawyer?' asked Clarissa, unable to keep the surprise out of her voice.

He smiled grimly. 'Yes. It was what I always intended to be and maybe, later, to go into politics – but life is under no obligation to give us the things we want.'

She looked at him curiously. 'What happened?'

'My father and older brother were killed in a riverboat accident,' he said quietly. 'That was when I suddenly found myself the owner of a plantation with no time for such things as law and politics.'

'Oh – I'm so sorry,' she said softly. 'How awful it must have been for you.'

'Yes – at the time. You see, before they died, Tamasee – that's the name of my home – didn't need me. With father and Andrew to run things, I was free to come to England to study law, but I was impatient for the years to come when I would be able to immerse myself in the politics of America.' He sighed deeply, and Clarissa could detect a faint hint of bitterness in his tone. 'But – it was not to be. At first I did think of selling Tamasee and going to live in New England, but Mother didn't want me to. She couldn't bear the thought of selling – and so I had no choice but to accept with as good grace as possible to be a planter.'

'Was that very difficult?'

'It was. I had no more brothers or sisters. There was only me – and Mother, of course, but she died some months back.' He sighed, taking a sip of his brandy, and, sitting back in his chair, crossed one booted leg over the other before going on. 'At first I was haunted by those days when I was here in London, but then, as the years progressed and because I wanted so much to do well – to make my father, had he lived, proud of me – I became determined to put those early years behind me – not to look back, because,' he said, suddenly seeming to look at something beyond Clarissa and speaking softly, almost to himself, 'if you do it drags you down so that you're incapable of picking yourself up.' He smiled ruefully. 'Since then I have lived and breathed cotton and become thankful for what I have. Nothing else has mattered – until now.'

He stopped speaking and they looked for a long, quiet moment into each other's eyes, and something of his mood conveyed itself to Clarissa, but the implication of his words again caused her to lower her eyes.

'H-have you ever been to Portsmouth before?' she asked, quickly changing the subject.

'No. I'm looking forward to seeing my friend and his family, but I had hoped to go north, to take a look at your cotton factories. However, I regret I do not have the time.'

'Oh – you surprise me. I admit that I know very little about the textile industry, but I thought we kept our machines and what goes on in our factories a jealously guarded secret,' she smiled.

'That might have been so ten years ago, but not any more. Your Parliament could not hope to keep the plans for the machines invented over here a secret forever. Wanting to keep the advantage over other manufacturing countries, they may have refused to export the machines or the plans of them, but people crossed the Atlantic, Clarissa, with plans and ideas carried in their heads, and as a result we now have our own mills in the northern states.'

'Why not in the south? Would it not be to your advantage to have them where the cotton is grown?'

'Yes, I agree it would, but there are many in the south who do not want change or industrialisation. Besides, all our time is turned to the raising of raw cotton.'

'Don't you grow anything else but cotton?'

'Yes, tobacco, and grain for our own use. We also leave some land fallow, rotating the crops every year, otherwise the land will become exhausted. But the main crop is cotton. There is an ever-increasing need for it because it's so cheap and easy for us in the south to grow. The climate and conditions are perfect. Believe me, Clarissa, raising cotton is the most profitable business in America, and this is only the beginning.'

Later, when it was time for Christopher to leave, Clarissa walked with him through the hall and out on to the top of the steps, noticing a carriage waiting below. A haze of moonlight filled the square and, looking up, she studied his face in the silver light, deeply touched by what he had told her of his life in America. How dreadful it must have been for him to have to abandon his life's dreams and ambitions in such tragic circumstances, and she wondered if, regardless of his firm resolution to become a planter, he still clung to those dreams, and she was saddened, but understood all the disappointment and bitterness he must have felt.

He looked down at her upturned face, as pale as the moonlight that washed over her. 'Thank you for supper, Clarissa. You were a wonderful hostess.'

'I'm glad you were able to stay.'

'I think I was the most fortunate man in London tonight,' he said softly.

At his words she smiled but said nothing.

'I must go.'

'What time do you have to leave for Portsmouth?'

'I have to be away early.'

'I hope you have a good journey.'

'When I return to London, Clarissa, will you permit me to call on you?'

'Of course,' she said without hesitation, feeling a sharp pang of dismay that he was leaving so soon, and this puzzled her. 'How long do you think you'll be gone?'

'I don't know. That depends upon a number of things,' he said meaningfully. He saw the questioning look in her eyes and he had an impulse to reach out and touch her, to caress the softness of her lips with his own, and he thought with yearning of the time when they would know each other better. To divert his thoughts from what was at the moment an impossible dream, he took her hand in his own and raised it to his lips, placing them gently on her cool fingers, but his eyes remained fixed on hers, a warm glow in their depths.

Clarissa trembled slightly at the feel of his lips on her fingers, and she experienced strange sensations and emotions and was sorry when he released her hand and stepped back, his voice low and husky when he spoke.

'Goodnight, Clarissa,' and then he turned sharply and went down the steps. He turned and looked at her just once more before climbing into the carriage and disappearing into the night.

Clarissa was only faintly aware of Betsy as she moved, as if in a trance, back into the hall, so preoccupied was she with her thoughts and the strange evening.

Betsy smiled at Clarissa's entranced state and moved

to close the door, which she had absent-mindedly left open. 'What a nice gentleman,' she said.

Clarissa looked at her and frowned, considering the word. 'Nice? No. Nice is not a word I would apply to Mr Cordell. Perhaps to someone like Richard or Mother, but no – certainly not to the American.' Smiling, she turned to go up the stairs, only to be jolted back to reality when told by a maid that her father had left the house while they were having dinner. He had gone to his club.

She went to bed with a heavy heart, unable to sleep, troubled about her father and the day's events – but also about Christopher Cordell, and when she thought of him it was such a host of contradictory feelings that she was quite lost.

It was in the cold grey light of dawn that her father's valet came to fetch her to her father's room, and it was with heavy, mechanical footsteps that Clarissa walked along the landing. The door was open and she went inside. It was totally quiet, the smell of death filling the room. Her eyes were drawn to and focused on the limp form of her father strewn grotesquely across the bedclothes. She stared as one hypnotised. His face was a mask of blood, his head lying in a sticky pool, showing rusty brown against the stark white of the bedclothes. His pistol was still in his hand. Slowly Clarissa crumpled to her knees, her hand rising to her lips to stifle the scream that rose in her throat. Now she knew what he had meant yesterday. Oh – she should have known. Unable to live with what he had done, her father had shot himself.

It was late when Christopher passed beneath the broken sign of the unwelcoming-looking inn outside Winchester and went inside. The taproom was small and low-ceilinged, and if the hour had not been late he would have travelled on to look for another. It took a while for his eyes to adjust to the dim light from a couple of oil lights hung from the ceiling. He was met by the nauseating reek of tobacco smoke and alcohol combined with the unappetising odour of cooked food. A fire struggled to survive in the hearth, black with soot, and the scrubbed wooden tables, their greasy surfaces slopped with pools of ale, were occupied by what he would only describe as a drunken rabble and two soldiers in a similar state, in uniforms of scarlet coats and tight white breeches, having seen much service, creased and unwashed, obviously on their way home from the Peninsular War, their cocked hats and sabres on the bench beside them.

Christopher sat down at a table near the wide chimney piece and a young serving maid came to him. She was small, lacking the lusty sensuality of the other serving girls. He saw that she had caught the eye of one of the soldiers, who reached out to try to touch her as she moved past his table. His advances were unwelcome, and swiftly she darted away; as Christopher ordered food and a room for the night her pretty young face beneath the starched white cap was scarlet with embarrassment and shame, and her large, liquid brown eyes held the same kind of fear he had seen in those of a frightened young doe facing death.

After he had eaten he settled into the corner of his seat, slowly savouring his brandy, shutting out the coarse drunken singing and shouting, his thoughts turning to Clarissa – in fact, he had thought of little else since leaving London, and how bewitchingly lovely she had looked when he had left her on the steps of Milton House. She had become an enigma to him and he had no intention of remaining for the four weeks in

Portsmouth as he had originally intended, however disappointed David might be.

His attention was again drawn to the young serving girl, still trying to avoid the clawing hands of the soldier who had been making a play for her all night, his face flushed with drink, his scarlet tunic stained with it. Christopher studied him. He had the superior attitude and the trimmings and facings on his uniform of a young officer. He recognised that he belonged to the privileged class, to that arrogant breed of English aristocracy, the type who wasted both time and money, his life, more than likely, given over to the pleasures of women and gaming – the type he despised.

His thick pale blond hair fell in a heavy wave over his boyishly handsome face and his eyes were grey with heavy lids, giving him a lazy, insolent look. His fleshy pink lips were parted as he leered and groped for the serving girl.

At first Christopher watched with amusement as the young girl eluded his clawing hands as best she could, but gradually he became irritated and then angry by the distress the soldier's persistence was causing her. Suddenly, with a yell of triumph, and much to the glee of everyone present, the soldier at last succeeded in pulling the girl on to his knee and thrusting his hand down the front of her low-necked dress, his hand gripping her firm young breast, but with a wordless cry and unusual strength for one so young the girl pushed his hands away and scrambled from his knees; reaching out, she grasped his tankard full of frothing ale and flung it in his face before turning and fleeing from the inn.

At this, silence fell and all eyes became fixed on the young soldier. His manner changed immediately and his eyes became splintered with ice. It was clear to Christopher that here was a young man who was not used to being rejected or bested by someone he would consider his inferior.

The whole place suddenly erupted in a volley of shouts and coarse jokes as the soldier rose, his hair dripping with ale, which he made no attempt to wipe away. His voice, full of a desperate violence, thundered above the din.

'I'll wager any man here that she's a virgin, and I'll tell you now that I intend to find out.'

At this a roar of approval went up, and the soldier staggered drunkenly towards the door, dragging one of his legs, which indicated that he'd been wounded in the war with France.

Christopher watched and listened, suddenly remembering the fearful look he had seen in the eyes of the girl, thinking she couldn't be more than fifteen years old at the most, and, as he was all too aware of the soldier's evil intent, it wasn't long before he followed him outside.

The night was dark and cold when he stepped into the yard but he paid no heed to it, hearing the strangled cry of the girl pierce the air, cut off as a hand was clapped over her mouth. He turned towards the sound and quickly went across towards the stables, where a light spilled out from the open doorway, pointing on the ground like a long orange finger.

The soldier had seized the terrified girl and dragged her inside, where he had brutally flung her to the ground, pushing her back on to a pile of straw, crashing down on top of her and pinning her beneath him, ripping the thin fabric of her dress from neck to waist, exposing her small, immature breasts. Though she screamed and managed to struggle frantically against him as if her very life depended on it, it was no use. She was no match for his brute strength, his muscles honed to perfection on the battlefields of Spain.

At first her resistance surprised him, but then it excited him and he laughed, a low, merciless sound. 'Fight me all you like, my little beauty. I like a girl with spirit – but I'll have you in the end,' and, gripping her chin with fingers like steel, he pressed his lips on to hers.

Struggle as she might, she was forced to submit to his loathsome kiss while his hand fumbled greedily under her skirts, exposing the soft flesh of her white legs. Her last reserves of strength were almost exhausted when Christopher's tall shadow fell across them from where he stood in the doorway.

In surprise the soldier paused for a moment and turned, favouring him with a mocking grin, a glazed expression in his eyes. 'Come to watch the sport, have you? Well, you can have her when I'm done.'

'Enough,' said Christopher with an ominous coolness, noticing the mute appeal in the girl's terrified eyes. Something in his tone made the solider turn again and look at him.

'Indeed, it is not,' he growled. 'Enough, you say – for what reason? Perhaps it is that you want this baggage now – for yourself. Well, I will tell you this – I do not care for anyone to interrupt me in my pleasures. So – whoever you are – be gone. Find your own amusement – or wait till I'm done.'

Undeterred, Christopher stepped closer, glowering down at him. 'Then allow me to present myself – Christopher Cordell, at your service, and I told you to release the young lady. She has made it quite plain that your over-amorous advances are not welcome.'

Recognising his soft southern-American accent and that each word was enunciated slowly and carefully, the soldier staggered to his feet, his clothes dishevelled and his expression deadly. He stood and faced Christopher, several inches taller than himself, who was making a visible effort to control his anger, a faint, scornful smile on his lips that only added to the soldier's rage.

'This is not your affair and I resent your interference.'

'Really?' he mocked. 'But you are bothering the young lady and I am making it my affair.'

'Young lady?' sneered the soldier. 'She is nothing but a common trull.'

There was a faint, animal-like whimper from the straw as the girl, as pale as death and shaking from head to foot, struggled to get up, modesty causing her to pull her torn skirts over her naked flesh with trembling fingers. The soldier turned as if to go back to her.

'Touch her again and I'll break your neck,' drawled Christopher.

The threatening quality in his voice caused the soldier to look at him again, anger blazing from his eyes, and suddenly, unable to restrain himself, he sprang at Christopher with clenched fists; perhaps, if his brain had not been fogged with drink, he might not have missed his target, but, as he raised them to strike, Christopher deftly side-stepped and struck out, hitting the soldier on the side of the face. His eyes rolled in his head and he staggered and fell to the ground, his face bleeding from a cut caused by the blow. All vestige of pride was stripped from the soldier, who was enraged to find himself so humiliated by the American. His body shook with the intensity of his anger and sheer hatred blazed from his eyes.

'Get out,' said Christopher, his voice like steel.

The soldier struggled to his feet and in the doorway he turned. 'If ever I have the misfortune to meet you again I'll make you pay for that. I'll get even – I swear it.'

'Oh, I doubt our paths will cross again, but perhaps you'll think twice the next time you're intent on raping anyone.'

Muttering curses beneath his breath, the soldier turned and stumbled out into the night, dragging his injured leg behind him.

When he'd gone Christopher sighed and, reaching out, put his arm about the girl's shaking shoulders. 'Are you all right?'

She nodded, smiling at him gratefully, too shocked to speak. A woman suddenly appeared by her side.

'Oh, Sal——' and, taking in her torn clothes, she looked at Christopher in alarm. 'Is she all right?'

He nodded. 'Yes. I came in time.'

She sighed with relief. 'Thank the Lord. Come on, love – I'll take you home.' She looked up at Christopher. 'She came instead of her sister tonight. She's ill, you see, and they need the money bad.'

Christopher nodded, understanding. 'Tell me – how old is she?'

'Thirteen.'

He looked at her, horrified. 'Then this is no place for her. Take her home, and here,' he said, pressing some coins into her hand. 'This should more than cover her night's work. Make sure she doesn't come back.'

The following morning Christopher continued his journey to Portsmouth, but no sooner had he arrived than he heard of the death of Lord Milton. He returned to London immediately.

For Clarissa the days following her father's death passed like a nightmare. There was a dull lethargy about her so that for a time, after the dreadful shock, she couldn't think clearly, her mind was numb, but she knew that later, as the numbness wore off and her nerves struggled to make themselves felt, there would come the sharp, searing pain of reality.

The fact that she would have to travel to Ashton Park and break the news to Richard about their father and tell him that the house would have to be sold was tearing her apart. How could either of them bear to lose it? But there was nothing else for it. Ashton Park would have to go. At last she had to admit defeat, to bow to the inevitable. She had pinned her one hope on Christopher Cordell, that, given time, he would offer her marriage, but now that was not to be. He had left London and would not be back in time to be of any help.

With Betsy's help she somehow managed to function, to do all the things she should, even arranging for her father's body to be taken back to Ashton Park, where it would be laid beside her mother in the village church at Ashton, but it was as if it were happening to someone else. No one came to offer their condolences. It was as if she had suddenly become shipwrecked upon some desert island as the outside world retained an embarrassed silence over her father's death. The only person she saw, apart from Mr Palmer, was Letty, and she thanked God for that. Without her support and Betsy's she couldn't have carried on.

CHAPTER FOUR

IT WAS the following evening, after a journey that had seemed endless to Clarissa, that the carriage passed through the huge iron gates of Ashton Park with their heraldic bearings, indicating that they were entering the grounds of a noble family.

She walked wearily into the house, into the lofty hall with its fine, gracefully arched timber roof, where servants were rushing about in haste because of her unexpected arrival. Thankfully she sank into a chair beside the hearth, where a welcoming fire blazed.

She was cold, but only now did she realise it and, taking comfort from the fire's warmth, she gazed into the hot coals while she waited for Richard, feeling the heat seep through her veins and the great house wrapping itself about her, acting like a balm, soothing her troubled heart.

As quickly as she could she told Richard why she had come home, regardless of the pain it caused her to do so, knowing she was about to bring his whole world tumbling down. She told him about their father's gambling and his enormous debts and about the way he had killed himself. For a while Richard was at a loss for words. Horror flared in his eyes over the manner of his father's death, but as the full meaning of her words sank in he looked pale and shaken, his whole attitude being one of despair.

'Dear God,' he said weakly, staring into Clarissa's eyes. 'I didn't know. I had no idea things were as bad as that. Why didn't you tell me?'

'I was going to – if and when I could get him to come home.'

'Is there nothing we can do? What about his holdings in the tin and coal mines and all the others?'

Clarissa shook her head resignedly. 'No. They're all gone.'

A deathly pallor spread over Richard's face as the implication of her words sank in. 'All?'

She nodded. 'We have nothing left, Richard. After we have sold the house in London and the rest of Father's properties – including Ashton Park – and paid off the creditors we may just have enough left to buy somewhere small to live and enough to live on until we can find work.'

'How long have we got?'

'Not long. Some of the creditors have agreed to wait, but they won't wait forever.'

He stared at her in disbelief. 'It's as bad as that?'

'Yes. The only alternative is that we go and live in Buckinghamshire with Aunt Celia.'

Angry emotion flared in Richard's eyes. 'Never – never that. I will not accept her charity.'

He was not ignorant of his father's passion for gambling and his presence at the endless gaming parties, where huge fortunes changed hands and where many were lost, but it had never occurred to him that his own father would indulge in such follies – to sink so low as to allow himself to lose all he owned and then shoot himself. His hurt tone when he spoke tore at Clarissa's heart.

'How could he do it, Clarissa?' he cried with a forlorn desperation in his voice. 'How can anyone lose so much at the tables?'

'Father could have told you,' she said bitterly.

'But to throw away everything like that. I always knew I could never mean the same to him as Simon –

but to do this. In the name of God, Clarissa – how could he do it? He has destroyed us both with his drunkenness and gambling – his weakness and stupidity.' His eyes were suddenly blinded by a scalding rush of angry tears. 'Well – I'll be damned and in hell itself before I see Ashton Park sold to someone else. The Miltons have lived here for generations. They have been the only family to live here.'

Clarissa rose from her seat and went to him, placing her hand tenderly on his arm. 'I know, but there is nothing else we can do,' she said gently. 'I have been over it all with Mr Palmer. He will be coming down to see us after – after the funeral, to tell us what has to be done. There is no other way we can pay off the debts – believe me, Richard.'

He turned and looked at her, a mixture of anger and grief filling his eyes, but his voice held a kind of bitterness she had not heard from him before; bitterness over the fact that he had been cheated out of what was his by right now that Simon was gone. 'Oh, I do – I believe you, Clarissa, and you are right. In the end Ashton Park – our home – will have to go unless I can find some way of raising the money, which is damn near impossible. But then,' he said, his lips twisting scornfully, 'I suppose I could look for a rich wife – an heiress. But no doubt it would have to be someone old and ugly, who has been passed over, to even consider taking me on with such enormous debts.'

'Don't. Please don't,' whispered Clarissa. His suffering was almost too much for her to bear. 'What – what about Laura? Tell me about her.'

At the mention of Laura's name his expression suddenly softened, and he sighed, running his shaking fingers through his untidy hair. 'Laura, poor love, has no means. I'm afraid she's as poor as a church mouse.

Her father is our new minister at Ashton. No doubt you will meet him shortly.'

'But you love her – don't you, Richard?'

'Yes – yes, I do. Very much.'

Clarissa sighed and looked back into the flames, feeling the heat on her face and all the sadness of her own lost love. 'Then be content with that and marry her. You know – I did consider marrying someone myself. Someone who is immensely rich – an American, who is over here looking for a wife.'

Richard gave her a puzzled look. 'But I thought – you – you said when Edward died that you'd never marry.'

'I know. I said a lot of things when he was killed and I meant every word I said – then. But now I have the future to think about and, like you, I cannot think of a future without Ashton Park.'

'What happened to your American? Where is he now?'

'In Portsmouth,' she said quietly. 'He will have no idea about all this – not that it would make any difference if he did. You see, we had only just met and didn't have the chance to become well acquainted, but for a time all my hopes for the future were in him. However distasteful the prospect, Richard, I thought that, if I must marry, if it's not for love then it must be to someone I could respect. But the most important thing of all was that he must be rich. Christopher Cordell was all that, but he won't be returning to London for quite some time. I fear it will be too late for him to help us.'

Richard didn't ask her any more questions about the American, but he was sure he detected a note of regret in her voice.

* * *

Harry Milton's body was brought from London, and it was with a leaden heart that Clarissa saw him placed beside her mother and other ancestors in the family vault in Ashton church, feeling that already a part of her life was receding into the past as his body was sealed in the darkness of the tomb.

Afterwards she remembered little of the service conducted by the new minister, the Reverend Mr Greenwood. The little church had been filled with their tenants, although they had not come to pay their respects to a Lord they scarcely knew, who had spent most of his time away in London, but to his son, who they considered was the mainspring at Ashton Park, who was the embodiment of all the qualities of a young gentleman, who, regardless of an extremely efficient bailiff, shouldered most of the responsibilities of the estate, making their troubles his own, the welfare of the workers and tenants being important to him. They all held him in the highest esteem, but none could know that the suffering and anguish etched in deep lines on his young face were not those of grief over the death of his father but over the inevitable loss of Ashton Park – which was like a death in itself.

It was over a week later, and Mr Palmer had just left Ashton Park to return to London, where he would begin selling off what was left of Lord Milton's property.

Driven by a compelling need to be by herself, Clarissa quickly changed into her riding habit and, after saddling her horse, Melody, was soon riding through the park. As she dug in her heels her horse bounded forward, and she galloped hard, trying to ease the misery and hurt that filled her, that was real and definite, echoing with the thunder of her horse's hoofs in her ears as it pounded over the turf.

It was late afternoon and already the last of the sun

had gone, and a band of darkness spanned the horizon. The wind had risen and overhead were swirling black clouds, which had been gathering all that day, and at last it began to rain, sharp and cold, stinging her cheeks already awash with her tears. Her hair became undone from its pins and began to blow about her face. She rode with reckless abandon over the springy wet turf, unable to determine in which direction she rode, so intolerable were her thoughts. The harder she rode, the more the wind screamed past her ears, and in her desperate need to escape her tortured mind she became forgetful of time and stopped thinking altogether.

This was how Christopher found her, seeing her through a dark veil of rain, her horse galloping at full stretch.

Clarissa was first aware of his presence when she heard the distant sound of his horse's hoofs galloping behind her. She pulled her horse to a halt and turned, listening to the rhythmic drumming coming closer, sounding louder, and then, in a moment, her sharp eyes saw the dark, ghostly shape of a rider looming, enormous, out of the rain, shrouded in a black cape with the stiff collar turned up and his hat pulled down so that his face was in shadow. She strained her eyes to see who it could be but he was too far away for her to see his features. Suddenly her attention became riveted on him and for a moment she thought she must be seeing things, brought on by some kind of a delusion, recognising the strong set of his broad shoulders and, as he came closer, the dark bronzed features of his face.

Quite inexplicably her heart gave a joyful leap when she saw it was indeed the American – Christopher Cordell – and for a brief moment all her terrors were forgotten. He drew rein beside her and she stared at him, at a complete loss for words. He pulled his hat back from his face and she looked into those dark brown eyes.

He smiled, his lips curving in a crooked smile as he took in her appearance. Her wet hair was drawn with a severity from her face, which only served to heighten her beauty, drawing attention to the fine lines of her cheekbones, the brilliance of her eyes and the proud curve of her lips. She sat straight and slim in the saddle. Her severely cut habit was soaked, her small waist and the round swell of her hips emphasising her femininity far more than all her dresses of satin and lace.

'Hello, Clarissa.'

'You – you must forgive me,' she stammered. 'I did not expect you. How did you know where to find me?'

'Your brother told me.' He had to shout to make himself heard over the noise of the wind. 'I want to talk to you. Isn't there somewhere we can go out of this infernal rain?'

She turned and pointed towards the dome of a summer-house which rose above the trees, one of several that dotted the park. 'Over there.'

Together they rode quickly towards the small round building, its walls bare but for the dust and festoons of spiders' webs that hung from the roof. It was not the most welcoming of places, being cold and damp, with the smell of decay from the sodden undergrowth, but at least it was a shelter from the rain. Clarissa shuddered, feeling a trickle of icy water run beneath her collar and down her back, and, clasping her arms about her, she was suddenly conscious of the extreme cold caused by her wet clothes.

To Christopher she seemed drained of all her strength and, touched by her sorry state, he immediately removed his cape and wrapped it about her, his hands oddly gentle as they rested on her shoulders. She began to relax, feeling its comforting warmth, and stood facing him, her eyes captured and held by his. He looked at her long and hard, catching a glimpse of her almost desperate sorrow. Neither of them spoke for several moments. Curiously Clarissa felt an insidious feeling of peace stealing over her. Christopher sighed and shook his head slowly, keeping his eyes fixed on hers, plumbing their innermost depths.

'How are you, Clarissa?'

'I am well – considering what has happened. Why are you here, Christopher? Why have you come?'

'I believe you know why,' he said, his voice low and serious. 'And I think you know that I want more from you than friendship.'

She nodded. 'Yes – although why I can't imagine. You scarcely know me.'

'As I told you before, that can soon be remedied. You must forgive my haste, but I did not have the time to remain in London kicking my heels indefinitely. I do not intend remaining in England for more than a few weeks. I learned of your father's death only when I reached Portsmouth. I'm very sorry, Clarissa. It must have been harrowing for you.'

'Yes – yes, it was,' and Christopher sensed a bitter note in her voice. 'But Father did not just die. It was suicide – there is a difference – but I think you already know that, don't you? Anyway, it's over now – or it will be when…when…' She faltered, unable to go on, and turned from his penetrating gaze as hot tears welled up in her eyes. Angrily she dashed them away with her clenched fist and moved towards the door, looking out over the park, but everything was a blur.

Christopher moved towards her, wanting so much to reach out and draw her into his arms. Her suffering almost broke his heart.

'Tell me why you're here,' she asked quietly. 'What do you want of me?'

'I came to ask you to be my wife,' he replied simply.

At his words she closed her eyes tightly, remaining frozen, like a beautiful marble statue. 'Wife?' she whispered. 'You would not ask me to be your wife if you knew what marriage to me would mean.'

Gently he placed his hands on her shoulders and turned her to face him, his eyes grave but calm, his fingers brushing away the wet strands of hair clinging to her cheeks. 'Oh – I believe I do,' he said softly, 'and please believe me when I say that it was not my intention to pry into your circumstances, but it is no secret that since your brother's death in Spain your father has squandered money in every direction, leaving you hopelessly in debt, that in order to survive you will have to sell that which you hold most dear – Ashton Park.'

She nodded dumbly.

'Clarissa, I am offering you a chance to be happy – a future. I promise you that if you marry me I will secure your home – if it is so precious to you, and if it is to be a condition of your acceptance.' He saw the relief flood her eyes and sighed. 'So – I was right. Ashton Park does mean that much to you.'

'Yes – everything,' she replied quietly. 'But why should you want to marry me?'

'Because, as Lady Holland told you, I need a wife.'

'But there are thousands of women in London. Why me? With all my debts, I can only be an encumbrance to you.'

'Because you are the only one who interests me. The only one I want – debts and all,' he smiled. 'I want to make you smile, to laugh, and I want you to savour all I have to offer.'

She looked at him, at the serious expression in his eyes, and thought how unfortunate it was that she did not love him. She owed it to him to be completely honest. 'I must be frank with you, Christopher, although I suspect you already know what I am about to tell you. After all – you do seem to know everything else about me,' she said not unkindly. 'But until a short time ago I was betrothed to someone I loved a great deal. He – he too was killed in Spain, shortly before we were to have been married,' she finished quietly.

Christopher nodded, noting how her face changed when she spoke of him, bringing to it a softness, a mistiness in her wide eyes, and he felt a sudden rush of resentment towards this unknown love of hers. His face remained impassive when he next spoke. 'Yes, I did know. But time is a great healer, Clarissa. You were both very young – you will forget.' Immediately he had said the words he regretted them, for her eyes were suddenly charged with anger.

'No. Never,' she said fiercely. 'I may not have the benefit of your experience, but I know that I shall never forget – ever.' Her anger melted and she sighed, lowering her eyes. 'I shall never love you, Christopher. I shall never love any man – and so if you,' she said, her face white and tense, 'knowing this, still want to marry me and if you will promise to secure Ashton Park, then... I accept.' As she said these words a sudden peace and an enormous feeling of relief that soon her problems would become his descended on her spirit, but she had every intention of paying back the money it would take to pay off the debts. 'You must realise that whatever it costs it must be considered a loan. Richard, I am sure, will pay it all back, given time – and good harvests.'

Christopher smiled, a strange, crooked smile, and placed his fingers gently beneath her chin, tilting her head, forcing her to meet his gaze. 'I am sure he will, Clarissa, but believe me when I say that marriage to you will be payment enough. You do realise that if you marry me you will have to go with me to America, don't you? That we cannot live here, at Ashton Park? But I assure you that my home, Tamasee, is a place that will be worthy of you.'

She nodded as she looked at him, feeling strange emotions stirring in her breast. 'Yes,' she answered. 'I do know that, but I hope that I shall be worthy of Tamasee. I shan't mind going to America, knowing Ashton Park is safe, and I promise to do my best – to make you a good wife.'

Christopher's lips twisted in a thin smile. 'I am sure you will, but I have to admit that it does nothing for my pride or self-esteem, knowing it's my wealth and not my charming self you want. However – I do think we both have something to give.'

His face suddenly became a hard, inscrutable mask, and something Clarissa could not recognise flickered behind his dark eyes, and again she sensed in him something purposeful, something vital that made her feel uneasy, and it came to her that Christopher Cordell was not a man to run afoul of. Ignoring this moment of insight and preferring to think instead of the kindness he had shown her and his obvious sincerity, she fixed him with a steady gaze. Yes, she would marry him. With everything collapsing about her ears, she had no choice. But how different it had been when she had loved Edward, with all the passionate intensity of her youth. How she had yearned to marry him, to learn all the overwhelming joys that love had to offer. But this was to be a different kind of marriage – positive and cold. It was to be a union of two people drawn together by circumstances. She wouldn't think about what would come later but be content for now, knowing Ashton Park was safe.

'Come,' he said, taking her hand and moving outside. 'It isn't raining quite so hard now. Let's go back to the house – otherwise, if you don't get out of those wet clothes, you'll be in no fit condition to marry anyone.'

CHAPTER FIVE

RICHARD could not believe their good fortune when Clarissa told him she was to marry the American Christopher Cordell, and that he had agreed to loan them enough money to secure Ashton Park after the remainder of his father's property had been sold. His relief was enormous and he lost no time in making it quite clear to his sister that he thought she had done well for herself. Better, he thought, than if she had married Edward. His feelings regarding Clarissa's one-time betrothed had been far from favourable and, like Letty, he had kept his opinion to himself.

The gloom and despondency hanging over the house was lifted, and as the days passed and the two men got to know each other a strong friendship developed between them. It was with pride that Richard showed the estate to Christopher, who, on observing the shining brown earth of fallow fields awaiting spring for the planting of the corn, jokingly told him that it was a pity they couldn't grow cotton. Their financial worries would be at an end.

In the days after she had told Christopher she would marry him Clarissa's life had taken on a strange feeling of unreality. But why, she asked herself, why should he want to marry her? It couldn't possibly be because he loved her – not on so short an acquaintance – nor could it be because he felt sorry for her or out of kindness, for he was not the kind of man to tie himself to anyone out of pity. But whatever the reason she was acutely aware of how attractive he was and found herself watching for him, listening for his footfall on the hard tiles of the hall floor, which would set her pulses racing, and when she thought of him, of the way she often found him watching her, his gaze dark and intent, she couldn't stop the trembling that came over her.

The wedding was to take place two weeks hence, just one week before they would have to leave Ashton Park for America, this date now earlier than Christopher had intended after hearing of the meeting of Congress, which had been brought forward by a month.

The younger, more aggressive members of the ageing, peaceable President Madison's party, mainly southerners and westerners who had newly entered Congress, with all their passionate ardour had enumerated the many grievances against Britain, among them being the continuing indignities inflicted upon the American flag by arrogant British sea captains and the injuries done to American commerce. But greatest of all was their anger over Britain's continuing insistence upon the navy's right to board neutral vessels, impressing into their service any British subjects found on them. Unfortunately they were often unable to distinguish between an Englishman and an American and there was no doubt that many of them were unquestionably American.

And so these newly appointed members of Congress – the 'War Hawks', as they were called – clamoured for revenge, for America to clad itself in armour, becoming determined to rid themselves of the British from the north-American continent – including Canada, Britain's most prized colony. But sentiments against further hostilities with Britain were high in the north-east, in New York and New England, where the Federalists were bent on avoiding war, knowing all too well that it would end a trade from which they profited enormously if just a few ships, their holds crammed with raw cotton and other supplies, they sent across the Atlantic escaped seizure by the British.

It was with reluctance that Christopher made his decision to leave for London to arrange for their departure to America. He was to return to Ashton Park the day before the wedding.

It was the evening before his departure that he and Clarissa talked at length of what going to live in America would mean to her, of what she could expect and the many duties and responsibilities that would be hers at Tamasee. They had just finished dinner and were in the drawing-room. Christopher was grateful to Richard for tactfully arranging to be elsewhere so they could be alone.

It was only then that Clarissa began to realise what marriage to Christopher would really mean and that there was a gulf between them wider than the Atlantic Ocean, their backgrounds being completely different. He came from a world she could not begin to imagine with its semi-tropical weather, where life revolved around the plantation with its rolling acres of cotton, where ideas and customs would be alien to her and where the economic and social survival of the southern states depended solely upon the blood, sweat and tears of the Negro slave.

This was a system Clarissa had only heard about and considered a crippling evil. Nothing Christopher said to her would ever be able to justify it, but some deep feminine instinct told her to keep her thoughts to herself. Whatever doubts she might have regarding any aspect of what her life in America would be like, she must learn to put them behind her, to accept it, because the survival of Ashton Park was as important to her as was the survival and preservation of their way of life to the plantation owners of the southern states of America.

But Christopher had read those confused and often angry emotions clouding her eyes when he talked of the slaves, and it might have surprised her to know that he understood and sympathised with what he knew she must be thinking, but he was glad she had the good sense to keep her opinions to herself upon a subject she was not yet personally acquainted with.

With his back to the fire and his hands folded loosely behind him, he gazed down to where she sat on the sofa, her eyes upturned to his. He smiled gently. 'You do understand why I have to return to London so soon, don't you, Clarissa?'

'Yes, of course I do.'

'I had hoped for us to spend the weeks before our wedding getting to know one another better.'

'Never mind,' she said, smiling softly. 'I do have plenty to occupy my time, not only for the wedding but also in preparation for our going to America. Letty is coming in a few days, so she will help me. You probably don't remember her, but she was with me at Lady Holland's party – the night we met.'

'And a night I shall never forget,' said Christopher softly, meaningfully. 'And I do remember her. We met briefly when I got back to London and called to see you. One of your maids directed me to her house. She told me you had come down here. And I must say,' he said, his lips twisting in a smile, 'she did seem very keen that I come and see you.'

'Oh, yes, she would,' remarked Clarissa, smiling a little to herself in amusement when she pictured how startled and surprised Letty must have been when Christopher had called on her. Letty's curiosity about what he wanted with her had obviously got the better of her because only yesterday a letter had arrived, informing her of her intended visit to Ashton Park. There had been no mention of her meeting with Christopher, but Clarissa could well imagine her reaction when she learned they were to be married – and so soon. Her gaze settled on Christopher again. 'You do realise, don't you, Christopher, that because it is so close to Father's funeral it must be a modest wedding? I don't want any fuss. Normally so short an engagement would be unthinkable, but because we must leave England quickly there is nothing else for it.'

'I do understand, believe me, Clarissa, and it suits me perfectly – although if you were at Tamasee everyone in the state of South Carolina would expect to be invited and would be mortally offended if they weren't.'

Clarissa looked at him, horrified. 'Everyone?'

'I'm afraid so,' he said softly, a glint of teasing laughter shining briefly in his eyes. 'And those who weren't invited would come anyway.'

'Even after a bereavement?'

'No – perhaps not. When a member of a family dies then the plantation is in mourning for months.'

'Will you be bringing your uncle, Lord Buckley, back with you for the wedding?'

'Would you mind?'

'Of course not. He is your closest relative and was a good friend of my father's. I would like him to be here. I – I just wish we had more time – that we didn't have to leave quite so soon after the wedding.'

All trace of amusement vanished from Christopher's expression and his voice sounded grave. 'I know, but if we delay much longer we may have difficulty getting back.'

'What do you think will happen, Christopher? Do you think there will be war?'

At her question his face became tense and his tall

figure seemed to dominate the room. 'Yes, I do, and once it begins it will have to be fought. But America is so unprepared. It is a war that will be fought largely at sea. No one can dispute the quality of our navy – it is superb – but it has so few vessels, twenty at the most, nothing that can compete with the might of your British ships. It will be fortunate for us that Britain will be unable to concentrate her full force on America because she is still at war with France.' He sighed and looked at Clarissa, who had paled at his words. 'But how will you feel, Clarissa, if war does break out between our two countries? Will you not think it an act of betrayal, leaving England for a country that has declared war on her?'

'I don't know. In truth I haven't thought about it. My mind has been so full of other things of late. The French wars have been a fact of life since I was a child, but,' she said softly, looking away from him into the heart of the fire as her thoughts suddenly evoked painful memories of the past, 'it is only in the past few months that, as a family, we have been touched by the cruelties of it. I can't envisage a world without a country being on a war footing. At the moment I have to admit that war with America doesn't make any difference to me one way or the other, although how I shall feel when I get there I cannot say.'

'And it won't make you change your mind?'

She stared at him with surprise. 'What – as regards my marrying you?'

He nodded, watching her face closely.

'No, of course not.'

'How will you feel when the time comes for you to leave Ashton Park? It will be a terrible wrench.'

'I know, but I don't think it will be long before the house has a new mistress, and I'm glad it's to be Laura. But you will let me come back, won't you?'

'Of course you can come back. I don't wish to give you any reason to regret marrying me.'

'I don't think you'll do that. I only hope I don't give you cause for regrets. I do promise to make you a good wife and pray that we shall be tolerably happy.' She smiled wryly. 'After all you've done for me, the last thing I want is to prove a poor investment.'

Christopher looked at her sharply and his eyes suddenly flamed with anger, at which Clarissa immediately regretted her thoughtless, impulsive words, and for the first time since she had known him she felt fear in her heart. He moved quickly and sat beside her, taking both her hands in his own hard grip. His eyes were dark and compelling, forcing her to look into them, and his voice was stern when he spoke.

'Tolerably? An investment? I intend for us to be more than tolerably happy and I never for one moment considered you an investment. I am not given to pretty speeches, Clarissa, and, unlike young Edward Montgomery – whom you professed to love more than life itself – I cannot offer you a title, but what I can offer you is a home and an estate, the like of which you have never seen.'

'If you knew me you would know that none of that matters,' she whispered with a sinking heart, wishing he had not made that reference to Edward. She hadn't even known that Christopher knew the name of the man she would have married had the war not taken him from her. Was there nothing about her he didn't know?

'Perhaps, but you must understand that I asked you to be my wife because it was you I wanted and for no other reason. The fact that your family was hopelessly in debt was unimportant. You have told me that you will never love me, that your heart went with the soldier you were betrothed to to the grave, and I accept that – for now – but time heals many wounds, Clarissa, including the invisible ones, and when it does you will love again. When you become my wife, when you bear my name, which to me is as proud and noble as any of your ancient aristocratic ones, I shall expect some affection from you and respect, but more than anything else I want you to be happy.' His voice softened when he looked at her sad, downcast face, and he placed his fingers gently beneath her chin. 'Look at me, Clarissa.'

Slowly she raised her eyes to his, the candle-light shining into their sapphire-blue depths. Despite himself, Christopher was touched by the grief he saw there, which brought a bitter taste to his mouth. He sighed deeply, shaking his head slowly, his eyes never leaving hers.

'I am a fool,' he murmured, 'and I have a distinct feeling that I am going to make an even bigger fool of myself where you are concerned, but you cannot live your life searching for something that is gone, that is dead. It is like chasing the wind. You have to let go, Clarissa. Do you think you will be punished if, instead, you look for happiness among the living? That you will have to pay penance? For I can tell you that no amount of tears can bring back the dead.'

Clarissa stared at him, lulled into a curious sense of well-being by his words as a rush of warmth and gratitude completely pervaded her and her lovely eyes became blurred, shining like stars with her tears.

'I really do not deserve you,' she whispered, 'and I know you are right – only. . .it's just not that easy to let go.'

'Then perhaps this will help,' he murmured, and very slowly he lifted his lean brown hands and placed them on either side of her face. His brown eyes darkened so that they were almost black as he leaned forward, and at his touch Clarissa trembled slightly – with fear or

excitement, she didn't know which, but she did not
draw away as he placed his mouth on her soft, quivering lips, cherishing them with his own, slow and so very
tender. His gentleness kindled a response and a warm
glow spread over her, but also a fear began to possess
her, a fear not of him but of herself and the dark,
hidden feelings he aroused.

When he finally drew away she remained unmoving,
as though still suspended in that kiss, her lips moist and
slightly parted. She gazed wonderingly into his eyes
and for the first time since he had known her some of
the grief had gone from hers, which were very bright
with tears. They spilled over her lashes, rolling slowly
down her flushed cheeks and over his hands, which still
held her face. Tenderly he wiped them away with the
tips of his fingers. She was utterly lovely, breathtakingly so, and he was moved by emotions almost beyond
his control, wanting so very much to kiss her again but
this time with all the hunger and passion that threatened to engulf him. He controlled himself with an
effort lest he betray how deeply he felt.

Early the next morning it was with reluctance that
Christopher left for London, and a few days later Letty
arrived. She swept up the steps, her bunches of auburn
ringlets bouncing wildly as she moved, her bright eyes
shining. Clarissa ushered her inside, out of the cold.

'It's lovely to see you, Letty, but I must say that your
letter was something of a surprise. How are things in
London?'

'Oh, much the same. As you know, nothing of
interest happens until the season gets under way.' She
paused and studied Clarissa with concern and was
relieved to see that the strain of the past weeks had left
her face. Now there was a somewhat settled air about
her, a new strength of purpose that had not been there

before, and she suspected that Christopher Cordell could have something to do with that. She made up her mind not to tell her about Edward until she discovered what had transpired between them. 'I know you told me not to come down to Ashton Park but I thought, now the funeral is over, you might be glad of some company.'

Clarissa smiled and squeezed her friend's hand fondly. 'Thank you. I am, Letty, and I'm so glad you've come. Now, take off your cloak and come into the drawing-room. You must be dying for some refreshment after your journey.'

Over tea they talked of inconsequential things, neither of them mentioning Christopher until Letty could stand the suspense no longer, suspecting that Clarissa was deliberately avoiding the subject. And so, unable to wait any longer and taking the bit between the teeth, she set her cup firmly on its saucer and fixed her eyes on Clarissa.

'Well – where is he?'

'Who?'

'Why – the exquisite Christopher Cordell, of course. I know he came down here to see you.'

'Oh, him,' said Clarissa, making a pretence of indifference and trying to stop her lips from quivering into a smile. 'You're too late, I'm afraid. He went back to London a few days ago.'

Letty's face fell with disappointment. 'Oh – he didn't?'

'Mm, he did – but don't worry, he'll be back.'

'He will?'

'He'd better be. We're getting married in less than two weeks.' At last her face broke into a smile.

Letty's jaw dropped in astonishment; then she gave a little squeal of delight and clasped Clarissa to her.

'Oh – love – I don't believe it,' but then she held her at arm's length. 'It is true, isn't it? You're not jesting?'

'Would I jest about so serious a matter?'

'I guess not. I knew he was coming to see you. Did you know that on learning of your father's death while in Portsmouth he immediately went straight back to London to see you?'

'Yes, he told me.'

Letty sighed, a kind of wonder in her green eyes as she looked at Clarissa, hardly able to believe that what she had told her was true, and now she knew that she could not tell her that Edward was alive. May God and Clarissa forgive her but she could not tell her, not until after she was safely married to Christopher. She would pray that Edward wouldn't change his mind and decide to come down to Ashton Park sooner than he intended. But her instinct told her that what she was doing was right. Clarissa would be far happier with Christopher than she ever would with Edward. If he had been anything like decent she would not be deceiving her in this way and, besides, she thought as renewed anger possessed her when she remembered how he had assaulted and tried to rape her, it would serve him right when he finally condescended to come down to Ashton Park and found Clarissa had married someone else, someone richer even than his own arrogant, conceited self, and with any luck she would be on her way to America.

'I can hardly believe it. To think that just three weeks ago you were on the point of penury and now – well, look at you. Your position is most enviable.'

It was almost dark when they strolled on the terraced lawns, their arms linked together and a light cold wind blowing their cloaks and hair. Soon the gardens, their beds and borders bereft of flowers, would be bathed in moonlight. Only the tall black evergreens showed any sign of life, casting their velvety shadows on the lawns. Their eyes strayed beyond to the park and they paused, each aware of the complete silence that wrapped itself about them.

Letty sighed wistfully. 'I do love Ashton Park, Clarissa. You are so lucky.'

'Don't I know it. But I didn't realise just how much it meant to me until it was almost gone. I have a lot to thank Christopher for. What he has offered me is a lifeline, Letty. I have to take it. He's been so kind, so considerate, and I believe he is genuinely fond of me. Why else would he have asked me to marry him?'

'Why else indeed? You know, you've changed, Clarissa.'

'Changed? I dare say I have changed a little. You see, I've made up my mind to put the past and whatever dreams I once had behind me and look to the future.'

'I'm glad to hear it, but I have to admit that I'm going to miss you when you go to America.'

'I know, and I'll miss you too, but you must come over and visit.' She sighed and again let her eyes stray lovingly over the countryside. 'I'm going to miss all this, but I know it will be well taken care of with Richard. It's his now, his and Laura's when they marry. I'm only sorry I can't be here for their wedding.'

'Laura? Who is she?'

'Our new minister's daughter, and she and Richard are hopelessly in love. I like her and I know she'll be good for Richard. I'm sure you'll agree with me when you meet her tomorrow. It does make going away that much easier – although theirs will be a different kind of marriage from mine.'

Letty frowned. 'Why do you say that?'

'Mine will not be clouded with romantic thoughts like theirs and, if I can help it, I don't intend being a captive of my emotions ever again. I've known love and lost it, so I must learn to come to terms with it. From now on all my aspirations must be realistic, but you know, Letty, it is important that I marry someone I can trust, someone I can lean on, who will protect me, and if Christopher can do that then I shall try very hard to love him, although I have to admit that when I think of America and being his wife it scares me.'

'You'll soon get used to it, and you'll have Betsy with you.'

'I know, and thank goodness she's agreed to come with us – in fact, she's positively looking forward to it. Oh,' she sighed, 'I'm being silly. I do realise just how lucky I am, but everything has a price – even happiness, and if I have to leave Ashton Park in order to preserve it then I am ready to pay that price.'

The wedding took place the day after Christopher returned from London, at noon on a cold January day and, because Clarissa wanted as little fuss as possible, the only people present in the little church at Ashton, which had so recently witnessed the interment of her father, were Richard and Laura and Letty, who acted as maid of honour. Only a few of the servants from Ashton Park occupied the pews and, much to Clarissa's regret, due to a severe chill, Lord Buckley had been unable to be there, but sent his good wishes.

Clarissa was a vision in a simple gown of white brocade, embroidered with tiny seed-pearls that matched to perfection the glorious creamy pearls around her throat, a wedding gift from Christopher. A fine veil was drawn over her face. She took her place beside him; he was handsome and impressive, his black coat hugging his broad shoulders and narrow waist with not a crease anywhere. His dark good looks were a striking contrast to her delicate beauty. He turned and looked at her, and his throat constricted at the picture she presented. Pray God, he thought, let me be worthy of her. Before she had been lovely, but today, as his bride, she was exquisitely perfect.

Along the walls of the church lay effigies on the tombs of long-dead Miltons, there to witness the marriage of one of their own, offering little comfort in the cold, dank church. After the ritual sacred vows had been said and the Reverend Mr Greenwood had pronounced the final blessing, it was with relief that Clarissa, now enveloped in a warm velvet cloak, left the church with her husband – and with Letty dabbing at her eyes with a lace handkerchief.

She soon found herself alone with Christopher in the coach taking them back to Ashton Park. The whole day had taken on an air of unreality and she found it almost impossible to believe that the man sitting next to her was now her husband. She had married him but did not know him. She glanced obliquely at him, telling herself how fortunate she was when she gazed at his bronze, clean-cut profile and proud features, and realised, not for the first time, how incredibly handsome he was, and began to think of the physical side of their marriage, of her duty, and all that would come later, and she experienced a curious mixture of terror and excitement and prayed she wouldn't disappoint him.

She remembered his kiss and how he had made her feel suddenly alive, rekindling desires she had suppressed for so long, desires that she had told herself she would never experience again, which proved how little she knew her own body. The memory of that kiss brought colour flooding to her cheeks and she looked away, but too late, for at that moment Christopher looked at her and laughed softly. Taking her cold hand in his own, he lightly touched the narrow golden ring on her finger before raising it to his lips.

This simple act of reassurance released her from her anxiety and she began to relax. The icy numbness that had gripped her from the moment she had left home for the church began to melt, and the feel of his lips on her fingers sent a strange thrill soaring through her.

'Tell me what you were thinking – that made you look away?'

'Oh – nothing really, only how lucky I am.'

'Are you happy?'

She nodded. 'Yes.'

'No regrets?'

'No – none that I can think of.'

He contemplated her for a moment and Clarissa was riveted by his gaze. 'Did I tell you that you look adorable?'

'Yes, before we left for the church.'

'Then I will tell you again. You are beautiful, Clarissa – like some perfect work of art.'

She laughed shyly. 'I'm sure every groom says that to his bride on their wedding-day. I am no more beautiful than any other.'

His eyebrows rose. 'I think I should be the judge of that, and perhaps they don't all mean it as sincerely as I.' His eyes darkened as they fastened on her soft pink lips, moist and slightly parted, revealing her small white teeth. His voice was husky when he spoke, which sent a tremor through Clarissa. 'Would you mind if I kissed my wife now we are alone, for I fear that when we arrive back at the house I shall not have you to myself for – let me see – at least eight hours?'

Clarissa's eyes widened in mock amazement and her mouth formed a silent 'Oh'. 'That long?' and she smiled softly. 'Then in that case I think you should.'

Christopher's gaze was intent and he was looking at her in a way he had never dared look at her before lest he betray how he really felt, and he prayed by all he held sacred that he would be able to bring her all the joy and happiness she was meant for.

Sliding his hand beneath her cloak and around her waist, he pulled her towards him, his eyes dark and full of tenderness. He did not kiss her at once but studied her face, close to his, with a kind of wonder, his eyes gazing intently into hers before settling on her parted lips, which he at last covered with his own, his arm about her waist tightening, drawing her closer, until their bodies were moulded together and Clarissa could feel the hardness of his muscular body. Her heart was beating so hard that she was sure he must feel it. His lips, moist and warm, caressed hers, becoming firm and insistent as he felt her respond, kindling a fire inside her with such exquisite slowness, a whole new world exploding inside her. She raised her arms, fastening them around his neck, returning his kiss, her lips soft and clinging, moving upon his in a caress that seemed to last for an eternity.

Christopher's lips left hers and he buried them in the soft hollow of her throat. He heard the sharp intake of her breath but she did not pull away from him, and when he lifted his head and looked at her his eyes burned with naked desire. Clarissa trembled inside, feeling as if she was on the threshold of something unknown, which caused fear to course through her but also something else, a longing so strong that she wanted to pull him towards her, for him to kiss her with all the savage intensity of his desire.

She had been kissed before by Edward, but never like this. His kisses had not aroused the passion that Christopher's did, a passion so primitive, which swept through her, a passion almost beyond her control, evoking feelings she had never felt before, and this new awareness of her own desire shook her to her very core.

Seeing the hunger in her eyes, Christopher sighed deeply. 'So – I was right.'

'Right?' she whispered. 'What do you mean?'

'That first time I saw you, to me, as a stranger, you seemed to have everything – beauty, wealth, every young man in London at your feet – but you seemed to want none of it. You seemed so cold, so remote, as if only part of you was alive. You became an enigma to me, Clarissa, and I was determined to get to know you better, convinced that behind your cold façade there beat the heart of a warm and passionate woman – and, it seems, I was right. I hope you will never regret your decision to marry me.'

'How could I? You have given me everything I could possibly want.'

His dark brows knit together as he considered her thoughtfully, a shadow of doubt darkening his eyes. 'Everything?'

Just for a moment her eyes clouded but quickly they became clear, as if she had suddenly come to a decision, and she looked at him directly, a determined tilt to her chin. 'Yes – everything,' and, smiling, she leaned forward and kissed him gently on the lips, just as the carriage came to a halt at the bottom of the steps of Ashton Park.

CHAPTER SIX

THE wedding breakfast at Ashton Park was a prolonged and happy affair, a festive air prevailing throughout. The food was exquisite, the champagne cold and delicious, the toasts numerous. Christopher was charming, regaling them with fascinating stories of his native America, smiling softly when he caught Clarissa's eye, silently reminding her of their kiss and the night to come. Richard acted the perfect host, an adoring Laura looking rather fetching by his side.

They chatted and laughed and sipped champagne until, what seemed like hours later, they sat back in their chairs, replete and exhausted. Richard left to escort Laura and her father home. Clarissa sighed and looked at Letty, who had seemed unusually preoccupied and quiet throughout the meal, nervously toying with her napkin, and on reflection Clarissa thought she had behaved rather oddly all week. She had blithely helped with the arrangements for the wedding, but at times she had been nervous and slightly agitated. Something was wrong, she could sense it, and she reproached herself for being too consumed with her own affairs not to notice.

Christopher poured himself another brandy, and Clarissa stood up.

'Come on, Letty, let's take our coffee into the drawing-room, shall we, and then I'll go and change?' She smiled at Christopher. 'Join us when you've finished your brandy.'

Clarissa relaxed on the sofa, watching Letty with concern as she slowly paced up and down, sipping her coffee. They made small talk for several minutes about the wedding and preparations that had to be made for going to America, until Clarissa could no longer ignore what was on her mind.

'What's wrong, Letty?'

'Wrong?' she asked, somewhat surprised.

'Yes, something's amiss – I can tell.'

'Nonsense. Nothing's wrong,' she replied, trying to sound casual.

Clarissa rose and went to stand beside her, studying her face closely. 'Come, Letty. It's me – remember? I know you too well. You cannot deceive me. You've been on edge ever since you got here. What is it?'

She shrugged. 'Nothing. But if you think I've been a little on edge then it's probably just excitement over the wedding. It came as quite a shock, you know.'

'Are you sure that's it?' asked Clarissa, not convinced. 'And that it doesn't concern me?'

'You? Of course not.'

Clarissa shook her head and sighed. If there was something wrong and Letty didn't want to tell her then she couldn't make her. 'Well – if you're sure ——'

'Yes, I am sure – don't trouble your head about me; you have other things to think of now and I think you should be with your husband – not me. He's a wonderful man, Clarissa. You're so lucky.' She lowered her eyes, hating herself for her deceit. She would tell Clarissa about Edward before she left for London, but not just yet. It would be too cruel to tell her now. She would not be responsible for spoiling her first night of love and, besides, perhaps tomorrow, after a night spent in the arms of the American, Clarissa would not care one way or the other whether Edward was alive or dead. But how Letty wished that Clarissa could sail away to America and never find out the truth.

'Yes – you're right, I am lucky, aren't I? But

although you say otherwise I am still not convinced there isn't something you have to tell me.' She turned and glanced out of the window at the gathering dusk, noticing the long shadows slanting through the branches of the tall elms, and she sighed, about to turn away, but her eye was drawn to a large carriage travelling up the drive. She watched it come closer, the horses lathered and the carriage travel-stained with dust, indicating that it had come a long way. 'If there is something, Letty, then I'm afraid it will have to wait. I think we have a visitor – although I have no idea who it can be. I'll go and see.'

Clarissa went out into the hall, followed by Letty. She too had seen the carriage and an awful premonition as to who it could be filled her with foreboding. Clarissa flung open the big double doors and stepped outside, the wind catching hold of her skirts and whipping them about her ankles. The carriage came to a halt, an elegant black carriage, and Clarissa suddenly went icy cold when she recognised the familiar coat of arms emblazoned on the door panel. It was the Montgomery crest.

She stared at it, unable to believe what she saw, but then she told herself that it must be Edward's father and reproached herself for not having written to tell him of her marriage. She watched one of the footmen step down from the front of the carriage and open the door, and she moved, as if to walk down the steps, but then froze, one hand rising to her throat, the colour draining from her face, her lips, and her eyes fastened on the man who emerged from the dark interior, a gold-handled walking cane in his hand.

He was quite tall and stepped out of the carriage with a languid, aristocratic grace, his attire elegant, to say the least. He wore a dark blue coat with paler pantaloons encasing his muscular legs, embroidered silk waistcoat, and there was white linen spilling from his neck and wrists.

Clarissa stared at him, unable to believe her eyes, remembering so vividly the pale blond hair falling in a heavy wave over his forehead and the handsome features, the cynical smile on his lips and hooded, lazy grey eyes. She stared at him with all the incredulous horror of one who had seen a ghost, unable to believe it. She must be dreaming. It could not be true. How could fate play such a cruel trick? Edward was dead and she was married to someone else.

He looked up at her and smiled lazily. Clarissa's face was whiter than death, one hand frozen at her throat, and she watched, feeling a terrible, agonising wrench at her heart. She scarcely breathed as he slowly climbed the steps, and then she knew her eyes were not deceiving her, that this was no dream.

'Edward,' she breathed, a hazy mist floating before her eyes, darkness threatening to engulf her. 'It cannot be you. They told me you were dead.'

'Dead? I assure you, Clarissa, that – as you can see – I am very much alive.'

It was then that Clarissa gave a desperate cry and crumpled on to the steps at Letty's feet. Alarmed, Letty fell to her knees beside her, taking her cold hand in her own while raising her face to Edward, complete and utter hatred blazing from her eyes.

'Why? Why did you have to come here? Why couldn't you leave her alone?'

Very slowly he smiled, a thin, cruel smile, his eyes like ice. 'I shouldn't have thought it necessary for me to have to explain my reasons to you, Letty, and, besides, London is a trifle dull just now – as well you know. Why did you not tell Clarissa I am alive?'

'Because I didn't want her to know. I hoped and

prayed to God she'd never find out. She's better off without you.'

'How could she not find out that I'm alive? Unless – God forbid – she intends staying down here forever and, anyway, shouldn't she be the judge of whether or not she's better off without me? I doubt she would agree with you,' he drawled.

On his way to join Clarissa in the drawing-room, Christopher heard Clarissa's strangled cry and halted in shock. Seeing the open door, he hurried outside, to find her lying in a crumpled heap on the top of the steps with Letty by her side. His dark face clouded with concern.

'Clarissa!'

'She's all right,' said Letty quickly. 'She's fainted, that's all.'

'Let me take her inside,' and, bending down, he picked her up effortlessly, cradling her in his arms, her head resting against his shoulder. It was only then, as he straightened up, that he became aware of the man who had paused halfway up the steps.

At first, taken unawares, Edward was startled by the tall man's sudden appearance and the familiarity he showed to Clarissa, and it was when their eyes met that recognition came to each man simultaneously.

'Permit me to introduce you,' said Letty, standing beside Christopher.

'I think the social distinctions can be ignored, thank you, Letty. We are already acquainted.'

'So,' said Edward, his cold grey eyes narrowed with murderous fury, 'it is you. The American I had the misfortune to encounter on my journey back to London.'

'The same, and I observe you have discarded your uniform.'

'Temporarily, I assure you,' he replied, his voice like

steel. 'We have an account to settle, you and I. You cannot have forgotten.'

'I have not forgotten, and neither have I forgotten the sordidness of the situation in which we met. As I remember it, the account was settled. Now – permit me to take Clarissa inside. It appears she has received quite a shock, and I suggest you leave this house before I do something I would not regret.'

'Wait,' cried Letty as he was about to turn away, her face a picture of confusion, wishing she knew what they were talking about. 'Wait, Christopher. Have you no idea who this is?'

'No, and nor do I wish to.'

She ignored his cutting remark. 'It is Edward. Edward Montgomery. He was betrothed to Clarissa before he went to Spain and was reported killed.' She looked from one to the other, feeling the tension between them, aware of an ominous, eerie silence wrapping itself about them.

Christopher did not reply at once; he just stared at Edward, showing neither shock nor surprise, his face a hard, inscrutable mask, the muscles tight. 'Dear God,' he said when he finally did speak, his voice not without contempt. 'How unfortunate for Clarissa.'

Still holding Clarissa, who was beginning to stir in his arms, he walked inside and into the drawing-room. Gently he laid her on the sofa and stood looking down at her, relieved to see that some of the colour had returned to her face. He was well aware of all the torment, the suffering she would feel when she came to, and it tore at his heart.

The first person she saw when her eyes fluttered open was Christopher, his dark form staring down at her, his eyes full of pain and concern but also something else, which puzzled her – understanding and pity. Letty stood beside him, anxiously worrying a handkerchief in her fingers. Clarissa blinked her eyes to clear the mist, wondering what she was doing, lying on the sofa, and then she remembered Edward and that he had come back to her, and her heart leaped and began racing as her eyes moved round the room, searching for him.

He stood, seeming very much at ease at the far side of the room. She stared at him, unable to speak for what seemed to be an eternity, and her eyes shone with the unbelievable comfort of knowing he was alive, and yet why, when he looked the same, did she feel that she was looking into the face of a man she did not know – a stranger?

Seeing her open eyes, he moved towards her, ignoring Christopher, whose face wore a hard mask of disapproval. With Letty he stepped back to observe the reunion between his wife and her one-time betrothed.

Aware of and slightly amused by his audience, Edward dropped to one knee beside the sofa and took Clarissa's hand in his own. Slowly she reached out with the other and gently touched his cheek with the tips of her fingers to convince herself that it really was him.

'It is you,' she whispered. 'It really is you.'

'Yes. I must apologise if my sudden appearance came as a shock, but I came as soon as I could.'

There was an impulse in Letty to rush forward and drag him away from Clarissa, and Edward heard her sharp intake of breath at this barefaced lie, but he ignored it.

'I'm sure you did, but – but you were reported killed.'

'That I didn't know until later.'

'What happened? Please – tell me.'

'It was during the battle at Albuera that my horse was shot from under me, and afterwards grapeshot shattered my leg. I was also injured in the chest. I lost consciousness, and I knew nothing else until I came to, only to find myself a prisoner of the French.'

A deathly pallor spread over Clarissa's face. So often she had pictured him lying wounded on the field of battle, his life's blood ebbing away. She couldn't bear to think of it. 'How did you get back to your regiment? Did you escape?'

'No, it was later, when I began to recover, that I was rescued by the partisans.' At this he remembered how they had come under cover of darkness and freed several prisoners. They were an odd-looking bunch, the partisans, dressed in a variety of uniforms, armed with carbine, pistol and lance, red flags tied to them, and it was with a stirring in his loins that he remembered in particular the black-haired beauty who had wielded lance and carbine like a man but who had also made his time spent in their camp more pleasurable. 'They returned me to my regiment,' he continued, 'but it was only to find that most of it had been wiped out.'

'How awful. Are you going back?'

'Yes. I was sent home to recuperate and shall return when the officers who returned with me to England have recruited fresh men.'

'I – I missed you so much, Edward. You and Simon.' Even as she said this she was vividly aware of Christopher standing behind Edward as if turned to stone, his hands clenched by his sides, but she did not look at him; she dared not.

'Yes, I know about Simon,' he replied, and the memory of Clarissa's brother touched a forgotten chord in his selfish heart. 'I'm sorry, Clarissa.' He looked at her pale face resting against the cushions, thinking she looked different somehow, different from when he had last seen her, before he had gone to fight with Wellington's army in Spain. Perhaps it was because of the deprivations over the past months that he noticed, although he had seen to it that he had not been without female distractions. His attitude to love and women had always been easygoing, take it or leave it, but, looking at Clarissa now, he was almost bowled over by his desire for her.

It had been his father who had insisted that he marry Clarissa. He was a fiercely proud man and would not have the ancient line of Montgomerys sullied by having his heir marry just any woman. Clarissa Milton, the daughter of his good friend Lord Milton, was the kind of woman he wanted him to marry, to bear his grandchildren, not one of those unsavoury doxies he kept company with in London. Edward had taken his father's advice and also taken advantage of Clarissa's naïveté and innocence and wooed her, having to admit that his father was right. She would make a perfect wife. One he could keep tucked away in the country while he continued to pursue the kind of life he had become accustomed to in London. Yes – they would get on well, providing she did not interfere with his passion for women and entertaining his friends and the green baize tables. He raised her fingers to his lips.

'Would you agree for us to be married before I return to Spain?'

Before she had time to reply Christopher's voice lashed the air like the crack of a whip. 'I think not,' he said, unable to watch a moment longer this intimate, touching scene and the possessive way Edward was holding Clarissa's hand. 'And I would be obliged if you would take your hands off her.'

Edward turned and stood up, fixing him with a cold stare, wondering, not for the first time, as to this American's presence here at Ashton Park. At first he had thought he must be a friend of Letty's – after all, she had a reputation for keeping an odd collection of friends. 'Oh, no – not this time. Clarissa is mine. We are to be married.'

Christopher stepped forward and he smiled, an absolutely chilling smile, his eyes gleaming with a deadly purpose, his voice cold and lethal. 'I don't think so. Clarissa is no longer free to marry you. She is my wife. We were married today.'

Christopher's words hung like a pall in the air, and an unearthly silence fell on the room. The moment was tense. The expression on Edward's face did not change, but his skin paled and a tiny muscle began to throb at the side of his eye. There was a cold glitter in his grey eyes when he fixed them on Christopher.

'You lie,' he spat.

'I am not in the habit of lying.'

Edward spun round to Clarissa, who had risen to a sitting position on the sofa, and his eyes, when they rested on hers, were merciless, his tone cutting. 'Is this true? Is this – this man your husband?' When she hesitated his voice rang out impatiently. 'Come, Clarissa – what have you to say?'

She nodded, gazing up at him, all her wretchedness and pain staring out of tear-filled eyes. 'Yes,' she whispered. 'It is true. But – I thought you were dead.'

'Dead or alive, I can see you lost no time in filling my place. How long is it – eight months? Were you in such a hurry to be rid of me? The next thing you'll be telling me is how much you love him,' he sneered, 'how you couldn't wait the decent interval of at least one year to marry. Well – for God's sake, spare me that.'

'Edward, please,' cried Clarissa in a terrible anguish, rising to her feet, one hand stretched out to him in her need to make him understand. 'You don't under-stand——'

Cutting short her protestations, Edward dashed away her hand. Christopher stepped towards them. The tone of this over-dandified Englishman had been deliberately offensive and had provoked his anger further, and he was torn by Clarissa's piteous defencelessness.

'Whether he understands or not is of no consequence. Six months or a year is neither here nor there. You were not married to him, so what does it matter? Clarissa is *my* wife.'

Edward's face was set hard, and a terrible hatred and jealousy directed at this American smouldered just beneath the surface that threatened to burst like a raging volcano, but an inborn caution told him to stay calm, to overcome the overwhelming lust to reach out and tear the man apart with his bare hands. 'Damn you for forcing your attentions on her, knowing she was spoken for.'

'You were dead,' he drawled flatly, 'or so everyone thought.'

'I am very much alive.'

'So I see. The devil has a way of taking care of his own, and if you intend to remain that way then I suggest you stay away from me – and especially Clarissa. So let that be an end to it.'

'An end to it? As far as I am concerned, there will never be an end to it. You have offended my honour – I have a mind to call you out. I want revenge and I will stop at nothing until I have obtained it.'

Clarissa gasped with horror at his words. 'No – Edward – please, you must not.'

Both men ignored her pleas and their eyes clashed with all the violence born of hatred. Christopher was all too well aware that beneath Edward Montgomery's cool exterior there was a ruthless vindictiveness that would know no bounds.

'Honour,' he scorned. 'I dispute that. There isn't an honourable bone in your body, and do not try and fool me. We both know that the revenge you talk of is not,

as you would have me believe, for my marrying
Clarissa. As I remember, you have the disgusting
morals of a tom cat, and you make me sorry I didn't
kill you when I had the chance. Your sort can only go
one way and I thank God that by marrying Clarissa I
have prevented her from being dragged down into the
mire.'

Clarissa's eyes passed from one to the other in
puzzlement as she tried to comprehend what they were
talking about. None of it made any sense. That they
should feel prejudice towards each other was under-
standable, but Christopher was talking of another
matter which had nothing whatsoever to do with her or
their marriage.

'You know each other, don't you?' she asked in
shocked disbelief.

'Yes, we have met,' said Christopher. 'But I shall not
offend your ears by telling you of the circumstances.'

Letty, who had stood apart, watching and listening
to all that was being said, went cold when she saw
Edward's eyes light on her for the first time in minutes,
suddenly smiling, a thin, knowing smile, and now she
braced herself. The moment of truth, the moment she
had dreaded had come. He would take malicious
pleasure in telling Clarissa of her deception. Oh, yes,
he would glory in telling her. When he next spoke it
was to Clarissa, but his eyes were fixed on her.

'Tell me, Clarissa, would you have gone ahead and
married him – this American. . .?' and he flashed
Christopher a mocking smile. 'Forgive me, but I do not
remember your name. You did tell me, but it has
slipped my mind. Would you have married him if you
had known I was alive?'

The echo of his words lingered in the stillness of the
room as all eyes became riveted expectantly on her. It
was a question she had preferred not to ask herself

because she could not endure knowing he might have refused her when he discovered she didn't have a penny to her name.

'I – I don't know,' she faltered. 'Please – don't ask me that.'

Slowly and with a deadly purpose Edward sauntered to where Letty stood, his limp not quite as pronounced as it had been. Considering the severity of his injured leg, he was lucky in the fact that he had kept his where others had lost theirs. His smashed bones had knit with remarkable speed due to the punishing series of exercises he had put himself through, determined to regain full strength quickly. He fixed Letty with a cunning stare, aware of what the impact of his words would be.

'Why didn't you tell her, Letty? Why didn't you tell Clarissa that I was alive and back in London? That you saw and spoke with me yourself and that my intention was to come down here to Ashton Park?'

Clarissa's heart suddenly missed a beat and she thought she was going mad. She stared at Letty in disbelief. 'No – no, Letty. Tell me it isn't true. Tell me Edward is lying.'

Letty looked into her eyes, seeing the hurt, the pain, and knowing the accusations would come later, but she firmly believed that what she had done was right. She squared her shoulders, meeting her gaze unflinchingly. 'No. He is telling the truth.'

'So,' breathed Clarissa. 'That is what you've been keeping from me. I knew there was something.'

Edward laughed, a low, cruel sound. 'And you are supposed to be Clarissa's friend – her closest and dearest friend,' he sneered. 'What kind of friend is it that would practise such deceit?'

Letty looked at him steadily, reading the mockery on his face, but her gaze did not falter. 'I am her friend,' she said coldly. 'That is precisely why I did not tell her. You are a liar and a cheat, Edward, and many more things besides. I couldn't begin to list them all. You are a man without morals or principles, and dishonour the very name you bear. You could have written to Clarissa, letting her know you were still alive. You had your chances, and then when you returned to London – at least three weeks ago – you could have written or come straight down here, but you chose not to,' and her eyes glittered with contempt. 'I don't know who it was that kept you in town – but I hope she was worth it.' She heard Clarissa gasp and moved towards her. 'God knows, I wanted to tell you, Clarissa, but I couldn't. I truly believed – and I still do, I might tell you – that he would have brought you nothing but heartache. For you to marry the likes of him would be like casting pearls before swine.'

'That is not true,' snapped Edward, beginning to lose some of his control. 'She is lying.'

'Stop – stop – please stop,' cried Clarissa, covering her ears with her hands. 'I cannot bear it. Oh, Edward – you should have written. You can't know what it was like for me. I have lain awake night after night, fighting battle after battle, not knowing whether you were alive or dead. Thousands were killed or wounded, yet I heard nothing of you – never a word. All I could do was wonder and pray and – and then your father...he...he told me you had been reported killed. I was devastated, but I had to come to terms with that. You must understand.'

'You came to terms with it a mite too quickly for my liking, Clarissa,' he said with brutal sarcasm. 'However,' and he turned from her sharply, 'I do realise the impropriety of my coming here today. I am well aware that this is your wedding-night and I should hate to rob you of a single minute of it, so I shall leave you to get on with it.'

'But where will you go?' cried Clarissa. 'You cannot go back to London tonight.' She suddenly looked imploringly at Christopher, her eyes bright with tears. 'Christopher – please——' But there the words froze on her lips and she suddenly felt very afraid. His dark face had paled and his narrowed eyes held a frightening glitter, and she realised that what he felt for Edward went deeper than anger, deeper even than hate. It was something she did not recognise and therefore could not understand.

But Christopher had read her mind, that she wanted him to stay at Ashton Park for the night, and the look he gave her was hard and unyielding, his tone low with contempt. 'No, Clarissa. How dare you ask that of me? He will not share the same roof as me tonight – or any other night. He can go and rot in hell for all I care.'

Edward laughed, a light, brittle sound, but there was no hiding his underlying tension. 'Worry not, Clarissa. I shall stay at the Black Boar here in Ashton tonight and should this...husband of yours not reach your expectations then you will know where to find me,' and he turned and strode out into the hall.

Clarissa noticed his limp and was brutally reminded of all he must have suffered in Spain, and her tender heart went out to him. A tearing sob broke from her. He couldn't leave, not now that she had found him again, and, gathering up her skirts, she hurried after him, avoiding Christopher's hand when he reached out to stop her. 'Edward – wait. For pity's sake, please – wait.'

He stopped and turned, and she came to a halt in front of him, her face awash with tears. 'I'm sorry,' she gulped. 'I know how much I must have hurt you. Please – you must forgive me.'

He looked at her hard for several moments and his eyes travelled with a lazy insolence over her white wedding dress, from the warm glow of the pearls around her slender neck down to her slippered feet before fastening on her face. 'Tell me, Clarissa, is that the dress you would have worn at our wedding?'

She stared at him in horror. 'Oh, no – no – that would not have been fair.'

'Fair on whom?' he said scathingly. 'Me or your American husband?' He looked back at Christopher, a cynical curl to his lips. 'As you will know, I am a gambling man,' he said slowly, 'and I will lay odds that Clarissa will come back to me in the end.'

Christopher's sleek black brows rose mockingly. 'I am a gambler of some skill myself, and I would not bet on that,' he replied.

'Oh – I would. You see – I hold the trump card.'

'And that is?'

'It is me she still loves. Think of that when you lie with her tonight. I shall have her in the end.' With a satisfied smile he turned and left the house.

Clarissa watched him go, without a smile or a word of affection or even farewell, and she bowed her head, thinking that he might just as well be dead to her. The sound of the closing door and his feet dying away down the steps was like a death-knell to her already breaking heart. She stared at the closed door for several moments until, filled with panic that she might never see him again, she hurled herself forward. She couldn't let him go – not like this.

'Edward,' she called, crushed with misery, but suddenly hands caught her, holding her in a hard grip, pulling her back, and she was enraged to find herself helpless.

'Clarissa, are you out of your mind? Let him go,' Christopher commanded sharply.

'No,' she cried, whirling round in his arms, a wild expression in her eyes. 'No – I have to make him understand why I married you. I cannot let him go like this. I may never see him again.'

'And for that I will thank God,' he growled.

'That's unfair, Christopher,' she said, her voice quivering with anger. 'We were to have been married. Can you blame him for being angry, coming home after what he's been through, only to discover that the woman he should have married has married someone else? I don't know what he's done to make you speak of him as you do, but whatever it is it cannot possibly justify this terrible hatred you feel for him.'

Christopher remained silent, his expression hard, his hands clenched by his sides, wanting to tell her what had taken place between them at Winchester but at the same time not wanting to be the one to shatter her illusions.

She stepped back and looked at them both, her eyes full of pain and accusation. 'You deceived me – both of you. You should have told me.'

'Oh, Clarissa,' said Letty. 'I wanted to – you've no idea how much – but I just couldn't. Do you really believe Edward would have married you when he found out about your father and the fact that you no longer have a penny to your name? He wouldn't. He would have dropped you like a stone.'

Clarissa's lips curled scornfully. 'What a low opinion you have of him, Letty. What can he possibly have done to make you hate him so? And yes – yes, I tell you, he would have married me, but you tricked me, both of you, and you had no right. I shall never forgive you for keeping this from me – either of you. I had a right to know so that I could choose for myself,' and with a choked sob and a swirl of skirts she turned sharply and fled up the stairs to seek the sanctuary of her room, but not before Christopher had seen fresh tears shining in her eyes.

CHAPTER SEVEN

CHRISTOPHER entered Clarissa's room and moved towards the bed, where she lay face down, with utter disregard to the ruin she was doing to her wedding finery, her face buried in the pillows and sobbing as though her heart would break. He looked down at her and his throat constricted with pain at her sheer loveliness. As she lay there in the flickering golden glow of the fire and candle-light, her pale blonde hair a wild tangle about her, he thought no one in the whole world was as lovely as she and he cursed Edward Montgomery with every fibre of his being. His very presence had withdrawn her a distance of a thousand miles, and what was in Christopher's heart was like death itself.

As he saw her despair, rage rose inside him against Montgomery, and he wondered what manner of man he was that could inspire such a love as hers, but also so much devastating misery. He let his gaze wander around the tastefully furnished room, this room he was to have shared for the few nights they were to remain at Ashton Park, an essentially feminine room, but, he thought bitterly, that was unlikely now. His gaze rested on the tantalising fine white lace nightdress Clarissa's maid had left draped over a velvet armchair near the fire, and he groaned inwardly, knowing he would not make her his wife in the true sense of the word until she had cleansed her heart of Edward Montgomery.

Sensing his presence, she turned her tear-drenched face and peered up at him, huge droplets hanging on her lashes like diamonds. He was so still, watching her, his face a hard, unreadable mask, and, seeing him, she felt renewed anger surge through her and her tears became frozen on her flushed cheeks.

'What do you want?' she asked coldly.

'Want?' he drawled with a hint of sarcasm, her anger inciting his own. 'Do I have to have a reason for entering my wife's bedroom?'

'Wife?' she scorned, feeding her anger with her words. 'I might not be your wife if you'd been honest with me.'

'What do you mean?'

'You know perfectly well what I mean. No wonder you were in such a hurry for the wedding to take place, having me believe it was because you wanted to get back to America when all the time it was because you knew Edward was alive and he ——'

'Enough,' he snapped coldly. 'Hear me out first, Clarissa. Your accusations are unjust. I do not deny that I met him just the once, and I swear to you that I did not know who he was until today.'

'And I am expected to believe that?'

'Believe what you like but, as I told him, I do not lie. What a low creature you must think me, Clarissa – but not as low as Edward Montgomery. But this I do know. Letty spoke the truth when she said he was a cheat and a liar. He is utterly corrupt, rotten to the very core – and this worthless libertine is the man you say you love and wanted to marry.'

Clarissa leapt quickly off the bed, beside herself with fury, and her eyes blazed into his. 'How dare you make the one thing I have loved so vile?' she flared. 'I will not listen to your accusations. I do not believe you.'

'Because you don't want to believe me. You cannot get it into your head that your beloved Edward is anything other than what you know of him – which, it seems, is very little.'

'Little?' she flared. 'I knew him well enough to say I'd marry him.'

'I doubt that – but, just supposing you had married him, do you think for one minute that he would have loaned Richard the money to save this place, your home? Because if you think that then you are a fool.'

His mention of Ashton Park and the cold disdain with which he uttered the words were like having a bucket of cold water poured over her, and she was suddenly reminded of all he had done for her and was full of contrition. He had offered her strength, security and understanding, which she had accepted gladly. She couldn't throw it back in his face. She sighed deeply, some of her anger evaporating.

'I'm sorry, Christopher, and perhaps I am a fool. You must think me extremely ungrateful.'

'The last thing I want is your gratitude,' he said coldly.

'Is it true – that you didn't know Edward was alive?'

'Yes.'

'But Letty knew. She could have told me.'

'Letty loves you more than anyone else in the world and she would not hurt you intentionally. Because of her past knowledge of your so-called betrothed – which, I might add, seems anything but honourable – she considered that what she was doing was right. She went through hell, keeping it from you, but she truly believed she was doing it for your own good.' Smiling crookedly, he moved away from her, pausing halfway to the door and turning to look at her again. 'You should thank me, Clarissa, for by marrying you I have saved you from an infinitely worse fate than death.'

'Where are you going?' she asked as he again turned away from her.

'To my room. And you needn't worry,' he said, his lips twisting cruelly. 'I shan't be bothering you tonight.'

'What do you mean?' she whispered in bewilderment.

'You know what I mean plain enough,' and when he turned and looked at her again his dark eyes began to gleam oddly and one sleek black brow went up. 'You can keep your chaste sanctity, my dear. Do you think I would stay with you tonight as, I might remind you, is my right, lie with you, touch you, all the while knowing you were wishing it was your precious Edward who was beside you?' He looked at her long and cool. 'It is obvious by the way you rush to his defence that you still care for him a great deal, so until the time when it is otherwise I will bid you goodnight.'

He went out, leaving Clarissa staring at the closed door, feeling so utterly bereft, thinking what an awful mess everything was.

A merciful numbness filled her mind as she listened to his footsteps dying away on the landing and she wanted to run after him, to appeal to his emotions, but she knew that while ever Edward was uppermost in her heart he would remain implacable; he would not yield from his cool verdict and she would continue to sleep alone. He had been angry and with good reason, and as she stared into the dying embers of the fire she took stock of all that had happened since she had returned home as his wife, suddenly feeling so very tired and drained of all emotion. Her feelings towards Edward were all confused and her mind seemed to be going round in circles. Why had she been so ready to believe him dead? Why hadn't she waited before rushing into marriage with someone else? But, she told herself, she couldn't have waited if she'd wanted to. Not with her father's creditors baying at the door.

Her thoughts turned to Christopher. Of her own free will she had married him, nothing could change that, and, she thought sadly, it was too late to weep for

Edward and what might have been. She and
Christopher were man and wife and she would honour
that, but what her feelings were towards him she
couldn't say – only that they were different from those
she felt for Edward. Christopher had asked her if she
believed Edward would have married her, knowing of
her circumstances, without a dowry and with the added
shame of her father's suicide. And would Edward have
secured Ashton Park as he had done? For her own
peace of mind she had to know so that she could put
things right, and to do this she must see him tonight,
for tomorrow he would return to London and she
might never see him again. It was a problem only she
could resolve.

Christopher, lying fully clothed on the bed and
hearing the soft thud of horse's hoofs, crossed over to
the window and, looking out, saw the dark silhouette of
a horse and rider galloping hard across the park.
Moonlight picked out the silver flanks of the horse,
which he recognised immediately as Clarissa's horse
Melody, and he was filled with a dreadful suspicion that
she was in the saddle. Cursing softly, he hurried to her
room, flinging the door wide open. On finding it empty,
he became consumed with a cold, blinding fury, knowing then, without doubt, that the rider had indeed been
his wife and that she was going to the Black Boar to see
Edward Montgomery. He paused only to don his cloak
and it wasn't long before he was riding after her.

The wind had risen, plucking strands of hair from
beneath Clarissa's hat, whipping them about her face
as she rode her horse hard, driven by a compelling
need to see Edward for one last time. The confusion in
her heart drove her on through the park until at last
she saw the dark buildings of the village of Ashton,
and looming above the houses was the square, battle-

mented tower of the church, standing stark and ghostly against the night sky – the church where she had been married that very day. She rode up the straggling street until she came to the Black Boar.

Only a few men were inside the inn, seated on the crude wooden benches that flanked the long tables. Edward was one of them, sitting with his back towards her. He turned, feeling the cold draught from the open door, and she moved into the centre of the room, the soft glow from the oil light shining full on her. He recognised her at once and surprise caused his eyes to widen, but then he smiled thinly, a smug, self-satisfied smile, and he rose, sauntering to where she stood.

He looked untidy without his jacket, his shirt open at the collar, the fine white linen stained with alcohol. Clarissa was disappointed, never having seen him like this; he had always been so immaculate. It came as some surprise to her to find he had lost some of that magical power to stir the old attraction that had kept her love attached to him for so long. He had also drunk a considerable amount, for his eyes were bloodshot, his aristocratic countenance flushed. She had always been aware of his capacity to absorb large amounts of alcohol – what man didn't? But this was the first time she had seen him lose some of his dignity. When he spoke his voice was slow and a little thick. He gave her a profoundly mocking bow.

'Why, Clarissa – this is an unexpected pleasure. I did not expect you quite so soon.'

His lack of elementary politeness irked her somewhat. He had not tried to hide the sarcasm in his tone. 'Why were you so sure I would come?'

'Because I knew you would be unable to resist the temptation of seeing me before I left for London in the morning. But isn't this a little irregular – I mean, isn't it supposed to be your wedding-night?'

An embarrassed flush spread over her face when she noticed the men at the tables had ceased their talking. She had become the object of curiosity and, whether they recognised her or not, she didn't want to stand there long enough to find out. 'Isn't there somewhere we can talk, Edward? Somewhere less public?'

A sly smile curled his lips. 'Of course – that is, if you don't mind my room.'

'No – anywhere.'

Still smiling, he led her up the narrow stairs and along a dimly lit landing. She entered his room, taking little notice of its shabbiness and the big four-poster bed that dominated it. Edward went over to the fire, kicking the logs alive, their orange sparks shooting up the blackened chimney. He turned and faced her.

'Well, Clarissa,' he said softly, a strange light entering his eyes as they travelled insolently over her slender form, over her close-fitting habit, emphasising the slimness of her body. S'truth, he thought, what a shape, and he realised, as the blood pounded in his temples, that she had more to offer than he had realised. 'Tell me why you are here. Can it be that your husband does not live up to your expectations?'

'Please, Edward – don't,' she said, choosing to ignore the implication of his words. 'He has no idea that I'm here.'

'Of course he hasn't – otherwise you wouldn't be. But why are you here?'

'You know why.'

'No. Tell me. Is it because now, after finding out that I am alive, you are sorry you married your American?'

'I don't know – truly.'

'But then, perhaps if I had been dead it would have saved you the embarrassment of your betrayal, your treachery.'

She gasped, angered by his accusation. 'Treachery? No – never that.'

He moved closer to her, his eyes fixed on her face, having narrowed to thin slits. 'I find it hard to believe how easily you forgot me, Clarissa.'

'I never forgot you,' she said emphatically. 'You have no idea how I wanted so much for the reports of your death to be lies. I tried not to believe it and you can have no idea how I dreamed of your coming home – so that we could be married, but. . .' She sighed, lowering her eyes. 'Oh – what's the use in talking now? It's too late. I am no longer free.'

A cunning glint appeared in Edward's eyes. The American had made a fool of him, had touched his honour in a way no other man ever had, not only when he had intervened in the matter of that young trollop at the inn in Winchester but also by taking Clarissa from him – which was too much to be borne. He knew that his success in winning her back, therefore exacting his revenge, depended upon all his powers of persuasion. 'A sermon doesn't make a marriage, Clarissa. You can be free of him – the wedding can be annulled if you swear it has not been consummated.'

For a moment she dispassionately studied this man she had once sworn to love forever, and shook her head slowly. 'No, Edward. Nothing is the same as when you left. I am not the same – although I am only now becoming aware of it. My marriage cannot be annulled. The vows I made are sacred. I married Christopher of my own free will and I will not betray him. He is my husband in the sight of man and God.'

At her words there was a sudden change in Edward's manner and his features became taut with a strange glow in the depths of his eyes, which was beginning to make Clarissa feel uneasy. She moved away from him, remembering why she had come, the question she must ask for her own peace of mind.

'Edward, there is a reason why I had to see you – something I have to know. Since – since coming home, what do you know of my circumstances?'

'What do you mean?'

She looked at him directly. 'Would you have married me – without a dowry?'

He looked slightly nonplussed. 'Dowry?' He ran his fingers through his untidy hair, irritated by her question. What had her dowry got to do with anything? 'What are you talking about, Clarissa?'

'When my father died he left Richard and myself nothing but a mountain of debts. He lost all his money gambling. Everything had to be sold to pay off his creditors.'

A look of genuine shock and amazement spread over Edward's face. So, thought Clarissa with a sinking heart, he didn't know.

'Good Lord. I had no idea. I knew he had debts – what gambler doesn't? But to be fool enough to lose everything——'

'Yes – everything,' she replied, fixing him with an unwavering stare. 'And do you know how my father died? Did no one tell you? Because I find it hard to believe you have not heard the scandal – which rocked London at the time.'

'No. I knew he was dead – Letty Davenport told me – but I haven't been home to Buckinghamshire for longer than a couple of days——' He faltered, having no wish to disclose how he'd spent his time in London with the highly delectable young actress, Lucy Marchant, who was appearing at the Theatre Royal in Drury Lane. They had hardly left her rooms in two weeks. 'Father was in Brighton, you see, and——'

'My father shot himself, Edward,' she said quietly, cutting him short. 'He committed suicide.'

Edward was stunned, and she watched the play of emotions on his handsome face.

'Well, Edward,' she continued, giving him no time to put his thoughts in order, 'would you have still married me – penniless and with the shame of my father's suicide? I need to know. Did you love me enough to do that?'

He was taken aback by her question and for a moment they looked at each other as if both were carved from stone.

'Marriage,' he murmured at last. 'Good Lord – why – of – of course I would. . .' But his voice died away, flat and unconvincing.

Clarissa wanted to believe him, but she knew with a sickening sense of reality that he was lying, and the face that looked into hers was not that handsome, beloved face it had once been. That was a sweet fantasy, a cherished illusion that had been shattered forever. Edward did not love her, had never loved her, not in the way she had wanted to be loved. He would have used her to serve his own interests, nothing more. It should hurt, but, strangely, it didn't, and if it didn't hurt then could it be that she didn't love him either?

She smiled bitterly. 'Don't try and fool me any more, Edward. I can see the truth in your eyes. You wouldn't have married me – even had you wanted to – and I very much doubt that now. Your father would never have allowed you to marry me anyway.'

He remained silent, looking at her hard, swaying slightly on his feet, the unspoken truth staring from his eyes. She turned from him, suddenly eager to leave this sordid room, the oil lamp making grotesque, monstrous shapes on the whitewashed walls. She wanted to get back to Ashton Park as quickly as possible – and to Christopher, and she prayed he would never find out that she had come here tonight. He would never forgive her.

'I don't think there's anything more to be said between us – do you?' and she moved towards the door, but in an instant he covered the distance between them, as light and fleet as a cat. He stood in front of her menacingly, blocking her path to the door. There was a dangerous, threatening glint in his cold grey eyes and she could not repress the icy fear that crept through her. When he spoke his voice was low and each word he uttered precise, but underlying them she could sense a violence that threatened to erupt at any moment.

'Before you go, Clarissa, tell me about your American and how it was that he came to marry you. Did you have to lie about your circumstances to him?'

'No, I didn't have to. Christopher and I have always been perfectly honest with each other. He has loaned Richard enough money to secure Ashton Park.'

For a moment his face did not change its expression, but suddenly what she had told him caused him to laugh mirthlessly. 'You mean, he bought you? You sold yourself to the highest bidder?'

'There were no other bidders,' she said drily. 'Only Christopher.'

'And he promised to pay all your father's debts for your own sweet self,' he scoffed. 'How very touching, and how unworthy of you.'

'Unworthy? No – I don't think so. I had no choice.'

'And – do you love him?'

'He – he has been very good to me.'

'I asked you if you love him,' he persisted.

'He is a wonderful man——'

'But you don't love him,' he said with an odious smile of triumph, with such finality that she stared at him unbelievingly, noting the immense satisfaction he derived from this knowledge, and she wished with her whole heart that she could have said otherwise.

'Please – move out of my way, Edward. The way you talk, you cannot blame me for thinking you are jealous of Christopher.'

Suddenly his face changed and his lips curled viciously. 'Jealous? And why shouldn't I be jealous? He's taken the woman I would have married.'

'No,' she replied coldly. 'Only the woman you did not love. And now,' she said, breathing deeply, seeing the fire in his eyes, that she knew spelt danger, knowing it had indeed been madness to come here, 'please move out of my way. I am leaving for America within the week. I doubt we shall meet again.'

'Then I tell you that this, our last night together, will be one to remember. I know you still love me, Clarissa, not that – that American you've so foolishly married, so come, why not show it?'

He moved closer to her and she could feel his breath hot on her face and the smell of spirits, which made her stomach churn. She stepped back, her face showing revulsion.

'No. What you suggest is an adulterous love – the sort I despise,' and she smiled scornfully. 'You talk of love, of my love, of not being loyal and accusing me of treachery – but what of your love, Edward? Not once in all the time I have known you have you mentioned that.'

'Haven't I? Then permit me to show you. I'm going to love you, Clarissa. I'm going to make you so happy that you'll never want to leave me to go back to your American. You'll beg me on your knees to let you stay.'

'No – never,' she cried angrily. 'I wish to leave now. Let me go.'

'No.'

'Do you intend to hold me here by force?'

'Only if I have to.'

Panic and fear overcame Clarissa and she began to tremble. He noticed and smiled with smug satisfaction.

'Why – you're trembling. Come, Clarissa,' he drawled, his voice thick with passion, 'you think I don't love you – but I do.' He placed his hands heavily on her shoulders, looking deeply into her eyes. At his touch she struggled, trying to free herself from his grip, but they tightened, refusing to relinquish their hold. 'So,' he hissed, 'you want to fight me – well, all the better. I like a woman with spirit – one to match my own.'

Clarissa was suddenly filled with fear, but it was a different kind of fear from any she had ever known. Never, in all the time she had known him, had he been anything other than charming, and she had always believed that nothing could touch him, that nothing mattered, but as she faced him, his expression dark and ruthless, she knew that at last something had touched him enough to bring about this ill-mannered, drunken stranger. She was now in no doubt that it was Christopher who had brought about this change and, whatever had passed between them that first time they had met, it must have been something terrible. She knew with a sinking heart that she could have married anyone and he wouldn't have cared one iota – but because it was the American it was a different matter. He would destroy her if he could to get back at him.

The full consequence of what she had done by coming here swept over her and she was gripped by panic. Edward saw her fear, feeling her quivering body beneath his hands, but he only laughed, a deep, horrible, mocking sound that curled his lips, and a look of madness filled and dilated his eyes, which told her that his mere triumph over her, her very resistance, excited him much more than all her passive docility. He wanted her whatever the odds, and the very fact that she belonged to Christopher made him even more determined to possess her wholly. He would settle for nothing less than that she surrender herself to him completely – absolutely. She knew that she could expect no mercy from him. He would not be cheated out of his ultimate pleasure.

The very sight of Clarissa aroused a violent, unfamiliar desire in Edward, such as no woman had before, and his lust, combined with hatred, made him like a man possessed of the devil. Brutally he pushed her back towards the bed. She cried out and stumbled, but he caught her, throwing her on to the covers. An icy terror gripped her and she tried to get up, but he fell upon her, crushing her with his weight, his face close to hers, contorted with fury and passion as he began tearing at her clothes, his hands expert from long practice.

A fierce, merciless struggle began between them and he became like a mad beast tearing at its prey. Now that she was faced with the terrible prospect of being raped and possibly killed, renewed strength surged through Clarissa and she fought as if her life depended on it, like a wildcat turning on its tormentor, and in her blind fury her nails raked his face, his eyes, anywhere she could see his flesh, feeling an immense, unholy satisfaction when she drew blood.

He laughed, a fierce, demonical sound that sent a chill through her. 'That's it – fight, my beauty,' he hissed. 'Fight all you want. I shall soon have you crying and pleading for mercy. I shall enjoy teaching you to obey me – breaking that stubborn Milton pride.'

When she opened her mouth to scream his own covered hers, brutal and demanding, nothing left but lust and need, and he kissed her as he would a whore.

By some miracle she somehow managed to tear herself away and scramble to the edge of the bed, but he seized a handful of her thick hair, which had come loose, pulling her back with such force that she cried out, tears of helpless rage filling her eyes. Savagely he continued tearing at her clothes, and as he forced her legs apart he cursed loudly at the encumbrance of clothes. But she was finding it harder to defend herself, reality slipping further and further away, and despair overpowered her as she reached the limits of her strength and her struggles became feeble.

And then, abruptly, something happened and his weight left her. There was a dull thud and she ceased struggling, trembling in what remained of her clothes, the taste of blood in her mouth from a cut on her lip. Through a mist she looked up and discerned a terrifying, faceless figure looming over her. Instinct made her draw her defiled body into a ball and shove herself back against the head of the bed, where she huddled, quivering like a terrified child, clutching her torn bodice. In the wild tangle of her hair, her eyes, enormous and full of fear, accentuated the transparent whiteness of her face, streaked with blood.

She peered up at Christopher, who was in a towering jealous rage, his face contorted out of all recognition as he glared down at her, beside himself with fury. The spectacle of the vile and contemptible Edward Montgomery forcing his attentions on Clarissa and the pitiful state he had brutally reduced her to made him feel physically sick. He thanked God he had found her in time.

Clarissa did not ask herself by what miracle he happened to be there, to save her from what she had been about to suffer at Edward's hands; it was enough for her that he had come, regardless of the fury and anger he would be sure to vent on her. He glared down at her half-naked form bitterly. In the flickering glow of the lamp she was still lovely, although now tragically so, and he knew the sight of her should sicken him, but it didn't.

'You brainless little fool,' he hissed. 'Is there no room in that head of yours for sense? How dare you come here, looking for him? Did you think I would not find out? What did you imagine would happen when that animal got his hands on you? You could ask for nothing better – believe me.' His eyes took in her soft white flesh showing through the tattered remnants of her bodice and quickly he removed his cloak, throwing it to her contemptuously. 'Here – cover yourself.'

Clarissa seized it and clutched it to her. He turned and looked at Edward, who had got up from the floor, where, in his rage, Christopher had thrown him. He stood glowering at the tall American, his fists tightly clenched by his sides, and the trace Clarissa's fingernails had left on his face trickled blood.

'Damn your filthy hide, Montgomery,' spat Christopher, his voice like a naked blade. 'She no longer has anything to do with you.'

'Perhaps not – but she did come looking for me, like a bitch on heat.'

Pure madness flamed in Christopher's eyes and he sprang at his adversary, grasping the front of his shirt and pulling his face close to his own, full of revulsion. 'And you should know all about that – being the dog that you are. Your methods of seduction leave a lot to be desired. I could kill you now but I will save that pleasure until later.'

Edward's lips twisted in an arrogant sneer, his grey eyes spitting venom as he knocked Christopher's hands away. 'Why, you are jealous – jealous because she preferred my bed to yours. But then, why shouldn't she? And how do you know she hasn't shared it with me before?'

Christopher eyed him with unconcealed scorn. 'Judging by what has happened here tonight, I doubt very much she would come back a second time.'

'At least I have given you a wedding-night to remember. You must have paid quite a price to get her to leave England and her home for that land of savages. Perhaps after tonight you'll consider she wasn't worth it.'

'Savages?' scoffed Christopher. 'That's a fine word, coming from you. You, who, it is said, belong to one of England's most noble families, are out of your class. You haven't an honourable, decent bone in your body. You are a low, stinking animal – not worthy of the blade with which I shall kill you.'

An ugly smile spread across Edward's features. 'No – it is I who will kill you. Nevertheless, if Clarissa had married me I would not have had to buy her as you have done. But then, you should know all about that – buying people.'

'What do you mean?'

'I've learnt quite a lot about you since this afternoon – and isn't that how you plantation owners in America get rich? By buying and selling human flesh, black flesh – slaves? Because as I see it there's nothing noble or honourable in that. How many Negro slaves do you own, eh? Fifty, a hundred, a thousand – or don't you know?'

'It's none of your damned business. Where I come from it's a perfectly normal practice.'

'I wonder if Clarissa will see it that way.'

'Whatever she thinks or feels has got nothing to do with you.' He turned back to Clarissa, who hadn't moved, and, pulling her towards him, wrapped his cloak about her trembling form before again facing

Edward. 'I'm taking my wife home, but be sure I shall return. You and I have a score to settle. I demand satisfaction for this night's work.'

Edward went very pale. 'You surprise me. I was under the impression that you Americans shot people in the back. However – you shall have it. It will give me immense pleasure to kill you. I shall not be cheated a third time.'

'Don't be too sure. Whatever you might think, we Americans are not all backwoodsmen. Like many of my fellow countrymen, I am an expert with pistol or blade, and I aim to make damned sure you rape no more defenceless women – high or low born.'

CHAPTER EIGHT

NOT a word was spoken between Clarissa and Christopher until they reached her room. She was oblivious to everything around her, utterly broken by all that had happened to her at Edward's hands. Her body felt bruised and defiled and weighted down with a terrible misery and despair, and the thought that she had to go on living after this night was inconceivable.

She stood in the centre of the room, still clutching Christopher's cloak about her, as if afraid to let it go. Christopher was suddenly overwhelmed with compassion. He wanted to go to her, to hold her, but he couldn't. He could not yet forgive her for going to Edward Montgomery. The memory of this night would live with him for a long time, longer than the sight of Clarissa's bruised and broken body. Because he had placed her on a pedestal her act of betrayal became harder for him to bear.

He turned from her and left the room to fetch Letty, and, when he returned with an anxious-looking Letty hard on his heels, Clarissa was still standing where he had left her, swaying slightly and pitiful to look at, wild and unkempt with her hair falling about her face, pale and frightened, her blue eyes wide open and staring.

'Oh, Clarissa,' breathed Letty. 'By all the saints – what has that monster done to you?' and, going to her, she gathered her in her arms, guiding her towards the bed, where she sat like an obedient child. Letty turned to Christopher, who was striding towards the door. 'Where are you going, Christopher? You're not leaving?'

He turned and looked at her, his face immobile. 'Yes. There is something I have to do. Something I have to take care of.'

Letty nodded, understanding, knowing without having to ask that he was returning to the Black Boar to settle the score with Edward. She couldn't blame him but thought, in his anger, that he had underestimated Edward. However confident Christopher might feel about his own prowess, Edward was a superb marksman and an expert with a sword.

His words penetrated Clarissa's tortured mind and realisation of where he was going and what he intended dawned on her. She tore herself from Letty's comforting arms and flung herself across the room, the cloak she had been so reluctant to relinquish falling to the floor, revealing the shameful ruin Edward had wreaked on her body. Her eyes were full of a desperate pleading when she looked into her husband's formidable face, gripping his arm fiercely.

'No,' she cried. 'Please don't go back there – you mustn't.'

He looked down at her, a cold glitter in his dark eyes. 'Don't try to stop me, Clarissa,' he said curtly. 'I have to. My honour is involved.'

'No, please – I know why you're going back, what you're going to do. Promise me you will not kill him. Whatever he has done, he does not deserve that.'

'No? Then perhaps you should have thought of that before you went looking for him.'

'H-how did you know I'd gone?'

'I heard you creep from your room and saw you ride off across the park towards Ashton. Where else would you be going if not to the Black Boar – and him? Did you think you could creep into his bed for a few hours and I would never find out? You underestimated me, Clarissa, if you thought that.'

'I – I'm so sorry——'

'The fact that you have betrayed me, have incurred my displeasure, does not seem to matter,' he said with heavy irony.

'Of course it does, and you have every right to be angry, but I did love him, Christopher, only I realise now that I did not know him, what he was capable of. . . I – I was so afraid——'

'Please – don't try explaining,' he scorned, 'and spare me the sordid details. What a pity I disturbed you before you could indulge your appetites for each other further.'

Clarissa stared at him in disbelief. 'It wasn't like that and you know it. You saw what the situation was, what he was doing to me. I had no idea he would behave as he did. It was as if some kind of monster had been unleashed.'

'And yet you want him to live. Clarissa, that man has abused you and damn near destroyed you. Don't ask me to ignore what he did tonight – I would rather hang.'

'And hang you shall if you kill him.'

He looked down at her, feeling her hand clinging to his arm with all her strength as tears began running unheeded down her cheeks. 'The minute he walked through the door earlier today he addled your wits. Come, now, tell me, if you had known he was still alive, would you have married me? Tell me, Clarissa – I have a right to know.'

'I don't know,' she cried miserably. 'Truly.'

'Do you still love him?' he went on remorselessly.

'Whatever love I had left he killed tonight.'

'I see,' he said, not totally convinced. 'However, because of your stupidity you have forced me to avenge you.'

'No,' she cried. 'I beg you not to. I no longer love

him but I cannot be the one to bring about his death.
If you kill him I shall blame myself. As surely as if I
had pulled the trigger I shall have killed him, and I
cannot live with that. The guilt would be too heavy for
me to bear. Please,' she whispered softly, 'if you kill
him his death will be between us forever.'

The anguish and pain on her pale face had their
effect, touching some hidden chord deep inside him.
He didn't know how to react to this terrible display of
grief, but he had to acknowledge the sense of her
words, fully aware that he had allowed his hurt masculine pride and anger to cloud his judgement.

'Haven't you thought what will happen if you do kill
him?'

He considered her intently and nodded slowly.
'Yes – I have. But put it another way, Clarissa. What
if Edward proves to be stronger than me? Have you
thought what will happen if he kills me?'

At his words she stared at him hard, not having
thought of this. Tonight her feelings had undergone a
considerable change so that she no longer knew what
to think, but when she thought of her life without
Christopher – her husband – on whom she had come
to depend like the very air she breathed, and whose
quiet strength she valued a great deal, she was bewil-
dered and confused. She covered her face with her
trembling hands. 'Dear God, no. Please, not that.
After all that has happened – after all I have lost – I
could not bear that too.'

Christopher sighed, deeply touched by her words.
'Very well, Clarissa. I promise you that I shall not kill
him – merely teach him a lesson he will not forget,'
and he turned from her and strode out of the room.

Back in his room, Christopher flung his jacket on to
the bed and, moving to the fireplace, rested his arms
on the mantelpiece, gazing into the fire.

He sighed, thinking over the night's events. Perhaps his anger had made him hasty. If he was honest with himself then he had to admit that he didn't want to kill Montgomery. He was a villain and he despised him, and it was right that he should be punished for what he had done, but he did not deserve to die for it. And Clarissa was partly to blame. She should never have gone looking for him. Anyway, the last thing he wanted was his death on his conscience. He would prefer to put the whole ugly episode behind him. But that was before one of the footmen brought him a note that had just been delivered to the house. It was from Edward, and the short missive told him that he would meet him at dawn in Huntsman's Quarry, where they would settle their differences with swords. Christopher uttered a sigh of resignation. So, he had no choice. He would have to fight. If he did not meet him he would be branded a coward, and that was unthinkable.

It was just before daybreak that he went to rouse Richard, urging him to get dressed quickly and meet him in the hall. It took him just a few minutes to tell him all that had happened.

The world as the two men rode through the park in a thick blanket of grey cloud was cold, everything about them dormant, gripped by a beautiful desolation. The ground was hard, the young shoots of spring held captive beneath a white, hoary frost, spread like a mantle over the land, showing tracks of rabbits and hoofprints of deer. The wind snaked a pathway round the naked trees, pointing their branches like gnarled fingers up to an as yet invisible sky.

They rode hard, staring straight ahead, grim-faced, the only sound being the blowing of their horses and the rhythmic pounding of their hoofs. As they approached Huntsman's Quarry nothing moved; it was oddly silent and deserted, the park hereabouts deeply wooded and, as Christopher looked into the semi-circular glade, he couldn't help thinking that it was aptly named and he remembered with an icy chill what Richard had told him before they had left the house, and could well imagine that this was where many a hunt had ceased. This was where, after spilling over the land like quicksilver, frenzied by excitement and their lust for blood, the liver- and white-coloured hounds, the death pack, trapped its quarry with a terrible ferocity, and with blood-curdling howls brought it to the ground, savagely tearing at the convulsive body.

They slowed their pace, advancing with caution deeper into the glade, the branches of the huge trees joining overhead, forming a tunnel. They scanned the dark shadows not only for Edward and his second but also for others, for the constables, for if the law had got wind that a duel was to be fought then it would spell disaster for them all.

Edward and his second, a servant who had accompanied him from London, were already there, and rode out of the dark shadows as they entered the glade. Quickly all four dismounted, Christopher divesting himself of his cloak and handing it to Richard, eyeing Edward carefully as he moved closer. In the cold light of dawn there was no trace of the drunken creature of last night, when the fumes of alcohol had clouded his mind. Now he met Christopher's gaze coldly.

'I trust you slept well,' he said with sarcasm, 'and that you said farewell to your bride, for I doubt you shall see her again.'

'No, I did not, for I do not expect to die.'

Edward smiled almost pleasantly. 'Then you were too confident, for, I promise you, you will not live to see another dawn.'

'We shall see,' said Christopher, taking off his jacket and throwing it on the ground.

The two men faced each other in shirts of fine lawn, and Christopher read clearly the evil intent to kill in Edward's eyes. Both men loosed their swords, freeing the naked blades from their sheaths. Edward saluted his opponent with a sardonic smile.

'*En garde.*'

They circled each other warily before their blades engaged, ferociously slicing the air. The swords clashed and at first neither bore the initiative, but they fought with all the violence born of hatred.

Richard watched fearfully, realising both men were evenly matched although Christopher was taller and appeared the most powerful of the two with his strong, muscular frame, but Edward possessed a lithe agility and fought with all the skill of an experienced duellist. As he watched he was certain that one of these men would not emerge from this encounter alive.

It was only after Edward stumbled slightly on stepping back, his injured leg letting him down, that Christopher seized his chance and immediately took the initiative, lunging, pressing home his attack. Enraged at finding himself at a disadvantage, Edward fought like a man possessed and their blades clashed faster and faster. A fierce, determined light shone in Christopher's eyes, but not a muscle in his dark face moved as his sword flashed, the clash of steel on steel rending the air. Edward began to fight dementedly, with everything to lose, but however hard he tried to attack he could not penetrate that unwavering guard and was constantly driven back as Christopher proved the stronger, his blade fiercely hissing the air.

Pure cold fury filled Edward's eyes at being held constantly at bay, and in desperation he began lunging wildly, carelessly, while Christopher retained his calm, and at last pressed home his advantage, sliding the point of his sword through the soft flesh of Edward's shoulder.

Edward's eyes opened wide in absolute surprise, his sword slipping from his hand, bright red blood staining the white purity of his shirt as he stumbled and fell, crumpling on to the ground. Christopher stepped back and stared down at him. Richard was beside him in a moment.

Edward cursed softly and attempted to get up but, his chest heaving, the effort proved too much and, smiling bitterly, he looked up at Christopher. 'Well, what are you waiting for? Aren't you going to finish me?'

'No – I shall not kill you, but only because before I came here Clarissa begged me not to. It is she you have to thank for your life, though God knows why after what she suffered at your hands. But be under no illusion, because it would give me immense pleasure to finish you for good.'

'Then do so,' hissed Edward. 'Because I swear that while ever there is breath in my body I shall hunt you down. I shall be avenged – I swear it. You shall regret not killing me – this I promise you.'

Christopher favoured him with one last contemptuous stare. 'I doubt that. Come, Richard, our business here is done. He is not dead and it was a fair fight. Whatever he threatens, I doubt he will bother us again,' and without paying further attention to the recumbent figure he turned and strode away, firmly believing as he did so that he would never set eyes on Edward Montgomery again.

At the house Clarissa waited anxiously for them to return. When Christopher stepped into the hall, having left Richard stabling the horses, he stopped for a

moment and looked at her, so still that she might have
been carved out of stone. Her face was white, one
hand at her throat as she waited, taut with suspense,
for him to tell her what had happened. Slowly she
moved towards him and stared into his face, set in hard
lines, his expression grim. She swallowed hard, reluctant to ask the question uppermost in her mind but
knowing she must.

'Is he – is he dead?'

She trembled inwardly with fear at what he might
tell her, and the intonation in her husband's voice was
cold and distant – he might have been a stranger – as
he replied, 'No. When I left him, I regret to tell you,
he was very much alive.'

At the relief that flooded her eyes his face hardened
and he was conscious of a sudden surge of anger.

'Thank you. Was – was he badly wounded?' she
whispered, her voice dying away into the silence of the
great hall.

Christopher looked at her incredulously. 'You
astound me, Clarissa. Does it matter to you so much?
Is it possible that, after all the harm he has done, you
can still feel compassion? Your concern for him is quite
touching, but did it not occur to you for one moment
that I might not return? That I might be the one lying
out there?' and then he smiled suddenly, a thin sardonic smile and his eyes narrowed cruelly. 'But then,
how convenient for you if I had been. I shudder to
think how quickly you would have flown to your
precious Edward then.'

'No – no,' she gasped, staring at him in disbelief. 'I
couldn't.'

'Why not?' he mocked. 'Do you mean because of
last night? Did his violent lovemaking give you no
pleasure?' and he laughed mirthlessly, a low, horrible
sound. 'But isn't that how women like their lovers to

be – violent? Don't they glean pleasure from the pain and humiliation inflicted on them?'

Clarissa shook her head. 'Christopher, don't – please don't talk like this.' She looked down at her hands. What could she say, she thought despairingly, to make him understand the torment she had been through after he had left her? How could she make him believe that she never wanted to see Edward again – ever – but that neither did she want him to die at the hands of her husband? And how could she make him believe that, after much soul-searching, she had realised that if one man had to forfeit his life during the course of the duel then she would rather it have been Edward? She stared up at him, unable to put her thoughts into words, and as she met his gaze miserably all she said was, 'This has been one of the most terrible nights of my life. I shall never forget it as long as I live.'

'Then you must forget it. For your sake – as well as for mine,' he replied cruelly. 'And I will tell you this, Clarissa: I never want to hear the name of Edward Montgomery mentioned again. Do you understand? You are my wife now and I expect you to behave as such. So the next time you feel the inclination to go running off in the middle of the night to meet your lover, perhaps you would be wise to think again. I will fight no more duels on your behalf.'

She was stung by his unjust accusation and the contempt in his voice, and some of Clarissa's fighting spirit rose to the fore and her eyes met his, flashing defiance. 'No – he was never that and you know it.'

Christopher's face became taut, his dark eyes boring into hers, plumbing their innermost depths, searching for some sign that would tell him she was lying, but there was none. He reached out and gripped her wrist as she was about to turn away, anger flushing her cheeks. 'Swear to me,' he rasped, glaring down at her mercilessly. 'Swear to me that what you say is true, because if he was and I had known earlier then I would have done all in my power to kill him.'

A violent, hidden force seemed to erupt inside him, and Clarissa was seeing a side to him she hadn't known existed. She felt afraid but her eyes did not fall beneath his gaze. Could this cold, angry stranger be her husband? The man she had married – who had asked her to go with him to America? The hideous events of the past twenty-four hours had unleashed in him all the fury of his passionate nature, and all the more terrible because she knew that due to her blind stupidity she was the one to blame. The pain his fingers caused her as they gripped her wrist suddenly made her cry out and tears start to her eyes.

'For pity's sake, Christopher. You're hurting me – please – let go——'

'Swear it,' he said between clenched teeth, forcing back a rage that threatened to consume him.

'Yes – yes, I do swear.'

He glared at her for a long hard moment, seeing the tears in her eyes, and only then did he release his terrible hold, flinging her hand away from him. 'Very well. But God help you if you are lying.' He took a deep breath. 'And now – perhaps you would be good enough to be ready to leave for London as soon as possible.'

At his words her eyes opened wide in alarm. 'Leave? But – but you said we could have a few days here at least before we had to leave.'

'I've changed my mind. I've wasted too much time already and have no wish to remain here a moment longer. Must I remind you that my country is on the brink of war and I have to get back?'

'But – but a few days,' she pleaded, rubbing her sore

wrist. 'We're not due to sail for a week – we could stay here a little longer.'

'No,' he said with such finality that she stepped back from him.

'Very well. If you insist then I shall instruct the maids to begin packing my things.'

She said this with such doleful resignation that Christopher sighed, some of the hardness leaving him, knowing just how difficult it would be for her to leave Ashton Park. But however much she pleaded he would not relent. The past twenty-four hours had made him heartily sick of the place and he was impatient to leave. They would spend the time left in London with his uncle before it was time to leave for Bristol, where they were to board a ship for Charleston.

'I'm sorry, Clarissa, but you have to leave some time – you knew that when you married me, so what does it matter whether it is today or tomorrow?'

She nodded and, swallowing back her tears, squared her shoulders, a determined little tilt to her chin as she looked at him directly. 'I know, and you are right – one day is much the same as any other.'

She turned from him and he watched her walk across the hall and disappear up the stairs to her room, aware of all the wretchedness she must be feeling, detesting himself for venting his anger on her, knowing that the manner in which he had spoken to her was unforgivable. He strode quickly into the dining-room, cursing angrily, and, taking a decanter, poured a generous helping of brandy into a glass; but not even when he drank deeply, feeling the fiery liquid course through his veins, did it lessen his self-loathing.

When Clarissa considered what her life would be from now on she felt that it would be like spinning about in some great vortex, without the stable influences of

Ashton Park, on which she had always depended and from which she was about to be wrenched, and she was totally unprepared for the scale of misery that engulfed her. She took refuge in silence, withdrawing inside herself, helping Betsy and Letty to pack her belongings with care, gazing at all that was familiar to her a little longer than usual, for whatever she saw now would be imprinted on her mind for all time.

It was the morning following the duel and she stood on the steps of Ashton Park, the wind blowing in sharp gusts across the wide expanse of the park, sending threatening black clouds scurrying across the sky. She looked up, feeling the wind brush her pale cheeks, and, breathing deeply, there came to her the pungent smell of pine needles. The first sharp drops of rain began to fall, stinging her skin, and she shuddered, feeling that the cold wind was like an act of terrible ill omen.

Servants, footmen and stablehands were all milling about and, straight-backed and dry-eyed, she said goodbye to them all, but it was with a heavy heart that she embraced Letty, who wet her with her tears, and Richard, who held her tight, hugging her to him so that she could feel the pounding of his heart, telling her to be happy. However much she wanted to, she did not cry; not even when she was in the carriage, sitting across from her husband and leaving the graceful lines of Ashton Park behind, wondering if she would ever come back, did she cry. But she would not allow herself to look back, for if she did it would break her heart.

CHAPTER NINE

THE American coastline was dotted with islands separated from the mainland by salt marshes, and the skyline over Charleston was dominated by numerous church steeples. Clarissa and Betsy, standing at the ship's rail, watched enchanted as the *Endeavour* drew closer to land, gliding through the tranquil waters, weaving its way between other vessels. They entered the broad, sparkling bay with snow-white sand and sailed up the harbour to the waterfront. It seemed an age before the *Endeavour* finally slid into her berth in this seemingly sleepy town, often called the mother city of the south, the focal point of social culture and economic and political activity of South Carolina, one of the smallest of the southern states. It occupied a narrow peninsula overlooking a large natural harbour created by the confluence of the Cooper and Ashley rivers.

It didn't take them long to disembark. Their baggage was to be brought ashore and sent on to the hotel here in Charleston where they were to stay overnight before travelling on to Tamasee. They soon found themselves in an open carriage, Clarissa's and Betsy's skin protected from the glare of the afternoon sun by lacy parasols. They travelled away from the docks, moving past warehouses piled high with bales of cotton, rice and tobacco, and Clarissa found herself wondering what would happen to it all if, as Christopher expected, a state of war was declared between England and America. He had told her gravely that if this happened then America's foreign trade would be almost destroyed. She wondered if most of it would go north to New England, where merchants were taking their capital and investing in new machinery, eager to manufacture their own goods and so reducing their imports from Europe. She sighed, wondering if she would ever understand the complexities of this strange new land, which, regardless of how she might feel, she must learn to adopt as her own.

After the winter in England she was quite unprepared for the light-hearted excitement of Charleston, with its sudden explosion of colour. It had been when the *Endeavour* had sailed closer to America, when the climate had changed considerably, that she and Betsy had taken to wearing their lighter dresses, more suited to the balmy clement weather. The warm sun and sultry air was filled with the sweet delicate perfume of tropical flowers and she was struck by the careless, languid atmosphere and the soft blur of the southern speech that fell pleasantly on her ears.

Pavements swarmed with people, people of all colours ranging from white, passing through every shade of brown to black. Their clothes were gaily coloured, their dark skins glowing as if they had been rubbed with oil. Clarissa looked at them curiously. The only black people she had seen before had been in London. Several of her acquaintances kept black servants, whom they dressed in brightly coloured silks with turbans on their heads. But all at once she was acutely aware of a cold, sickly feeling in the pit of her stomach, which told her that this was different. This was slavery, which, she told herself, she must learn to accept if she was to live here. It was this obscene trade in human flesh that kept the southern states and men like her husband rich. Her embarrassment was evident and she did not know how to react, hence it was with great difficulty that she avoided Christopher's questioning eyes, his close scrutiny, as he waited expectantly for her reaction, and so she remained silent.

The carriage came to a halt in front of their hotel and immediately three bell boys dressed in blue velvet emerged from inside to assist them. The manner in which the manager and the hotel staff greeted Christopher, ushering them inside, seeing to their every comfort at once, left Clarissa in no doubt as to his importance and the high regard in which they held him. It was almost as if he were royalty. But then, she thought, having learnt a great deal about South Carolina and its people from her fellow passengers on board the *Endeavour*, wasn't that what these southern planters considered themselves? Wasn't there a conspicuous upper-class gentry, an aristocracy, as some liked to call it, with old established names like Rutledge, Lauren and Pinckney? And she was in no doubt that the Cordells could be listed among them. In fact, these people, this planting upper class who had a right to this class, were relatively more numerous in South Carolina than in any other part of north America.

The room to which they were shown was large and cool and, she thought, quite correctly, probably the best the hotel had to offer. The creamy lace curtains moved gently with the soft, refreshing breeze blowing in through the open window. Betsy was to occupy the smaller, adjoining room, to which she disappeared immediately to change, and it was only then that Clarissa, staring at the large bed, felt a sudden dart of panic when she realised that Christopher was to share it with her.

He had followed her inside and, seeing her standing quite still in the centre of the room, staring at the bed, and noticing the sudden pallor of her face, he smiled thinly, angered by her reaction. 'Does it displease you to know this room is for both of us?'

She spun round, startled by the sound of his voice. 'No – no, of course not,' she stammered. 'Only – I – I thought——'

'Thought what?' he said brusquely. 'That I didn't wish to share a bed with my wife? Well, whatever thoughts might have passed through that pretty head of yours, Clarissa, I can tell you now that I find the possibility quite appealing, although on board ship was hardly the place to begin married life,' he said drily.

He moved to the window and stood looking down into the street. Clarissa stared at his stony profile, his jaw set firm, and a sudden surge of longing to go to him and run her hands over the broad set of his shoulders welled inside her, but she didn't move. She swallowed hard, sensing the tension inside him. This was the first time they had been alone, truly alone, since their marriage, which now felt as if it had happened in some other lifetime. But one thing was clear to her and that was that they couldn't go on like this. They would have to talk, to bring down this invisible wall he had erected between them. At last she moved towards him.

'Please, Christopher,' she said softly. 'We have to talk. We can't go on like this.'

'No – you're right, we can't. But tell me,' he said without turning, his voice low and controlled, 'why did you go to him that night? I have to know, Clarissa.'

He had told her he never wanted to hear Edward's name mentioned again and since the duel neither of them had, but she knew he remained uppermost in his mind.

'I went to him,' she said quietly, 'because I had to know if he would have married me – knowing my circumstances. I had to know, before I went away, for my own peace of mind.'

He turned sharply and looked at her, and she cringed inwardly at his cold expression. 'And would he?'

She shook her head. 'No.'

'Then it was fortunate for you, after all, that I came along, wasn't it?' he said cruelly.

'That wasn't fair,' she gasped, stung by his words. 'You knew my situation when you asked me to marry you. I made no secret of what my feelings were for Edward.'

'Of course,' he said, his lips twisting with sarcasm. 'You must forgive me for forgetting. But do you expect me to believe that you went to him on our wedding-night for no other reason than to talk to him?'

'Yes, I do.'

He shrugged. 'Whatever your reasons, you should not have gone.'

Clarissa's cheeks suddenly flamed, and she raised her head high as anger rose inside her, anger at his stubborn male pride, his refusal to accept what she had told him. 'Perhaps not, but if I remember correctly it was you who left me. It was you who turned from me on our wedding-night.'

'I will not make love to my wife, or any other woman, come to that, while her heart lies elsewhere,' and he threw her a mocking smile. 'Rather like having three in a bed, don't you think?'

'As far as I am concerned, Edward is dead, and if we are to find any happiness in our marriage then he must be dead for you too. Nothing can change what has happened, so we must learn to put it behind us. I no longer love him – I think I realised that before I went to see him at the inn – and, in fact, I don't know if I ever did. This I have told you, so why can't that stubborn pride of yours let you accept it?' She sighed deeply, her anger of a moment ago leaving her. 'Please,' she murmured, placing her hand timidly on his arm. Summoning up all her courage, she gazed beseechingly into his angry eyes. 'Have you made up your mind to hate me all your life? How much longer will you continue to spurn me? Can you not find it in your heart to forgive me? It hasn't been easy for me either, you know.'

Christopher looked into the imploring softness of her eyes, so bewitchingly beautiful, and he was moved in spite of himself. She looked so piteous, so defence-less and she spoke so passionately that the hard gleam went from his eyes and there was a softer tone to his voice when he spoke. 'You little fool,' he said, taking her hand from his arm and tenderly drawing her close. 'I don't hate you, Clarissa – don't ever think that. No man in his right mind would spurn you intentionally. You are far too lovely for that.' He smiled slowly. 'I've been a selfish brute, haven't I? You deserved better after what you've been through.'

She smiled with relief at the tenderness filling his dark eyes, and she trembled with a quiet joy. 'Then we are friends again?'

'More than that, I hope. But how does it feel to know you have the power to make me suffer, to make my life hell? You have bewitched me, Clarissa. No other woman has ever done that.'

'I – I'm sorry, Christopher.'

'What for?'

'My stupidity. Did I hurt you very much?'

'More than you will ever know, but you are right. We will put all that has happened behind us. We must not allow it to poison our happiness and, besides, the days ahead will be difficult enough for you without that. It is very important to me that you learn to love Tamasee as I do.' Gazing down into the magnificent blue depths of her eyes, he raised her hand to his lips, feeling desire surge through him, and he was impatient for the time to come when he could make her his wife in flesh as well as in name. But, however soft and inviting the large bed looked, now was not the time. 'I have to leave you for a while,' he said huskily. 'Much as I hate to.'

Disappointment clouded her eyes.'Oh – must you?'

'Yes. Ralph Benton, my overseer, should be here in Charleston. I have one or two things to attend to before we leave for Tamasee tomorrow.' He lowered his gaze, moving from her, unable to tell her that the things he had to attend to concerned the buying of slaves at the auction to be taken back to Tamasee.

'When will you be back?'

'Later. If I'm not back in time for dinner, you and Betsy go ahead and eat without me.' He turned back to her, drawing her once again into the warm circle of his arms. 'Don't worry, I'll be back later,' he said, bending his head and brushing her soft lips with his own. 'Wild horses won't be able to keep me from you tonight.'

Clarissa watched him go, her heart pounding as she awaited the night to come with all the sweet anticipation of a new bride.

Ralph Benton was a tall man in his mid-thirties, with a big muscular frame and a loud deep voice that gave the impression of his being more intimidating than he actually was. He'd been the main overseer at Tamasee for as long as Christopher had been the owner, and a great mutual respect and friendship had developed between them over the years.

Unlike many other plantation owners, Christopher abhorred unnecessary brutality where the slaves were concerned, and he had not hired Ralph for his skill in exhorting labour from the slaves with brutal methods. He was tough, and his commanding presence could galvanise any one of the Negroes at Tamasee into work without the use of the lash. Both men managed the plantation and Christopher only surrendered everything over to Ralph when he had to make business trips up north or to England.

The two men greeted each other warmly and, ordering refreshment, made themselves comfortable in the hotel lounge.

'How are things at Tamasee, Ralph?'

'Just fine. Young Mitchel's running things until we get back. Must say, your letter came as something of a surprise. Didn't expect you back so soon. Why the haste?'

Christopher lounged back in his chair indolently, crossing one booted leg over his knee. 'With the continuing unrest, I had no intention of being stuck on the wrong side of the Atlantic if war breaks out.'

'As it surely will if these new members of Congress have their way,' said Ralph.

'What's the situation here, Ralph?'

'Much the same as when you left. Many people in the south, and especially here in South Carolina, still clamour for war with the British – including that dynamic young pup from the back country, John Calhoun. He's one of these so-called "War Hawks".'

'Then they are fools,' said Christopher grimly. 'All of them.'

Ralph shook his head in disagreement. 'Are they? I'm not so sure. Ever since the Chesapeake incident in '07, when the British opened fire on her, you know yourself the demands for vengeance have been nationwide. Britain's continued harassment since has done nothing to reduce their anger.'

'Then they should learn to temper their ardour. Don't they realise that we shall be the losers?'

'It's no longer a matter of money, of dollars and cents, but one of national honour. War is inevitable. As I see it, we have two choices – fight or submit. We really do have to teach Britain a lesson. If we don't fight then everything we achieved during the revolution will be undone. She cannot go on treating us as one of her colonies. We are a free, independent nation, and the sooner she realises that and accepts it the better.'

Christopher sighed deeply. 'Yes, and I do agree, but war achieves nothing. I believe negotiations are the best way to sort things out. Surely people can't have forgotten so soon that the embargo we exacted on Britain three years ago all but ruined us? Don't they realise that if we are unable to ship our cotton to Europe then we will be totally dependent on merchants in New England, and they will take advantage of our helplessness and offer us such ridiculously low prices that we will be forced to accept? Unless,' he smiled with a touch of sarcasm, 'we learn to spin and weave it ourselves.'

'And would that be such a bad thing?' asked Ralph. 'Wouldn't it be a good thing for us to stop being what Britain wants us to be – exchanging our raw materials for their manufactured goods? Wouldn't it be a good thing for us to pour more of our labour into learning to make things for ourselves? We have nothing in the south but slaves and cotton. Ah, Christopher,' he sighed, 'you have the mind of a lawyer. By the way you think and talk, I reckon you're more in tune with the Federalists up north. Maybe you'd be better off selling Tamasee and opening a law practice in Washington.'

Christopher grinned, not in the least offended by Ralph's words. There was no one else in the world who could speak as openly to him as Ralph. 'And we both know I won't do that. I shall never sell. Tamasee is where I belong.' He looked across at his overseer and the serious expression on his face. However much they argued, they would never see eye to eye, and he laughed suddenly, knowing from past experience and the many nights they had sat in the library at Tamasee after a hard day's work in the fields, relaxing and drinking their port, how Ralph loved nothing more than embroiling himself in political discussion, and, reaching out, he slapped him good-humouredly on the shoulder. 'Have you never considered joining the "War Hawks" yourself, Ralph?' he joked light-heartedly. 'Bet they'd like to have someone with your political enthusiasm on board.'

Ralph frowned seriously. 'Nope. But I bet they'd welcome you.' He grinned, and his expression relaxed. 'As for me – well, I'm quite happy doin' what I'm doin' and letting others sort the nation out. Now,' he said, looking across at Christopher and squinting thought-fully, 'what about this other matter you mentioned in your letter? Didn't you write somethin' about a wife?'

Christopher nodded, the expression in his dark eyes softening when he thought of Clarissa. 'I did, and her name's Clarissa.'

'Well,' said Ralph, scratching his head. 'You could have bowled me over when I read that. Never thought you'd do it,' and he frowned suddenly, although a merry glint danced in his eye as an amusing thought struck him, and he looked at Christopher sideways. 'Does Marie know?'

Christopher looked at him long and hard, smiling slowly. 'No, not yet – but she will.'

'Then I sure hope I'm not there when she finds out. All hell will break loose – that's for sure.' He didn't tell Christopher that he had his doubts about him bringing a girl out from England to live at Tamasee. If he'd said he was looking for a wife and asked his advice then he'd have told him to marry a girl from the south. There were plenty just waiting to be asked. Girls who'd been born and bred to plantation life and who would manage Tamasee and the slaves in a way no girl from England ever could. Still, he'd bide his judgement until he'd met her, for, knowing Christopher, he wouldn't have married her if he hadn't thought she'd be suitable.

There was a more pressing matter Ralph had to mention to him, one that he knew would upset him, and a serious note had entered his voice when he spoke again. 'There's something I have to tell you, Chris, and I'm not goin' to beat about the bush. Sam's run away.'

'Sam?' Christopher looked at him in amazement, but as the full implication of his words struck him he paled and he was filled with a cold dread. Sam was his valet and meant a great deal to him. 'Why on earth would Sam want to run away?'

'Because I sold Della. You remember, that young Negress you bought in Georgetown just before you left for England – the one from Louisiana.'

Christopher nodded slowly. He did remember her – about twenty years of age, slender as a willow with short-cropped hair about her well shaped head, held high and proud, and he remembered the way she had met his gaze defiantly, her dark eyes spitting hatred, lacking the humility of other slaves. Oddly, this had appealed to him and, lacking his better judgement, he had bought her, intending to have her work in the house to help Agatha, whose aged bones were almost worn out. It had been obvious from the outset that the two did not see eye to eye but, unable to do anything about the situation because he was about to leave for England, he'd deliberately put Della out of his mind, hoping they would have resolved their differences by the time he returned home.

'I do remember her, but why should Sam run away because of her?'

'He became mighty smitten by the girl. I tell you, Chris, she was nothing but trouble. Even Agatha couldn't do anything with her in the house. She was forever complaining about her insolence and how uncooperative she was. Gave me the creeps, that one, with that strange practice these blacks have brought with them from Africa of worshipping the devil. As the Negroes say, she had the power to know things seen and unseen. She was both feared and respected. Sam certainly came under her spell – although I have to admit I didn't know he'd got it that bad.'

'He must have if getting rid of her caused him to run away. Nearly every plantation has one like her, Ralph. I don't think we need worry on that score. The Negroes at Tamasee aren't as deeply immersed in witchcraft as they are down in Louisiana and the Caribbean islands. Couldn't you have turned a blind eye?'

'No. There was too much general unrest, with strange rituals and incantations taking place at night, scaring the drivers out of their wits. She's different, that one, I tell you. Whatever you might think, her powers are not fanciful and nor can they be ignored.'

Christopher sighed. 'Nevertheless, it's years since a slave ran away from Tamasee. God help Sam if the slave patrol gets wind of this. Their brutality is renowned throughout the state. They'll show him no mercy, that's for sure. They've long had an eye on Tamasee, anxious to find an excuse to flog one of our "pampered slaves". We'll have to get to him first.' He glanced sharply at Ralph. 'I take it the patrol doesn't know about this yet?'

Ralph shook his head. 'I'm not sure. Slaves talk, and

when someone as important as Sam goes missing it's hard to keep it quiet.'

'I value Sam above any of the others, Ralph,' he said quietly. 'You know that. He was born at Tamasee on the same night as myself. My brother, Andrew, was so much older than me that I never really knew him as a child and, besides, he lived in Father's shadow. It was Sam I grew up with. If I manage to find him I want to make sure he'll have no reason to run away again – even if it means buying back the girl. Who bought her?'

'Robert Wheeler. His place is just north of here.'

'Yes, I know him and, from what I remember, he's a reasonable man. Perhaps if I offer him enough I might be able to buy her back.'

'If he's having the same trouble we had then he might be glad to be rid of her by now,' said Ralph wryly, but doubt filled his eyes. 'Do you think it'd be wise having her back? Everyone's breathed a lot easier since she went.'

'I don't know until I see her. Have you any idea where he might be?'

'I reckon he'll have headed for the Wheeler place – trying to get to her.'

'When did he leave Tamasee?'

'Two days ago.'

'How long will it take us to ride to the Wheeler plantation?'

'About an hour, I'd say.'

'Right, then have me a horse saddled and we'll leave here in half an hour. I'll go and change and tell Clarissa.'

They rode their horses hard, spurred on by thoughts of the slave patrol and what they would do to Sam if they got to him first. By the time they arrived at the Wheeler plantation the moon was already high in the sky, lighting up the driveway and the house. They rode towards the foot of the steps, but no one came out of the house to meet them. An uneasy, unnatural quiet hung over the place and just a few lights flickered through the windows; in fact, the whole house seemed devoid of life. The men glanced at each other apprehensively.

'Let's go round to the rear quarters,' said Ralph. 'There has to be someone about.'

Immediately he'd said these words the peace of the night was disturbed by the high, piercing scream of a woman, and suddenly the night became hideously unreal. A sinking feeling of dread knotted Christopher's insides. Hearing a commotion coming from the direction of the slave cabins, they set off quickly to investigate.

Away from the street of crude wooden slave huts was a large gathering of Negroes, with little isolated groups pressed against buildings, men, women and children, their eyes riveted on a huge wooden stake, to which a Negro was tied with ropes. They stood in silent obedience, but Christopher could smell the stench of fear emanating from every one of them. A dozen or so white men stood guard, some with guns trained on the Negroes, while one was administering the flogging of the man tied to the stake, his face twisted with sadistic pleasure as he brought the lash down slowly and with relish, to inflict the worst possible pain.

As the lash came down Christopher saw the body give one last agonising jerk before collapsing against the stake, his head flung back, the muscles of his arms bulging as they took the strain. A woman he recognised as Della was on her knees close by, her face in her hands, sobbing brokenly. In her despair she was the one who had screamed out her anguish into the night.

The man at the stake was filthy and bleeding profusely. The flesh had been reduced to a crimson jelly where the lash had fallen with such dreadful precision, but Christopher would have recognised him in any condition. It was Sam, and at the sight of him, a prisoner of these blood-thirsty slave catchers, he went white to his lips and could feel himself trembling with a terrible anger and indignation. That they had dared to flog one of his Negroes senseless was almost too much.

Robert Wheeler stood on the far side of the gathering and, from the hard expression on his face, he clearly disapproved of what was taking place on his plantation.

Before the patrol leader – whom he now recognised as Ned Stone, a thoroughly nasty piece of work – could raise his tired, bloodied arm to bring down the lash one more time on to Sam's back, scraps of human flesh stuck to the leather thongs, Christopher rode into the crowd, and it was with a great effort of will that he kept his fury in check, but his face was set hard and grim, a deadly gleam in his dark eyes. Ralph remained on the outer circle while Christopher rode forward, unafraid of the menacing threat posed by the gun-wielding patrol. The atmosphere became tense, and the crowd parted to let him through, his whole manner radiating a strength of purpose. None tried to stop him. The slave catchers all looked at him in amazement, and no one uttered a word as he slid from his horse.

'Cut him down,' he commanded to the nearest of the men.

The tone of his voice and his expression brooked no argument and, taking a knife from his belt, the man hastily did as he was told and severed the rope that bound Sam to the stake. He crumpled to the ground, unconscious. Christopher looked accusingly and with unconcealed loathing at Stone, who had derived such an unholy pleasure in flogging Sam. The others in the patrol closed ranks around their leader, waiting for Christopher to speak.

The face of Stone was lean and cruel, with deep-set pale grey eyes that had narrowed slightly. His features were savage with rage and disappointment at this untimely interruption.

'Well,' he snarled, unperturbed, unlike everyone else, by Christopher's presence, refusing to be intimidated by him. 'If it isn't Mr High and Mighty Cordell himself. Come to see what we do with runaways, have you?'

Christopher felt a shiver of revulsion at the cold cruelty in Stone's eyes. 'I see I wasn't in time to cheat you out of your sport, Stone, but raise that whip once more and I'll give you a taste of it myself.'

Stone's sallow face reddened with rage, and pure madness flamed in his eyes. 'Damn it all, Cordell, this 'ere's a runaway. I was giving him his just deserts – that's all.'

'Just deserts? You call flogging a man to death for running away giving him his just deserts?'

'He isn't a man, he's a Nigra,' he rasped, 'and catchin' runaways is my bizness. They have to be flogged as an example to others who harbour grand ideas in their heads of freedom – and, anyway, how do we know he isn't an insurgent, inciting other slaves to riot? They have to be put down – taught a lesson – and there's only one way to do that. We don't want a rebellion on our hands, now, do we?'

'Sam is not an insurgent and you damn well know it, and *I* say what has to be done with slaves who run away from Tamasee. You have no authority there, and if you set foot on my estate again I'll sure as hell kill you.'

Stone laughed, a ragged sound, and he glared at

Christopher. 'I beg your pardon,' he mocked, 'but he
wasn't where he should've been, at Tamasee, and it's
right what I've always suspected – what everyone
always said of you,' and he thrust his vile face closer to
Christopher's, 'that you're a nigger lover.'

'When it comes to filth like you, Stone, I'd as soon
love the devil. You're scum, the worst possible kind,
and it's not in the too distant past that I retain
memories of your handiwork, your sadistic tendencies,
where Negroes are concerned. I remember all too well
how you hanged those four runaways from the Stanton
place in cold blood, and I also remember the tortures,
the unimaginable cruelties that were inflicted on them
by you. For them death was a merciful release. You
are a butcher, Stone, and you should be horsewhipped
for this night's work.'

Stone glared at him furiously, but before he could
hurl further insults Robert Wheeler had come to stand
beside Christopher.

'I don't think there's any further reason for you to
be here now, is there, Stone? You've done what you
set out to do, so be gone – and take your henchmen
with you. I don't want you here any more than Mr
Cordell wants you at Tamasee.'

Stone turned and spat into the dust and with a
gloating triumph looked down at Sam, who raised his
tortured head, allowing Della to place it on her lap.

'You're right, Wheeler,' he said smugly. 'I've done
what I set out to do – for now – so I'll go, but you'll
come to thank us. This'll cool his appetite for runnin'
away, just you see if it don't.' He pointed his whip at
Della. 'She was to have been next. All nice an' cosy
they were in her little hut. Harbourin' runaways is
almos' as serious as runnin' away, but I'll save her for
a later date. Anyway, I wouldn't want to outstay my

welcome, now, would I?' And with an ugly-sounding laugh he sauntered to where his horse waited.

Everyone was silent and watched as the slave catchers mounted their horses and rode away, the night closing in around them. Christopher knelt beside Sam's body, taking in his pitiable state, and he was stricken to the very soul. He was certain Stone would have killed him had he not come when he had. He got to his feet when Robert spoke, clearly shaken by what had taken place.

'I can't tell you how glad I am to see you, Christopher. I would have done anything to prevent this, but it was impossible. I've been away for most of the day and the flogging was already under way when I got back. He is one of your slaves, isn't he?'

'Yes – he's from Tamasee.'

'Then I'm sorry. You know how much I deplore this kind of punishment. I don't hold with ill-treating slaves. That way you don't get the best out of them. I find they need kindness and understanding. Put terror into their hearts and it incites them to run away.'

'You're right. I abhor flogging. I believe the Negro requires skilful handling. Like you, I've always found they normally respond to kindness. They need firm guidance, but not with whips and chains.'

'Why do you think he came here?' asked Robert.

Christopher sighed and indicated Della, her head bowed, with Sam's head still cradled in her lap. 'There's your reason, Robert – a woman. He came to find her.'

'I see. She's the one I bought at auction a month back. Wasn't she one of yours?' he asked, eyeing Christopher curiously.

'Yes. I don't suppose you'd consider selling her back, would you?'

'Yes. As a matter of fact, I'll be glad to be rid of her.

She's trouble, that one – but then, you'll already know that.'

'No. I've been away in England and only arrived back today, but my overseer thought so. That's why he sold her.'

Robert scratched his head thoughtfully. 'Ah, well – I should've taken note of that when I bought her. It's well known that you never sell any of the slaves from Tamasee unless there's something wrong with them. And you're prepared to take her back?'

'Yes. I value Sam highly, Robert. He's my man-servant and an important part of Tamasee and my life. If it stops him running away I'll have her back.'

'Then she's yours and I'll ask for nothing more than the price I paid for her. Now come into the house. I don't know about you, but after this I feel the need of some strong liquid refreshment.' Seeing Christopher hesitate and cast a concerned glance at Sam, he smiled. 'Don't worry, I'll have Sam tended to. Send a wagon over in the morning for them both.'

CHAPTER TEN

ALONE, Clarissa moved aimlessly to the open window, thinking of Christopher and what it was that could be so important as to keep him from her. She gazed down at the street, letting her thoughts turn with longing to Ashton Park and Richard. In the clarity of her mind's eye she saw it all, the graceful sweep of the park and ancient, noble trees. How she wished she were there, to savour it all, instead of in this new, unfamiliar place. But then, she thought wistfully, if she were back in England then Christopher wouldn't be with her, and suddenly all those girlish dreams of Edward and the bulwark of her security – Ashton Park – began to slip into the past and didn't seem to matter now.

Suddenly, without her noticing, Christopher had become a very important part of her life. He had stood by her, offering her his name, risking his money and his reputation. Letty had been right when she had said that no man would do all these things for a woman he did not care about, and she knew she would rather be here with him than without him at Ashton Park. But what did she feel for him? Did she love him? This she did not know. After Edward she would never trust her judgement again, but when she thought of him, of his darkly handsome face and flashing smile, her body trembled with an unaccustomed desire to have him hold her, to feel his strong arms about her and to rest her head on his broad chest – to have him love her. She was more than ready to become his wife in every sense of the word.

At last her vigil was rewarded when she saw him

come riding down the street towards the hotel accompanied by another man, larger than he was, who she assumed must be his overseer, Ralph Benton. They rode slowly, their bodies slumped in the saddle as if they had ridden far. After a few words they parted company and the other man rode off down the street, taking Christopher's horse with him as he entered the hotel.

With feverish anticipation she turned towards the door, expecting him to come in at any moment. Her heart began to beat quickly and her mouth became dry, the palms of her hands clammy, and then suddenly he was there, standing in the open doorway, his face etched with tired lines, his hair falling untidily over his forehead.

He was pleasantly surprised to find her not in bed and looked at her for a long moment before stepping inside, closing the door softly behind him. All thoughts of Sam and Della vanished as he stared at Clarissa, neither of them speaking, standing just a few feet away from each other. The only sounds Clarissa could hear were the sounds from her own heart, and in that one marvellous moment everything was forgotten but the immense joy they each felt in knowing of their mutual need.

'You needn't have waited up, Clarissa.'

'I wanted to, and, anyway, I wasn't sleepy,' she answered softly.

As he moved towards her she began to feel slightly light-headed, and then he was beside her, reaching out with one hand and letting the tips of his fingers run gently over the filmy lace of her nightdress.

'I remember this,' he said huskily. 'I saw it draped over a chair in your room on our wedding-night.'

Clarissa moved closer to him, her eyes wide and clear, her lips moist and slightly parted. Very slowly she wound her soft arms about his neck, drawing his head down to hers and breaking down any resistance he might have had left. 'Let this be our wedding-night,' she murmured, her warm lips against his. 'And I promise you there will be just the two of us, with no room for anyone else.'

Having waited too long for this moment, Christopher took her into his arms and clasped her to him. Like a starving man, he kissed her, feeling the awakening of his desire. It was a kiss that seemed to last forever, that went on and on, until gently he pulled away, gazing into the velvety softness of her eyes.

'I love you, Clarissa. As God is my witness, I love you. From that first moment I saw you at Lady Holland's party I have loved you, my sweet Clarissa – my wife. I have nearly died of wanting you.' At her soft smile he again bent his head, kissing her eyes, her lips, her throat, as though he could never have enough of her. His hands moved over her thin nightdress, realising that beneath it she was as naked as the day she was born.

She didn't stop him when he slipped her nightdress off her shoulders, whereupon it fell in soft folds around her feet. She stepped out of it, and his breath caught in his throat at the splendour of her beauty, her body drenched in the intoxicating sweet scent of roses. His eyes devoured her pale loveliness in the soft light emanating from the lamp and the moon shining in through the window. He reached out and removed the pins from her hair, plunging his hands into the long silken tresses as they tumbled about her shoulders, drawing her close, his lips finding hers yet again.

Clarissa's need for him shook her to the very core. 'Please, Christopher,' she breathed against him.

'Please what, my love? Please make love to you – is that what you want? Oh, my darling, I shall make love to you until you beg me to stop, I promise you,' and with that he swept her up into his arms and carried her to the bed. After divesting himself of his clothes he lay beside her.

It was without shame or shyness that Clarissa wound herself about him, seeking his lips with her own, his hand caressing her with exquisite slowness, stroking the firm swell of her breasts and down over the smooth curve of her belly, bringing her flesh aflame as ecstasy and passion swept through her such as she had never known.

With his lips close to hers he murmured tender, passionate endearments and she closed her eyes, allowing his words to wash over her, experiencing a fierce, primitive hunger that threatened to engulf her completely. With his mouth covering hers she felt his weight crushing her, and she stretched beneath him so that he could feel every inch of her body as joyfully she allowed him to possess her, abandoning her body to his will completely, rejoicing in the delicious sensations of pleasure. In his arms she was filled with an ardent desire that matched his, and as they became one flesh she was plunged into a glorious oblivion.

They made love until towards dawn, when at last they fell into a short but blissful sleep, but before Clarissa closed her eyes, curled within her husband's warm embrace, she knew with a feverish joy, as surely as night followed day, that she loved him. She accepted the truth with a kind of wonder. She loved him with every fibre of her being, he was a part of her, branded on her very soul, and she would never be free again. With this glorious revelation everything she had found so difficult to understand suddenly seemed so simple, so uncomplicated, and now she had only one desire – to stay by his side for always.

* * *

She came awake suddenly when he stirred beside her, and when she opened her eyes he was sitting on the edge of the bed, pulling on his clothes.

'What's the matter?' she murmured sleepily, rolling towards him, and, reaching out, ran the tips of her fingers provocatively down his bare spine.

Christopher shuddered involuntarily, her mere touch sending him dizzy, and, turning, he looked at her as she stretched sensuously among the ravaged bed-clothes, her pale, silken mass of hair spread about her. Unable to resist her, he reached out and tenderly gathered her into his arms, placing his lips in the warm hollow of her throat. 'I have to leave you for a while, my love. There is urgent business to attend to before we can leave for Tamasee.'

She nestled drowsily into his embrace, finding his lips with her own, winding her slender arms like wands about him, bent on conquering him. 'But why must you go?' she murmured. 'Stay here with me – for just a little while longer. Don't you want to?'

'God help me, Clarissa,' he replied hoarsely, placing his firm hands on either side of her face and gazing with longing into her dark, sleepy blue eyes. 'You know I do. You are beautiful – wonderful beyond belief. You are like a witch – a temptress.'

'Then stay with me,' she pleaded.

'No,' he replied, gently but firmly, feeling renewed passion stirring inside him, and, disentangling her clinging arms, he held her away from him. 'There is nothing I want more than to stay here with you and make love to you all day – but unfortunately I cannot. We must leave here before midday. Now,' he said, laughing lightly at the cross frown creasing her brow, 'be good, will you, and go back to sleep?' and, standing up, he continued dressing.

Lying back on the pillows, Clarissa watched him

from beneath half-closed lids, and when he was ready to leave she raised herself on one elbow, the sheet slipping down to reveal one firm white breast. Christopher's breath caught sharply in his throat at her sheer loveliness.

'Won't you kiss me before you go?' she asked.

'No,' he answered, laughing lightly. 'You know damned well what would happen if I so much as touched you. In a moment I would be in that bed beside you and Ralph would be knocking on the door in no time to see what was keeping me.'

Defeated, Clarissa sighed and sank back against the pillows, pulling the covers up to her chin. 'Oh, very well. Go, then. When will you be back?'

'Soon – I promise,' and, laughing softly, blowing her a kiss from the open doorway, he left her alone.

With sunlight streaming in through the window Clarissa no longer felt the desire to sleep and hurriedly climbed out of bed, noticing her nightdress still lying in a crumpled heap on the carpet. Striding over it, she gazed at herself in the dressing-table mirror, seeing her lips slightly swollen from Christopher's kisses and her skin, which seemed to glow from his touch. At the transformation a sense of triumph swept through her, for the face reflected in the mirror was the face of a woman, all trace of innocence having disappeared, and when Betsy tapped on her door and entered, smiling broadly, one look at Clarissa's face and she too noticed the transformation and welcomed it. Never had she seen her look so radiant, so happy.

Later, having dressed and eaten, they were delighted to discover that Christopher had arranged for them to see the town in a very elegant horse-drawn carriage, which had been sent out from Tamasee, driven by an ageing Negro. He had a cheerful face and the broadest smile Clarissa had ever seen, and he delighted in telling them his name was Amos and that he was one of the main coachmen at Tamasee. He sat up front with an air of dignified authority as he prepared to give them a grand tour of Charleston.

Eagerly they climbed inside, travelling along narrow streets, attracting many an admiring glance, especially Clarissa, in her lemon silk day dress. Betsy stared about her, awestruck, treating it all as one huge adventure. The streets swarmed with people and in parts were jammed with carriages and wagons, many loaded with bales of cotton, making for the wharves. Mules and horses alike champed at the bit in sheer frustration as they attempted to force their way through the congestion.

They passed bustling stores, unexpectedly quaint, and bar-rooms, with Amos pointing out places of note, travelling along streets with long rows of dwellings with names like Broad, Queens, Tradd and cobblestoned Chalmers. Blossoms topped garden walls, and houses were of mellowed brick and weathered wood, often two-storeyed open-galleried homes with delicate iron filigree on gateways and railings. There were mansions with long piazzas and elegant white columns looking inward towards shaded courtyards filled with pots of brilliant geraniums, flowering magnolia and azaleas in a variety of colours, their sweet scents filling the air.

Clarissa was enthralled, but she didn't remain that way. The carriage slowed almost to a halt as the jumble of carriages and horses became dense, and curiously she glanced around for a reason. What could it be that had brought so many people to this place? Her eyes were drawn to some posters on the wall of a building in front of them, and she strained her eyes to make out what was written on them, just managing to read the bold print at the top. She read, 'To be Sold'; the writing below was too small for her to read further, but it didn't matter, she'd read enough. These posters were advertising the sale of Negroes – this was a slave auction.

Despite the warmth of the day, a creeping chill stole over her, and she shuddered instinctively when she suspected that this might have something to do with why Christopher had delayed his departure to his home.

Betsy too had read the large print and understood only too well what it meant but thought it sensible to ignore it and drive on. How she wished Clarissa could have done the same, but when she ordered the carriage to stop she looked at her in alarm.

'Clarissa, you're not getting out? You mustn't – you can't – not here.' –

'Why not?' she said sharply. 'If I have to live here I shall have to learn all I can about it, so I consider this an appropriate place to start. I shall probably learn more in there during the next few minutes than I shall in a whole year in Tamasee.'

Seeing that Clarissa was determined to go into the building, Betsy sighed. 'Very well – then I'd better come with you. You can't go by yourself,' and, climbing out of the carriage, she followed her inside.

Neither of them noticed the look of abject disapproval on Amos's face at their unseemly behaviour. No respectable lady would go into that place, but his long years of servitude had taught him to hold his tongue. It wasn't his place to tell white folks what to do.

The two of them attracted many a curious glance, especially from Ralph Benton, who, having recognised the carriage and Amos, assumed, quite correctly, that the beautiful young woman disappearing inside the auction-room must be the new mistress of Tamasee. What she was doing in this place he had no idea, but one thing was certain: when Christopher found out he'd be livid.

Clarissa was right. She did learn a lot about slavery in the following minutes and saw it in a light she had never considered before. She watched the scene, transfixed, the moment seeming so unreal, as if she was suspended in some other world, intruding on something positively evil, as slave after slave emerged from the stalls, where they waited before stepping on to a balcony, the auctioneer's voice ringing out above the noise of the crowd.

'Bid up – bid up, gentlemen,' he shouted before proceeding to recount their age, characters and capabilities. They were paraded miserably, their sad, mournful eyes downcast, their whole look being one of despair, but Clarissa wondered at the anger and hatred that must fester in the hearts beneath their black skin for their white masters. Some were scantily clad but most were naked, all human dignity having been stripped from them as planters degraded them, examining their bodies closely to make sure they were healthy.

Owners' initials were branded on their skin, mostly the shoulder of a woman and the chest of a man, and Clarissa could almost feel and smell the brand, as the red-hot iron seared their soft flesh. How many of them would have her husband's brand on them? she wondered, and at this thought bitterness like bile rose in her throat until it almost choked her.

The people shifting restlessly about her regarded everything that was taking place as a perfectly normal practice, talking among themselves, buying and selling these Negroes dispassionately. Wives were separated from husbands, parents, weeping with deep sad sorrow, from children, which, to Clarissa, was against all humanity and reason. They were nothing to these cold southern planters but mere commodities.

A man came out on to the balcony with a woman, and when they were sold separately he cried out at the cruelty and, reaching out, grasped the woman, his wife, to him, tears and sobs and the terrible anguish of broken hearts rending the air. Clarissa watched their piteous pleading with their buyers, wanting to cry out at the injustice.

Unable to watch this spectacle in human misery pass before her eyes any longer, and much to Betsy's relief, she turned and went outside, climbing back into the carriage, her face white and expressionless. This town, which only a short while ago had seemed so warm and exciting, had suddenly taken on a whole new sinister meaning. She no longer had any desire to see through wrought-iron gateways at the beautiful houses and piazzas, whose foundations were the product of the dungeons and slave pens of Africa and the stinking ships that had carried them to America. All this civilised beauty had only been made possible by the oppressive society of South Carolina.

'Drive on,' she called to Amos. 'Take us back to the hotel.' She closed her eyes, breathing deeply as she tried to compose herself, to still the angry beating of her heart and the trembling inside her. 'Dear Lord, Betsy, what have I let myself in for?'

'Are you sorry you went in there?'

'No – no, I'm not. But how can they do it? How shall I be able to endure living with people who treat their fellow human beings with such cruelty, worse than animals, with whips and fetters, their only crime being the colour of their skin?'

'I don't know. It seems to be a state of affairs that's perfectly natural to them. Perhaps when we get to Tamasee things won't be so bad.'

'I hope not. Somehow I find it strange to think of Christopher being involved in anything so evil.'

'I know, but you mustn't forget that he was born a southerner – surrounded by slaves all his life.'

'No – not slaves,' said Clarissa, her lips twisting with irony. 'They prefer them to be called servants or hands. You see, at least I've learnt something. But you know, Betsy, after what we've just seen I know – now more than ever – that, no matter how abominable, how absolutely shocking I consider slavery to be, it's wise to keep my thoughts to myself. I must learn, however hard that might be, not to criticise this way of life, but I shall never be able to accept it. Never. But, like that of the south, my own subsistence depends on it.'

She fell silent as the carriage continued on its way back to the hotel, painfully slowly, but before they reached their destination Betsy suddenly gripped her arm.

'Look,' she said, 'over there – coming out of that store. Isn't that your husband?'

Clarissa directed her gaze to where Betsy indicated and saw that it was indeed Christopher, his arms full of packages, and her heart gave a joyful leap. His name was on her lips in an instant and she was about to call out to him, but she stopped, suddenly thrown off balance, staring at him uncomprehendingly. There was a woman by his side, the most beautiful woman Clarissa had ever seen, with a powerful sensuality. She was quite tall and slender, her long hair, as black as midnight, woven about her head, her skin pale and stretched smoothly over high, angular cheekbones, bringing a slant to her black eyes. The dark green of her silk dress accentuated the hidden charms of her supple, perfect body beneath, and a small matching hat with a dancing plume, set at an angle, was coquettishly perched on her head.

Clarissa watched her walk a little way along the pavement to where an empty carriage waited, noticing that she moved with the grace reminiscent of a cat, while her manner was the image of southern hauteur and arrogance.

Unaware that Clarissa was watching them, Christopher placed the packages inside the carriage before turning again to the woman. They talked for a moment and for some reason the woman was angry, their words heated. But Clarissa watched in horror, turning to rage, as the woman, with her head flung back, slowly slid her gloved hand over his chest, placing it about his neck and pulling his head down to hers, fastening her full red lips on his, kissing him passionately, to which he didn't seem to object in the least. When at last they drew apart, which to Clarissa seemed like a lifetime later, he offered the woman his hand to help her up into the carriage, but she ignored it coldly. Looping the reins through her long fingers and without looking at him again, she urged her horse on, a thin smile on her lips.

Like her carriage, which had conveniently become stuck in yet more congestion, enabling her to witness this touching scene between her husband and a woman she hadn't known existed until now, Clarissa hadn't moved as she struggled with the anger raging inside her, her blood seething. So, this was his urgent business. How dared he? How dared he leave her arms to go to this woman? And to think he had the gall to consort with her in public. Oh, what a stupid, vulnerable fool she'd been, letting him make love to her, believing he loved her, when all the time he must have been thinking of this creature. How he had deceived her and how she had succumbed to his embraces, letting him love her and then toss her aside. No wonder he'd been in such a hurry to get back to Charleston, she thought bitterly. How could she ever forgive him his treachery?

Christopher had disappeared into the crowd and the woman's carriage came close to her own. Glancing casually in Clarissa's direction, instantly she recognised the carriage, and frowned, her pencilled black brows drawing together like wings, her eyes darting to the occupants and fastening on Clarissa, who, stiffened by pride, had managed to dominate her anger and, raising her head, favoured this other woman, whom she saw as a threat to her new-found happiness, with a cool, level stare.

A heavy scent of jasmine wafted across to them from her body as her dark eyes examined Clarissa with curiosity, well aware of who she was and that she must have witnessed the scene. Slowly her eyes narrowed and glittered triumphantly, and she smiled dangerously, her red lips curling scornfully. Clarissa caught a flash of sharp white teeth from between her parted lips, knowing this woman derived a vicious pleasure from the discomfort and anger she knew Clarissa must feel.

Clarissa was convulsed with jealousy, and she had a primitive desire to reach out and strike this creature down. She was relieved that, with a brusque movement of her head, the woman turned away, and with a quick flick of her wrist laid the whip on her horse with such force that it jumped forward at once; then she was gone, leaving Clarissa staring after her, still swamped with anger.

'Well,' gasped Betsy, 'I never. I wonder who she can be?'

'I don't know, Betsy, but I certainly intend finding out.' Breathing deeply, she leaned back on to the soft upholstery as the carriage moved on. 'So, it seems I have another problem. Not only do I have slavery to contend with, but also a faithless husband.'

* * *

However much Clarissa's anger burned inside her, it could not match that of Marie's as she brutally laid the whip on the soft flesh of the horse with such ferocity that it leaped forward. Her beautiful face was convulsed with rage, her heart filled with a fierce hatred, hatred for the woman Christopher had dared to marry and bring back to South Carolina. How dared he deceive her and humiliate her in this way? He belonged to her – she was the one he should have married and taken to be mistress of Tamasee.

Well, this woman, with her insipid looks and simpering English ways, might be his wife, but so much the worse for her, she thought, and a deadly smile distorted her features as her jealous heart hungered for revenge.

Marie was Spanish, born of poor parents in New Orleans, and had dragged herself up from the gutter, making full use of the only assets she possessed – her looks and her body. She had come to Charleston and met Christopher Cordell, one of the wealthiest, most handsome men in South Carolina and, fortunately, unmarried. Determined to entrap him, she had lost no time in luring him into her bed.

Marie had always believed that one day he would marry her, but when the months of waiting had slipped into years she was filled with a growing doubt and impatience. But she had not been prepared for this insult, this humiliation, and, she thought with a sudden savagery, she would teach him a lesson he would never forget for his total rejection of her – casting her aside as if she had meant nothing to him. She might not have the genteel breeding of his cold English wife, but no one treated her like that. No. Not even Christopher Cordell, however rich and powerful he was.

Back at the hotel, Clarissa still seethed as she waited for Christopher. When he strode into the room he didn't at first notice her anger, being too full of his own. His face was set hard, the lines around his mouth tight, and when he stood glowering down at her she asked herself if this was the same man who had left just a few short hours ago, declaring his undying love for her – this angry, impersonal stranger. There was nothing lover-like about him now.

'What did you think you were doing, going to that auction?' he thundered.

For a moment his words distracted Clarissa from her own anger and she flinched, her eyes snapping wide open at his surprise attack. Surely she was the one who should be chiding him? Her heart contracted at his tone, merciless and cutting.

'If I'd known what you intended I would never have arranged for Amos to drive you around Charleston.'

'That isn't fair,' she replied indignantly, her anger restored. 'When I left here I had no intention of going into that place. Anyway, who told you? Amos?'

'No, he didn't have to, and, besides, he wasn't there to forbid what you might do. He knows better.'

'Yes, I'm sure he does,' said Clarissa tersely. 'Then who?'

'Ralph – my overseer,' he answered, preferring to ignore the implication of her remark. 'He recognised Amos and the carriage waiting outside. Clarissa, have you no sense? Can't you see it was the height of folly for a woman of your station to attend a slave auction?' He turned from her, running his fingers through his hair, which had fallen over his forehead, in exasperation.

'No, I can't,' she cried. 'And, whatever you say, it makes no difference. What I saw in that place was inhuman. To rob a man of his freedom is a sin. Black people were bought and sold just like cattle. It was horrible – an experience I shall never forget.'

Christopher rounded on her angrily. 'Please, don't start preaching to me of liberty and the rights of man, Clarissa. How can you argue about something about which you know nothing? Perhaps when you've been at Tamasee for a few weeks you might see things differently.'

His eyes darkened and a hard glitter appeared in them, which should have told Clarissa that his patience was wearing very thin, but her anger was such, brought on by his shameful behaviour with that black-haired woman earlier, that it matched his own, and as she threw back her head her eyes blazed into his defiantly.

'I doubt that.'

'Why?' he growled, his voice low, his face close to hers so that she could feel his warm breath on her face. 'What are you expecting to find? Negroes in shackles? Living in cringing submission of their white masters? Living under the shadow of the whip with the constant dread that they may be sold to more cruel masters, where their situations become even more hopeless? Well, let me tell you that the Negroes at Tamasee have no need to complain of their treatment. They are well fed, well clothed and housed, and the whip is seldom, if ever, used, and once bought they are never resold.' As he said these words his thoughts flew to Della. She had been the first Negro to be sold from Tamasee for a long time, but he believed Ralph had been justified in his reasons.

Beneath his withering gaze Clarissa sighed deeply, suppressing, with effort, the hot, angry words that threatened to burst from her lips. Suddenly everything was going wrong. The last thing she had wanted was this kind of conversation regarding the treatment of slaves. She had never intended becoming involved in an argument about slavery, however unjust she considered it, knowing she must reserve her judgement until she had seen it for herself.

'Christopher, let me explain——'

'There's no time,' he snapped, turning from her abruptly and striding towards the door. 'I want to leave here for Tamasee within the hour, so tell Betsy to get your things together. We'll deal with this matter later.'

His harsh dismissal of her caused Clarissa to summon all her self-control to stop herself bursting out of rage. But it was impossible. 'No,' she said, throwing all caution to the four winds, drawing herself up proudly. 'That is something I'm going to have to deal with in my own way, but what I cannot deal with, what I cannot come to terms with, is your faithlessness.'

Her words arrested him and he turned and looked at her, and for the first time since he had entered the room there was an element of surprise in his eyes, and he stared at her for a long moment before speaking slowly.

'Faithlessness? What on earth are you talking about?'

'You know perfectly well,' she said in a controlled voice, moving slowly towards him, her look as cutting as ice. 'I saw you earlier, Christopher, so don't try denying it. I saw you with a woman in the street.' Desperately she searched his rigid features for some hint of denial – but there was none, and a sudden revulsion filled her, a spasm of pain shooting through her heart. She glared at him with burning resentment.

At her words his face darkened and a look of guilt flashed into his eyes, but it was gone almost as soon as it appeared, and the shadow of a smile crossed his face, softening his expression, which only added fuel to her anger.

'What's the matter?' she fumed, stopping in front of him. 'Don't you remember? Then let me refresh your memory – black hair, a green silk dress? Why, yes,' she sneered, 'of course you remember, for you had the affrontery to kiss her in public.'

To her chagrin, the smile on his lips broadened. It was the first time he had seen her so angry. It seemed he had married quite a little spitfire, and in that moment, with the flush of fury on her soft cheeks and her magnificent eyes blazing, to him she had never looked more lovely. 'As I remember it, I wasn't the one doing the kissing.'

She found his teasing intolerable. 'I do not find it amusing, Christopher. Your behaviour was highly reprehensible, to say the least. No wonder you were so eager to leave my bed – after all, she is very beautiful.'

'Yes, she is,' he agreed infuriatingly.

'And was her bed warmer than mine?'

He sighed. 'Marie and I are old friends, Clarissa.'

'Ah, Marie – so that's her name. And do you deny that you are lovers?'

'Yes, I do deny it. We were – a long time ago – but not any more. The charms of Marie's bed long since ceased to hold any attractions for me.'

'Why didn't you marry her?'

He shrugged nonchalantly. 'Quite simple, really. I didn't love her.'

Clarissa's lips twisted with angry contempt. 'Don't take me for a fool, Christopher. I saw you with my own eyes. Have you any idea how I felt? The humiliation I felt?'

At her persistence a hard, disquieting line settled between Christopher's black brows and a spark of anger flamed in his eyes. The teasing note in his voice disappeared as he reached out and gripped her shoulders, pulling her towards him so that his face was close to her own, his fingers biting into her soft flesh.

'Yes, I do know how you felt,' he hissed with brutal

sarcasm, 'and I don't want to bring up old grudges, Clarissa, but wasn't I in the same position once? Do you remember that, or can it be that you have forgotten so soon how I might have felt, finding my wife with another man in his bedroom? God forbid – do you think I lived the life of a monk before I met you?'

'No,' she flared, 'I most certainly do not, but if you think for one minute that you are going to keep me on your plantation with the servile obedience of one of your slaves while you continue one of your unsavoury affairs here in Charleston then you are very much mistaken. I have too much self-respect for that.'

'Damnation, Clarissa,' he thundered, his fingers tightening their hold on her shoulders. 'Marie is not my mistress. What more can I say?'

'Then tell me what you were doing with her,' she cried, hot, angry tears threatening to engulf her at any minute, 'letting her kiss you like that.'

'After I had finished my business with Ralph at the auction we ran into one another quite by chance.'

'And you expect me to believe that?'

'Believe what you like, but you are making a mountain out of a molehill. She means nothing to me. She is of no consequence. Can't you see?' he said, his face full of both fury and desire as he tried to make her understand. 'Are you so blind, you stupid little fool, as not to see that it is you I love? Since I first set eyes on you there has been no room in my heart for any other woman. What Marie and I had was finished before I ever laid eyes on you.'

Clarissa stared at him, tears starting to her eyes as her nerve finally broke and her anger began to drain away. He sounded so convincing, and how she wanted to believe him, to know for certain that that woman meant nothing to him any more, but his words could not repair the hurt that seeing them together had inflicted on her. Her image was still there. It still stood between them. Tears ran from her eyes. 'Is it true?' she whispered.

His fingers relaxed their painful grip on her shoulders, but instead of letting her go he pulled her closer still, his breath fanning her cheeks, his dark face suffused with passion as his eyes fastened on her soft trembling lips.

'Idiot,' he murmured. 'But I'm sorry, and you have a perfect right to be angry. The last thing I want is to hurt you. But do you think I could want any woman but you after last night? You are a part of me now, my love, branded upon my heart forever, and I shall never be free of you.' Unable to resist her any longer, he bent his head, covering her mouth with his own, tasting the salt of her tears and feeling her lips quivering beneath his own as he kissed her tenderly. 'Now come,' he said, his lips leaving hers. 'We must prepare to leave Charleston. I want to show you Tamasee – our home – before dark. I want your first glimpse of it to be one you'll always remember.'

CHAPTER ELEVEN

Tamasee lay some three hours west of Charleston. Leaving the coastal swamps behind for a while, they followed the Cooper river, travelling further inland. The carriage bore them along the dusty road, driven by Amos, and a wagon sent out from Tamasee followed with the three field hands bought at auction. Having gone to the Wheeler plantation for Sam and Della, Ralph would not be arriving at Tamasee until much later.

They travelled through forests with hardwoods such as oak and hickory, the shade of their foliage and huge branches offering them welcome relief from the warm sun. Behind gateways were the stately houses of plantations, which owed something in both their design and the leisured, sophisticated lives of their owners to the gentry of eighteenth-century England. Spring in all its glory was spread before them, the woods clothed with varicoloured blossoms, white dogwood, yellow jasmine and wild azalea, the ground carpeted with purple violets and the sweet scent of honeysuckle carried on the soft warm breeze.

The carriage passed through a huge stone gateway, without the heraldic bearings of those at Ashton Park, but no less grand. They travelled slowly up a hill, the drive lined on either side by giant twisted oaks, dripping with moss, offering a cool, gentle shadiness, but before they topped the rise Christopher ordered Amos to stop the carriage. He climbed down, holding his hand out to Clarissa.

'Come – I'll show you Tamasee.'

Holding her hand, he led her to the top of the rise, the carriage waiting behind, Amos's face split in a broad smile. Without realising she was doing so, Clarissa held her breath when she gazed in wonder at what she thought must be a dream, an illusion, at the gentle sweep of the valley unfolding before her eyes. Acres of fields stretched almost as far as the eye could see, with straight furrows of well ploughed earth waiting for the spring planting of the cotton. Everything looked fresh and green, with pastures full of horses and cattle.

Clarissa gazed with wide-eyed enchantment at Tamasee, her husband's domain, and when her eyes at last rested on the house, white but glowing rose-pink in the red glow of the late-afternoon sun, she gasped in awe. It rose like a jewel out of the cool, dark shade of tall, moss-draped cypress and oak, surpassing anything she had seen so far in South Carolina. It stood stately and supreme, surrounded by lawns like green velvet and orchards of peach blossoms covering the countryside like a delicate pink cloud. The house had tall, gleaming windows with shutters to close out the sun. In front the roof rose to a point above tall Doric columns, with a wide, spacious veranda, reached up a flight of impressive marble steps. Beyond the house were the outbuildings and neat rows of slave cabins.

Watching her reaction, Christopher smiled slowly. 'I'm glad to see you're not disappointed.'

'Disappointed? How could I be?' she sighed. 'Oh, Christopher – I never imagined Tamasee being as beautiful as this.'

'Yes – I think so,' he replied with pride. 'Are you happy?'

She nodded without taking her eyes off Tamasee, which held them like a magnet.

'No regrets?'

'No, not one. But tell me – what does Tamasee mean? It's such a strange name.'

'Yes, it is. It's Cherokee and means "the place of the sunlight of God".'

'Yes,' she whispered, 'and I can see why.'

'It was my great-grandfather, Jonathan Cordell, who founded Tamasee. It wasn't easy for him in the beginning, having come from England, the regions being uncivilised with constant battles with the Indians, who, as more and more whites came, found themselves being pushed further and further back. Feeling a natural resentment, they fought to retain their homelands and hunting grounds. And yet,' he said quietly, gazing far into the distance, 'it is an Indian, a Cherokee chief, we have to thank for Tamasee.'

Clarissa looked at him curiously, waiting for him to go on, wondering why she had never asked him about his home before.

'During a storm my great-grandfather saved the Cherokee's daughter from drowning. In return for her life and knowing he was looking for a place to settle, the Indian chief rewarded him by bringing him to this place, and it was here that he put down his roots, feeling that he had come home.'

'What a lovely story,' said Clarissa.

Christopher grinned down at her. 'You might think so now, but then it was hard. It was only after many trials and adversities that he at last achieved success and created a rich estate, the one you now see. One to be handed down with pride to his descendants – and one, my love,' he said, 'that you and I shall one day hand down to our children. All this is yours now and I want you to feel for it as I do.'

She smiled up at him. 'I don't think that will be too difficult.'

'Come,' he said, turning and slowly escorting her

back to the carriage. 'We'd better get back before Betsy comes to see what's keeping us. I'm glad you brought her with you, Clarissa, that you haven't abandoned everything from your home in England. If you're wondering about a maid, don't, because I think I have just the girl. Her name's Della, and before she came to Tamasee she'd been on a sugar plantation in Louisiana and, I regret to say, was mistreated. Before I left for England she was helping Agatha in the house, but by all accounts they didn't get on and she wouldn't settle down. Because of this Ralph felt it necessary to sell her. For reasons I shall go in to later, I have since bought the girl back, although what Agatha will have to say when she finds out I shudder to think.'

'But – but I thought Agatha was a – a —'

'A slave?' and he grinned. 'Wait till you meet her. She's a formidable lady, is Agatha, and feels she owns the Cordells body and soul. She was born at Tamasee and presides over the house and other Negroes like some kind of matriarch, and her code of conduct is such that it would match any of your matrons back in England. Believe me, Agatha is a force to be reckoned with.'

Clarissa frowned. 'How will she take to me? It could be that she is unwilling to hand over the position that has been hers for a good many years. Will she not feel threatened and resent me – a total stranger?'

Christopher laughed lightly at the worried look on her face. 'Of course not, and don't worry. She told me long since to find myself a wife to ease her burden. She'll love you – just as I do. She may not show it – but she'll love you just the same.'

Although Christopher had told her all about Agatha, his housekeeper and one-time nurse, Clarissa was quite unprepared for the woman who came out on to the veranda to welcome them home with an air of dignified authority. She was quite tall and extremely thin, and her skin, stretched tight over her bones, was as black as ebony, but in stark contrast her grizzled hair was as white as driven snow, pulled with a severity from her face and squeezed into a large bun at the back of her head from which no rebellious strands dared to escape. Her features were fine, and as she saw Christopher her thin lips broke into a welcoming smile, transforming her stern expression to one of loving tenderness.

He strode forward to embrace her, wrapping his strong arms about her, and Clarissa thought that if he was not careful his housekeeper would snap in two.

'Ah, Agatha,' he sighed. 'You've no idea how good it is to be home again. I sure missed you and your cooking, but come – I have someone I want you to meet.' Turning, he brought Agatha to where Clarissa stood with Betsy a little way behind. 'Agatha – I would like to present my wife. Clarissa, this is Agatha.'

The two women were of the same height and their eyes met, blue ones meeting black ones. Agatha stared at Clarissa quite openly, although there was nothing insolent about her stare. It was as if she was trying to read there the answer to a question she had been asking herself ever since Christopher's letter had arrived from England, informing her of his marriage. Would this woman make him a good wife and would she prove to be a suitable mistress for Tamasee? It was important that she would, on both counts.

She was not disappointed and, having made up her mind, smiled slowly. Her black eyes held a gentle kindness and were now full of complete admiration for this fair-skinned, beautiful young woman from England, with the cool self-assurance of someone who had suffered and come through. Yes – she would be glad to have her shoulder some of the load at Tamasee.

'Welcome to Tamasee,' she murmured with a smile

of real pleasure, her voice as deep and rich as velvet. 'This sure is a happy day.'

Clarissa smiled, sighing with relief, some of the apprehension and tension she had been feeling over her meeting with Agatha disappearing. She wasn't nearly as formidable as she'd expected and, unlike that of all the other Negroes she had come into contact with since arriving in South Carolina, Agatha's mode of speech had been affected by her long years of servitude to the whites so that she had come to talk like them with the deep southern drawl.

'Thank you, Agatha, and I can't tell you what a pleasure it is to meet you at last. Christopher has told me so much about you.' She turned slightly and, grasping Betsy's hand, drew her forward. 'This is Betsy. Betsy is my companion.'

Still smiling, Agatha bowed her head slightly to the smaller, dark-haired woman. 'The welcome extends to you too, Miss Betsy. I hope you'll be happy at Tamasee.'

'Would you show Clarissa and Betsy to their rooms, Agatha?' asked Christopher. 'I'm sure they'd welcome a bath and a change of clothes after the journey.'

'Yes, Massa Chris, and I have refreshments ready and waiting.'

What seemed like dozens of black servants suddenly appeared and began unloading the baggage from the wagon while the two women followed Agatha's straight back in silence, looking dazedly about them, their feet sliding easily over the marble floor of the flower-decked hall, large and light and surprisingly cool. Doors led off to other rooms and, as Clarissa was to find out later, all were tastefully furnished with pieces from England and France. In general the colour of the hall was white with gilt-edged scroll-work on the ceiling, from which hung a single, magnificent crystal chandelier. They mounted a staircase, which rose grandly, its carpet a deep blue with a gold pattern. Clarissa was overwhelmed by it all. The interior at Tamasee was no less grand than the exterior.

A servant appeared to show Betsy to her room, close to the master bedroom which Clarissa was to share with Christopher. This room was no less startling than what she had already seen. But here, instead of the stark white, this room was decorated in softer, more restful shades of beige, the walls hung with ornate baroque mirrors and pictures, with a huge four-poster bed occupying the centre of the room.

Agatha stood to one side, showing pleasure at Clarissa's obvious delight.

'This is a lovely room, Agatha, and look,' she exclaimed, moving towards the slightly open french windows leading on to a balcony with curtains like gossamer blowing gently in the soft breeze. She opened them wide, stepping out on to the balcony, letting her eyes travel over the lawns to the fields beyond. 'What a lovely view.' For a moment she let her gaze rest contentedly on the rich acres of Tamasee before, sighing and turning, she went back inside, where servants were beginning to carry in her trunks.

'I'm glad you like it,' smiled Agatha. 'Massa Chris wrote and told me from England how he wanted it.'

'Then he chose well. Has this always been my husband's room?'

'No, miss. His was further down the landing. This was Miss Rosalind's room – his mother's – until she died.'

Clarissa noticed how her voice trembled when she mentioned Christopher's mother, and she detected a hint of sadness. 'Were you very fond of her?'

She nodded. 'Oh, yes. She was like an angel – a

remarkable lady and, like you, she came from England.'

Clarissa looked at her, intrigued, her curiosity about her predecessor increasing all the time. 'Did she find it easy to adjust to life here, Agatha?'

'Oh, yes – but then, she and the massa were so much in love. It did take her a while to settle down, but as soon as she learnt how to run a household as big as this she was just fine.'

'What was Christopher's father like? Did he look like him?'

'No. Massa Chris is like his mother,' and she shook her head slowly, her black eyes clouding over as her memory slipped back over the years. 'It sure was a terrible day when his daddy and young Massa Andrew died on the river boat during a storm – one of the wust storms I remember. Do you know about that?'

'Yes – he told me.'

'Massa Andrew was such a handsome young man – just like his daddy. Miss Rosalind was so distraught that I thought she would surely die of a broken heart. Mebbe she would have if Massa Chris hadn't come from England so quickly. He took charge of everythin' right away – even though his heart wasn't in it – and him bein' so young. I could see what he was goin' through but, you see, he had to take over, forgettin' everythin' else. It was either that or sell Tamasee, and to him that was unthinkable. If he'd done that the soul of Jonathan Cordell and all the others who came after him would have risen up and condemned him.' She moved to where Clarissa stood, giving her a sudden keen look, a serious expression in her wise old eyes. She nodded slowly. 'I think Tamasee is in for better days. You'll make Massa Chris a good wife – I know, I feel it here,' she said, placing her clenched fist firmly over her heart. 'But it will not be easy for you. A woman's lot is never easy at Tamasee.'

'I know it won't, Agatha, but I am more than willing to learn. I only hope you will teach me – and be patient, I am afraid there are many things about this land that I am going to have to get used to.'

Agatha nodded but remained silent, understanding by her quiet words that by this she was referring to slavery, something she herself had been forced to accept at a very early age. But then, she had not had a choice, and hadn't Miss Rosalind said the very same thing to her when she too had come to Tamasee as a young bride? Although Rosalind Cordell had never breathed a word to her husband or Agatha, the old woman knew the young miss never had come to terms with this evil that was necessary to keep the south alive. But not a word of this would she utter to this new miss. Like Miss Rosalind, she would have to bow to the inevitable – to cope with the realities of slavery in her own way.

Clarissa saw nothing of Christopher until dinner. He was waiting for her in the dining-room, having washed and changed, looking strikingly handsome in his calf-coloured pantaloons and a black jacket, which was stretched smoothly over his broad shoulders.

Despite Christopher's attempts during dinner to make everything appear normal, there was an unease and tension about him, an alert, waiting look. Instinctively Clarissa knew he was worrying because Ralph hadn't arrived from Charleston.

When dinner was over Betsy tactfully retired to her room. Christopher took Clarissa out on to the veranda, the draught from the open doors causing the candle flames to waver. He moved towards the balustrade, staring silently up the drive, which in the silvery moonlight was like a long white ribbon disappearing into the night, a rosy tint on the horizon. Strange noises of insects that had come with the night could be heard along with the soft chant of the Negroes from where they rested in their cabins after their long day of toiling in the fields.

Clarissa looked up at the grim profile of her husband, noticing how tense the muscles were in his face. 'What's worrying you, Christopher?'

He turned suddenly and smiled down at the concern filling her deep blue eyes and, bending slightly, placed a kiss gently on her soft lips. 'Now why should anything be worrying me when I consider myself to be one of the most fortunate men in South Carolina?'

'Because I think I know you well enough to know when something's bothering you. Can't you tell me what it is?'

He sighed, no longer trying to hide his anxiety. 'Yes, there is something, but it shouldn't concern you.'

'Christopher, I am your wife now,' she said sharply, 'and if I am to be mistress here, how do you expect me to learn if you constantly keep things from me? It's Ralph, isn't it? Are you worried because he isn't back yet?'

He nodded. 'Yes. I had expected him before now.'

'Where did he go when he left Charleston this afternoon?'

'To collect two Negroes from a plantation just north of the town.'

'Are they two you bought?'

'No. One is the girl I told you about – Della's her name – the one Ralph saw fit to sell while I was in England because of her disruptive influence on the others.'

'Then why did you buy her back? And what makes

you think she'll make a suitable maid for me if she's so disruptive?'

'Because that's what she was trained to be in Louisiana – a lady's maid – and, besides, I liked her. Because there was no lady at Tamasee she was put to work in the kitchen, which she no doubt considered beneath her and which led to conflict between her and Agatha. She was also immersed in witchcraft, which unsettled the other Negroes.'

Clarissa stared at him, feeling a quick stab of superstitious horror. 'Witchcraft?'

'Yes. Devil worship and things like that. When the Africans were brought to America they brought with them their own traditional beliefs, a dark knowledge of obscure, insidious things that, unfortunately, are no longer confined to the Caribbean islands and Louisiana. Coming from there, Della practised those strange rites, which aren't recognised as much here in South Carolina, but nevertheless it unnerves the other slaves. Negroes are a strange lot, Clarissa, as you will soon learn for yourself, and they have a way of communicating with each other that we whites will never be able to fathom. I suppose that's something in their African background. Those who live and work in the house consider themselves to be way above field hands, and no doubt Della thought herself way above any of them – her position, next to Agatha's, of course, being higher than any of theirs. Maybe this time she'll be able to settle down when she finds she has a lady to work for. But I bought her back because the other Negro Ralph has gone to collect, who is called Sam, ran away from here a few days ago to try and find her.'

'I see,' said Clarissa quietly. 'Was she his wife?'

'No.'

'Couldn't anyone have stopped him running away?'

'No. His feelings were such that he couldn't live without her. She meant everything to him.'

'Then I can understand why he ran away,' she said softly. 'You must think highly of him to risk buying back the girl.'

'Yes, I do. Sam is a fine man, Clarissa. We grew up together. He's my valet, my friend – call him what you like. But he's as much a part of Tamasee as I am.' He was silent for a few moments and when he next spoke his voice was low, and he had great difficulty in keeping it from quivering with anger as he remembered how he had found Sam at the Wheeler place. He looked straight ahead, avoiding Clarissa's eyes. 'There's only one thing. The slave patrol – who can only be described as a sadistic, murderous rabble who spend their time tracking down runaway slaves – somehow got wind that Sam had run away.' He swallowed hard, a vivid picture of Sam hanging from the stake, his life's blood dripping to the ground, flashing before his eyes, and he was unable to keep his voice from shaking with anger when he next spoke. His fingers were white, gripping the balustrade. 'Unfortunately, they got to him before I did.'

Clarissa felt a cold hand clasp her heart. 'What did they do?'

'Flogged him. But they'd have damned near killed him if Ralph and I hadn't turned up when we did – Della, as well, for harbouring him.'

Clarissa stared at him, aghast. 'But – but she's a woman. Surely they——?'

'That doesn't make any difference,' he rasped, turning his angry, pain-filled eyes to her. 'And for precisely that reason they would have subjected her to all the indecent indignities it is possible for a woman to suffer before flogging her half to death.'

At his words Clarissa's throat constricted and she

stared at him in horror. 'Dear Lord – that's dreadful,' she whispered.

'Yes. I'm afraid it will take Sam a long time to get over this. I will not countenance cruelty towards any of the slaves at Tamasee, Clarissa, please believe that, and I don't know how the others are going to react to this. The slave catchers proclaim they are doing a service, hunting down runaways with their dogs, and I am ashamed to say that there are those planters who employ them and support their filthy work, those who consider their slaves to be lower than animals. I can well imagine how smug they will feel over this. When a slave has reason to run away it does nothing to suggest contentment. Like the patrol, they have long awaited an opportunity like this – for an excuse to flog one of the slaves from Tamasee – especially one with a high standing like Sam. I'm not sure if they flogged Sam to punish him or as a way of getting at me because I have different ideas from theirs concerning the treatment of slaves.'

Hearing the grinding wheels of a wagon accompanied by the hoof beats of a horse on the gravel, they fell silent. Their eyes discerned that it was being driven slowly by Ralph so as to cause Sam as little discomfort as possible. They watched it come to a halt at the bottom of the steps. As though she had been waiting for this moment, Agatha came to stand beside them on the veranda, her face expressionless. Christopher moved away from Clarissa and she made as if to follow, but he turned to her sharply.

'Can't I come with you?' she asked.

'I'd prefer it if you didn't. Not for anything do I want you to witness what they've done to Sam.'

For a moment she hesitated, on the point of doing what she was told and stepping back, but she noticed Agatha watching her carefully, curious as to how she would deal with this situation, her eyes seeming to bore right through into Clarissa's innermost heart, holding a challenge, daring her to defy her husband on this matter, and as Clarissa battled with her decision those eyes never faltered in their gaze. Suddenly Clarissa saw with dreadful clarity what her life would be like at Tamasee if she did obey her husband and stand aside while others did the work. It would be something everyone would expect her to do whenever an unpleasant situation arose and that was not the way she wanted it. If she was to take on the responsibilities of this house and earn the respect and trust of everyone in it then she intended knowing everything that went on under its roof, and if that included nursing slaves who had been flogged mercilessly she would do that too, but she would not stand back while others did the unpleasant tasks in whispers lest they offend her.

Gently but firmly she stepped towards him, meeting his gaze squarely. 'No, Christopher,' she said with a suggestion of pride and defiance, 'and will you please stop trying to spare my feelings? Perhaps I can be of help to Agatha.'

The ghost of a smile appeared fleetingly on Agatha's lips and she nodded ever so slightly, obviously pleased with the way Clarissa had asserted herself.

Seeing the determined set of her jaw, Christopher did not contradict her. He nodded slowly, a brief flash of admiration entering his eyes. 'Very well. I'm sure Agatha will be glad of all the assistance she can get but, I promise you, the slave catchers' handiwork is not for the squeamish.'

'No. I didn't expect it would be.'

Christopher turned to Ralph, who was climbing into the back of the wagon in order to lift Sam out.

'Sorry I'm late,' he said, 'but I couldn't hurry. Every rut was agony for Sam. Luckily he passed out an hour or so after leaving the Wheeler place, which made it easier. Let's get him inside.'

The dark silhouette of a girl was bending over Sam as he lay on the boards of the wagon and Clarissa's eyes were drawn to her, realising that this must be Della. No sound passed her lips as she climbed out of the wagon and stood aside as the strong arms of Christopher and Ralph and two footmen lifted him out and carried him carefully up the steps and into the house. They bore him to a room in the servants' quarters, which Clarissa presumed must be his own. They placed him on the bed, and everyone stood around uneasily until Agatha came in, taking charge immediately.

'Water – get some water and bandages,' she ordered. The footmen left to do her bidding and she looked at Christopher and Ralph. 'You can leave us. We'll see to him now.'

Left in the room with Sam were just the three women – Clarissa, Agatha and Della, her still, silent presence oppressive. After glaring at her with a deep, profound hatred, which did not go unnoticed by Clarissa, Agatha now ignored the girl completely, not at all happy at her reappearance at Tamasee. She alone was the one she blamed for Sam's running away and being caught by the patrol; no one else.

Unintentionally Clarissa found herself studying Della, admiring her lithe, slender form. Seeing her close to, she found her strikingly beautiful, having a strange, savage kind of beauty, her Negroid ancestry showing in her large nose and full ripe lips, her skin black and flawless. The only emotion Clarissa could discern in her was the unconcealed love and anguish in her misty, sloe-like eyes, almost beyond any woman's endurance, as they rested on Sam lying unconscious and face down on the bed as Agatha began cutting away at the shirt stuck to his back, stained with crimson patches of fresh blood.

Clarissa tore her eyes off Della and began to assist Agatha as she cut away at the thin fabric. But, however determined she had been when she had insisted on helping her, when the fleshy pulp that had once been Sam's back and buttocks lay exposed she had to turn away as nausea threatened to engulf her. Only Agatha's hand placed firmly over her own stopped her from running out of that room, and it was on seeing this that Della moved soundlessly towards the bed, falling to her knees and beginning to help Agatha.

After taking several deep, gulping breaths Clarissa pulled herself together and turned back to the bed, meeting Della's challenging stare, but also something else – a flicker of understanding.

For Sam, slipping in and out of consciousness, the pain was excruciating. Each time he opened his eyes and tried lifting his head he groaned wearily. The source of his pain was indiscernible. It had invaded and seemed to occupy every inch, every nerve in his battered, punished body.

Horror and revulsion brought a bitter taste of bile to Clarissa's mouth, and she tried not to let her eyes dwell on the places where white, glistening bone shone through the deep welts cleaved into his back. Conflicting emotions about this new land and its people ran riot inside her head and she wondered what sort of men could inflict such torture on their fellow humans. In her anger she prayed that the wrath of God would strike them down, for surely this was the devil's own handiwork.

It was almost two hours later when she emerged from that room and went in search of her husband. She found him alone in the library, just staring out of the window. When she entered he turned and, seeing the strain etched on her lovely face, he stretched out his arms; like a child seeking succour, she walked straight into them, letting him wrap his arms around her while she laid her tired head thankfully on his broad chest, breathing a deep sigh.

'I think he'll be all right,' she whispered.

'Thank God,' said Christopher, his lips against her hair.

'He's lost an awful lot of blood and he'll be horrendously scarred, but I believe he'll come through. We've done what we can, and Della will stay with him tonight. She must be worn out, but she won't leave him.'

'Is he still unconscious?'

'No. He's in terrible pain, but Agatha's going to give him something for that.'

'What did you think of Della?'

'She's a strange girl.'

'How do you feel about her being your maid?'

'I don't know. Honestly, Christopher, I don't. I can't help remembering what you told me earlier. I find it disquieting and do not understand. Call it what you like, but I find witchcraft and magic alien, something I cannot begin to comprehend. It scares me. But not only that – she seems to have so much bitterness inside her, so much resentment.'

'You can't blame her. Be patient with her, Clarissa. She's had a tough time and has no cause to love the whites, having suffered only cruelty at their hands. I can't send her to work in the fields, nor can I ask Agatha to take her back in the kitchen, and for Sam's sake I can't sell her.'

Clarissa raised her head sharply and looked at him. 'No, you can't do that.' She sighed resignedly. 'So that leaves just me. All right, Christopher – she can be my maid – at least for now. We'll see how it works out. And,' she said, placing her head back on his chest and closing her eyes, 'can we talk about this in the morning?'

'Of course,' he murmured, placing a kiss on the top of her head. 'And I promise that as soon as Sam's well enough I'll get him to have a word with her about those strange practices of hers – that they cannot be allowed to continue if she wants to remain at Tamasee. You must be tired; I'm sorry.'

'What for?' she asked, a wave of tiredness sweeping over her.

'This was hardly the kind of welcome I'd intended. I doubt you'll forget your first day at Tamasee in a hurry.'

'I shall never forget,' she whispered. 'Ever.'

His arms tightened about her. 'Is there anything you want before we go to bed?'

'No – all I want is to go to bed and for you to hold me.' She sighed deeply and, raising her head, half opened her eyes; lifting her arms, she brought his head down to hers, placing her lips lightly on his, recognising the passions she had aroused in him in his dark eyes. Her mouth against his, she whispered, 'Please, take me to bed.'

This he did, and they made love while all Tamasee slept. All, that was, except Della, keeping a sad, silent vigil over Sam.

CHAPTER TWELVE

THE days after Clarissa's arrival at Tamasee were full
and long and far from easy, beginning at sunrise, when
the gangs of Negroes, with their drivers and white
overseers, went out into the fields. Under Agatha's
tuition Clarissa learnt surprisingly quickly how to
supervise the slaves and how the household was run,
which wasn't much different from Ashton Park; but,
whereas at Ashton Park she would merely discuss with
the housekeeper what had to be done, here she did
many of the tasks herself. There was always so much
to do, and with five hundred slaves at Tamasee their
food rations and clothing had to be organised and sick
Negroes had to be tended.

Sam's recovery was slow, and Della refused to leave
his side. As the days passed an understanding grew
between Clarissa and her new maid, and the quiet,
contemptuous attitude and hostility Della seemed to
have for everyone at Tamasee began to crumble. At
last she started to realise that the courtesy and kindness
of her new mistress was genuine and that the land she
came from was so much different from this, where
people were not kept in bondage, and she even began
to understand how difficult these early days at Tamasee
were for her too.

Clarissa missed Ashton Park, but in spite of this she
was happy, and the times she treasured most were the
nights when she and Christopher would close their
bedroom door on the outside, and the busy, hectic
world that went to make up Tamasee was forgotten
and she would become a woman of pleasure. She would

lie in his arms and experience bliss, sweet, sweet bliss as his lips burned her skin, his fingers searching, caressing her gently, urgently, until senses soared and sweet dark oblivion claimed them both.

His lovemaking took her to such heights of pleasure she had never even dreamed of. He was a potently sensual male and he showed Clarissa a side to her nature she had never known existed. Their need for each other was desperate, a torment, crying out for release, and Clarissa would tremble with sweet anticipation, a warmth glowing and spreading in the pit of her stomach as her body arched to meet his.

They loved, they slept, then loved again, and when they awoke with sunlight invading their privacy, their legs entwined, their skin warm and moist, Christopher would lean over and kiss her, her eyes opening momentarily, and she would smile before sleepily closing them again, and then he would leave her and she would turn and nestle into his warm, vacant place, the aroma of his body mingling with the sweet scent of jasmine on the sheets.

Before she had come to South Carolina she had known how much he loved his home, but it was only now that she understood just how much. On many of their rides he didn't bother changing out of the clothes he wore for his work in the fields, and Clarissa saw a side to him she was not used to seeing, casually dressed in calf-coloured breeches tucked into his black leather boots, and loose white shirt, open to reveal his strong, muscular chest, his hair falling untidily over his forehead, but it was a Christopher she found extremely appealing.

On one occasion they paused to watch the Negroes planting cotton. Clarissa returned to the subject of slavery and her words caused a knot to form in

Christopher's stomach but his expression did not change.

'I suppose,' she said, 'that the more cotton that is grown and the bigger the plantation then the demand for slaves increases.'

'Yes. Negroes are necessary for the plantation system to survive.'

'But surely that will become difficult now that slaves can no longer be imported?'

He nodded. 'Yes, and as a result the prices have gone sky-high.' He avoided telling her that because of this, Virginia and Maryland had found it more profitable to become slave-breeding states, to raise not cotton but Negroes, as one would mules or horses, a system he found abhorrent.

'Don't any of them read or write?' she asked. 'Don't they have any kind of education?'

He looked at her sharply. 'Of course not. Negroes are like children, with the same unpredictability.'

'They're like children because they're not permitted to be anything else,' she quipped.

'That's not exactly true.'

'Isn't it? Well, how can they be anything else when they've never been given the opportunity? Teach them and they will be able to read and write as well as you and I.'

Christopher found her questioning disconcerting, and frowned. 'That may be so, but there are many here in the south who believe the more the Negroes learn, the more aware they become and the greater the likelihood of revolt.'

She turned and looked at him, her lovely blue eyes open wide. 'Why should they do that if, as you say, they are treated with kindness? Why should they want to revolt and run away?' She asked this calmly, fixing him with a level gaze, with no sign of accusation in her voice, only a deep need to understand a system she was going to have to live with for the rest of her life, but when Christopher replied she sensed a note of anger.

'I've never tried to fool myself about slavery, Clarissa, or justify it, and there are those who believe that keeping them in ignorance will keep them down. I know only too well how some planters employ brutal methods to exact the most from their Negroes. Some have different ideas about keeping order among slaves, but ultimately even the paternalist and the patriarch, however sincere, will have to be capable of asserting their authority from the barrel of a gun, forcing them to respect and fear their white masters. They instil into them the notion that they are inferior, and even some ministers of the church preach to them that it is right and proper for them to be slaves, that if they are neglectful of their duties towards their white masters in this life then they will suffer hell and damnation in the next.'

Clarissa stared at him in horror. 'But that's dreadful.'

'Yes. It would be ridiculous of me to say most are content with their lot, but we have been lucky at Tamasee. We haven't had the insurrections that occur on other plantations, but,' he sighed, 'it does make me wonder, especially when I hear how some blacks prefer horrendous punishment and even death to subjection. Already I am criticised for treating the Negroes at Tamasee with humanity – and you have seen for yourself,' he said, referring to Sam, 'what they are capable of when I put a foot out of line. Can you possibly imagine what would happen if I began teaching them to read and write? There are exceptions, of course, especially when slaves are constantly in close contact with the whites. Sam can read and write, elementary stuff, I know, and so can a few others at Tamasee, but usually they are taught the basic physical tasks and no more.'

'Please forgive me, Christopher. I didn't mean to sound critical. It's just that I am trying my best to understand your ways and you must realise that this way of life is so different for me.'

'I do, and must confess that I've always felt uncomfortable about owning slaves. I've learned from my visits to the north and abroad, where there is no slavery, that the system must be questioned and changed. It won't always be like this. America is making such rapid technical advances, especially in the north, that there will come a time when there is no justification for it. Perhaps it will take a war to bring about nationwide emancipation – who knows? What I do know is that it won't happen yet, but when it does I hope I can be a part of it.'

Christopher's reference to war brought another thought to Clarissa's mind, of this other war everyone talked about and seemed even more imminent as the days passed, a war she thought of with cold dread.

'What about this war that is being talked of between England and America?' she asked quietly. 'Will – will you go and fight if it does come?'

Christopher glanced across at her, at the troubled frown on her brow as she looked straight ahead, and he smiled to himself, drawing his horse to a halt beneath the trees. Dismounting quickly, he strode towards her horse, holding out his arms, which she slid into with ease.

'I cannot bear to think that you'll have to go – to leave me so soon.'

'If war comes then I must.'

'But why? You're not a soldier.'

'Maybe not in the sense you mean, but I have long served in the militia, and if South Carolina goes then I must go with her.' He sank on to the grass, pulling her down beside him, trying to dispel her fears. Reaching out, he removed her hat, tossing it on the ground beside him. 'Now, no more talk of slavery or war, Clarissa, it's too nice a day. Instead let us talk about us and your introduction into society.'

She sighed, lying back on the soft, sweet-smelling grass, in the wide circle of his arms, the shadows spread about them, hearing the lazy hum of insects. 'Do we have to? I'm quite happy as we are.'

'So am I, my love, but people are beginning to talk and I have kept you to myself for far too long. The neighbourhood is agog with curiosity – all are impatient for me to introduce you. You cannot say you are not aware of the invitations to social functions that have been pouring in since your arrival at Tamasee.'

She gazed up at him in wide-eyed amazement, a slow, teasing smile curving her lips. 'You mean they don't come all the time?'

He laughed softly. 'You know they don't, you minx,' and, rolling over on to his stomach, he rested his weight on his arms, looking down into her lovely face, her pale blonde hair spread about her on the grass like a giant halo. 'Oh, my love, there is nothing I want more than to keep you here at Tamasee all to myself, forever. But I cannot. That would be too selfish.'

She reached up and placed her hand lovingly on the side of his face. 'I know, but I'm so nervous about meeting everyone.'

'There's absolutely nothing for you to worry about,' he said, turning his head slightly and kissing the palm of her hand. 'They'll adore you.'

Clarissa gazed up at him, at the sun filtering through the trees, feeling its balmy warmth, and she revelled in the luxury, stretching contentedly, squinting up at him through half-closed lids, tiny flecks of light and shade dancing on his hair. He leaned down and planted his lips in the warm, pulsating hollow of her throat and she sensed the desire stirring within him. Feeling his warm lips on her flesh, she laid her hand on his thick unruly hair, feeling the familiar, urgent ache for him in the pit of her stomach, an ache he never failed to arouse in her. She tried to resist the warm, tingling sensations, but it was useless.

Lifting his head, he looked down at her with undisguised passion, his eyes dark and pleading. 'I want to make love to you,' he breathed, 'here and now.'

She laughed softly, shakily, trying to still her wildly beating heart. 'Later,' she sighed. 'It would not be seemly if someone saw.'

'Why not?' he murmured. 'They'd only envy me.' He looked deeply into her eyes, his own filled with the intensity of his love. 'Ah, Clarissa, when I first saw you you were the most beautiful, most captivating woman I had ever seen.'

'And now?'

'Now you are even more so because you are my wife, and I love you so much that I cannot bear the thought of another man touching you. I swear I shall kill any man who does. I have said this before, but never did I mean it as much as I do now.'

He spoke with much intensity, and Clarissa was aware of an underlying seriousness, knowing instinctively that he was remembering Edward. It would be a long time, if ever, that he would be able to put him from his thoughts.

'Don't worry,' she said softly. 'No one shall.'

'Whatever happens, Clarissa, whatever is to come, know that I love you.'

She gazed at him with something like awe and she knew he loved her, really loved her in the true sense of

the word, as she loved him, and she was overwhelmed
by it.

'And I love you,' she whispered, knowing as she said
these words that it was not the first time she had
admitted it to herself, let alone said it to Christopher
– and it would not be the last. With each day that
dawned all the chains that had bound her to the past
began to fall away.

And so began the endless round of social events as
Clarissa was swept along as if on a tidal wave. She
never failed to look stunning, and Christopher proudly
escorted her to all the parties and balls, introducing
her to all the people who were someone in South
Carolina. She was undoubtedly the biggest attraction
at any event she attended and was received warmly.
Never had she believed she could be so happy.

The lives of the people in this new society in which
Clarissa mixed were varied and full. Most of them
managed their estates and slaves, visited their neighbours, hunted, danced and gambled, making frequent
visits to the race-track, and many of these privileged
landowners also engaged in politics, dominating society
and local government. Christopher was no exception,
although he was not as deeply committed as some.
There was no reason why he couldn't be both planter
and politician but he chose not to, knowing that
eventually the political side of his nature would take
over, and, no matter how much this appealed to him,
his decision to be a planter, making a success of it, had
been made when his father had died.

Among his friends Christopher was a man respected
for the way he had taken over and wrestled with the
responsibilities of a large plantation after the tragic
deaths of his father and older brother, but he was also
a man respected for his integrity and intellectual clarity.

He was conscientious and hard working and amply endowed with common sense. He had also developed a keen knowledge of military science during his long service with the militia and had gained influence and popularity, and as the talk of war with Britain gathered momentum he could not remain uncommitted. His more frequent attendances at political meetings were both noted and welcomed.

Anti-British feeling in America was strong. Tempers were inflamed because of Britain's continued harassment of and interference with American ships and America's right as a neutral nation to trade with legitimate markets in Europe and the West Indies. This, along with the matter of impressment, the seizing and detaining of vessels, touched a raw nerve of the people of this new, independent nation.

In England itself the economy was crumbling, with widespread unemployment, and British exports had fallen considerably. Britain realised that quarrelling with the United States was not in her best interests, this country being her best customer, and peace with her was cheaper and less troublesome than war. But, however many complaints America had, Britain considered she had her grievances too. Under her neutral flag, America was supplying France – with whom Britain was still in a state of war – with goods that Britain needed badly, and this alone made Britain more hostile and resentful towards the gathering strength of America as an independent nation.

But the central issue was impressment, and Britain asked why America should complain if the Royal Navy asked for its own men back, men the Americans had encouraged to desert to American ships, so what matter if some Americans were mistakenly taken? Surely it was fair exchange? Britain was not unduly worried by America's complaints and most British people did not see her as a threat, considering her utterly incapable of offensive warfare. But they had not reckoned on President Madison and his newly elected members of Congress, the so-called 'War Hawks', led by Henry Clay of Kentucky and John C Calhoun of South Carolina, just two of the new rising generation of politicians. They retaliated against Britain, making military threats, stating that unless she altered her navigation laws then the most valuable of all her colonies, Canada, would be torn from her grasp.

America continued to be patient, endlessly negotiating with Britain, asking her to change her policies, hoping that common sense would prevail in the end, but their patience was growing thin. They were doing everything they decently could to avoid war, although provocations continued to be endless and unreasonable. Britain treated America as if she were still part of her colonial system. The choice facing President Madison was either war or submission. America either had to fight or undo one of the main fundamental achievements of the revolution by accepting total submission in international affairs to England.

War was unnecessary but from America's point of view inescapable. No alternative was left but war or the abandonment of their right as an independent nation.

It was in June '12 that Britain at last agreed to cancel restrictions on American trade, and it finally did so in July '12 – but it did not dispose of the impressment of British soldiers from American ships. Unfortunately, by the time they'd made up their mind it was too late. By mid-June, in ignorance of Britain's relaxation, President Madison finally gave up in response of a Congressional vote and declared war on Great Britain.

* * *

Clarissa's idyll was shattered when Christopher told her he was to leave Tamasee on a business trip to the north to consult some of the factory owners with whom he did business and to find others, hoping they would take more of his cotton while he was unable to ship it to Europe because of the war. Unable to bear the thought of being without him, Clarissa asked if she could go with him, but he steadfastly refused. With all this talk of war he considered she would be safer at Tamasee.

But then he told her that she couldn't go with him because, along with more of his friends who had seen long service with the militia, he was also going north to enlist, where recruiting and preparations were being made for the invasion of Canada. Clarissa was stunned. There was absolutely nothing she could say. Regardless of his views, stating that war with Britain would ruin them all, he felt duty bound to go and, however hard it was to even contemplate being without him, she was determined to make his few remaining days at Tamasee happy ones.

She had just changed for dinner and was in her room, sitting at her dressing-table brushing her hair, when Della brought her the letter from Letty, the second she'd received while she'd been at Tamasee. Excitedly she placed the brush down and opened it, knowing Letty would give her a long account of Richard's marriage to Laura. She avidly read Letty's writing, which flowed over the page, and yes, the wedding had gone well, but her presence had been missed. It had been a quiet affair at Ashton Park, rather like her own wedding. She gave a detailed account of the whole day and ended by saying that bride and groom were immensely happy.

Clarissa paused in her reading, trying to visualise what it must have been like, and she felt an ache in her heart at the thought of Ashton Park having a new mistress, but she was happy it was Laura.

She read on. Most of what Letty wrote was gossip about what was happening in London, but unlike in her first letter, when she had made no mention of Edward, knowing how much both Clarissa and Christopher must want to forget him and that terrible day, in this one she felt it was in their best interests that they know what he was about.

As Clarissa read a coldness crept through her and her expression became a hard mask. It appeared Edward's father had died and, as he was the oldest son, the estate had passed on to him. He had resigned his commission in the Dragoons and spent little time in London. Letty went on to say that since the duel and the time when Clarissa had left England for America Edward had become a changed character. As far as she was aware, he had stopped drinking and gambling and he hadn't been seen with a woman since. Some said it was because he was taking his new responsibilities seriously – but Letty felt differently.

Since that terrible incident she had only come face to face with him once and she hoped she would never have the misfortune of doing so again. He was cold and unyielding – it was an Edward she hadn't recognised – and by his attitude he had made it quite plain that he would neither forget nor forgive Christopher's making a fool of him. Seething with hatred and resentment, he was a man with a burning desire for vengeance but, she went on,

I believe he's fallen in love with you, Clarissa, and he is consumed by his own obsession to get you back. Nothing will persuade him that you love your husband. He is convinced you married him for no other reason than to secure Ashton Park.

Shortly afterwards Letty had heard news that had alarmed her, that Edward had left England, for how long no one seemed to know, not even his brother, whom he had left in charge of the estate, but it was almost certain that he'd taken a ship bound for America.

The very words struck terror into Clarissa's heart, which seemed to have stopped beating. She felt weak, and the fear she hadn't felt since the night, that terrible night, when he had tried to rape her returned.

'It cannot be true,' she whispered. 'It cannot possibly be true.'

Della paused in what she was doing and looked across at her mistress, at the deathly pallor on her face, and swiftly and silently she crossed the room to her side, where she hovered without speaking, but she might just as well have been invisible, for Clarissa was oblivious to everything but the pounding inside her head. She continued to stare at the letter. Surely Edward wouldn't come all this way to America to settle an old score? But would he? Surely she knew, now more than ever, that he was capable of anything, and yes, a voice screamed inside her head, yes, he would, but what did he hope to achieve? Nothing but revenge for his own hurt pride, and surely that wasn't worth coming all this way for?

Grasping at straws, she asked herself if Letty could have been mistaken. He could have gone anywhere, and she knew he had friends in the West Indies. But, she thought wryly, what was the use of fooling herself? Of course he was coming to find them, to exact his revenge. However, one thing she was certain of – she couldn't tell Christopher about this, not now, not when he was about to leave for the north. He had enough to worry about without this. Like everyone else in the south, he was worried as to where he was going to sell his cotton now the European markets were closed to him – and he was leaving her to fight for his country. She couldn't let him go knowing Edward was at liberty in America.

Gazing into the mirror, thinking of this, she didn't hear someone come into the room or Della go out until suddenly a voice broke into her thoughts, making her start. It was Christopher. He placed his hands on her shoulders and, bending his head, met her eyes in the mirror.

'Thinking of me?' he asked fondly.

She smiled nervously, hoping he hadn't noticed the alarm in her eyes. 'How did you know?' she said, hurriedly folding the letter, trying to still her shaking fingers as she opened a drawer and placed it inside.

'What has Letty to say?' he asked, bending his head and gently nuzzling her neck with his warm lips.

'Oh – mainly gossip,' she laughed, trying to sound normal. 'You know Letty. And she wrote about the wedding.'

He looked up, once again meeting her gaze, sensing her unease, mistakenly believing it was because of the wedding and that she might be feeling homesick. His fingers tightened on her shoulders. 'So, Ashton Park has a new mistress. Does it worry you very much?'

She shook her head. 'No. How could it? It was always my home and perhaps you, more than anyone else, know what it meant to me, how much I loved it, but I could never be mistress of Ashton Park – at least not in the sense Laura can be as Richard's wife. God certainly did me a favour, providing me with you and Laura. I might miss Ashton Park but I don't have to worry about it any more. This is my home now, here, with you, and – I love you so very much.' There was a catch in her voice as she struggled not to think of the implications of the words Letty had written, and gently Christopher turned her round to face him.

'Convince me,' and, pulling her to him, he kissed her long and deep. She melted into his arms.

When they finally drew apart she stood up, seeing the desire in his dark eyes, his lips parted ready to kiss her again. Playfully she pushed him away.

'Come along, Christopher. Don't start something we haven't the time to finish, and don't forget Ralph and Betsy will be waiting to start dinner. They'll be wondering where we've got to.'

'Damn dinner,' he murmured, ignoring her pleas and pulling her towards him once more. 'And, besides, I doubt they'll miss us – in fact, I think they'd be more than happy to be without us for once.'

Clarissa smiled, knowing he was probably right. Anyone would have to be blind not to see what was happening between his overseer and Betsy. 'I'm sure you're right, Christopher, but nevertheless I'm hungry. First we'll eat and then,' she said, kissing him lightly and extricating herself from his arms, 'we'll continue this later.'

CHAPTER THIRTEEN

As they went down the stairs neither of them saw Della silently watching from the shadows, her sharp instinct telling her that her mistress was more anxious than she wanted her husband to know. She went back into the room, making straight for the drawer containing the letter. She opened it and, taking out the white paper, unfolded it. Without any qualms whatsoever she began reading Letty's bold handwriting.

Della was fortunate, having learnt how to read and write when she'd been a lady's maid in Louisiana, sitting through lessons with the mistress's two daughters in case one of the young misses should need anything fetching. Secretly she had taken the opportunity to learn her letters, absorbing almost everything their tutor taught them, so determined had she been to rise above the other slaves. She'd never met any other who could read and write – not, that was, until she'd met Sam.

Della was a slave. She was born a slave and no doubt would die a slave, and the only thing she wanted in his life, apart from her freedom, was Sam. Sam – so strong and yet so gentle, the only person during her brutal and miserable existence, apart from her new mistress, who had shown her any kindness. Sam who, on hearing she was to be sold, had fiercely promised that he would find her. When she had pleaded with him not to, reminding him he would be hunted down and shot, he had simply said, 'What does it matter? I have only my life to lose.' She had been sold and he had run away, and he had found her and almost died for it. But they

were together now and in return for what he'd done
she gave him all her love and would do all in her power
to see that no further harm came to him.

Quickly her sharp eyes scanned the pages in an
attempt to find out what could have upset her mistress,
but it wasn't until she came almost to the end of the
letter that she began to understand what it was. She
read on to the end before calmly replacing the letter
inside the drawer, knowing as she did so that this man,
this Edward Montgomery, was someone her mistress
did not like. He was coming to find her mistress, to
take her away, back to her own country, and if she
went then Agatha would see to it that she, Della, was
sold away once again from Tamasee and Sam.

Della had seen and recognised the fear in her mistress's eyes of this man – the same kind of fear she
herself had felt of her master in Louisiana whenever he
had looked her way, and if this was so then she was
determined to see that he would not harm her. Miss
Clarissa was the only truly good person she had ever
known; in fact, she hadn't known such people existed,
and by keeping her from harm she would be protecting
her own and Sam's existence at Tamasee.

She had promised Sam she would no longer practise
her African rituals but when the need arose, to protect
her own, she would not hesitate in turning to it and her
absolute belief in the power of the fetish. White people
might laugh, treating them as harmless African
superstitions, saying that the fetish objects they used
were nothing more than scarecrows and toys, but,
living in Louisiana on plantations alive with
superstition and distrust and lurid acts of cruelty, she
had borne witness to all the violent results.

Clarissa tried not to think of Edward at this crucial
time, having convinced herself that he couldn't possibly

be in America anyway now that war had been declared. She was busy making preparations for Christopher's departure, trying hard not to think of what it would be like to be without him. He spent hours with Ralph, going over what had to be done in his absence, until the moment she had been dreading, when he had to leave, finally came, and their painful farewell was said in the privacy of their room before going downstairs, where everyone would be gathered on the steps.

Clarissa felt his arms holding her tightly and she was determined not to cry. He cupped her face lovingly in his hands and kissed her lips, cherishing them with his own.

'Goodbye, Clarissa, and, as I've said a thousand times before, know that I love you.'

'Yes,' she gulped, 'and I love you. But it isn't goodbye – never goodbye. You will come back – I know you will. I couldn't bear it if anything happened to you. Take care, my darling.'

'I shall, and of course I'm coming back,' he said, folding her once more in his arms as if he was trying to make them one person. 'We shall be together again, my love. It's only a matter of time,' and after one last kiss, into which he infused all the passion of his love, they went downstairs.

Clarissa watched him go, having absolutely no idea when she would see him again.

As the days turned into weeks the suspicion that had been growing inside Clarissa that she might be with child turned into reality. She was deliriously happy, but how she wished she could tell Christopher. She wrote to him, but it wasn't the same. Agatha was overjoyed at the prospect of having a baby in the house again and immediately began turning out the nursery, which hadn't been used since Christopher was a child.

She also suggested that Clarissa take a trip to Charleston to do some shopping for the baby while she was able, taking Betsy with her and, of course, Della. Anything to get the girl out of her way for a while. But she had to admit that she wasn't as difficult as she had been that first time she'd come to Tamasee, and she reckoned she had the mistress to thank for that. She certainly seemed to have a way of handling the slaves, who adored her.

Considering Agatha's suggestion a good idea, and that it was best they go now before the start of the cotton picking at the beginning of August, which could last for anything up to three months, Clarissa, with Betsy and Della, left for Charleston. Besides, the summer was so hot at Tamasee that it would be a welcome relief to feel the cool breezes blowing in from the Atlantic.

Rooms had been reserved for them at the Planters' Hotel, the one she had stayed at when Christopher had first brought her to South Carolina. It felt good to be away from Tamasee, if just for a little while, to feel the cool breezes of Charleston, the energetic restlessness of this fine coastal city, proudly conscious of its importance as the capital city of South Carolina.

It was the day after their arrival, after a morning's successful shopping, when they were in the carriage returning to the hotel for lunch that Clarissa glanced casually in the direction of the people on the pavement, her eye drawn to one man in particular. He was quite tall and tastefully dressed in a dark blue suit, his thick fair hair gleaming like spun gold in the sun. His handsome face was familiar, becoming even more so, and then, suddenly, she recognised him and was overcome with terror.

He glanced idly in her direction, and when he

recognised her his eyebrows arched and his lips curled in a thin, cynical smile that made Clarissa's blood freeze in her veins. She stared at him with incredulous horror but apart from the pallor on her face her expression did not change, although at this one cruel blow she saw the beautiful life she had built for herself shattering into tiny pieces at her feet – for this man was indeed Edward Montgomery, the man she had thought never to see again.

The carriage passed on. Betsy had been too preoccupied to notice anything amiss, exclaiming rapturously over some articles she had just bought, but Della, sitting beside her, hadn't. She noticed her mistress's sudden pallor and, following her gaze, her keen eyes had observed the stranger staring openly at her, and his smile was not so much insolent as knowing. She knew immediately that this was the man in the letter, the man who had come to take her mistress back to England.

As the carriage moved away the man looked directly at the beautiful slave girl sitting ramrod-straight beside Clarissa, her black eyes narrowed with open dislike as she stared at him, without the humility usually found in a slave, but something in her look took the smile from Edward's handsome face. If he could have seen the first of the small, crude wooden effigies she made when alone in her room later, her gaze transfixed, her expression intense, relentless as she watched it burn, he would have fled from Charleston, taking the first available route back to England.

Back at the hotel, Clarissa pleaded a headache, wanting desperately to be alone so that she could think properly. Surely she must have been mistaken? It must have been an illusion. It could not possibly have been Edward she had seen, but she knew, the instant one of the bell boys came to tell her there was a gentleman waiting to speak to her in Reception, that she had not been mistaken and that as she made her way mechanically down the stairs, seeing him waiting with ease by the desk, it was indeed no illusion. As she moved towards him her reaction was not one of surprise but of indifference and revulsion – that he had dared come all this way to try to ruin what happiness she had found.

Her proud eyes met his without flinching. Letty had said how changed he was. Physically he looked the same except that there was a maturity about him that hadn't been there before but, she thought wryly, she suspected that beneath all this he was still the same arrogant, conceited Edward, with no thought for anyone save himself. After all she had suffered at his hands, she felt surprisingly calm. The unspecified terrors she had experienced since Letty's letter disappeared now she was face to face with him, and she realised she had reached a state of mind in which she no longer had any reason to fear him. The harm had been done and she had only one desire, which was to get this meeting over and done with as quickly as possible.

She moved towards him, cool and serene, the steadiness of her gaze unflinching. He smiled crookedly and bowed slightly, his eyes never leaving hers for a second, as if trying to unnerve her, but it must have been disconcerting for him to receive nothing but a stare of profound boredom.

'Well, Edward,' she said, her voice as cool as ice. 'What do you want?'

'Want? Why, I merely wished to pay my respects. Why should I want anything?'

'Don't play games with me. What do you hope to achieve by coming all this way? I would have thought, after our last encounter, that we had nothing left to say to each other – that I'd made it quite plain I never wanted to see you again.'

Edward stopped smiling and wore an expression Clarissa had never seen before, unmarred by arrogance or pride – which was totally out of character and did nothing to allay her suspicion that it was merely a ruse to soften her, to throw her off guard – but it did nothing to dispel the hardness in her eyes.

'You're wrong, Clarissa,' he said, glancing about him, suddenly conscious that they were attracting attention to themselves. 'Please, can't we sit down and talk a little? I think we're attracting too much attention.'

Clarissa saw he was right. People were beginning to look curiously their way. Although since coming to Charleston she had caused many a head to turn and look at her, merely because she was married to Christopher Cordell. 'Very well, but say what you have to say and then be gone. Although whatever it is that is so important as to prompt you to cross the Atlantic – especially now, when we are at war with England – I wish you'd written.'

Edward raised his eyebrows in surprise. 'We? You surprise me, Clarissa. Surely your loyalties should lie with England at a time like this – not this barbarous nation.'

'This "barbarous nation", as you call it, is my home now, and my loyalties are with my husband. Anyway, if you feel that way you can always leave,' she said tartly.

They seated themselves in a room off the foyer where several people were taking tea, although Clarissa paid slight attention to them. Settling back on the cushions, one booted leg lazily crossed over the other, Edward let his eyes linger appreciatively on Clarissa's lovely face, noticing, as if for the first time, the long slender column of her neck and the soft swell of her breasts beneath her lemon dress, and his breath caught in his throat. She was certainly lovely and he cursed himself for not having taken notice before. What a fool he'd been to let her slip away. But, he thought, he was here to get her back and he was determined he would. Whatever methods he had to use to get her away from that pompous Cordell, he would use them. He would make him regret not killing him when he had the chance.

'Would you care for some tea?' he asked suddenly.

Clarissa stared at him in stupefied amazement. 'Tea? This is not a drawing-room in England, Edward. You have the effrontery to ask me to have tea with you after all you have done? That you have the audacity to approach me at all astounds me.'

He smiled, but it did not reach those cold grey eyes. 'Why not? You were to have been my wife. You cannot have forgotten.'

'I'm hardly likely to do that,' she replied coldly. 'I am indeed fortunate to have been saved from such a fate. When I first saw you, in my innocence and naïveté I thought I loved you. I trusted you. I believed in you. For me you could do no wrong,' and she laughed harshly at the memory, studying his face dispassionately. 'How stupid and childish I must have seemed. What a pity I couldn't see you for what you really were.'

A look of irritation crossed Edward's face. 'I can only suppose you have listened too much to Letty.'

'No. My mistake was in not listening to her enough. If I had I would never have become betrothed to you in the first place. And can it be possible that you have forgotten the circumstances of our last meeting? How you almost destroyed me? How you tried to rape me – showing me just the kind of animal you are?'

'Would you believe me if I said I wish to apologise? That I deeply regret what happened? I realise my conduct that night was inexcusable – certainly not the conduct of a gentleman. My only excuse is that I was shocked to find you'd married someone else.'

'Especially when you discovered that the man I'd married was Christopher Cordell, a man who'd already crossed you. And no, I would not believe you,' she scorned, not taken in by his unusually contrite manner, 'and you're right. Your behaviour most certainly was not that of a gentleman. But tell me, was the shock you felt over losing me or – more to the point – over the damage done to your arrogant male pride?'

'Whatever it was, I deeply regret it.'

'That is your misfortune,' she said coldly. 'Now, say what you have to say. I have no wish to prolong this meeting.'

He nodded slowly, a steely glint entering his eyes, a hard note to his voice when he spoke. 'Very well. It's quite simple really. I want you to return with me to England.'

She stared at him in shocked amazement for a long moment before speaking. 'You are incredible. Have you forgotten that I am married to Christopher – the man you would happily have killed?'

'No, but I am willing to overlook the fact. You will be able to divorce him easily enough. Come back to England with me, Clarissa. My father is dead – the estate is mine. You can have anything you want.'

'Anything money can buy,' she scoffed.

He looked at her hard. 'If that's what it takes to get you back, then yes. After all, you allowed yourself to be bought once. Remember?'

Clarissa looked at him with complete loathing. She felt herself trembling inwardly with anger and it was with great effort that she controlled herself and managed to speak. 'How callous you are. I would as soon associate with the devil as you. But tell me, why this sudden change in you? Why should you want me to go back with you? Can it be that you've discovered you love me after all?' she asked with sarcasm.

'Yes,' he replied, matter-of-factly, 'I think I do. Since you left I've found myself thinking of you constantly. I haven't been able to get you out of my mind. I've known many women, I admit that, but none have affected me like you. So, if that is love, then yes, I do.'

'Love? You don't know the meaning of the word, and why is it that I have the feeling you are not sincere? Besides, is it really me you want, or am I part of some squalid, hideous scheme you've hatched to get even with Christopher? When will you realise that I cannot stand the sight of you?'

Edward nodded slowly, his eyes becoming like ice, his face taut. Clarissa could sense his anger mounting but he managed to remain infuriatingly calm, looking at her with a faint deprecatory smile on his lips.

'Be that as it may, I have no intention of leaving without you. I would as soon see you dead than for you to remain married to him.'

Nothing could have blatantly underlined his determination to get her back as those words, but she refused to let him intimidate her. 'I could make things very difficult for you – you do realise that?' she said.

'Really? In what way?' he asked, unperturbed.

'How many people here in Charleston know who you are?'

He shrugged. 'I really don't have the faintest idea. I presume everyone thinks I'm here from the north. But what does it matter, anyway?'

'Don't be a fool, Edward. This is America and you are an Englishman – out of uniform. What do you think would happen to you if you were found out?

You'd be thrown in gaol or – even worse – executed as a spy.'

He laughed mirthlessly. 'Me – a spy? Don't be ridiculous, Clarissa. There are hundreds of English over here, caught up one way or another in the war. So you would denounce me.'

'Yes, if I have to. I think the authorities would take my word against yours, don't you?'

'Maybe, but that would do more harm than good.'

'Really? How?'

'Why, your husband's standing in the community, my dear. I might just have a tasty little story or two of my own to mention before they...execute me,' he mocked. 'What matter if I elaborate a little here and there? Think of the scandal.'

'I am,' she said. 'And I'm thinking how it would make Christopher laugh. But do your worst, Edward. Nothing you can say or do frightens me any more.'

'Nevertheless, know this,' he hissed, suddenly sitting forward, the anger and emotion he had kept in check beginning to show itself, 'when I'm finished with him he'll have nothing. He'll be a pauper – yes, I'll strip him of everything: wealth, power, position, even you. I am going to destroy him. I shall burn his southern palace to the ground – he will have nothing left but ashes – and when I am finished you will come crawling back to me.'

When he'd finished speaking he waited for her to say something, but she remained coolly silent, which was far more effective than any words could have been, and a look of pure madness flamed in his eyes. She rose abruptly, about to leave him, but his next words held her attention.

'Your husband's in the north, isn't he?'

She looked at him sharply. 'How do you know that?'

'I've made it my business to know. He'll be gone for

quite some time, I believe – a long time for you to be alone. Why, anything might happen.'

'Nothing is going to happen. Why can't you accept that I despise you and go back to England? You have no place here. If Christopher should return he would not spare your life a third time.'

He ignored her threat and sighed deeply. 'I like Charleston. I have a mind to spend a little time here before I move on.'

As Clarissa was about to move away he caught her wrist, his fingers closing round it like a vice, forcing her to turn and look at him again. Their eyes met and held.

'But be sure that when I do, Clarissa, you will come with me.'

'No. To me you are dead. You died in Spain and shall remain dead.' Snatching her hand from his grasp, she strode out of the room, unaware as she did so of the woman sitting alone at a table in the corner of the room, whose beautiful sharp black eyes had watched the whole episode with a great deal of interest.

Marie watched as Clarissa walked out of the room, poised and elegant, every other woman's eye turning to her in envy, and Marie's black eyes narrowed dangerously. How she loathed that golden-haired woman with her charming ways and typically English manner, hating her with such vicious savagery that she wanted nothing more than to see her dead.

She glanced across at the man still sitting where Clarissa had left him, and a malicious smile curved her lips at the evil thought that had been growing while they had talked. Christopher was in the north. Could it be that his precious, darling wife was carrying on an intrigue while he was away fighting for his country? Could it be that the mistress of Tamasee had a lover? Although there had been nothing lover-like in their behaviour. As far as she knew, Christopher's wife had never accompanied him on his trips to Charleston. Strange she should wait until he'd gone away to come here.

Suddenly her heart lurched with an exultant sense of triumph that at last the moment had come when she might get her own back, to repay Christopher for all the mocking, jeering smiles and comments, the slights and insults she had had to endure, which had touched a raw nerve, when he had brought his English bride to Charleston.

She looked at the man with the thick blond hair with renewed interest. A mite too fancy for her liking, she thought, noticing the elaborate waistcoat and neck-cloth, but handsome just the same – arrogant, too – which appealed to her baser instincts. Yes, she might just make it her business to get to know this fine gentleman, and she was certain that what she might discover would be of interest to Christopher.

She rose and moved across the room towards him, triumph shining in her eyes, in every line of her beautiful body, and exultation that at last she could pay the mighty Christopher Cordell of Tamasee back for rejecting her. She stood looking down at the stranger, her eyes hard and shining, like a cat poised to spring.

When Edward looked up his expression was one of hauteur, and then he smiled in frank appreciation of her dark beauty. His features were perfect in every detail, his smile engaging, but Marie was not deceived, for when she looked into the depths of those cold grey eyes she recognised that which was in herself – that they were two of a kind and, however dubious his friendship might be, she realised he would make a mighty dangerous enemy.

* * *

Edward wasn't too perturbed when he learned that Clarissa had hastily departed for Tamasee. He waited and listened and bided his time, learning as much as he could concerning Christopher Cordell. The hatred he felt for this man festered in his mind so that he could think of nothing else, and the fact that he was highly respected, one of the leading citizens of Charleston, wealthy and all-powerful, was all the better, for, the more he possessed and the higher his standing in the community, the further he would have to fall – and the greater would be Edward's own satisfaction when he'd succeeded. He would then take Clarissa back with him to England – he would stop at nothing to achieve this.

His greatest asset at this time was Marie, and it didn't take either of them long to make their minds up about the other – that they were too much alike to be friends. They were full of vindictive malice as they plotted and schemed to bring about the downfall of their most hatest enemies, each making full use of the other to gain their own evil ends. But, thought Edward smugly, Marie could plot and scheme all she liked to find a way of disposing of Clarissa and he would help her, but he knew that, even if she succeeded, Cordell would not take her back. It didn't enter his head for a moment that the same could be applied to himself where Clarissa was concerned, so convinced was he that she would come back to him in the end.

They needed someone to help them put their devious plot into operation, someone who could watch Tamasee without attracting too much attention. Marie immediately suggested Ned Stone, the leader of the slave patrol; he was a thoroughly unsavoury character, but she had a feeling he was just the man they were looking for.

Edward found Ned Stone in one of the seedy bars he frequented near the docks, discovering to his immense satisfaction that Marie was right, that Ned Stone's hatred of Cordell was something akin to his own, having many an old score to settle. He was only too eager to offer his services – for a price. Although Edward knew he was just the man he needed, he neither liked nor trusted him and would be relieved when the job was done and he was shot of him.

Feeling the throbbing ache from the wound in his shoulder, a result of the ill fated duel, only added fuel to his desire for revenge, and inwardly he felt a warm glow of satisfaction and certainty that at last the time had come to bring about Cordell's downfall.

CHAPTER FOURTEEN

BY AUTUMN Tamasee was like an island in a sea of white cotton. After the long weeks of cultivation cotton picking began in earnest. Beyond Tamasee, hundreds of miles to the north, was the war and Chistopher. Clarissa counted the days they were apart, trying not to worry, trying not to think he might be lying wounded somewhere – or, even worse, that he might be dead. This was too awful to contemplate, but in her heart of hearts she knew he was alive. So imbedded was he in her heart and mind that if he had ceased to live then in some way she would be aware of it.

In spite of the shock of seeing Edward, she refused to let her mind dwell on him and the fact that he was still at liberty in Charleston, or his threat to burn Tamasee to the ground, but it hung over her like an ugly black cloud. She knew from Ralph, who made frequent visits to Charleston, that he hadn't left and that he'd become more than friendly with Marie Pendleton.

What Ralph didn't tell Clarissa, however, because he did not wish to worry her unduly, was that this Edward Montgomery had also been keeping the company of the odious Ned Stone, the slave catcher, who had been seen on and around Tamasee more often of late – searching for runaways, he said, but Ralph had a gut feeling that he had some other motive, that there was something going on between him and that Montgomery fellow, and he would do well to keep his eyes and ears open.

Clarissa had neither seen nor heard of Ned Stone, so

when he rode up to the house with half a dozen men and a pack of yapping, snarling dogs she was facing a complete stranger.

Her eyes settled on the man in front of the rest as he halted his horse and looked up at her. She knew at once that she didn't like him. He was rough-looking, dirty and grizzled, chewing on a wad of tobacco, his small, deep-set eyes squinting in the glare from the sun, travelling over her body with a bold insolence, lingering on the swell of her pregnancy beneath her loose-fitting cotton dress, knowing perfectly well who she was but treating her with utter disregard to her station.

Della had come to stand close behind Clarissa, and at the sharp intake of her breath she turned and looked at her.

'What is it, Della?'

'Dis man is Ned Stone, Miss Clarissa, de man dat beat Sam. He evil, dat one. Evil.'

A rush of memories of the night when she had witnessed the mindless cruelties inflicted on a slave by the patrol, of Sam's wretched condition, flashed into Clarissa's mind, and she was incensed by an anger so strong that she shook, feeling sick inside. She fixed Ned Stone with an ice-cold stare, freezing him in the saddle as he was about to dismount.

'What can we do for you?' her voice rang out.

'My name's Ned Stone ——'

'I don't care what your name is. I know perfectly well who you are. What do you want here?'

Stone slouched forward in his saddle and pushed his hat further back on his head, revealing more of his lank hair. He shifted the wad of tobacco to the other side of his mouth and studied Clarissa, this proud mistress of Tamasee he'd heard so much about, finding her as high and mighty as that husband of hers –

beautiful, too, and he could see why Montgomery wanted her so bad, although she was a mite too uppity for his liking.

'Well, now, I reckon you might just have a runaway we're lookin' for hidin' here. He was last seen headin' this way, so, if it's all the same to you, I'd like to take a look around.'

'No, it is not all the same to me,' Clarissa replied in a voice with cutting contempt. 'And the only Negroes at Tamasee are the ones who belong here. Now – please go.'

'It's my job to find runaways, Mrs Cordell. Got to make an example of 'em. Show 'em what 'appens when they take the law into their own hands.'

'I've already seen one of your examples and I would be obliged if you would leave this property.'

'Still like to take a look around.'

'Do you doubt my word, Mr Stone?'

'Why, no, ma'am, only——'

'Good. Then, seeing as there is no reason for you to remain, will you please go?'

At that moment, and much to Clarissa's relief, Ralph came riding round the corner of the house. Working in the fields, he'd seen the patrol heading in this direction and came as quickly as he could.

'What Mrs Cordell says is the truth, Stone. There are no runaways at Tamasee – as I've already told you. Hell, man, what more do I have to say to convince you? Now get off this property before I throw you off. You've no business here.'

'Now, Mr Benton,' said Stone in an irritating, wheedling voice, 'no cause takin' that attitude. Catchin' runaways is our bizness, as well you know, and I've reason to believe some of your Nigras might be harbourin' one of 'em.' His eyes narrowed as they came to rest on Della, whom he'd already recognised, and his thin lips twisted in an evil smile as he pointed a steady finger at her. 'Ask that there nigger wench. She knows – and she knows I still 'aven't forgot that she's to be punished for harbourin' slaves. No, suh – I ain't forgot.'

Infuriated by the threat, Ralph moved close to Stone and his hand lashed out, gripping the man's arm tightly, glaring into his cold eyes. 'Feel you're safe, don't you, making threats and riding around here while Mr Cordell's away at the war? Well, let me tell you something: if you dare touch her or any of the Negroes at Tamasee, Stone, then I'll kill you myself. Now do as Mrs Cordell says and get off this property.'

Stone glared at him and nodded slowly. 'For now, mebbe – for now. But I'll be back. Mark my words – I'll be back,' and with a last meaningful look at Della he turned and, surrounded by his companions and yapping dogs, rode off up the gravel drive.

Ralph looked at Clarissa with concern. Like everyone else at Tamasee, his liking and admiration for her had grown immensely over the months and it hadn't taken him long to admit that Christopher had made a perfect choice. Those early days hadn't been easy for her, but he'd liked the way she'd squared her shoulders, determined to take her part in the running of Tamasee. 'You all right, Clarissa?'

She sighed with relief. 'Yes – yes, I'm all right, Ralph. Thank you for coming when you did, although I can't say I like Mr Stone much.'

Ralph grinned. 'Don't worry about him. No one does.'

Clarissa turned to Della, who hadn't moved, and put a comforting hand on her arm. 'Don't worry, Della. We won't let him harm you.'

'Yo' don' know him, miss. Dat man evil – an' yo' see, he do as he says.'

* * *

The cotton picking was over and the sheds beyond the slave cabins stacked high. An invitation came for Clarissa to attend an engagement party over at Fairlawns, the Whitaker plantation, their closest neighbours.

On their arrival a smiling Mrs Whitaker met Clarissa and Betsy on the veranda, taking them under her wing with a friendly warmth, ushering them inside to introduce them to the other guests. At first Clarissa was slightly ill at ease, knowing just a few neighbours, the rest of the gathering, more than she had anticipated, having come from Charleston, but she soon began to relax in the easy, friendly atmosphere and was glad she'd taken Agatha's advice to get away from Tamasee for a while.

Footmen circulated with trays of food and champagne while people chatted, exchanging news and views about the war. Guests continued to arrive as the afternoon wore on, the atmosphere warm and vibrant, noisy laughter ringing out as more champagne was drunk.

Feeling tired and needing to relax somewhere quiet, Clarissa excused herself and wandered out into the gardens, the party receding into the distance. She turned a corner, hoping to find a quiet, secluded spot, but suddenly she stopped, and, despite the warmth of the day, she went cold all over, feeling the colour drain from her cheeks, for there, sitting on a bench, was Marie Pendleton, as stunning as she had been that day in Charleston.

She showed no surprise at Clarissa's sudden appearance and stood up, a hard glint in her black eyes, looking exquisite in a gown of black lace, a sharp contrast to Clarissa, who wore a flowing ivory silk dress, although it did not conceal her pregnancy; she noticed a faint look of surprise cross Marie's face, but it was gone in an instant, replaced by something else, which Clarissa recognised as jealousy.

Immediately Clarissa turned to go back to the house, the mere thought of confronting this woman, Christopher's one-time mistress, making her feel physically sick. But before she could do so Marie's voice rang out coolly, halting her in her steps.

'I do hope you're not leaving on my account?'

Clarissa turned and faced her. 'Of course not,' she replied calmly. 'I simply did not wish to disturb your privacy.'

'How considerate of you,' said Marie with false casualness, slowly sauntering towards her, her dislike obvious and the thin smile on her crimson lips insincere. Her black eyes shone ruthlessly like those of a cat, her claws coming out to play. 'But don't you think you and I should talk?'

Clarissa returned her stare, intending to remain calm, refusing to be intimidated. 'I don't think we have anything to say to each other. Now, if you will excuse me, I really would like to go back to the house,' she said with a quiet dignity, about to turn away.

'No, wait,' said Marie, halting her yet again.

Clarissa sighed. 'What do you want? Why did you come here today?'

'Because, like you, I was invited. I am a friend of William Markham, Amanda Whitaker's fiancé. What other reason could there be?'

'What indeed?' said Clarissa drily. 'However, I doubt you would have come to Fairlawns had it not been so close to Tamasee. You knew I'd be here, didn't you?'

Marie laughed harshly. 'Don't flatter yourself – of course I didn't. How could I?' She looked at her steadily. 'But – so you know who I am?'

'Yes – and who you were.'

'Who I was and who I still am,' purred Marie, malice

glittering in her eyes. 'Surely you must know Christopher and I never stopped seeing each other – that he's still in love with me?'

'If it suits you to think so, then do,' said Clarissa coldly. 'But what do you hope to achieve by telling me this?'

'Achieve? Why, nothing. I am merely putting you in the picture – that is all. I always think it is so mean of men not to tell their wives the truth about what they get up to when they're away from them, don't you?'

'What are you saying?' asked Clarissa stiffly.

'Why, that, whatever you may think, Christopher does still love me – he'll always love me, and he never stopped seeing me. Whenever he came to Charleston on business he made a point of seeing me. All those nights he wasn't with you he was with me.'

'I do not believe you – they are just wicked, jealous lies. If he'd loved you he would have married you and, whatever you say, I have never had reason to doubt my husband's fidelity to me.'

'Why, even in his letters he says——'

Clarissa looked at her sharply, her face turning white. 'Letters? He writes to you?'

A fierce surge of pleasure shot through Marie, knowing one of her arrows had hit its mark, that this was the reason she had come here today, to humiliate and shatter this woman's most sensitive feelings, to make her cringe and feel how she had felt when she'd discovered Christopher had spurned her. There was a note of triumph in her voice when she spoke.

'Of course he writes to me – all the time.'

Clarissa shook her head, still refusing to believe her. 'No – I still don't believe you.'

'Only because you don't want to,' and Marie twisted her mouth in an ugly sneer, bringing her face close to Clarissa's, staring into her eyes so that Clarissa had an overwhelming urge to strike the impudent twisted features, but she shook her head slowly, trying to remain calm, which only infuriated Marie further. 'Don't deceive yourself,' she snarled. 'He doesn't love you. He never has.'

'You're mad to think that,' said Clarissa quietly. 'Quite mad, and I pity you.'

'Pity? Ha – don't pity me, madam. It is you who is to be pitied. It is you who will be lying in soon, and when you are remember this. If Christopher is home and decides to visit Charleston – think of us then. Think of him in my arms – in my bed. He never was a patient man, so don't imagine for one minute that he'll be waiting by your bed for you to get well again so he can share it, because he won't.'

Clarissa stared at her with a coolness that astounded Marie.

'How coarse you are. There's not one shred of decency in you. I can understand now why Christopher didn't marry you. When he stopped seeing you you got just what you deserved, and whatever lies you attempt to fill my head with you will not destroy my faith in him.'

All of a sudden Marie laughed, somewhat hysterically. 'Oh, you're so smug,' she said, and her voice dropped, low and intense. Her eyes narrowed, glittering as she thrust her face forward. 'So high and mighty. But then, I suppose you can afford to be – being mistress of Tamasee.' Her lips curled cruelly. 'How I despise you, and you were right: I did come here today knowing I'd see you. I came to tell you something, not only that Christopher still loves me – and, however much you refuse to believe it, it's true – but also that I'll get him in the end, you see if I don't. I've been patient but you'll pay a hundred times over for stealing him from me. I swear it.' Pure cold madness flamed in

her eyes and her chest heaved beneath her black lace
dress with angry emotion as she glared at her rival –
two women in love with the same man.

Clarissa looked at her in amazement. 'You are mad,'
she breathed. 'Anyone who behaves as you do has to
be.'

At that moment a shadow fell between them and it
somehow came as no surprise to see Edward emerge
from the trees and pause beside Marie, but it was
Clarissa who held all his attention.

'So,' said Clarissa, gazing from one to the other with
cold contempt. 'I might have known you'd be here.
After all, what is it they say about birds of a feather?'

Edward ignored her sarcasm and, bowing his head
slightly, smiled, but when his eyes took in her condition
he froze. His mouth tightened and his eyes narrowed
dangerously, glaring at her, his fists clenched tight as
he struggled to control his impotent rage.

'So,' he said, a scornful curl to his lips, his voice like
steel, 'you are to have his child.'

Clarissa met his gaze squarely, defiantly. No longer
had he the power to frighten her. 'How observant of
you, Edward. Perhaps now you will realise the futility
of your revenge, that there is no sense in remaining
here any longer, and go back to England.'

His eyes darkened, his nostrils pinched. 'Don't waste
your breath and don't think you're getting rid of me
that easily, for, in spite of this and the revulsion I feel
at your coupling with him, I shall learn to overcome it.
As far as I am concerned, nothing has changed – only
that he has one more thing to lose that will make my
revenge sweeter.'

Clarissa stared at him, horror-struck, trying to
understand why he should want to continue treating
her like this. 'Why? Why do you hate me, Edward?'
she asked in a last attempt to reason with him, reaching

out her hand in supplication. 'What have I done that makes you want to treat me this way, apart from marrying Christopher, believing you were dead? And, besides, you didn't love me, so why should you object?'

Edward moved to stand directly in front of her, looking like a man possessed of the devil, his face twisted out of all recognition. Clarissa shrank back, for the man before her was a stranger and the eyes that bored into hers were those of a madman, and she knew, with a sinking heart, that this was indeed what he was, for only a madman would behave this way.

'I told you, I don't hate you – in fact, quite the contrary. But he has made a fool of me, shamed me, dishonoured my name, and for that he will pay. My purpose is strong, Clarissa. I shall kill him.'

'You are out of your mind, Edward. You have lost your senses. Go back to England before you regret your actions.'

'Regret?' and he laughed insanely. 'I shall regret nothing I do where he is concerned.'

Clarissa swallowed hard, looking from one to the other. 'Then there is nothing more to be said to either of you. You have descended into the very realms of evil, so you know nothing else.'

Clarissa and Betsy passed Ned Stone and his companions on the road back to Tamasee, but Clarissa paid him no heed, having too much on her mind, and it was with immense relief that she climbed out of the carriage at Tamasee and turned to Betsy.

'I must find Ralph. It's important that he knows what's happened.'

'No,' said Betsy firmly. 'I'll go and find him and send him to you. Go along into the house. You look tired.'

Clarissa smiled gratefully. 'Yes, I am. I don't know if it's the heat, the party or the ordeal of meeting

Edward. When I've had a word with Ralph I'll go and lie down for a while.'

As she climbed the steps she noticed one of the grooms leading a horse that was lathered, having been ridden hard, towards the stables, and she wondered curiously whose it could be. Agatha appeared on the veranda just as she reached the top of the steps, her black face wreathed in smiles. Clarissa looked at her in surprise.

'Why, Agatha, what is it?'

'He's home, Miss Clarissa. Massa Chris is home.'

Clarissa stared at her with incredulity, a rush of joy pervading her whole being, and Edward, his threats and Marie were all swept away in the glorious realisation that her husband was home. 'What?' she whispered. 'Christopher? Home? Oh, Agatha. . .' and the next instant she picked up her skirts with both hands and went flying into the house, her weariness forgotten, tears wetting her cheeks, calling his name incoherently as she sped through the hall and into the library and then, with a cry of joy that was almost a sob, she was in his arms, locked in his embrace, clinging to him without speaking.

She hung there until at last she was able to lift her head and look at him, observing joyously that he hadn't changed. His eyes were heavy with fatigue, his face strained and more clearly defined and his clothes travel-stained, but he was still the same, and she reached out her hand, her fingers as light as air as they touched his face as if to reassure herself he was real. She smiled softly, her eyes bright with tears.

'Oh, Christopher,' she whispered. 'I've missed you so much.'

His hands cupped her face and he looked wonderingly down at her, almost overwhelmed by her beauty. Seeing the quiet joy in her eyes, he thought that nothing and no one in the whole world was as lovely as she and, bending his head, he covered her mouth with his own, devouring her lips like a starving man, making up for all the weeks and months they had been apart, when he had dreamed of this moment, and something like terror moved in the region of his heart when he remembered the moment Marie's letter had reached him, when she had written how Clarissa was keeping the company of one Edward Montgomery. But Christopher was no fool, all too aware of what she hoped to achieve with her malicious lies, and the very depth of his and Clarissa's love for each other was enough to crush any jealous words Marie might try to instil into his heart.

But the letter had made him mad with impotent fury and alarmed, knowing only too well that the very fact that Montgomery was in Charleston, of the torment he might subject Clarissa to, posed a threat not only to her but also to their unborn child; when he had imagined the terror Clarissa must be feeling he had immediately arranged for leave and come home as quickly as he could, pausing only long enough in Charleston to seek out Montgomery, but he was not there.

Now he studied Clarissa's face closely for some sign that he had harmed her but, thank God, there was none. 'How are you, Clarissa?'

'I'm well. How long can you stay?'

'A few days at the most.'

Disappointment clouded her eyes, but she nodded in acceptance. 'Then we shall have to make the most of what little time we have. What's it like where you are, Christopher? We hear so little about the war here in the south that it might just as well be on another planet.'

'It's like all wars, I suppose. Marching; trudging through forests and swamps, all potentially hostile and unmapped, unbridged territory; never enough to eat because supplies don't get through – but enough of war, Clarissa. Tell me about you and our child. I cannot begin to describe the joy I felt when you wrote me.'

'Yes – it is wonderful, isn't it? And he's just fine,' she laughed, placing her hand on the swell of her stomach. 'At least he's energetic enough.'

Christopher raised his eyebrows in mock surprise. 'He? What makes you so certain it will be a boy?'

'Because I know it, and he's going to look just like you.' But then she frowned at more serious thoughts. 'Why have you come home, Christopher? Is there a reason?'

His face suddenly became grave. 'Yes; I know about Edward – that he's here in South Carolina. It was fortunate I was able to obtain leave so quickly. May God help him if he's harmed you.'

'Harmed me? No. But who told you he was here? Ralph?'

He shook his head. 'Marie.'

Clarissa stared at him in silence. 'So,' she said at last, 'she was right. You have seen her.'

'No. She wrote me a letter, full of malicious intent, saying it was in my best interests that I should know what was going on between my wife and a certain Edward Montgomery. Of course, I dismissed it as the ravings of a jealous woman, but,' he frowned, eyeing her curiously, 'it appears you've seen her.'

'Yes, just this afternoon over at the Whitakers'. It was their daughter Amanda's engagement party. If I'd known Marie was to be there I would never have gone.'

'What did she say to you?'

'That you were still seeing each other, that you were sending her letters and that it's her you love and not me.'

'That's ridiculous. You didn't believe her?'

'No, of course not, and however hard she tried to destroy my faith in you she did not succeed, but she'll never forgive you for marrying me. If, as you say, you had stopped seeing her before you knew me, then it's unimportant. But at least,' she said, her cheeks dimpling as she tried to suppress a smile, 'it shows she has good taste.'

He smiled. 'I suppose you're right. Marie is so steeped in a morass of lies that she probably believes them herself; my only regret is that she might have hurt you.'

'No. I think I know you well enough now. I don't see her as a threat and I know you wouldn't try to deceive me – for two reasons. First, because you, my wonderful husband, have a true sense of honour and would never indulge in anything so low as deceit, and the second is that I would not let you, and when this son of yours has been born,' she said, indicating the swell of the child, 'I shall convince you that you will have no need for other women.'

Christopher stared at her for several moments and then laughed lightly, pulling her into his arms. 'You are wonderful, do you know that? I do not deserve you, and to me you have never looked more lovely. But,' he said, a serious note entering his voice, 'I must ask you about Edward. You have seen him? It is true he's here – in South Carolina?'

She nodded, swallowing hard, her lovely eyes clouding over. 'Yes – yes, it is true. I saw him in Charleston and then again today. He was with Marie. They seem to have formed quite an attachment, those two. Perhaps it's because they have much in common.'

'Tell me what's happened, Clarissa. I want to know everything.'

They sat close together while Clarissa haltingly told her story, of how she had met Edward in Charleston, and, when she spoke of his terrible threats and how he had repeated them earlier when they had met at the Whitakers' place, tears smarted and blurred her eyes.

Christopher's questions were gentle and he listened to her calmly, to cause her the minimum distress, but as she spoke, her soft voice faltering now and then, his face grew darker. 'So,' he said bitterly, 'again he shows his hand. Again he has dared threaten our happiness,' and what was in his heart was rage and murder against Montgomery that he had the gall to come to America, to his home, and cause Clarissa such distress that it might have resulted in her losing the child.

Clarissa stared at him with fear-filled eyes. 'He's changed, Christopher. There was something unrecognisable about him this afternoon – almost satanic – and I really do believe that his consuming obsession for revenge has caused him to go clean out of his mind. I don't know what he intends to do – but he means to ruin us. He'll kill you if he can – I'm sure of it.'

Christopher put his arm around her, calming her, bringing some measure of comfort to her trembling body. 'Not if I can help it and, besides, I do have the advantage of surprise over him. He'll have no idea I'm home.' But his eyes were hard as he thought over what Clarissa had told him, the hideous recollections of the events of the day he had married her and the duel all too vivid, the memory still fresh and painful inside his mind – for it would not go away – and he knew, with a certainty, that while ever Edward Montgomery was alive he would be a constant threat to everything he held most dear – Clarissa and Tamasee – so it was up to him now to make an end to it. 'How I wish I'd driven my sword into his fiendish heart and finished him for good,' he said fiercely. 'But one thing I am sure of – I will not be cheated out of the pleasure of killing him this time.'

'What will you do?' asked Clarissa in a small voice.

'Find him. Was he still at the Whitakers' when you left?'

'Yes.'

'Then I'll start there.'

'Please – please take care.'

'I will. But you do understand what I have to do?' he said, looking at her steadily. 'That I cannot let this pass?'

CHAPTER FIFTEEN

DUSK was gathering and the wind had risen to a frenzy when half an hour later, clad in clean clothes, Christopher, along with Ralph, rode off up the gravel drive. Clarissa watched him go and, much as she wanted to call him back, she couldn't, for in the back of her mind was a deep sense of futility, for the moment when he would meet Edward could no longer be avoided, and what would happen when the two men came face to face she didn't want to imagine.

Only when they were out of sight did she turn to Betsy and Agatha, suddenly feeling so very tired and weary. The events of the day were beginning to take their toll, but even now she had a terrible feeling of oppression, of impending doom, that the day was far from over.

Sighing deeply, she placed her hand in the small of her aching back, the child suddenly feeling so heavy. 'I think I'll go to my room for a while and have Della prepare me a bath. I think a good soak might make me feel better.'

Agatha suddenly frowned at the mention of Della. 'Della? Why, I don't think she's back yet. With all the excitement I'd clean forgot about her.'

Clarissa looked at her sharply. 'Why? Where did she go?'

'Over to Ralph's house with some clean laundry. I was going to send one of the others with it until she offered, having nothing much to do.'

'How long has she been gone?'

'About an hour.'

234

Clarissa felt herself going very cold, and a sickening fear gripped her heart. Her tiredness was suddenly forgotten. To get to Ralph's house she would have to go past the slave cabins, follow the path alongside the river and past the cotton sheds before reaching the house. 'But – but it should only have taken her half an hour at the most,' and she stared at Agatha, her mouth going very dry as the hint of a suspicion took root in her breast and became larger with every second until it became a terrible certainty. 'Oh, dear God,' she whispered. 'Ned Stone. I should have known he was up to no good. We passed him – do you remember, Betsy? – on the road back to Tamasee. Agatha – you don't think— Oh, dear, merciful God,' she said, her trembling hand gripping her throat.

Alarmed by Clarissa's stricken face, Betsy took her arm and propelled her into the drawing-room. 'Don't worry, Clarissa. She's more than likely gossiping somewhere.'

'No. Della isn't one for gossiping – you know that.'

'But what reason could Ned Stone have for harming Della? She's done nothing wrong,' said Agatha.

'We might not think so, but he does. When she was at the Wheeler place he accused her of harbouring Sam when he ran away to find her. When he came here not long ago he saw Della and recognised her. He made it quite plain then that he hadn't forgotten what she'd done and that she still had to be punished for her crime.'

At Clarissa's words Agatha's face tightened and she knew they had cause for concern. Lord knew, she had no liking for the girl, but she had no desire to see her brought back to the house in the same condition as Sam after he'd run away. But it would be worse for Della because she was a woman. Undoubtedly she would be raped before being flogged – and God help her if she resisted.

It wasn't long before their worst fears were realised when one of the field hands, breathless, his black, terror-filled eyes darting from one to the other of the three women, was ushered into the drawing-room to tell them that the slave catchers had got Della.

Clarissa stood up from the couch, her face ashen. 'Where is she?'

'Out near de cotton sheds, Miss Clarissa. De patrol er mighty drunk an' de's goin' ter flog 'er.'

'Then we must stop them.' She turned to Agatha. 'They'll kill her if we don't. Is there anyone we can send?'

'No. No one will dare interfere with the patrol. They're too terrified for their own skins.'

'Then I'll go myself. They must be stopped and made to realise that they cannot come on to other people's property and take the law into their own hands in this way.'

Betsy gasped, horrified. 'You can't go. You can't possibly go out and face them in your condition and, besides, you heard what the boy said. They're drunk. There's no telling what might happen.'

'Just try stopping me. I'm going, Betsy. I'm the only one here with any authority.'

'Please wait for Christopher and Ralph to get back,' she pleaded.

'There's no time. Della could be dead by then.'

Seeing that Clarissa was determined, Betsy relented. 'All right. But I'm coming with you,' she insisted. 'Just wait until I fetch our cloaks. It's enough to freeze you to death out there, and it's blowing a gale.'

Darker and darker grew the sky as the two women made their way past the neat rows of slave cabins, the doors tightly shut as the trembling Negroes hid behind them in stark terror of the slave hunters. The very name instilled fear into them, as tales had come to Tamasee of atrocities and persecution on others less fortunate. Although none had suffered at their hands at Tamasee, nothing would induce them to come out of their cabins until they'd gone.

They hurried along a narrow path that ran beside the river towards the cotton sheds, the wind bitterly cold, bending trees almost double, making their bare branches creak. It was an ugly, menacing wind and Clarissa hated it as it pulled relentlessly at their cloaks, whipping their hair about their faces, stirring up dead leaves at their feet and also a memory of another night – for wasn't it on a night such as this that she'd gone in search of Edward at the Black Boar? She quickly thrust the memory from her mind. They heard the first rumble of thunder followed by a vivid flash of lightning, and Clarissa shivered, clutching her cloak tightly about her.

The journey from the house seemed interminable as they battled on, fraught with worry, their nerves raw as they thought of nothing except reaching Della in time. They saw the dark, ghostly shapes of the cotton sheds ahead and the faint glow of burning torches amid the darkness of the trees becoming brighter the closer they got, the noise of drunken voices carried to them on the wind growing stronger with ever-increasing force.

Their eyes became riveted on the scene before them, which seemed unreal, and Clarissa felt a nervous quivering in the pit of her stomach, wishing Christopher and Ralph were here to deal with this. Bravely she moved towards the cluster of rough-looking individuals squatting and sprawling on the ground, kegs of cheap liquor passing among them, some already

drunk out of their minds, with slack mouths and glazed
eyes. She saw the unmistakable figure of Ned Stone
slouched against a tree and she suspected he was not
as drunk as the rest, but it was on a figure not far from
him that her eyes rested.

In the flickering torch-light she could see it was
Della, a piteous sight, but although her clothes had
been brutally torn, and her proud young breasts
exposed, despite her attempts to cover them with her
arms, while shivering from the bitter cold, she
appeared unharmed; however, several eyes rested on
her greedily, eyes that she met with admirable defiance.
There was something strange about the whole scene,
and Clarissa thought it odd that no one had touched
Della. It was almost as if they were waiting for something or someone.

As the two women stepped into the circle of light the
dogs suddenly bounded forward, yapping and snarling
ferociously, their fangs bared and eyes gleaming.
Clarissa paled but tried not to show fear as she looked
directly at Ned Stone. Fear had to be set aside if she
was to help Della.

'Call them off,' she commanded.

He looked up, showing no surprise at her appearance. It was almost as if she was expected. He let out a
low whistle. 'Stay,' he ordered, at which the dogs
reluctantly ceased their snarling but continued to growl
as they sat back on their haunches, still alert, still
threatening, waiting for instructions. He looked up at
Clarissa, his gaze indifferent, as if he was bored by the
whole incident and, turning his head, he spat on the
ground before again fixing her with a bold stare. 'Well,'
he drawled, 'come to watch the entertainment?'

'Release her,' said Clarissa icily. 'She's done nothing
wrong.'

He merely shrugged, unperturbed by her anger.

'Taint no use mixin' in our bizness, miss. We've a right to punish niggers what done wrong – no 'ceptions. You don' understand our ways, so it's best not ter interfere.'

A sudden fury seized Clarissa. 'Then what are you waiting for? Why haven't you flogged her? Or is it your way to prolong the agony?'

'Nope. Only waitin' for someone, that's all.'

Clarissa was about to ask who when at that moment a figure emerged from the trees, but he was too far beyond the light for her to discern who it was. She watched him come closer, purposefully taking his time. A trickle of cold sweat ran down Clarissa's back, and as the man stepped into the light, a shock of blond hair falling casually over his forehead, a sardonic twist to his firm lips, she felt the blood drain out of her face, but she refused to give way to fear as she faced Edward.

'So,' she said, 'it is you,' and with sudden clarity she knew the situation had been set up by him. Her eyes settled on him with complete hatred. 'It was you who sent the man to the house, wasn't it? Knowing Ralph, our overseer, was away?'

His cold grey eyes widened in mock surprise. 'How perceptive of you, my dear, and yes – it was me. I've waited a long time for a chance such as this, but,' he said, looking with distaste at Della, 'little did I know that she would be the bait. I have Ned Stone to thank for that, having an old score to settle with her himself. I had no doubt that you would come to the aid of your own personal slave, having learnt, of course, that no one, unless they are white, would dare interfere with the slave patrol and their work – although even then they have to be careful lest they be accused of being nigger lovers.'

'You learn quickly, Edward,' scoffed Clarissa. 'And are you also to stay and witness the flogging of an innocent girl?'

'I think not. Their methods of dealing with servants are really quite barbarous, don't you think? They lack the finesse, the refinement of us in England. Don't know how you put up with it – whole damn south is teeming with niggers. Don't mind if I never see one again, I can tell you.'

Hot words in defence of the Negroes rose to Clarissa's lips, but she restrained herself. 'Why are you here at Tamasee, Edward? What do you want?'

'You,' he said without hesitation. 'I have a carriage waiting to take us to Charleston. Tomorrow we will leave for the Indies and from there go on to England.'

Clarissa stared at him incredulously, and if the moment hadn't been so serious she would have laughed. 'And Christopher? Do you think he won't come after me?'

'I'm sure he will, but he is in the north. It will be a long time before he will be able to come after you. And when he does I shall be ready for him.'

'You make it sound so easy, Edward. But after all your plotting and scheming to kidnap me you have overlooked one important fact – that Christopher is here, at Tamasee. He arrived earlier today and at this very minute he is with Ralph – looking for you.'

Edward stared at her in disbelief and then his face twisted with sudden fury. 'You lie,' he spat.

'No, I do not lie, and it is Marie you have to thank. She is the one who wrote to him, telling him of your presence in Charleston.'

'The bitch,' he snarled. 'Well – no matter. We shall leave now.'

As he was about to grasp her wrist Ned Stone rose and stood between them. 'Not so fast, Mr Montgomery. There is a matter of unfinished bizness.'

Edward looked at him sharply. 'What do you mean?'

Ned Stone glanced meaningfully down at Della, and Edward, aware of his intent, glared at him furiously.

'There's no time now. We'll have to let her go.'

'Ye've a lot to learn 'bout our ways. We never let niggers go and, besides,' he grinned, a lop-sided evil grin as he indicated Clarissa, 'ye'll never git her back to Charleston without us. Minute you lay a finger on 'er she'll start kickin' an' hollerin' like a hell cat. Nope – way I see it, ye'll just 'ave ter wait 'till we're done.'

'But there isn't time,' persisted Edward.

Ned Stone ignored him and urged his men to their feet. 'Do your work,' he commanded, the wind snatching the words from his lips. He pointed towards the nearest of the cotton sheds. 'Take 'er in there and string 'er to one of the beams.'

Two men staggered forward and seized Della, hoisting her roughly to her feet, dragging her towards the already open door. Clarissa was about to run forward, but Betsy held her back.

'Clarissa,' she shouted, 'you mustn't. There's nothing you can do.'

They watched helplessly as Della struggled frantically, and when the remnants of her torn bodice was ripped from her she raked her nails down the face of one of her captors, at which he gave a yelp of pain and dealt her a mighty blow that sent her sprawling to the ground, senseless. The men bent over her as a gust of wind sucked at a burning torch and Clarissa and Betsy watched, horror-struck, as a spark, borne on the wind, was blown towards the cotton shed and through the open door.

At first it was only a spark that, if near enough, anyone could have extinguished, but, drunk as Ned Stone's men were, it was nigh impossible. The wind caught the living spark, becoming a living tongue, licking and feasting greedily on the dry bales of closely packed cotton. The wind caught the flame and the fire took hold, leaping and dancing, penetrating higher into the night sky.

Ned Stone's men stared at the fire, their mouths agape and eyes half crazed before turning and fleeing into the woods. Clarissa turned to Betsy, her body functioning automatically.

'Quick, Betsy. Go to the slave quarters and fetch as many as you can with buckets. They can get the water from the river. We have to stop the fire from spreading to the other sheds.'

Betsy didn't need to be told twice and fled back along the path. Turning her attention to the shed, Clarissa could still see Della lying on the ground and would have run towards her, but Edward barred her way. At the sight of him she vented all her pent-up fury on him.

'There,' she cried accusingly. 'Are you satisfied? This is what you wanted, wasn't it?'

'If you hadn't been so foolish none of this would have happened in the first place. If only you had waited for me,' he shouted over the noise of the wind and fire.

'Foolish? I, foolish? No, Edward, not me. It was through your foolishness that you lost me and I must thank you, for because of it I met and married Christopher and it freed me from you. I love him in a way you could never understand, and if you intend to dispose of his life then you will also be disposing of mine, for I would rather die than go back with you to England.'

At that moment two men came riding out of the trees, drawn by the blaze, and Clarissa gave a cry of relief when she saw it was Christopher and Ralph. She ran to them just as Negroes began appearing from the direction of the slave quarters. Dismounting quickly, Christopher turned to Clarissa, but at the same time he saw Edward, and his face darkened with a murderous fury.

'You,' he spat. 'I might have known. This is your work. You can be sure I'll deal with you when I've brought the fire under control.'

He turned away, taking command immediately, shouting above the roar of the fire and wind, which, mercifully, was blowing away from the other sheds, although it could change direction at any minute. Ralph and Betsy organised the Negroes, who formed a human chain to the river, passing buckets from one to the other, drenching the other sheds for fear of rogue sparks blowing their way, There was nothing that could be done for the burning shed but contain it.

Christopher turned back to Clarissa and, taking her hand, pulled her away. 'Go back to the house,' he ordered. 'This is no place for you.'

'But – I —'

'Go, Clarissa. I've enough to do here without having you to worry about.'

'Wait – please,' she cried, grasping his arm, and the intensity in her eyes made him pause.

'What is it?'

'Della's by the shed. We must get her away. It's because of her that I'm here. The patrol came and took her. They were going to flog her.'

'Good God.' Immediately he ordered one of the Negroes closest to him to pour a bucket of water over him before plunging through the wall of smoke.

The night was suddenly torn asunder as lightning ripped across the sky, and the noise from the fire was like the angry roar of an enraged animal. A hideous red glow filled the sky into which belched a pall of black smoke, and the crash of falling timbers could be heard from inside, sending up fountains of sparks as

mercifully, at long last, providence came to their rescue
and they felt the first drops of rain.

It seemed an eternity but couldn't have been more
than seconds before Christopher emerged with the now
semi-conscious Della, coughing and choking from the
effects of the smoke, in his arms, but as he stepped
through the doorway one of the scorched beams came
crashing down, pinning one of his legs to the ground.
He managed to throw Della clear. Ralph immediately
ran to his aid and tried raising the heavy beam,
uncaring that it blistered and burned his hands, but it
was too heavy to lift alone. Frantically he called for
help.

Clarissa watched it all, her mind blank with terror as
the shed became a blazing inferno, but, seeing
Christopher pinned helplessly to the ground, a wall of
burning bales likely to come crashing down on top of
him at any second, she came alive. Smoke smarted her
eyes and burned her nostrils and she could feel the
intense, searing heat, the smoke choking her, filling
her lungs so she could hardly breathe. She flung herself
forward with a strangled cry, calling his name, tears
flooding her cheeks mingling with the rain. But suddenly hands gripped her shoulders, pulling her back. It
was Edward and she struggled wildly against him.

'No,' she screamed. 'I must go to him. Let me go.'

'You little fool,' he spat. 'You can't.'

'Why?' she cried, staring at him, her eyes wide, filled
with madness. 'Why can't I? Whatever you intend
tonight, Edward, if Christopher dies then as surely as
if you had thrust the knife into his heart you will have
killed him. Are you prepared to burden your heart
with his murder – and mine? Because I will not go on
living without him. You will have my death on your
conscience too.'

For the first time since she had known him his face

expressed no mockery, no anger, only a complete and utter wretchedness, but after all he had done to harm her she could not feel sorry for him.

'No,' he said, so softly that she only just caught the words. 'I'm sorry, Clarissa. That I do not want.'

Clarissa laughed triumphantly, a half-crazed sound, full of a cruel sweetness at finding she could hurt him at last. 'Let me go,' she cried, trying to shake off his hands. 'I must go to him.'

'No – stay here. I'll go.'

As he left her Clarissa felt nausea rising inside her, and her head began to swim as darkness closed in. Her vision was obscured by a grey mist and she was conscious of a feeling of weightlessness as slowly she slumped to the ground. It was into a deep, merciful oblivion that she sank, merciful because she did not see Edward lift the beam with Ralph, who managed to pull Christopher free, or the wall of blazing bales which chose that moment to come tumbling down on Edward. Nor did she see Della's satisfied smile.

The blessed rain at last came lashing down, sizzling fiercely as it met the searing heat, and a cry of abject relief went up from the Negroes at this welcome help from heaven – but too late to help Edward, whose charred and blackened body was pulled from the ashes the following day.

For Christopher the war was over; for America it had two more years to run, though it was obscured throughout by the continuing conflict in Europe. An American attempt to invade Canada failed dismally, but neither were the United States successfully invaded. British expeditions were checked on the Great Lakes at Baltimore, but they managed to capture Washington, burning its public buildings, including the House of Representatives and the President's home, sorely injuring American pride. This was restored by General Andrew Jackson, the great American hero of the war, as the British invasion moved south in the hope of taking New Orleans. That offensive was blocked by Jackson, who repelled the attack, inflicting such heavy losses that the British were forced to abandon their attempt on New Orleans.

This was America's most decisive victory of the war, which had covered three years of scattered, indecisive battles, both on land and sea, with many lives lost. Only then were the leaders of both countries persuaded that it was preferable to compromise than to fight, though the peace treaty was little more than an agreement to stop fighting, for neither side would make concessions. Had that been possible, the war need never have been fought at all. Yet out of this peculiar conflict America obtained a new confidence, a self-awareness, and Britain at last learned, after all her bullying and inflexibility, that war with the United States was not worthwhile and had to admit a reluctant respect for her former colony.

After sending someone for the doctor, Ralph picked Clarissa up and quickly carried her back to the house with Betsy hurrying beside him. Christopher was transported on a crude litter and the pain he suffered from his shattered leg was sheer torture, intensified with each jarring step and, adding to his agony, he could scarcely breathe, his lungs were so full of smoke. He prayed he would lose consciousness to escape the crippling pain and mercifully his prayers were answered before he reached the house, where he was put to bed in his old room.

Clarissa was attended to by Agatha and Betsy, anxiously waiting for the doctor to come and examine her, fearful that because of her ordeal she would lose the child.

When she opened her eyes she didn't know how much later it was. Perhaps hours, days, weeks, when it was, in fact, just two hours and the doctor had left her to attend Christopher. The first person she saw was Betsy, her eyes full of loving concern, who smiled with tears of relief glistening on her lashes when she saw she was awake.

'Christopher – how's Christopher?' Clarissa asked with difficulty.

'Unconscious but alive. The doctor's with him now.'

'Thank God,' she whispered. 'And – and my baby?'

'Your baby's just fine, Clarissa.'

She smiled softly and then sank into a deep sleep.

The doctor, having been a military surgeon, was accustomed to broken limbs, and with Sam's help he worked for hours straightening Christopher's shattered leg, which was badly broken in several places, the bones having pierced the scorched flesh. Later, with Christopher's leg splinted and swathed in bandages, the doctor left, promising to be back the following morning, but after having a word with Agatha he left her in no doubt that even without infection setting in, which was always a danger in these cases, his recovery would be slow. It would be weeks before he would be able to leave his bed and months before he could attempt to walk. And when he did he would always have a limp.

When Agatha told Clarissa this when she awoke the following day she was sad but realised it could have been far worse, that a few seconds longer, pinned beneath that beam, and he would not be here at all. The wall of bales would have fallen on him instead of Edward, which was something she couldn't bear to think about. But when she thought of Edward and what he had tried to do she could feel only anger. In time she would write to his brother, telling him what had happened – he had a right to know that – but not just yet. At the moment she didn't want to think of Edward or what had prompted him to rush forward and save Christopher's life. Whatever his reasons, she didn't want to know.

The doctor was right: Christopher's recovery was slow and painful, which wasn't surprising, considering the severity of his injuries, and he would have gone clean out of his mind with sheer frustration at being tied to a sick-bed had it not been for Clarissa and Ralph, who kept him informed on matters concerning the plantation and the war.

He became reconciled to the fact that he would not go back to his regiment, and as his broken bones knit together he concentrated on regaining his strength, determined that when he was back on his feet, limp or no limp, there was much to do. He was looking forward to taking an active part in the politics of South Carolina, and who knew where it would take him once the war was over? He remembered the conversation he had had with his uncle, Lord Buckley, at his club in London, the day after he'd first seen Clarissa, when he'd told him of the great opportunities America had to offer and how he wanted his children to have a part in the building of their country. Then he had not considered that the opportunities were there for him too, having made up his mind to be a planter until the day he died. But not any more, and he became consumed with a driving ambition, a sense of elation and expectation, for at long last he accepted what his friends had been telling him for years, ever since the death of his father, that there was no reason why he couldn't be both master of Tamasee and politician.

He would be able to pursue the subject that was

uppermost in his mind – the question of slavery. As a politician he would be in a prominent position to help bring about a movement for abolition by moral and political action. He had inherited a labour system he was no longer able to live with and ever since he had returned from England ideas had been forming in his mind. To appease his conscience he would begin by freeing the slaves at Tamasee, and by paying them a wage he hoped they would remain and work for him. But he did not delude himself. The path he had set would be a hard, ceaseless struggle. This private act of manumission would most certainly be frowned upon as irresponsible by his neighbours, but if he was to make abolition his central issue he had no choice.

What the consequence of his action would be he could not foresee, but he had no doubt that what he was doing was right. But he wasn't doing it just for himself. It would be for his children and Clarissa, too, for, however hard she might try, she would never be able to accept slavery as a fact of life. Whatever he decided, he knew she would support him wholeheartedly and be with him every step of the way. She would even be able to put into effect her idea for educating the children. That would please her.

Clarissa was sitting on Christopher's bed when Ralph left them, having just returned from Charleston bringing them eagerly awaited news about Ned Stone. Knowing he was to be accused of starting the fire at Tamasee in which a man had died, he had fled the state. No one had set eyes on him since. The other news he brought was that Marie had also gone – back to New Orleans.

The relief Clarissa felt when he told them this was overwhelming. It was like having a heavy load lifted from her mind. All the old fears that had tormented her for so long began to fade into the past and the future stretched before her, bright with joy. A future she had once been too afraid to contemplate.

'So,' said Christopher, 'Ned Stone has evaded justice. Ah, well, it doesn't surprise me, but one day you can be sure he'll get what he deserves. And Marie – so she's gone too,' and he smiled. 'It seems all our enemies have deserted us.'

Clarissa nodded. 'Yes, thank goodness. But, you know, I'm not sorry Edward's dead, Christopher. Do you think it's terrible of me to say that?'

'After what he put you through? No.'

'You were only injured,' she said softly, 'when you could so easily have been killed. Edward paid for what he did with his life. But what I shall never understand is why he saved you. When you were pinned beneath that beam everyone could see the bales were about to fall.' She sighed, shaking her head slowly. 'I don't suppose I shall ever know why he did it.'

Christopher reached out and placed his fingers beneath her chin, lifting her face to his own, gazing steadily into her eyes, those beautiful blue eyes, which had so entrapped him from the start. Then they had been devoid of love – but not any more. 'Don't you? I think I do. Perhaps he remembered what might have been had he treated you differently. He set a trap for you but fell into it himself. When you became unattainable, in his own peculiar way and as much as Edward was capable of feeling love for any woman, I believe he fell in love with you.' He swept her into his arms, the very force of their love causing the child to stir within her. 'But he could never love you as I do, Clarissa. God, how I love you.'

The very tenderness on his face brought tears to her eyes. 'It's over now, isn't it, Christopher? Edward, Marie – neither of them can harm us ever again.'

'No, my love. You needn't be afraid any more. Everything is going to be all right,' and as he said this he knew the time had come for him to tell her of his plans for the future.

'I never believed I could be so happy,' she murmured through her tears, resting her head on his shoulder. 'I'm so happy I feel I could die of it.'

He laughed lightly. 'You'll soon get used to it – you'll see.'

It was the greatest day Tamasee had known for several decades when the master's son was born, beginning a round of festivities suited to such a happy occasion. Happiness reigned over the great plantation. All were celebrating at once the freedom of the slaves and the new heir.

Christopher sat on the bed with his arm around Clarissa, who was gazing down at the child sleeping soundlessly in her arms. He thought how changed she was. Happiness suited her. With the birth of their son her beauty bloomed with a new contentment and maturity as never before.

'What are you thinking?' he asked.

She sighed. 'About everything. About us and how happy you've made me.'

'Don't you think you deserve it after all you've been through?'

'Not only me – you deserve it, too. Oh, Christopher, this really is a time for celebration. I'm so proud of you. Just listen,' she said, looking towards the open window, through which drifted the sound of laughter and singing coming from the ex-slaves' quarters. The moon had risen and the celebrations would go on well into the night. 'They sound so happy. I hope many more plantation owners follow your example and free their slaves.'

'I doubt it, somehow. We've a long way to go before we see the end of slavery in the south, Clarissa. It may not be in our lifetime, but,' he said, gazing proudly at his son, 'God willing, it will be in his. The tide will turn one day.'

'Can Tamasee survive without it? Will it prove too difficult for us to live here?' She felt his arm tighten about her shoulders, and his voice took on a fierce determination when he answered.

'Yes, Tamasee can survive, and not only Tamasee but we also will survive – the Cordells as a family, with our pride and honour and our love. Whatever hardships are thrust at us, we will face the future together. Giving the slaves their freedom is only the beginning, but we'll win through in the end. You'll see.'

Please turn the page for a tantalising extract from
Helen Dickson's

BELHAVEN BRIDE

Out September 2004

Chapter One

Chapter One

1932

It was a wet winter's day in London. Rain lashed at the windows of Mr Rothwell's office, obscuring the forms of bustling pedestrians on the streets. The office was spartan and cold, Mr Rothwell large, solid and humourless. In brusque tones he introduced Anna to a man by the name of Mr Alex Kent.

Stepping forward, Mr Kent expressed sympathy for her bereavement. His voice was deep, resonant and slightly accented—East European, Anna thought. He had a patrician, almost arrogant air about him that suggested education, breeding and money. However, Anna was so nervous and awed by the occasion she paid no attention to him. She was only interested in what Mr Rothwell had to say.

When the letter had come, asking her to make an appointment to attend the solicitors Rothwell and Rankin's office in London for the reading of her mother's will, she hadn't known what to expect—though, of course, she didn't know enough about lawyers and wills to make comparisons. Since then she had worked herself into a knot of anticipation and foreboding.

Mr Rothwell gestured to a leather-covered chair across the desk. 'Please sit down, Miss Preston.'

Dressed in maroon school tunic, blazer, maroon-and-gold striped tie and sturdy black lace-ups, Anna removed her felt hat and placed it on the desk in front of her. Sitting stiff-backed on the edge of her chair, her lips compressed into a thin line, she faced the elderly lawyer across the desk. A shiver of apprehension ran through her. Glancing down at the folder in front of him, as briefly as possible Mr Rothwell explained the terms of the will. Apart from a few of her mother's personal items there was nothing of value—no money, no property.

This came as no surprise to Anna, but what did surprise her was that her mother had placed her in the care of Lord Selwyn Manson. Lord Manson was Anna's maternal grand-father, a man she knew practically nothing about—and the little she did know did not endear him to her. Because her mother had always spoken of him in the past tense, she had believed him to be deceased.

Anna listened in utter silence and in an agony of tightly corked emotion, her fingers tightening on each other in her lap. Her nerves were stretched, teetering on a scream.

'This has come as something of a shock to me, Mr Roth-well. My mother sheltered me all my life, kept things from me. She often spoke of my father, who was an artist and was killed in the war before I was born, but she told me very little of her own background, only the unpleasant circumstances that forced her to leave home. I was not aware that I had any family alive at all, let alone a grandfather—or that he was a peer of the realm.'

'Lord Manson has always been aware of your existence. I am in contact with your grandfather's solicitors—and I am grateful that Mr Kent, who is your grandfather's adviser and associate on several business matters, could take time off from his busy schedule to be present today.'

Anna kept focused on Mr Rothwell, feeling the eyes of the formidable Mr Kent, seated on the sofa behind her, burning holes in her back. 'Why did my grandfather not try to contact me?'

'Your mother forbade him to. However she stipulates in her will that on her demise, until you reach twenty-one, your guardianship must pass over to your grandfather.'

A coldness closed on Anna's face. She shifted uneasily and wondered why pain always had to be concealed in hard reality. 'I don't understand. Why would my mother do that? Why should he care about me?'

'You are his sole heir, Miss Preston, and when he dies— even after death duties—you will be an extremely wealthy woman.'

At that moment the amount of her grandfather's money didn't interest Anna—the disruption the terms of her mother's will would bring to her life did. 'Does he want to see me?' She felt depressed and there was a hollow feeling in the pit of her stomach.

'Eventually.'

'May I ask when?' she asked evenly. Her tone betrayed nothing, neither shock, outrage or pain, which was deeply felt.

'When you have completed your education.'

'I take my Higher Certificate examinations very soon. My teachers have been preparing me for university and I was hoping to sit the Oxford entrance exam. You see, I had set my sights on a career for which a university degree is essential. However, I do not have the means to go to university now, so I am considering doing a secretarial course instead. I must work to support myself, you understand.'

'My dear Miss Preston, you can forget about work.'

'Why? I have to work some time.'

'There is absolutely no question of that. You must reconsider your future. When you have taken your exams, your grandfather has expressed a wish that you continue your education in Europe.'

'And afterwards?'

'That you make Belhaven, which is in Buckinghamshire, your home.'

Mr Rothwell went on to talk further about Belhaven and Lord Manson's plans for her future—coming-out, a Season. Anna gave only monosyllabic replies. She asked a brief question now and then, showing no sense of curiosity about Belhaven or the man who was to be her guardian, and feeling nothing but abhorrence at his talk of a Season. They were interrupted when his secretary knocked and opened the door, beckoning to him that she would like a word. Murmuring an apology, Mr Rothwell excused himself and left the office.

Alex Kent, who had listened quietly and intently, now got up and came towards her. He stood looking down at her slim, informal figure. At seventeen years old there was still a trace of childishness about her; in fact, Anna Preston looked as aloof and virginal as a nun in a convent. She was calm, controlled, which, he thought, was her normal way of doing things, but beneath it all a kind of fierce energy seemed to burn.

When they had been introduced, she had looked at him uncertainly and taken his outstretched hand. Her grip had been surprisingly firm for her age, and when she spoke her voice was soft and cultured. His first reaction had been, 'what a prim miss', and then, more soberly, 'what a pretty—no—beautiful girl'. Her skin was pale, her features small and delicate, but it was the large violet eyes and upward slanting eyebrows that drew and arrested his gaze so that the rest was forgotten. Her hair was long, silken and black, drawn in a maroon ribbon at the back of her neck. Her expression was still and frozen, an expression he understood. It was the look of a girl who had never been happy—who was frightened to allow herself so frivolous an emotion in case it was taken away. He knew her mother had helped keep it there.

'Your grandfather and I have been close friends for many years,' Alex said. 'He realised the problems you would have to face today and asked me to come here to look after you. I have accepted that responsibility.'

'May I ask why he didn't come himself?'

'He suffers from a severe form of arthritis that prevents him moving about. He lives quietly, rarely leaving the house. Aren't you interested to know more about Belhaven—about your grandfather or your future?'

'No, sir, not very,' Anna replied, speaking politely and frankly and looking up at him from her fringe of dark lashes. As she did so she remembered the night when she had been six years old and she had walked in on her mother crying wretchedly for her long dead husband. In her anguished ravings and with half a bottle of gin inside her, her mother had told of the harsh, cruel treatment meted out to her by the very man Alex Kent spoke of.

Her mother, always careful never to show emotion or feeling, had never spoken of it again, but what Anna had seen and been told had affected her deeply. With all the anger and confusion of a child she had craved revenge for what her grandfather had done to her mother. And now that same man was arrogantly demanding control of her life.

'Any interest my grandfather shows in me now is seventeen years too late, Mr Kent. I have worked hard for my examinations in the hope that I can go on and further my education. Do you expect me to turn cartwheels over a house and a man I thought was dead—a man who was so unfeeling he turned his back on my mother for marrying the man of her choice?'

Alex Kent sat on one corner of the desk, gently swinging one elegantly shod foot, forcing her to look at him properly for the first time. Probably twenty-seven or eight, his skin was burned mahogany brown—suggesting an extended holiday in the south of France or somewhere similar where the rich and famous went—contrasting vividly with his silver-grey eyes. The planes of his face were angular, his gaze penetrating. His black hair, as black as her own, was brushed back, with the gleam and vitality of a panther's pelt. Anna noted the crisp way it curled in the nape of his neck, and the hard muscled width of his shoulders beneath his expensively tailored jacket. The firm set of his jaw confirmed her impression that he would stand no nonsense from anyone. He towered above her, making her at once guarded, vulnerable, and acutely uncomfortable as he considered her in lengthy silence.

'Not entirely,' Alex replied at length in answer to her question. 'When your father died your grandfather asked her to return home. She refused, allowing sentiment and not good sense to rule her emotions. If she was unhappy, she had no one to blame but herself. But what of you? Your mother was a secretary to an accountant in the city, living in a rented house in Highgate. You must have known she wasn't earning the kind of money to send you to Gilchrist. Did it ever occur to you to wonder where she found the money to finance your education at such an exclusive school, a school with high academic standards, admitting only the daughters of the very rich?'

Anna grew thoughtful. He was right, Gilchrist was expensive and exclusive, as befitted the daughters of people of class. She had puzzled on this, but, after a while, accepted it. It was easier that way. 'No. But I suspect I am about to find out.'

Alex nodded, his gaze hardening at her tone, which was offhand and with a hint of animosity. 'Your grandfather. Despite their estrangement, your mother was not averse to accepting his money to finance your education—but she would accept nothing for herself. She sheltered you, kept things from you. You never questioned her, which tells me you are either stupid or afraid of reality.' His eyes narrowed when her smooth façade broke. An objection sprang to her lips, which she checked, and her face became flushed, the blood running beneath her smooth skin in the painful way it does when one is young. 'The latter, I think.'

'If I am as stupid and naïve as you obviously think, then I would do better to harden myself in my own way, with my own kind of people,' Anna snapped.

Alex raised an eyebrow. Her remark stirred his anger, and when he spoke his tone was harsh and to the point. 'Your own kind of people have always resided at Belhaven. Harden yourself, by all means, but do it in the right place and with the right people. Perhaps a year at finishing school will help you acquire charm and confidence and, since you are to move in exalted circles, will help you develop a feeling of being the equal of any man or woman—which, being the granddaughter and heir of one of England's wealthiest men, is important.'

Anna blanched and for the space of half a minute she could not speak. 'Forgive me. I really had no idea my grandfather was that rich. So, it is his intention to turn me into a facsimile of a well-bred, well-connected young woman.'

'Which is precisely what you are,' Alex stated, with a distinctly unpleasant edge to his voice. He smiled his rather austere smile, one corner of his mouth curling.

With a sinking heart, Anna wished he didn't make her feel like the gauche schoolgirl she was. It was irritating to be judged on appearances and found lacking.

'You are impertinent, Miss Preston,' he went on reproachfully. 'Gilchrist may apply great emphasis to the values of academic ability, but where manners are concerned it appears to be somewhat lacking.'

Anger kindled in the depths of Anna's dark eyes. Tutored in rules of discipline and restraint, normally she would never dream of arguing with anyone, especially not with an elder. She was far too polite, far too dutiful, but this stranger had a way of getting under her skin and releasing something unpleasant in her. He also knew far too much about her and about her mother for her liking.

'I suppose I must seem impertinent to you,' she admitted, meeting his gaze unflinchingly, her sense of depression growing worse. 'With no family to speak of, with a mother who ignored me thoroughly throughout my life, with no brothers and sisters to keep me in my place and never having known my father, I say all kinds of impertinent things, Mr Kent. Am

I supposed to feel grateful to my grandfather? Because, try as I might, I can find no hint of gratitude within me.'

Alex's anger with her vanished and his expression softened. 'I apologise if I sounded harsh just now,' he said gently. 'I should have known better.' For the first time she had let her guard slip a little and truth over loyalty to her mother prevailed. He was strangely moved by her words. Anna Preston had lived her life in a tight discipline. The extent and intensity of her mother's unhappiness and bitterness at the death of her husband after just one year of marriage—the man she had loved above all else, including her daughter—had been with her through life. Sadly, its tragic effects were visible on the young face before him, and as a result Anna Preston was seventeen going on seventy.

For an instant Anna thought she saw a shadow of sympathy flit over Mr Kent's face. Before she could be certain it was gone, replaced by a faintly ironic interest. She was normally not the sort of person to go around revealing information about herself, let alone to total strangers. In fact, she would normally cut her own tongue out before revealing how things had been between herself and her mother, but there was something about Alex Kent that drew you into his rather intense personality. Realising she had given too much of herself away and that he'd picked up on it, regretting her outspokenness she lowered her eyes. 'I'm sorry. I shouldn't have said that. It's no concern of yours.'

'You're right, it isn't, but I'm a good listener—if you'd like to talk about it?' Alex prompted.

Anna shook her head, thankful that he didn't pursue it.

'Miss Bartlet, your headmistress, has always sent Lord Manson's solicitors annual reports of your progress. She says you've worked hard and done extremely well in class, that you are a credit to your school. Your grandfather is immensely proud of you. He was glad to see the money he provided was well invested.'

'So I'm an investment,' Anna remarked coolly, indignantly

tilting her chin a notch. 'I'm pleased he considers my good marks in class as value for money. I suppose taking his money all these years means that I have to give something back—that he expects it, that it is a debt to be repaid. But what if I choose not to go to school abroad, to turn my back on everything he offers,' she enquired, 'for I need no one's aid or protection?

'I do not in the least mean to sound ungrateful, but I find nothing at all pleasurable in the prospect of having my established order of things turned upside down. It has always been my intention to be self-sufficient, to make my own way in the world.'

'Which is a trait I personally admire in anyone—be it man or woman—unlike your grandfather. It is one of the few things we disagree on. It is his considered opinion that marriage and motherhood is the true career for a woman, that ladies do not take up paid employment.'

This unexpected revelation about Lord Manson was uttered quietly and accompanied by a smile. It was a smile that took all the harshness and offence out of Alex Kent's previous words, a smile that was instantly rueful, conspiratorial and incredibly charming, a smile that said he perfectly understood how hard the situation was for her. Anna was absorbed in the smile, a smile that drew her into a private alliance. He was sitting perfectly still, watching her. Something in his expression made her hastily drop her gaze, but the warmly intimate look had been vibrantly, alarmingly alive, and its effect would remain with her.

Raising her head, she looked at him hard. 'Such prejudice is stupid in this day and age. Women are no longer the weaker sex.'

'I couldn't agree more, but do I detect a hint of feminism in that remark?'

'I just happen to believe women should have the same opportunities as men. If that happens to be feminist then so be it. My mother was of that opinion, too. One thing I am thank-

ful for is that she believed passionately in the education of
women, which was why she went to great pains to have me
properly educated.'

'And you want to go to university?'

'Yes. I've set my heart on it. Domestic subjects are given
low priority at Gilchrist, as you will know, Mr Kent. Academic success is the main goal, with university entrance the
pinnacle of ambition—which my grandfather must have
known when my mother sent me there. However, I realised
when she died that I lack the means to go to university, and
if necessary I will take the Civil Service entrance examination
instead.'

'And do clerical work?'

'If I have to.'

'I can't see you drumming your brains out on a typewriter.'

'Needs must, Mr Kent,' she said, and her small jaw was
set in a way that Alex found so reminiscent of Selwyn he
almost laughed.

'Not in your case.'

Alex looked down on Anna's quiet composure, her certainty, and her absolute confidence in herself. 'The Belhaven
inheritance by tradition is rightfully yours,' he continued on
a more serious note. 'There is no other direct heir, no son or
daughter, no other grandchildren to carry on the ancient line.
You, Miss Preston, are the last of the line. Should you refuse
to have anything to do with your grandfather, on his death
the estate will be broken up, its treasures dispersed.'

'I see. So, in spite of his power and wealth, my grandfather
has no stake in immortality,' Anna remarked drily.

'No one has that.'

Anna fell silent and averted her gaze. She felt lost and so
very alone. She had no one to turn to. No one. Every avenue
of appeal was closed to her. Even this man concurred with
her grandfather. 'It appears I am left with no choice but to
adhere to my mother's wishes and do as my grandfather says,'
she said softly, without joy.

'You are his rightful heir, so my advice to you is to accept it with the grace and dignity of your noble lineage. Furthermore, the fact that it was your mother's wish that you make your future at Belhaven with your grandfather makes me fervently believe she would have forgiven him if she'd had the chance that you now have.'

Her ire coming to the fore once more, Anna tossed her head. 'I am not my mother.'

Alex recognised in her remark the same hostility he found whenever he negotiated with any business rival who was being forced by circumstances to sell something he wanted to hold on to. It was her pride that was forcing her to retaliate by making the whole situation as difficult as possible for Alex.

Fearing that she was vacillating, he said pointedly, 'I realise what the loss of your mother must mean to you in a personal sense and I respect your bereavement. But you must consider the effect her death has had on Lord Manson. His feelings for her were passionate and deep. She caused him unimaginable suffering when she defied him and married your father. The fact that she has died so suddenly without making amends, which your grandfather has tried to do since the day she walked out, has affected him deeply. He loved her more than you imagine. Whatever you may think, he is heartbroken.'

Refusing to be mollified and reluctant to change her opinion of a man she had spent her life hating because of the suffering he had caused her mother, suppressing the urge to remark that she doubted her grandfather had a heart to break, Anna said somewhat ungraciously, 'He'll survive.'

Stifling a sigh of impatience, Alex said with unintentional curtness, 'I am sure he will. You are an intelligent young woman, Miss Preston. You'll learn your grandfather's ways quickly. You'll soon come to terms with his system, his peculiarities.'

'My mother told me he insisted upon controlling her. He cast her out. After all he has done, am I to pretend it didn't happen?'

'You are not his judge, but even if you were, don't you think it would be best to be certain of your facts before you pass sentence? Are you to commit your grandfather without hearing his defence?'

Anna looked at him solemnly for a moment, then she said, 'I don't mean to. I will let him put his case. But are you saying my mother was lying, Mr Kent?'

'I hate to be the one to disabuse you of your illusions, but your mother walked out of Belhaven. It was her choice. There is more to the matter than appears on the surface.'

'Then I would be obliged if you would enlighten me.'

'It's for your grandfather to do that. Not me.' Standing up, he picked up her maroon mackintosh and helped her into it. 'There are details to be worked out, but they needn't concern you at this point. Your grandfather's solicitors will contact your headmistress when a suitable school has been found—perhaps in France or Switzerland. Do you have a preference?'

'No,' she answered, unable to keep the disappointment she felt about being denied the chance to realise her dream at university from her voice. But she had to be sensible and practical. 'Since you appear to know a great deal about me already—which, because you are a stranger to me, I must say I find quite unsettling and objectionable—you will know I have never been further than my school in Essex, so either will do.'

Alex was shocked into momentary silence. In his own world and wide circle of friends and acquaintances, everyone went everywhere, and often. It was difficult to accept this bright young girl had never been anywhere beyond Essex. 'All the more reason why you should continue your education abroad for a year or thereabouts. They do say that travel broadens the mind, especially at your age. Afterwards you will go to live at Belhaven. Your grandfather wants you to have the opportunity to enjoy a Season—to look over the eligible young men,' he added almost as an afterthought, a humorous twinkle glinting in his eyes.

Anna stiffened, finding nothing funny about that. 'Does he indeed? He is going to be disappointed. A Season is quite out of the question. I want no presentation at Court, no coming-out. The sole purpose of all that ghastly nonsense is for a girl to procure a husband. The manner in which she is put on parade for gentlemen to look her over like a filly in the ring at a race meeting is quite absurd and so outdated, don't you think?' She paused when she saw Mr Kent's eyes widen and a smile tug at his lips as he nodded his agreement. 'I have no inclination to marry in the foreseeable future—not for years and years, in fact, so it would be pointless.'

Suppressing the smile, Alex smoothed his expression into an admirable imitation of earnest gravity. 'I quite agree, but we will see what happens to you when you are of an age to decide—in a year's time.'

'Age has nothing to do with it,' Anna went on somewhat irately. 'I will not change my mind, but I hope my grandfather will change his. His ideas are stuffy and antiquated. I cannot see the point, or the purpose, of sending me abroad to an expensive school. It will be money totally wasted. If he must spend his money on me, I'd much rather he sent me to university instead.'

'The purpose of spending a year at school abroad is to enrich the mind, not to train it for some exacting occupation. But whatever you do in the future, your education will prove invaluable to you. Plenty of time when you return for university and to develop a career if you want to.'

'Even though my grandfather will oppose it?'

'I'm sure you'll be able to win him round,' Alex said, desperately trying to prove to her she wasn't as powerless as she thought she was. 'Your grandfather is a fine man, Anna—you don't mind me calling you by your Christian name?' She shook her head. 'It isn't natural for two people who are close to be strangers to each other.'

'But after all these years—'

'He wants to meet you. You could make him happy. He is

the finest man I have ever known. I admire him enormously.'
There were few people Alex admired. 'One day I hope you
will understand what I mean. There's no limit to what he can
do for you—if you let him.'

'The role of grandfather cannot be assumed by a total
stranger, Mr Kent, and I cannot be expected to love him to
order.'

'That is the last thing Lord Manson would expect of you.'

Anna found herself quite intrigued by Alex Kent; she
looked at him enquiringly, tilting her head to one side. 'I
suppose you went to university.' For a moment he looked
quite taken aback. Immediately she regretted her impulsive-
ness. 'I'm sorry,' she said sincerely. 'I didn't mean to pry.'

'Don't be sorry. You may ask anything you like—within
reason,' he added an almost imperceptible second later. Anna
perceived that second and she recognised what he was saying—not to pry too deep. 'I will be as honest and direct as I
can,' he went on. 'I did go to university—Balliol College at
Oxford.'

'And got a double first, I expect.' The smile that moved
across his lean brown face confirmed her remark. 'You must
have had to work unimaginably hard.'

'No academic achievement is automatic.'

'Mr Kent, I really don't want to go to school abroad and
the prospect of being thrust into an unaccustomed social life
in the company of hundreds of strangers appalls me,' she told
him earnestly. 'It's a worthless, frivolous life and I would hate
every minute of it. I don't think I will be able to stand it. I've
always known what I want to do with my life. I know
it…perhaps like you did.'

He nodded slowly. 'Ambition comes before everything.
That's a fundamental lesson I learned a long time ago. I can
see you're serious, that you have your heart set on it.'

'Yes. I've always been determined and single-minded about
what I want, and the fact that I might fall at the first hurdle—
that of lack of money and opposition from a man I've never

met—undoubtedly means I am losing both those qualities. Please will you try to make my grandfather understand how important going to university is to me? Don't forget that I don't have to do what he wants. I can still walk away.' Her gaze was steady and meaningful as it became fixed on his.

Alex was silent, studying her seriously, then he began very slowly to smile. 'That sounds to me like blackmail, Miss Preston.'

Anna's expression became sublimely innocent. 'Does it? It was not intended. I'm merely trying to strike a bargain.'

Alex cocked a sleek black brow. 'With Lord Manson? Several have tried—and failed. I must tell you that your grandfather hasn't considered university and will probably say it's an absurd notion, but I promise I will try.'

'Oh, my goodness,' said Anna, her eyes alight with hope, 'do you think you could? I would be most grateful.'

Alex saw her poignant look of gratitude before she masked her feelings with a smile. 'Leave it with me. I'll see what I can do. Now, come along, I'll get you something to eat and then drive you to the station.'

'Thank you, but there's no need.' Her smile broadened—a sudden, dazzling smile that hit Alex somewhere in the region of his stomach. He seemed to be looking at a different person. 'Miss Bartlet very kindly allowed Mr Cherry—that's the school chauffeur, to bring me to town in the car. Goodbye, Mr Kent. No doubt we'll meet again some time—at Belhaven, perhaps.' Placing her maroon hat securely on her head, she turned her back on him and marched briskly towards the door.

'Anna?' Alex called after her.

She stopped and turned. 'Now what?'

'You're doing the right thing—about going to Belhaven,' he said softly.

'I hope you're right, but whatever happens I'll cope—just as I always have.'

Alex watched her go. Never had he been so dismissed. He suppressed a smile. Anna Preston was a tough little madam and his admiration for her was acknowledged. Something warmed him as he watched her go. And the way her face had been transformed by her smile—hope renewed that he might be able to arrange it for her with her grandfather for her to go to university after all. He suspected that she didn't smile often, and when she did it was as if she were bestowing some kind of favour.

He began to wonder what she would be like after three years at university—if he could persuade Selwyn into letting her go—and if Selwyn had not made a grave mistake in what he intended for her. Reserved, proud and young as she was, it would be interesting to observe the maturing of Anna Preston—to assist in it, even. At that moment he didn't know whether she would be a curse or a godsend at Belhaven, but he was looking forward to finding out.

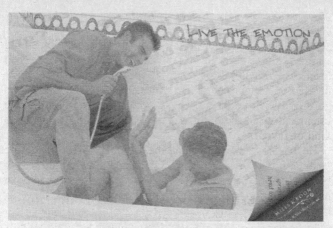

On sale 3rd September 2004

Available at most branches of WHSmith, Tesco, Martins, Borders, Eason, Sainsbury's and all good paperback bookshops.

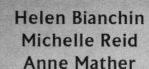

FOREIGN AFFAIRS

Sultry heat, sexy men – seduction guaranteed!

**Helen Bianchin
Michelle Reid
Anne Mather**

MILLS & BOON

On sale 3rd September 2004

*Available at most branches of WHSmith, Tesco, Martins, Borders,
Eason, Sainsbury's and all good paperback bookshops.*

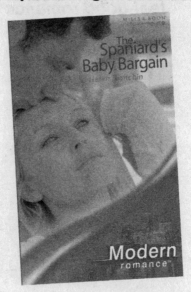